John W. Parsons

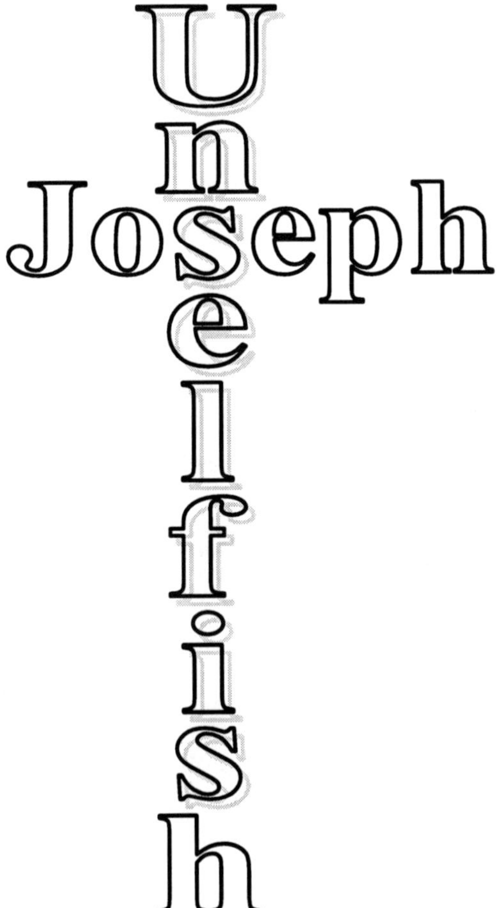

A Civil War Saga

Wasteland Press
Shelbyville, KY USA
www.wastelandpress.net

Unselfish:
A Civil War Saga
By John W. Parsons

First Printing – June 2010
ISBN: 978-1-60047-441-5
Cover illustration by Barbara Tyler Ahlfield

Printed in the U.S.A.

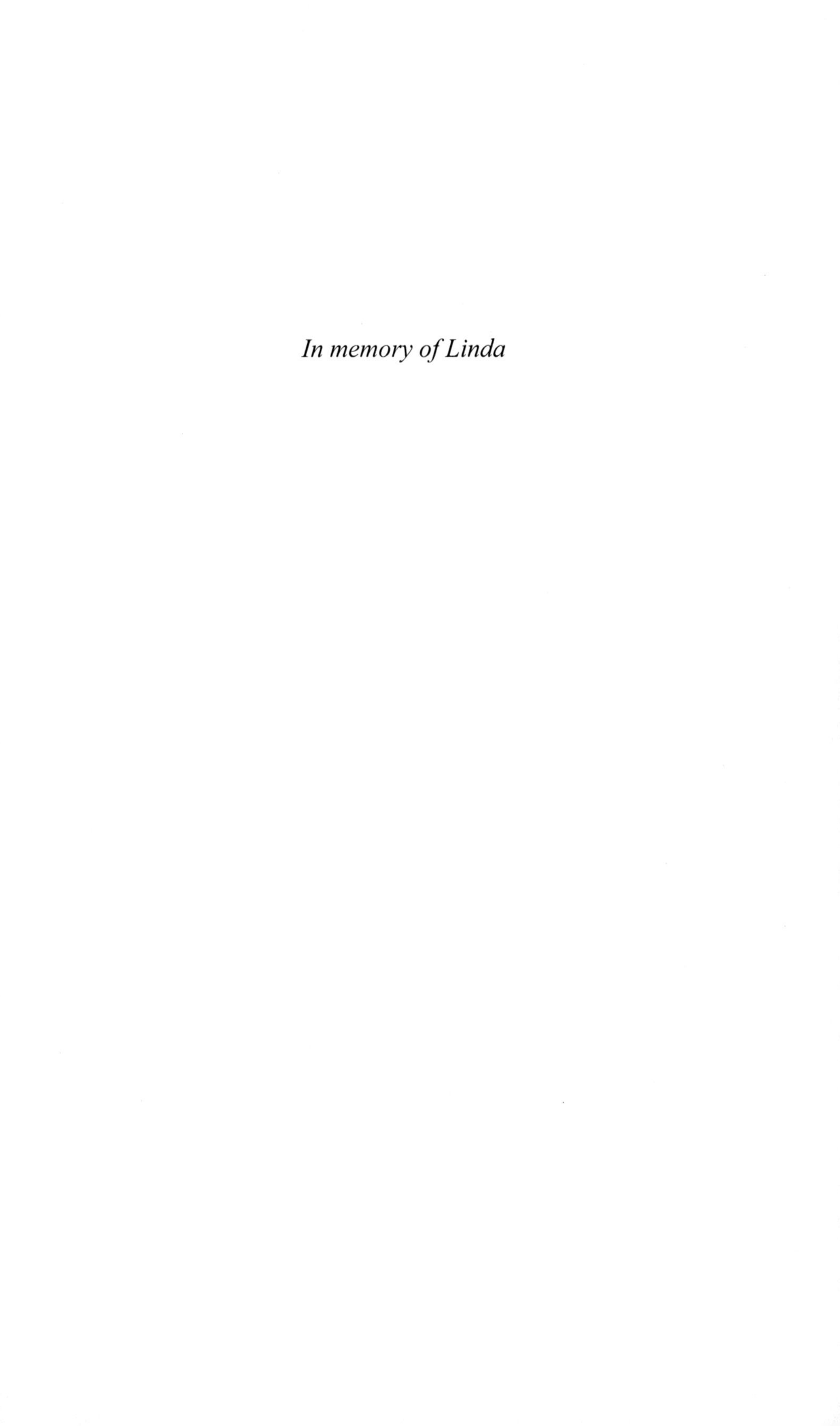

In memory of Linda

Preface

"I cannot believe that it lasted more than half an hour, but how we dropped them, I was astonished myself when the smoke lifted and I could look beyond and around us and see the number killed and wounded Rebels, and what appeared to me at the time to have been the work of a few minutes. And there at the same time so few killed or wounded on our side. The 7th and 6th Maine had some hurt; they were upon the right and left flanks. But this was an even chance, what fighting men call a fair fight, neither party having the advantage of position, being in open fields which had been very rare if at all before in this war. The Rebels having always fought us from behind walls of earth and wood and trees. I was informed today that there were eight regiments that made the attack on us. I saw prisoners myself from five different regiments, but this I do know that they had two lines of battle coming down on us, either of which was nearly the length of ours. They certainly had many more men than we had, and had brought them into the field for the express purpose, under the command of two generals, to drive us from the field and get our artillery. The same good result throughout the day along the line would have most effectively used up their army on the peninsula.

Our wounded men and most of theirs were brought in before dark, and as far as the surgeons could operate both parties were cared for. I was pleased to see our men without being ordered about, going over the battle field, helping up and leading those of the Rebel wounded that could walk (the stretchers at first being used to carry our wounded) and many a one I saw pouring water from their canteens in cups and giving it to others; instead of being maltreated, they were cared for and made as comfortable as the circumstances, time, place and their condition would admit, and early the next morning the colonel sent some of our companies into the woods, where our skirmishers had been, to pick up any that might be found there. They found several dead, and some wounded and brought them in yesterday. Parties detailed for that purpose buried the dead. If some Southern heartless witches can boast of having drum sticks and finger rings made from the bones of Yankees we have the gratification of saying in reply; we cared for and administered to the comfort of your dying and wounded as decently as civilized people ought to do, buried your dead, and would not allow loafers to insult your comrades when our prisoners."

CHAPTER ONE

Leaving Home

So much of getting ahead of oneself. My name is Joseph and my story begins in a small community in Nova Scotia, Canada in 1814. If one were to have asked me a few years ago if I would be writing such a letter as I just quoted to my beloved wife I would have told them, "only in your dreams." Unfortunately this country is now in the middle of a horrific Civil ??? War and I am in the midst of it also. This is not the place I intended to be and I often lay awake in our tent at night wondering why it is called "Civil" and also wondering if it was at all necessary. One especially wonders when they see the agony of the wounded and the piles of dead bodies after the fighting. I believe it was President Lincoln that said we must fight to "preserve the Union" or something to that effect. I also wonder as I lay here at night if one hundred years from now mankind will look back and ask, "Would the Union have been preserved without the sacrifice of so many that may be wounded or killed?" One will never know the answer to that question, as the road not taken was the one of diplomacy and time. I sometimes wonder if the issues that this war is being fought over would have worked themselves out over time without such a terrible toll on our nation.

I am in my mid 40's and come from good stock having been born in Nova Scotia, Canada and later on moving to New York State and marrying the lady of my dreams, Julia. One of the few things I remember as a youngster in Nova Scotia was when I was six years old and we were living in the Beaver River Settlement near Yarmouth and a wild fire came up and it moved so rapidly that our entire family and the entire community literally had to run for our lives from such an onslaught. I hope I never find myself in a situation like that again where I must run from an onslaught of either nature or man. Up until now I have been successfully enjoying myself with my lovely wife Julia and a family that God has blessed us with as I practice law in our fair town. I also was recently elected to the New York State Assembly where I served willingly for a short time and then returned to my law practice so that others with new ideas can now serve, which is the way government should function in my opinion.

There is more and more rhetoric being shouted around here in 1861 about the abhorrent practice of slavery, as is the norm in the Southern States in this country. I have heard recently that some slave owners and others have come to their sanity and have freed their slaves, as it should be. Unfortunately others cling to this way of life and do not seem to be willing to give it up at any cost. Our President, Abraham Lincoln, who recently took office has his hands full with the situation as it now stands with the Southern States threatening to pull out of the Union. As he recently said, "In your hands, my dissatisfied fellow countrymen, and not in mine, is the momentous issue of civil war. The government will not assail you. You have no oath registered in Heaven to destroy the government, while I shall have the most solemn one to preserve, protect and defend it." I sincerely hope and pray that he has thought through the consequences of what an appalling conflict this could be. It is often discussed around our dinner table, and my charming wife reminds me when I get carried away, as do many lawyers, that I am not making the decisions in this country and the last she knew, President Lincoln had not asked my advice. I won't argue with her but I often think he ought to.

It is April of 1861 and the entire issue I fear is coming to a head. President Lincoln has stated that secession is illegal and he said he is willing to use force if necessary to defend the Federal law and the Union. Unfortunately this all came to a head when Confederate batteries fired on Fort Sumter and forced its surrender. The president has called upon the States of the Union for volunteers to face what he sees as a grave threat to the very existence of the United States. I can only hope that he has thought this through as to the human costs of a mighty war.

Since as I mentioned, I am a local small town lawyer and also a recent state assemblyman, I have an unselfish duty to be a leader in the forming of a company that will assist in hopefully bringing this conflict to a rapid conclusion. I believe the radicals in the South when they see those of us in the North stepping up to the call of duty will soon put down their weapons and go back to the bargaining table to negotiate an end to our differences. I have put up posters and taken an ad in the local paper for volunteers and the government has indicated a willingness to give me the title of captain if I raise one hundred volunteers. The company will be called Company B and be part of the 33rd Regiment, New York volunteers, which will have one thousand men all of which will hopefully return home unscathed. We will then become part of the 3rd Brigade, 2nd Division, 6th Corp of the Army of the Potomac. I think it should be a relatively easy task since so many of us are caught up in the nationalism of the day and sure enough I have many willing to serve. Maybe they see a future of a small pension from the government or some other such benefit and I don't believe many of them, if any, think that this will become a serious confrontation. My wife and family have been encouraging; as I believe they also feel it will be safe and short-lived. I for one am not so sure and often I lay awake at night wondering what evil has been brought upon this land and I worry that this conflict might become much broader and much more deadly that the average citizen thinks at the present. It is amazing to me that so many good men are so willing to serve and have become caught up in the tumult of the times. God rest their souls and hope that this turns out to be a short conflict without many, if any, casualties. President Lincoln has called for seventy-five thousand volunteers and hopefully this will show the South that he is very serious about keeping the union as one and they will then back down and go to the bargaining table.

I have heard it said, that in times of peace, sons bury fathers and in times of war, fathers bury sons. I say this and feel it so deeply that no young person should have to serve that I am particularly dishearten when I came home from out first organizational meeting of the company and found out that our oldest son John had also become caught up in the patriotism of the time and had volunteered to join Company B. I have tried my most earnest to talk him into staying home and taking care of his mother and his sisters Martha and Sara and young Joseph Henry who has been somewhat sick of late, even though his mother has been supportive of his volunteering. Julia is even possibly expecting our fourth child and under the circumstances she still wants me to go. She said there isn't much I can do here anyway as far as the delivery is concerned and she said since no man has ever been pregnant we really don't realize what the women are going through. I have even had some second looks from our neighbors whose husbands have decided to join our company. Henry Brown's wife and Josiah Hucksley's wives were here for a visit with Julia and they were talking softly in the kitchen about their husbands having volunteered and what they thought about it. I hope they don't hold it against me especially since it is an act they themselves decided to take and they have not been forced to do it. I do believe most able-bodied men do feel, if they didn't step up, that the community would shun them. I also believe that most if not all have said a silent prayer that it will be a short and relatively safe service and that the South will fold quickly under the Union Army's mighty hand. Since I am in my mid 40s which most folks around here consider over the hill I don't think too many are that concerned about my going off to war but they are very concerned for the younger ones who are leaving young wives and children to be taken care of by the community. How rapidly lives can be uprooted by circumstances. We take everyday life for granted until something like this happens and then all hell breaks loose. Even Old Doc. Peterson has volunteered and since he is older than Methuselah, it seems I guess the government doesn't have any age restrictions on who can serve in this endeavor, even youngsters are being allowed to serve. Doc talked to me for quite a while after our meeting and he said he was more concerned about disease than bullets from the Rebels' guns taking a toll on all these brave fellows so he wanted to be there to see if he could ease their suffering. He mentioned that the rigors living off the land and in the open in all types of weather would surely take its toll. I reassured him as I have said before that this should be a short-lived conflict and we can all be back in our warm beds at home and not have to worry about either disease or bullets.

I don't recall the soldier that at one time in history was remembered as saying that in the army it is hurry up and wait situation. It is now July 14th in the year of our Lord 1861 and we have finally left our small town and our beloved ones and headed out on the train for Elmira where we are to meet up with more of the regiment and henceforth leave from there to our encampment in Washington, D.C. There is a great deal of joviality amongst the volunteers and you would think they are going to a picnic and most are all animated about it. I fear that many of them may be in for a rude awakening if this turns into something ghastly.

CHAPTER TWO

Camp Granger

We arrived in Washington and have set up camp, called Camp Granger, with the government issued tents about two and a half miles North of the city. It is a wonderful spot as we can see for miles the tended fields and the farms in every direction. The only problem with it is that I am sharing a tent with John, Henry and Josiah and it just doesn't seem quite fair my being a captain and all and John and Henry and Josiah all being lieutenants. It was even more aggravating when I saw that Old Doc. Peterson has a tent all to himself. I suppose since he is older than the hills he is entitled to it and I do hear his snoring can wake the dead; even so he is a blessing to have with us and he is a great doctor. I am sure there will be plenty of snoring in our tent and I'd better get used to it as things seem to be heating up and we may be living in a tent for a few weeks until this mess can be resolved. Josiah even complained that the government issued uniforms did not fit very well and then we all had a great laugh when we found out he had tried to put mine on by mistake and they were just a little snug on him. Josiah is a fine fellow and I would be happy to have him watch my back anytime but the truth is he hasn't missed many meals over the past few years and of course I only weigh about 140 pounds ringing wet?

I was so pleased to receive Martha's letter of the 15th instant and also the one from Julia that was sent to Elmira and forwarded on to us here at Washington. Julia did say as it turned out she is not expecting so that is at least one burden off my shoulders since I would not be there with her during that difficult time. I wrote them all back and thanked them and also expressed that my prayers have been answered that young Joseph is feeling somewhat better. There are so many diseases around in this day and age that we worry constantly about the young ones. I also told her that John has a furlough coming and may head for home in a few days. Hopefully this will all be over when he is scheduled to return and he can stay where he belongs. I ended my letter to my dear wife, "Hoping that through the protection of Divine providence you, I and our children may all be blessed with good health and that we shall be again united in our home, and that you will all in the meantime put your trust in God, and enjoy yourselves and be happy." It is easy for me to say while living in a tent and possibly shooting at our fellow citizens soon and being shot back at. A man once complimented a great army officer in a previous war for planning and carrying out a successful battle plan and said to him how brilliant he was. The officer replied, " If I was so brilliant I would have been able to achieve a peaceful solution to this conflict rather than a battle." These were words spoken by a very wise man and I wish the leadership on both sides would make the same effort towards resolving this conflict. Maybe if I survive what may well be around the corner I will run for president and see if I can't find peaceful solutions to mankind's differences. Wouldn't that be a change from the way men have lived in this world with all the past wars. I sent the following letter home to Julia and the family.

Courtesy of the Library of Congress

"My Dear Wife:
July 21, 1861:

I am writing you this epistle from our headquarters of the 33rd Regt., Camp Granger, Co. B in Washington. That all sounds so grand for a bunch of small town fellows that all volunteered when called upon to help resolve this conflict. There seem to be many an exciting event taking place in Virginia almost daily and from the many erroneous reports that at first are flushed along the vines and published in the papers may unnecessarily alarm you. Believe only a small amount of what you hear or read as even in the best of times rumors are passed on and printed and it is multiplied many times over. Be patient at all times and hope for the best. There has been heavy cannonading nearly the whole forenoon southwest of us, which undoubtedly was at Manassas Junction (Bull Run) which is about 30 miles southwest from our camp, and undoubtedly there has been a great battle fought there. I am praying that this will be the last battle of this conflict. However I am not optimistic as there is great anticipation amongst the soldiers camped here that they soon would be getting their shot at Johnny Reb. and they seem to a man to think when that happens the Confederacy will lay down their arms and give up their useless cause. We are on high alert and have been told we may move from here shortly but like any army it is hurry up and wait for orders to be issued. We are all well except some of the men have developed diarrhea and Old Doc. Peterson is trying to treat them the best he can. He mentioned to me that we have only been camped out here in relative comfort from what we might expect in the conditions we may well endure if we enter into hostilities and already men are becoming sick. He said again that he fears that this conflict could take as many men from disease as from battles if it continues long.

John will start for home as soon as we get our pay so be patient and he should be bringing some money home for yours and the children's needs soon. You may well hear that we have marched from here and if you do I beg of you to not borrow trouble about my safety. God will direct all things for the best, we may not get into any action at all but if we should, some of us may be wounded or killed, every man has his day, yet if one of us fall it will be where duty directs, and honor will cover the faithful and courageous.

I feel today as though I should like to step in and see you and take tea with you, but that cannot be, and I have to control myself by imagining myself there. I trust you are all well and having a pleasant day and give our little boy a great hug and kiss for me, God help him and all of you until my return.

Your affectionate husband,

Joseph"

Things are certainly heating up, as I mentioned they had a big battle down in Manassas and now one of the colonels from the New York City Fire Dept. who commanded the Fire Zouaves as they call themselves from New York has been shot. A damn Rebel shot Colonel Elmer Ephraim Ellsworth who was only 24 years old as he was removing a secessionist flag from the top of the Marshall House in Alexandria. I heard that upon hearing the news that President Lincoln wept and had Colonel Ellsworth's body ordered to the White House to lie in state. I would suggest that President Lincoln wept because he realized that this misunderstanding (I use that word hesitantly) will widen and many more are likely to die. John took the boat down the Potomac River to Alexandria and even got two pieces of the steps where the colonel was killed for souvenirs. I warned John not to go as things had heated up so much there but he took Henry and Josiah with him to cover his back he said and he did return unscathed as I prayed he would. If we are to engage the enemy we will show them what a real fighting man is all about as those of us from Upstate New York are sure to be feared in battle.

The entire regiment was ordered to go on parade today for the review of the colonel and low and behold in front of the entire group he announced that our Company B was the best of the lot. That makes me feel quite proud and I hope they perform in battle when called upon as well as they perform on the parade grounds. I also received another letter from home and it is with great anticipation that I wait for each letter. They cannot come too often and I try to write as often as my time here allows. How wonderful it would be to see my family if just for one night and hold little Joseph in my arms. Julia mentioned that he is better and growing stronger everyday and under the protection of Divine Providence he may continue to improve and live to cheer us in our old age, that is if I survive this conflict. Josiah and I managed to get into Washington itself today and we bought some cheese and sausage to enjoy with our other tent family this night. We are also having John Smith for supper as he was in the recent battle in Manassas or as it sometimes is referred to as the "Battle Of Bull Run." Some of our enthusiasm has been dampened when we heard that there were 481 Union soldiers killed and over 1000 wounded. The Confederate casualties were 269 killed and almost 1500 wounded. He also said we should not underestimate the battle readiness and the devotion to the South's cause that their soldiers exhibited. He said if the conflict widens and goes forth thousands may end up dying on both sides. For what will they die that couldn't eventually, even if it took years, be resolved at a bargaining table. Only God knows the answer to that question

Here it is the 4th of August in this year of our Lord, 1861. It is very sultry and heat oppressive and we have some sickness in camp with several fellows having to be taken to the hospital. As Old Doc. Peterson has said, he is concerned that some very infectious illness may strike the camp and spread rapidly. I pray that will not happen. There has been no particular movement of the Army since the battle a couple of weeks ago and I don't believe there will be another advance until this oppressive heat lifts and maybe not until September. When we are ordered to move it will be to conquer. There I go with that overflowing optimism and patriotism which when I think about it may be in the end regretted if many are wounded or die. I look out amongst all the tents that we can see from this vantage point covering every open field between here and the city, and hearing the roll of the drums and bands of music fill the ear from every direction. The vastness of all these volunteers and the combined furor make me feel that no army will be able to stand up to us for long. I hope I am right and we shock the Rebs. into submission and to the bargaining table shortly. I want to get home to my family. John is getting melancholy awaiting our pay and I hope I can send $100 home with him if and when our government comes through.

I wish we had the means so that I could bring all my family down here to Washington to see this vast army but alas I do not at this time. The money has stopped coming in from my law practice and I am sure those that choose not to serve are picking up my clients and hoping that I shall never return. I heard from Josiah that two letters were received from our town stating that one of my men, George Wheaton, had tried to shoot me and that I had shot him dead on the spot. Nothing can be further from the truth and I must write Julia immediately to set the record straight or she will be in a panic. As it turns out George is one of our most trusted men and I would put my life in his hands anytime as well as any member of the company. I believe I am as respected as I respect all of them. It would be disastrous if those of us in the Union Army began to shoot each other rather than the enemy, or the so-called enemy. Sometimes I think we are going to war against our brothers so to speak.

Well John and I went into Washington after we finally got paid and I saw him off on his trip back home. He is planning on stopping and seeing Jesse so it will most likely take him a week to get there. I wonder what the hurry would be anyway as we are all just sitting on our behinds almost a month now since we arrived here. I don't know who is figuring out the strategy for this conflict but I would suggest they get off their asses and make some decisions or we will be here all winter. The only down side of going into Washington and seeing John off was that it rained cats and dogs on my way back to camp and I had to take shelter several times under some porches and in a shed or two. I finally got back to our rain-soaked camp and what a chaos of mud and leaky tents some of us had to endure. It didn't seem to bother either Josiah or Henry, as they were both dead to the world when I finally got back. I wish I could sleep as soundly but unfortunately my thoughts drift off to the coming conflict and what it will mean to this country and all these fine men on both sides of the conflict. Wouldn't it be nice that in wars the leaders are the ones to fight it out rather then send us poor peons to do their fighting for them? I am feeling very fit and I truly believe that any of the other lawyers in our small town would have been totally stressed out if they were living and drilling under these adverse conditions. Who knows, maybe they were the smart ones and I was stupid for volunteering but I thought my country needed me so here I am. We will all have to answer to the Lord when our time comes so we shall see what he says about my duty and their lack of patriotism. I just hope my time does not come earlier than old age and that I die in my bed in Julia's arms while asleep, what more can one ask. I did manage to send some gold coin home with John and it should help Julia pay the rent and some other bills until we hopefully get paid again in September. I even managed to send home a flower, which I believe is from the Holly Tree that I picked when we were in town from the president's garden. I hope President Lincoln didn't mind but I am sure he has more on his mind at present. Julia had sent me a few of her geraniums in her last correspondence and I enjoyed them so much I wanted to return the love.

Lieutenant Hucksley has been assigned picket duty by the colonel and myself and he has gone up the river to stand picket. He will be on duty for 24 straight hours so I don't think anyone would be willing to say that army life is not trying. It is also raining so that will make it even more difficult for him. The regiment has also mounted heavy guns on the hillside and they have been practicing it seems night and day. If you think it is tough to sleep in a tent with three other fellows snoring each night try it with that and hearing the big weaponry going off all the time. I think our leaders are worried that the Rebels may well mount a direct attack on Washington and they want to be able to defend it. We have even had the 2nd Vermont Regiment join the brigade and they have camped out just south of the 3rd Vermont. There are so many men here I wonder what is going to become of us and if we are ever to be used in this conflict. The 2nd Vermont brought with them some fine peaches so I traded them 36 lbs. of coffee for a very generous supply of peaches. I believe we will all be enjoying them for many a day. We can also buy milk by the quart here for ten cents a quart but if we walk the mile we can get it for eight cents. I have dispatched several of the men in the company to rotate their duty and bring us the needed milk daily. Along with the peaches and milk we received a load of hominy and I showed the regiment cooks just how to cook it without burning it. It wasn't as good as Julia's but then again nothing is as good as hers.

The other day a photographer was here in camp taking pictures of as many of the soldiers as possible and he managed to get myself, John, Henry and Josiah before he left. What a fine looking group of fellows we are, all dressed up in our uniforms with our guns stacked up in the background. The artist said he would give us several copies and Henry and Josiah each want one and I will get two (rank you know) and another for John if they came out all right and as soon as we get them I want to send it home to Julia and the children so they can see firsthand how fit we look and how well we are. This should hopefully dispel any misgivings at the present time of our well being.

I reprimanded our company mailman today as he only brought two letters for the entire company and the day before he only delivered one. I don't think he waits long enough at the station for all the mail to come in before he comes up to deliver it. I warned him it should not happen again. I usually receive at least one letter daily either from Julia or the girls and of course John who is now at home. It is so important for all the men because they get downcast somewhat when the mail isn't handled in a timely fashion. All this waiting and living in the outdoors in tents and often having to put up with the mud is getting everyone on edge. I think President Lincoln could have waited a little longer to make the call for so many troops if he and his officers didn't have a clue what they were going to use us for. I believe this amounts to a substantial waste of fine talent, as the men have been anxious to go into battle. The enthusiasm is wearing off and eventually I believe if we are not used, some of the men will start to wander back to their homes. I am not sure as a husband and father that I can blame them but as their captain I cannot let on to any of them my feelings.

It's a good thing I keep these thoughts to myself as low and behold our brigade was notified that we would shortly be reviewed by not only the Secretary of War (what a wonderful title to bestow on someone, have I ever heard someone called the Secretary of Peace) and he will be accompanied by none other than President Lincoln himself and General McClellan. I have told the men to dress properly and shape up for such a momentous occasion. I have never seen any of these men close up and personal so I am looking forward to their arrival. I'm sure those three are not too thrilled about having to review the troops but it is part of their duty like it or not.

They were a little late but when they showed up and the entire brigade was in spit and polish, as much as was allowed under these cursed conditions. I believe the three big shots were properly impressed with us all. I was shocked by the gaunt look of the president and frankly I liked the looks of General McClellan for a commander and I thought that he had the look of a true ring of metal from his appearance and reputation. I believe the officers and men will have full confidence in him. Maybe I will try to invite him into our tent for a little liquid nourishment some evening if I get the chance. It is said that real fighting men are also true drinkers or something to that effect. I have heard a rumor that he is a teetotaler so I'm not sure if that bodes well for him as a commander, only time will tell. I wanted to stop them all in their review and ask them when the hell we would be finally going into battle rather than sitting around here forever getting sore feet and fighting off bugs of one sort or the other. I did notice that Old

Doc. Peterson gave all three of these gentlemen sort of a sour look and I wondered what he was thinking as they walked by. Old Doc. is a very bright fellow and I sometimes think he should be the one running this country, not these other fellows.

Courtesy of the Library of Congress

Since the army has not furnished us with any beds rather than a roll-up blanket that passes somewhat as a bed we decided to go into Washington and see if we could find some halfway decent beds. We did manage to find us three corn nap bottomed bedsteads and we have now used them for a couple of nights. Since there are four of us in the tent normally and only three beds John, when he returns, Henry and Josiah will be rotating with one of them nightly sleeping on the cold, wet, and hard ground. Since I am the captain I pulled rank and use the best of the three exclusively for myself. I have taken a lot of ribbing over it but it is all good-natured fun and we have had a few good belly laughs, which help to pass the time and boredom of waiting and waiting and waiting. I have even heard from John that some of the men have written home that they did not have enough to eat and that their officers kicked and abused them. I can't believe this has happened in this army and certainly not in this company. The only time I have even raised my voice to any of the men is when a couple of them snuck off into town and had a little too much of the bubbly and heaven only knows what else but never have I or any of my officers struck anyone in the company. As far as I know they have all had plenty to eat even though I am sure it is a far cry from home cooking it is still enough to keep a man on his feet. If it is fighting that we come to I feel many of the complainers will then wish they were back here at Camp Granger eating rations and being chewed out a little when they misbehaved. I asked the company cook for a report on the food on hand and he told me we have two full days of ration of pork and bacon and 50 lbs. of corn beef. We also have 84 lbs. of sugar, 48 lbs. of coffee and plenty of tea for those so inclined. He said we also have beans, rice, vinegar and soap and believe me if anyone in this army needs soap it is the 80 men at present in the company. It is difficult, to say the least, to get a decent bath in these surroundings and more than one fellow has ventured down to the river with his ration of soap. We have even had so much bread that we have been feeding it to the horses before it goes stale since the men cannot consume it all. Does this sound like deprived soldiers?

On top of all this food some I have heard complaining they haven't been given enough proper clothing. At Elmira each soldier was given a full suit with an overcoat, two woolen shirts, two pairs of drawers, two pairs of woolen socks and of course shoes. Our wonderful government supplied all of these so that we could someday be sent into battle to face our enemy properly dressed? Since we arrived here we have been issued more socks and shoes and so many that the quartermaster says the men aren't taking advantage of them as they already have all the clothing they think they need. Of course if one gets close to some of them you might wish to suggest they change their socks and britches a little more often. Even so I still, as I have often said, would rather have these men by my side and watching my back than anyone else I have seen in this man's army. They are solid folks from Upstate New York and not to be trifled with.

I happen to be a few good men short in the company as a few have been reassigned and unfortunately a few (very few) have taken to wandering off. I need to add about 20 good men to bring us back up to about 100 and I sent a note home to Julia asking her to talk to George and see if he would volunteer to come as our company butcher and the pay would be $22 a month. He would be required to kill and butcher every other day everything that is found. If that sounds good to him she will tell him to telegraph me here at the camp. John has returned and enjoyed his time away from here immensely.

CHAPTER THREE

Action?

Would you believe it we have finally been told we are going to see some action and the commander met with myself, John, Henry and Josiah to fill us in on the details of our engagement. Low and behold it is a campaign worthy of Napoleon himself. We were told that we are to take a dozen or so of our best men and raid the local Whorehouse in Washington where many of the soldiers have been seen entering for tea and afternoon delights. We have been ordered to clean it out, not harm anyone but scare the living daylights out of all the fine ladies that are there in the hopes that they will move on. Now a campaign like that takes a lot of pre-planning and I have called upon some of my best men to help us figure out the best way to storm this fort. Several of the fellows seem to have a considerable knowledge of the layout of the intended target and I questioned in my mind how they knew so much but I decided I would not ask them to many drilling questions. I did consult with Old Doc. Peterson concerning any medical problems we might encounter and he just snickered and said to say hello to the ladies for him. I'm not sure what he meant by that but he did seem to have a gleam in his eye when he told me. Old Doc continues to amaze me. A number of the men said they would act as advanced scouts to go in ahead of the main troop and evaluate the enemy's strength. It is surprising that so many of these fine stout lads are so willing to volunteer for this dangerous assignment with the risk of major injury incurring in the heat of battle. I decided it best to send half the troop in the back way and keep the other half for a main frontal assault but when it came time to carry out our mission I was not surprised to find this house of ill repute empty. I only wonder if some of the higher ups in the army warned the Madame of the upcoming assault and they decided to move their foundation of operation. Most likely they were worried that some high government official might be caught literally with his pants down and such an embarrassing situation would not be tolerated by the commander-in-chief. This assignment, even if it resulted in an assault on an empty building, will certainly help to keep the men's fighting edge honed as necessary when they do, if ever, have to face the Rebs. All I can say about this entire fiasco is that it gave us all some good laughs and kept our minds off the boredom of army life when we are constantly told to hurry up and wait. I don't believe this will go down as one of the biggest battles of this Civil ??? War and I don't expect any metals for our bravery in the face of overwhelming enemy firepower but we did our duty like good soldiers and if called upon again we will be trained and ready for the next assault on a Whorehouse.

After all this the colonel has received orders that our company has been chosen to accompany the 3rd Vermont across the river tomorrow and reconnoiter into Virginia. My company has been chosen for that duty, I am sure because of our vast experience in engaging the enemy, and all but Josiah will be going. Josiah is still up the river so to speak pulling his weight as one of the officers of the picket about four miles from here, he will certainly be upset when he finds that he missed this opportunity especially if we run into Johnny Reb and get a chance at him. As it turned out 300 of us made the excursion into Virginia and never saw a Rebel or anyone that in any way resembled any threat. It is a beautiful country and it is a shame if it ends up being stained by the blood of both the Union and the Rebel soldiers. Living in peace and resolving mankind's differences seems to be beyond man's abilities or they are just too damn stubborn, pig-headed and downright aggressive to follow that other road. We are to return to the outskirts of Washington to rejoin the rest of the vast Army of the Potomac and several of the men have indicated an eagerness to volunteer to search for any newly opened whore houses that we may be asked to raid. These fellows are sure eager fighters, or is it lovers.

I still am short several men for the company and I have written Jeremiah who is still at home and asked him again if he could raise about 20 able bodied men to join us here. The man who organizes them I can make sergeant and he will be paid $19 per month and the foot soldiers will be paid $13 per month, now who could turn down such a good deal especially when all your travel expenses are paid for and your keep is all paid for when you reach here. It seems that some of the patriotic fervor that was so prevalent early on in this conflict has waned some since some of the reports of fighting and dying of some of the troops. As I earlier said a lot of the fellows never felt this would last long and they certainly never thought they would be seeing any dangerous action so they were eager to join the ranks. Cooler heads are now prevailing and folks are thinking long and hard about any commitment. I still think we will be able to raise the necessary manpower but it won't be as easy as before. I did hear from Josiah's brother, who is still at home with a fever, he told us that poor Morrison is very ill at home and fears he will never be able to return to the field. Old Doc. Peterson's prediction may well be true about the toll that a long protracted campaign may take on all the men not only from bullets but also from disease. Asking Jeremiah to recruit about 20 good men reminded me so much of home when my mind went back and forth through our community and all the fine folks that live there and share the good times and bad.

One of the more difficult duties of an officer in this man's army is to sit in judgment of a fellow soldier. It is one thing to try and bring down the enemy, I use that word hesitantly, and another to sit as a judge in a court-marshal of someone supposedly on the same side as you are. This particular soldier who will go unnamed was not from my company but from one of the Vermont companies and I was ordered to be part of the military commission that will hear his case and set the penalty if found guilty. The penalty could range in this case from dishonorable discharge to hanging or of course be found not guilty. That is quite a spread when it comes to penalties and it will be interesting to see what defense his puts up. Another reason I was chosen, I believe, is because I was an attorney in my past life so they are in hopes I can be impartial and understand the ramifications of this case. It is hard to believe but this case has to do with the recent action we saw in raiding the house of ill repute in the city. It seems that this poor fellow after being ordered, along with the entire regiment, not to visit the ladies for afternoon tea and cookies was caught in the act of needless to say partaking. I do believe if we were to bring charges against all the fellows who had tea and cookies at this "Little White House" we would end up being thin in the ranks when we go up against the Rebs. When I told Old Doc. Peterson I was to sit on the court marshal panel he said they had asked him to serve and he said it might not be such a good idea since if they bring in some of the ladies to testify, they might recognize him. They say he has treated a number of them for various medical problems, sure he has.

There were five officers assigned to hear the case and the army provided a prosecutor who was also an attorney in his past life and they provided the accused with a defense attorney who we shall see if he is up to the task. As it turned out, none of the ladies of the tea and cookie society were called upon to testify, as I think some of the other officers there were afraid they might be recognized and thought discretion the better part of valor. The prosecutor's case was quite simple. This poor fellow was seen leaving this house of questionable character late one evening and was immediately arrested and thrown in the brig. The prosecutor suggested he be hung with a sign around his neck saying "WELL HUNG." Most likely we would have had to get the madam's opinion before going that far. When you are in the army, some moments of levity ease the boredom so I took the latitude of expressing my true feelings.

When he was brought into the court I thought he looked about 14 years old and it might have been his first encounter with the ladies. The defense attorney decided to present a very brief argument that a certain company that recently had been given the assignment to raid said house and close it down had failed in their task and therefore his client was not guilty since if said company had done its job properly the temptation would not have been there for his client. I thought I saw a number of eyes turn my way when he was speaking of this but I couldn't be sure. As I said before I didn't expect any metals for our efforts in this great raid but now I am worried that we may be reprimanded for our failure to find anyone there and thus close them down. After the case was presented, the five of us retired to our chamber to make our decision. One of my fellow officers wanted to hang the poor fellow for his indiscretions and make an example of him. Two others thought he should be drummed out of the army and I held out to acquit him with a slap on the wrist. I reminded the others that we would most likely soon be facing a much more disciplined and focused enemy and that we would need every able bodied man we had in case things heated up. The one officer still held out for the hanging but the other four of us resolved that this time he would get off with a warning to not partake again. Needless to say, when we read our verdict, he was extremely delighted. The one officer who held out for his execution just sat there scowling at myself and the defendant and his attorney. I never could figure that one out; maybe he also had been caught with his pants down at the Little White House and was afraid the defendant might divulge it in case he had seen him there. All's well that ends well and with relief we dismissed all those present and got on with more serious matters.

We have now moved on and we are at Camp Lyon, have been ordered to hurry up and wait again. Some days I can't believe the time we spend wasting time. Does General McClellan know what he is doing? He came across as such a spit and polish soldier when he reviewed the troops but it doesn't seem to me he is using his resources, as he should be. As I mentioned earlier on, these folks ought to turn to me for advice as I often tell Julia, but alas they do not. Since they do not, then I feel I can be critical of them if things do not work out, as they should. Time will only tell if he lives up to be the fine officer he appears to be.

As it turned out, I didn't have too much time to complain as we are camping out in the open and have set up some makeshift bush tents as best we can. We crossed the chain bridge and arrived at this spot much closer to the action. There is nothing like lying in the open air at night and having the bugs bite you, hearing a thousand fellow soldiers all snoring to make one wish for home and being with Julia in our warm bed. To add insult to injury it has started to rain and since we did not dig a drainage ditch around our makeshift tent the water is running right through it. I am lying on my oilcloth coat within the sand and mud and even awoke once and found my hip lying in a pool of water. Many of the fellows have been out on picket duty so they have had to endure the rain even more than we are. Laying in a pool of water when you are in your 40's certainly is great for the rheumatism and will certainly make a lasting impression on me I am sure. The colonel has ordered that at daybreak we are all to dress in full battle gear and be ready anytime to engage Johnny Reb. I believe when Johnny Reb gets close enough to the regiment they may decide not to engage us as most all the men have been sleeping and living in the same clothes for about ten days and I am sure if the fellows in the South whiff those of us in the North that they may head back to the sunny south. Of course they have been living out also as is the way with most soldiers. We have even set up the heavy artillery in case of an attack. I for one do not think they will attack and the colonel is saying that the general may order us into battle soon if we are not engaged. I am almost hoping for some action to take our minds off the miserable state we are currently living in. This is not fit for man or beast. Whatever happened to the negotiations table? If we don't enter battle soon I am going to request a furlough to go home and be with my lovely wife and children. I am concerned there may be more than one fellow thinking the same thing and wondering if they may never come back. After living in the open so long much of the early passion to get at the enemy is wearing off and I think more than one soldier is wondering why they are here rather than the leaders of both sides just having a duel to end this madness.

CHAPTER FOUR

Advanced Camp

We have been moved up to a position where the general thinks we might engage the enemy for the first time. For now I am taking advantage of a beautiful sunny day and have cleaned out my trunk and hung all the clothes out on a rope to air out. That is about the best we can do as far as laundry is concerned here in the open. I believe my dear wife Julia would cringe if she could see the way we look after a protracted time in the open, so is the way of the poor soldier. I have been assigned every other day to picket duty and I am taking about 250 men with me along with Lieutenants Brown and Hucksley. They are good men to have on your side when we are out on picket looking for the enemy and making sure he doesn't sneak up on us especially in the dark. It is nerve-racking duty especially at night since one never knows what lurks around the next bend or behind the tree or hedgerow. I think Johnny Reb is watching our movements and waiting for the opportune time to attack. They may also have some informants amongst our ranks, not in my company I am sure, and be getting information from the inside that way. If I am ever called upon to serve in court-marshal for anyone being caught as an informant to the enemy you can rest assured I would vote to have a very public hanging. One becomes very attached to each other in the regiment and especially in my Company B as we survive together in the field, tomorrow or the next day you may need each other more so than ever before in this life. Since John is still laid up I do not have him to worry about being out on the picket line along with all the other concerns at present. John has been feeling under the weather since his return and maybe it is for the better as far as I am concerned although he has expressed that he is anxious to rejoin the company but for now I will accept things as they are and be grateful to God for looking after John and all the family. I also told John that I think I can get a commission for him, which would mean a few more dollars in his pocket, when he is back in full health. I also have heard from home that the fellow that was raising the 20 good men to make this company full again has sold out his chance for captain to a man in the next village. I think some of the boys may be disappointed that the officers that the army is now appointing all have to take an examination and are not chosen by the company as it has been. One might argue that if someone can pass the exam they are better fitted for command but I personally think that men have more faith in leadership that has proven itself and is chosen by the men who will follow their officers. Whatever, they didn't ask me, even though they should have. I think if they had asked me we would have been engaging the enemy long before now and kicking some ass in the hope of ending this lunacy

We are now positioned well beyond Washington and are ready to repel any attack by the Rebels if it should come. I cannot believe their leadership would be so foolish to mount such an attack as much as they would like to occupy Washington. McCall's Brigade of Pennsylvania has built massive fortifications on the other side of the river and we have batteries set up to rake every road and field from which they may mount an attack so it would be suicide for them to try. In war however the unthinkable becomes the thinkable as one side senses their invincibility and feels that they can easily show the enemy what they are all about. I sometimes daydream that we are all sitting down, both soldiers from the North and South having a tall one in the local tavern rather than living in squalor and just waiting to put a bullet through the other fellow's head.

I have had a pleasant and an unpleasant surprise today as John has rejoined the company being considerably better than he has felt in some time. I sometimes wonder if I would be a more effective officer if I only had my own hide to worry about instead of having John here and constantly worrying about him. I realize he is a grown man and can take care of himself but one never sees their children as grown-up only as the blessings the Lord has bestowed upon us. Our pickets have had a small encounter with Johnny Reb and they say it didn't last long as he soon retreated to a less threatening position. I'm sure they were out scouting our strength and when they were close enough to get a sense of the massive army encamped here ready for battle they thought better of it which is certainly what I would have done if I were commanding them.

The leadership on both sides at this point is just starting to get their feet wet and I understand General Robert E. Lee is playing a major roll in the military movements of the South. He was a graduate of West Point and an officer in the army when the war started and he was asked to play a leading roll in the Union Army but he declined as he was a native Virginian and when hostilities started he went with his native state. He said when making his choice, "With all my devotion to the Union and the feeling of loyalty and duty as an American citizen, I have not been able to make up my mind to raise my hand against my relatives, my children, my home. I have therefore resigned my commission in the Army, and save in defense of my native state, with the sincere hope that my poor services may never be needed. I hope I may never be called on to draw my sword." This is a wise man and will be a formidable opponent and it is a perfect example of brother against brother in this ill-gotten endeavor. Wouldn't one think that if wise men like Robert E. Lee and President Lincoln were just to take more time to talk and try to calm down the furor present on each side we might have been able to avoid that which is ahead of us? God help us all, Northern soldier and Southern soldier.

More of the men are turning up sick from living out of doors so long in cramped quarters and the stress is certainly not helping any. Stress I have learned can be a large factor in everyone's lives, especially the soldiers. Henry has fallen ill but Old Doc told me that he should be up and around soon after he treated him. Old Doc has some kind of magical medicine he gives those that report to him and it is rumored it is so helpful that some of the men fake their illnesses just to get another slug of it. He may well need it soon to deaden the pain of severe gunshot wounds when he has to do surgery on some poor fellow. I sure hope it doesn't come to that. It is amazing also how the rumors fly about in the camp. We are adding to our strength everyday and even so it is often rumored up and down the encampment that Johnny Reb is advancing. If I had a dollar for every time we are told to be at the ready I would be a rich man, which at this point I certainly am not. Some of those other attorneys that stayed at home are most likely cleaning up and taking over most of my clients. I should not be dwelling on this as it was my choice to form the company and join the cause but this constant stress has made me sometimes wonder if I did the right thing. The road not taken may have been the road I should have taken.

Julia and the children have all written me fine letters and in the last one Julia told me that the family has gotten a dog especially for little Joseph. They are all wondering what to name him and asked for my suggestions. I wrote them back and suggested "Union" or "Mac" for General McClellan and I was going to suggest calling him "Battle" but thought better of sending that suggestion as I believe every time they called the dog they would think of John and I so close to danger. I also enclosed in my letter to Julia and the children what I believe is called Cocks-Comb, which is a beautiful flower, looking like velvet. How can so much beauty exist when we are about to try and slaughter our brothers and they upon us? Old Doc said maybe we ought to chew on the flower and it might help those of us with diarrhea, which is becoming rampant in the camp. These men with this affliction will certainly not be at the top of their form when called up. Julia also told me that little Joseph is starting to walk and he is lisping "Papa." If I were only there to see him but I have the next best thing as they have sent me a picture of this darling little boy and I carry it with me all the time and when I am out on picket duty I often take it out and look at it and it comforts me along with all the pictures of the family from home.

We have finally gotten the orders to march and those of us still healthy are ready to go. There are a few too sick to move but not as many as I would have expected. We marched over on the turnpike and regiment after regiment, artillery and cavalry have been forming and marching up the road. I had not received any direct orders from the commanding officers but I expect we are to drive the enemy from their camp south of Lewisville. As we came closer to Langley the regiments were spread out on the open fields and the batteries of artillery took positions on commanding points. When we were about three quarters of a mile from where I thought we would launch an attack we were ordered to take up defensive positions around Captain Mott's battery. Soon after this I was amazed to see wagon after wagon coming down the road towards our position. To my total surprise they were on their way to fill up the wagons with hay and oats from the farms of several Rebel soldiers for feeding the cavalry soldiers' horses in our command. I was relieved and also a little disappointed that we were not there to drive the enemy back but only to take his grain. This did not quite live up to our most famous campaign to date, that of our direct frontal attack on the House of Ill Repute, but it did come close. They loaded up full 100 wagons and we all headed back to the relative safety of our encampment. I again have to wonder why so many good men are being wasted on raids on whorehouses and barns full of grain but again the commanders didn't ask my opinion. Some of the men in the regiment wanted to burn the house and barns but I ordered them to leave it as we found it. If the shoe was on the other foot I wonder how they would like it if Johnny Reb were in our state and burning our property. The last I knew a house or barn could not shoot back at you. On the way back we did see a number of the Rebel Calvary at about three quarters of a mile distance but a few well placed shots from one of Mott's rifled guns soon sent them scurrying. When we were just about back to camp we did come under some long range fire but it didn't amount to much and no one was injured, thank heavens. On our way back we also noticed some grazing cattle on an abandoned farm and I asked the commanding officer if we could confiscate them and he said to go ahead. I sent ten men in and the rest of us watched their backs. They came under some shot and shell fire but only one close enough to make them jump. One of our batteries returned fire and on the second shot silenced one of their guns. Johnny Reb is not a very good marksman and fortunately missed everyone. The fellows also found two cases of very fine honey and we brought that back along with the cows. This evening I suspect we will dine on beef and honey.

Someone told me the honey and the cows came from the farm of the secessionist, Captain Bell of the Rebel Cavalry. We also managed to get a few of his horses for our cavalry and I confiscated one for myself. I think the rank of captain deserves a horse. My company and the division now have two immense campaigns behind us. The first I am calling the "Raid on The Well Stacked" and the second the "Raid on The Stacked Well." I will so note in my diary. I have grave misgivings about the latest so-called encounter with the hay and cows and I really wonder if that is how this many thousand-man army can be best used. I content myself with the knowledge that men of much more military knowledge and experience and with much better sources of information know what is best for us. I am content to abide by their judgment until they are proved to be erroneous, however I still wonder sometimes why we are not engaging the enemy. If the Southern Rebels are to be dealt with harshly, then why are we being wasted attacking whorehouses and barns full of hay? President Lincoln may well be wondering the same thing. I though General McClellan was cut from solid steel but I am beginning to wonder if he is the man for the job, only time will tell.

CHAPTER FIVE

Camp Of The Big Chestnut October 1861

I have written Julia that she should not worry herself about John's fate and mine. I told her she should not imagine that if we should go into action, that out of 50 or even 100,000 men that your husband and son will be amongst those killed. Trust in God that he will protect us both from sickness, injury or death in these hours. Trust that we shall both return unharmed to you and the children to live many years in peace and happiness, under the protection of our government and that we may be humble instruments in aiding to maintain and sustain against this wicked rebellion now being waged. I also enclosed in my letter to her some flowers I picked from the house the general has taken over as his headquarters. They were very pretty even though I didn't know their name and it reminded me of Julia and all the family.

Julia was also very kind and thoughtful in her latest correspondence as she included some of her famous cookies and also a new shirt she had sewed for me for the cooler weather ahead. I can wear it proudly under my uniform. Before I could hardly get to the cookies they were all eaten, especially by Josiah, as I have mentioned he loves his cookies and almost anything else that is put before him. Oh to sit down at home right about now for a home cooked meal but it can't be so at this time, hopefully soon. I am eager to get paid soon so I can send some more money home for the family and also that Julia can collect some of the money owed me from legal cases I turned over to some of the other attorneys that stayed behind rather than answering the call.

It is now my 47th birthday here on Nov. 4th, 1861 and by Divine Providence I am yet spared and in good health for an old fellow. I guess I was fortunate in our two major battles up to now that I was not injured. Hopefully those are the most serious of the battles we will ever be in. It is turning out that it is more dangerous to be out in some of this terrible weather than it is from Johnny Reb. I have been on picket duty and it has been cold, rainy and windy when I was out for about 16 hours straight and I don't think I will ever warm up again or be dry again. It is tough on the men and I am sure the Rebels are feeling the same way as they are standing on their picket lines.

I have asked Julia if she can spare it to give Josiah Hucksley's wife five dollars as I will send Julia my pay as soon as I get it. It has been awhile since we have been paid and Josiah said his wife and family are having a very difficult time without his being able to send any money to them. I told him we would lend him the five dollars and he said he would pay it back when we finally are paid. It is certainly tough on those of us living out in the fields, constantly worried about what is going to happen tomorrow but it is also very difficult for those families left at home who are trying to deal with the situation the best they can on almost nothing. This is when community is so important and as the word has been passed down, everyone at home, with the exception of a few that are too selfish to help, are trying to ease everyone's pain and make it easier to cope. There are always a few individuals that are all too wrapped up in themselves and their position in life that they seldom can see beyond their collective noses and offer a hand up to the less fortunate. I sometimes wonder if those are the ones we are sacrificing and fighting for. Hopefully it is the good folks that we are enduring this hardship for in the long run.

It has turned very cold here in November in Northern Virginia and last night we had a quarter inch of ice in the washbasin. If you think it is tough to live out of doors in the nice weather try doing it when the water turns to ice. Since it is only early November, I shudder, literally, to think what we are in for as winter lingers around the corner. Maybe with God's help the conflict will be ended soon. However I would more likely think that if we were to avoid the rigors of winter it would be because General McClellan orders us to drive into the Deep South to show the Rebels who is the boss. In either case it would be better than sitting here on our behinds freezing our asses off. My feelings are, use us or lose us general. As you can see I am getting more tired every day that goes by of just sitting around and not being ordered to engage the enemy. The general seems to be hesitant to commit his troops and since we have been waiting since July and it is now November I wonder if we will ever see action. I guess I shouldn't complain as we are relatively safe here but I sometimes wonder if this entire conflict would be ended sooner if we just made a move. I am sure the Rebels can sense our leadership's hesitation and are taking advantage of it to add to their numbers and re-supply themselves. The longer we wait, the stronger Johnny Reb becomes in my opinion. I have spoken with a number of the other officers and they have the same opinion and feel that we may well spend the next few months here at camp and may even be pulled back to Camp Griffin to await someone finally making a decision. Pray tell why did the country ask for so many volunteers to put down what they considered an insurrection and so many fine fellows stepped forward only to be left cooling our heals in camp week after week. Would someone in Washington please make a decision or end this madness. If this stalemate continues I am going to ask for a furlough so I can go home and see my beloved wife Julia and my wonderful family. I cannot imagine the powers turning down my request as there is little to do here but sit and wonder, worry and see so many of the fine fellows getting sick and needing treatment. Old Doc is most likely the busiest of all of us at present treating all the aliments running through our camp. I guess I should stop complaining, as it is better than having Johnny Reb's bullets sailing by our heads.

We were finally paid and I am sending home by express $310.00 thankfully. It includes $20 from Josiah for his wife and I have asked Julia to see that she gets it. It also includes money from a number of the other men to their family and Julia and the girls will be delivering it to them as soon as it arrives home. I did instruct Julia to hand deliver Mrs. Riley's personally to her and not to her sons who I fear might use it to buy some more spirits as they have a reputation of enjoying a nip or two. We used a small amount of our pay too, exactly $8.26 to buy a stove in town. John and I went in and bought it and it has four places on it for the teakettle, boiler, coffee pot and oven to bake in. It has all the comforts of home. We cooked a nice piece of roast beef in it for its first work out and it was well worth it. Today we also had a grand review. There were sixty or seventy thousand troops in the field for review and General McClellan, President Lincoln and their staffs road by and reviewed all the troops. I wanted to yell out to them as they passed our regiment, "Gentlemen, in all due respect why are we sitting on our behinds here rather than engaging the enemy and binging this conflict closer to a conclusion?" It was certainly a grand site to see so many fine troops assembled and I was within a rod of the general and president on several occasions. I don't think they would have appreciated my calling out to them my concerns so I kept my big mouth shut, reluctantly. It is said that some leaders come across as solid steel but have a very difficult time going beyond the hypothetical and actually ordering their plans to be carried out. Maybe the general is somewhat that way, I sincerely hope not.

Would you believe that the colonel came into our tent this morning and brought with him an order from Albany for John to be named lieutenant colonel of the 33rd New York Volunteers? To everyone's surprise and especially John's and mine, he was to be my superior officer from this point on. You can well imagine my concerns and the colonel soon realized that those in Albany that issued the promotion had put the wrong name on it and it should have read Joseph. The colonel is going to send it back with a memo to correct the name. This was a nice surprise and will mean a little more pay and of course some more responsibility which I consider myself up to. The only fellows that were really surprised by the promotion were the current adjutant and the major both of which thought they had this position locked up for themselves. John had a great time with myself, Josiah and Henry, giving us all orders even though it was all in fun. I will set him straight soon enough when the proper paper work comes through. I received hearty congratulations from them all and many of the men in the company and regiment. I appreciate the opportunity to be able to lead such a fine group and hope we all return safely and I will have not regretted a minute of it. With the new advancement, I am going to try and see that John is appointed Assistant Pay Master if possible. It will pay him more and possibly be a less dangerous situation for him if we ever see action. With my promotion I will have to invest in a new uniform and of course a horse, which I already have confiscated from Johnny Reb. I will be paid an additional $50 per month, most of which I can send home to Julia and the family since some of our needs here, the government is taking care of.

Here it is already Thanksgiving Day in this year of our Lord 1861. It is on days like this that I am so homesick and can only in my dreams imagine myself sitting at the table with Julia and the children and enjoying a fine turkey dinner to celebrate and be thankful for all of God's blessings. At the present rate of engagement with the enemy I think the government could well have waited until now to call up volunteers and save all that money they have had to shell out for the past six months and we could all be home with our families enjoying this and every other day. As it turned out I formed the regiment up at 10 AM and we had the Governor's Thanksgiving Day proclamation read and then some remarks by our Chaplin. I then led the men in singing "Say Brother, will you meet us on Canaan's happy shore?" A fine rousing song to put the spirit in the hearts of everyone. Old Doc sang along with all of us and has a rousing bass voice. After the singing and I had dismissed the troops, Old Doc told me he hoped that line of the song was not a premonition of things to come. We had a fine supper and our regimental baker made some most excellent bread for the two regiments he now bakes for. He bakes about 2000 pounds or 1800 loafs every 24 hours to feed all these hungry mouths. The rest of our meal consisted of stewed oysters, coffee and some of the butter Julia and the neighbor ladies sent down to us. Everyone was well filled after we partook.

We have had our first casualty, not from enemy fire but from disease. Poor old Killian succumbed to the virus he had picked up about a week ago. Doc said he tried his best, which I am sure he did, to save him but alas it was more powerful than Old Doc's medicines and the rest of our prayers. I trust Killian is in a much better place and all of the regiment attended the funeral service for him with myself and the Chaplin saying some words. I think even though I felt deeply about losing a fine fellow and feel even more upset about his poor wife and children I do not think my words were adequate for such an occasion, but then again when are man's words ever adequate when someone passes on? I was also saddened to hear from Chaplin Dr. Khenny that he will be returning to his parish in Rochester, NY shortly as his term of service is up unless he is recalled. I sincerely hope that the State of New York assigns us a new one very soon as the regiment has a great need for the council of a minister on many occasions. He has been a calming influence and that is certainly what we need in these difficult times. He did tell me that he would stop by and see Julia and the family and give them a good report on the continued good health and spirits of their husband, father and son. I believe Julia will be much relieved to hear it directly from him.

I so miss the family and often in my imagination I see myself looking in upon them. I often imagine that I am there watching little Joseph sitting by the stove on these cold nights and then getting up and running around the house until he settles in my dear wife's arms. I see him asking his Momma about Papa and Julia trying to tell him about the lunacy that is currently going on in this country. I'm sure his little mind cannot comprehend any of this and I am relieved that he can't. Hopefully when he grows up there will be no more war and such madness. I daily pray that that will be true. May God spare Little Joseph's life and that of all of us, that we may again rejoin the family circle and not one link be missing in my ever-silent prayer?

I found out today that Major Manna who I was fortunate enough to beat out for the lieutenant colonel's position is none other than a second cousin. He had heard of my name when I was promoted, did some inquiring and turned up in our tent one day to check it out. We had a fine conversation about some family members we both knew and some that I had heard of but had never spoken to. He is a fine fellow and very gracious about being passed over for the promotion. At first I thought he might be here to give me an earful about the officer's position but as it turned out he was only trying to bond some family ties together. If it hadn't been for the promotion we would have most likely finished our term without even knowing we were in the same regiment and also cousins. It certainly is a small world sometimes. He even mentioned the recent passing of another of our cousins that I was not aware of. It is a shame how families drift apart over time and lose track of each other. When I finish my term I am going to make a concerted effort to contact all of my cousins and renew acquaintances. He even mentioned that Elizabeth was now living in Elmira and I am saddened that I was there a few months ago and did not know it or I would have made it a point of visiting her.

Here it is Dec. 8th and we are still sitting in Camp Griffin twiddling our thumbs. I think we are all getting rusty and I know for sure that my joints are getting corroded and my rheumatism is sure acting up. It certainly doesn't help to be sleeping out of doors all the time and especially when the weather is turning cold and wet. The ground has now frozen up solid enough to support our horses and Blackjack, as I named my beautiful black stallion, seams to be enjoying it. I even rode him in the night to check on all the pickets, over roads, fields and through the woods and he is steady in foot and gently but he is willing to go well when called upon. I have been putting on a little weight and John is up near 165 pounds, which is heavy for him. It is all this easy living and eating those fine cookies the ladies from home send us on a regular basis. Julia even sent me some pieces of little Joseph's dresses and I especially liked the plaid one and I could even picture him in it. His Papa is certainly proud of him. Colonel Draime has gotten a ten-day furlough and is headed back home.

I had hoped on getting one also but with him gone I am in charge of the regiment so I can only see home and my lovely wife and children in my dreams. Maybe I can get one in January. On top of all this our Brigade Post Master is ill and therefore most of the mail from home is being backed up. I don't wish anyone getting ill but the last person I wanted this to happen to was the postmaster since that means all those uplifting letters from home and family will be delayed. I would almost wish that our cooks had fallen ill instead of him since I think I could exist for sometime without nourishment but not long without my beloved letters.

The weather has been fantastic here of late and we have taken advantage of it. As the commander I have ordered that the camp be cleaned up so that it is fit for man and beast. The men eagerly fell into the task since there is certainly nothing else to do while we wait for our orders, which at the present time may never come. As I have said many times before, lets get this dreadful conflict over with and get on with our lives both North and South. To sit here month after month makes no sense to me and many of the other officers and men. I am often asked about it and what can I tell the men but to be patient and sooner or later we will either be discharged or sent to engage the so-called enemy. I hope it is the discharge but I dare not speak that to the men. The troops even went so far as to decorate our camp by setting out evergreen trees and arches, etc. in preparation for celebrating the birth of Christ. The camp looks almost like home but of course would never come close to substituting for home. We will collectively celebrate Christ's birth even though we are in the field in the middle of a war with our fellow men. I do not believe the Lord will look down upon us with any blessings for what we are undertaking. Who is to say that God is on our side anymore than on the side of the Southern soldier? I guess each man must make his peace with the Almighty and hope for a swift end to this recklessness. If only Julia and the children could be here to help us celebrate this wonderful occasion but alas it is not possible. Even though I am making a little more money with my promotion I still do not have the funds to send for them and it most likely is for the best since some more illnesses are springing up in the camps almost every day. The colonel is expected back on the 17th and I was hoping to get a furlough then but the major's wife is very ill back home with inflammation of the lungs and liver and he must go and be with her. Old Doc says it sounds very serious and I pray that she will be all right but it may be his last time to be with her so he deserves the furlough much more than I do at this time. Maybe in January I can finally get my leave.

It is Christmas Day in this year of our Lord, 1861. John, all the men and myself are making the best of it. The men are visiting up and down the camp with their fellow soldiers and I would guess they are enjoying quite a bit of the homemade spirits that some of the fellows have a knack for making. That of course is strictly forbidden however on days like this when we are all away from loved ones, the officers and certainly myself are turning out heads. In fact I even turned my head and there was a bottle of that fine spirit that Charles makes. Of course I do not know anything of this officially, and I decided I couldn't let it go to waste so I partook. It was very refreshing. The colonel has of course returned but he is ill and has been taken into a Washington hospital for rest and care, I sincerely hope he will be well soon and back with the regiment. In the meantime I am in charge so I guess I can't be turned into a superior officer for enjoying a little of the spirits so I might even see if I can find another jug to drown my sorrows in. There I go starting to feel sorry for myself when I was the one that volunteered to be here. I just wonder about those stout fellows that stayed behind, chose not to volunteer and are enjoying this day with their families. Were they the smart ones or was I? I don't think if I live to be as old as Old Doc I will ever be able to answer that question. I also sit here thinking about my counterpart and all those Southern soldiers that are also sitting in their tents and trying as best they can to celebrate this birthday of Christ and wondering why they are involved in this conflict. I would imagine that they have the exact same feelings of loneliness for home and loved ones and the exact same uneasiness of what the future holds as we do on this side. I have said and I repeat I would love to be sitting with them at a tavern tipping a little of the spirits and having a mighty laugh over all this insanity. I still have not heard when our leaders are planning on having a duel with their leaders to decide this issue.

The men have taken up singing a new song recently introduced in the country and written by Julia Howe called the Battle Hymn of the Republic. It is still in development stages but some of the words and the tune are familiar and it seems to stir the men's patriotism. It starts out "Mine eyes have seen the glory of the coming of the Lord, etc." and seems to be a rousing marching song. Who is to say whether the Union or the Confederacy will pick up on it but I have a feeling it will live in history as one of the greater and more uplifting moments of this Civil War. The general invited all the officers to his headquarters for a continuing celebration of this holiday and I along with all the others made an appearance. We were served eggnog and plenty of cigars, champagne and Sherry wine. At about the time, 8 PM., that Julia and the children were going to church we were served a wonderful oyster supper with mince pie, sardines and other fixens. I was the only officer of the 33rd there as the colonel and major were away and the adjutant was under the weather. We broke up about midnight after having a very social time indeed, and with credit to the brigade I can say that not one officer was the worse for the spirits served. As I have mentioned before I sometimes wonder if a little more liquor and a little less talk might just be the medicine to get some of our leaders off their dead asses and allow them to make some decisions about how to best use all these thousands of troops.

I have been detailed as the Field Officer of the Picket Guard and at 4 o'clock this morning after not getting to bed until well after midnight I am up and at it even though I am dragging somewhat. I am sure it is not a hangover from the champagne and of course the special spirits available in camp. Some of the other men look a little hung over but I am not going to say anything as I think we are all in the same position this morning. I hope we do not run into Johnny Reb in our condition, however I have a feeling he may well be in the same fine state as most of us. I am taking 225 men and officers with me to go out on picket and relieve those that have been there this past night. I spent most of the night at what we call the reserve, two-thirds of the men are here while one-third are on the line as sentinels for four hour shifts. They are then shifted and the men that have been out are returned to the reserve while another group replaces them. Four hours out as a sentinel is very trying duty especially tonight as it has been raining, freezing on the trees, and of course they have even less shelter than we do when they are on the line. Each third are under the direct authority of a captain, two lieutenants, three sergeants and three corporals. At the main reserve the men can have fires but on the line as sentinels they are strictly forbidden. We are in thick pinewoods with plenty of cover and I am worried the cover may well entice Johnny Reb to take a stab at us to calculate our strengths and weaknesses. With all this rain it is hard to keep the fires going in the reserve and I have been sitting here with my rubber coat on, good rubber boots and a blanket over my head for what seems like a week. To try and keep somewhat dry and the joints limbered up twice during the night I rode Blackjack the entire length of the line and it seemed to do me some good as I felt better each time when I returned. I felt sorry for the men especially those out as sentinels but so is the fate of the poor foot soldier.

When I got back from overseeing the sentinel duties I was surprised to find out that Barns had received a large package of wonderful items from home and he asked me if he could set up a large table in the colonels' tent and serve us another fine dinner this day after Christmas. We ended up enjoying turkey and all the fixins and even frosted, candied and curlicued cake. The meal was similar to that which we have enjoyed at various weddings and reminded me again of home. I may need to curtail some of my mentioning to Julia and the children of all these fine meals, as they will begin to think we are all just sitting around, smoking cigars, our pipes and chowing down on all this delicious food. I will say that John continues to gain weight and I believe if he keeps it up he might catch up with Josiah in that department and they may be able to exchange uniforms without any problem. I think I am not drilling them enough or that it is agreeing with them. I humor them and myself sometimes by saying that it is all muscle and none of it is fat. We all get a good laugh over it and it helps relieve the tension.

Would you believe it is now January 1st, 1862 and we are still sitting here at Camp Griffin? I wonder more and more if I should not have been so hasty to volunteer my services so early but as I mentioned the patriotic furor was so rampant back in April of last year that many were anxious to go. I am sure that if it wasn't for those of us that volunteered that the South would have launched a raid on Washington and tried to end this conflict in their favor early on. Only the massive presence of so many fine men prevented this but the inactivity still wears away at one. In some of Julia's letters she has mentioned that most of my clients have gone to the attorneys that choose not to serve and she is afraid the few others will be wandering off soon. Several of the townsfolk have told her they are sorry but that they need the advice of an attorney and couldn't wait until I was mustered out. I worry that if and when this madness ends and we are all dismissed I will have a difficult time rebuilding my practice and providing for my wonderful family. Time only will tell and I find myself trying not to think about things like that as I lay in our tent each night, although it is hard not to worry. One thing that consoles me is that there are hundreds of thousands of other fellows in both the North and South that most likely have the same worry. All of the volunteers like myself and John share this concern, it seems the only folks in this man's army that are not concerned about their future are the career military officers who will just move on, if they survive, from a war time officer to a peacetime officer. Wouldn't it be wonderful for mankind if we only had peacetime officers and no wars for them to practice their skills at? I don't mean to belittle the regular army officers for without them most of us in the field would be lost and their bravery speaks for itself, I only wish that their skills in the field would never be needed. This day is very pleasant for January. It is almost like a day in May and we have enjoyed the weather conditions from some of the bad weather we have had lately. I would love to be spending this day home with my family but providence has ordered it otherwise, or at least I decided it for myself. I am a strong believer that nothing happens without the hand of God in it somehow so I feel that my being here was his plan for me. I don't think this war was his plan except the part to end the abhorrent practice of slavery. I do think however, as I have said, that given time we might well have seen the end to it and a strong and united America even without killing each other to decide it.

CHAPTER SIX

Furlough?

I have filled out the necessary papers for a 15-day furlough and sent them to headquarters. I should know in a couple of days if it will be granted. I can't imagine the officers not granting it as my services could well be taken over I believe by most anyone in the regiment since we continue to sit on our cold butts day in and day out. Leadership at this point consists of trying to keep the men occupied and their minds on the business possibly facing us and not let them become to melancholy thinking about home all the time. It seems that all the other officers have had furloughs, as I said I think I am due, and if I don't get it I may just hitch a ride on a slow freight train to home for a few days. Even though I think that way some of the time I certainly am not made that way and whatever my calling in life, let it be husband, father, attorney, state assemblyman or an officer in the Union Army I will always do the finest job I am capable of doing. Sometimes this might be a curse but that is the way I was brought up and it will not change even though we are living in the open with a great deal of monotony as companion. The furlough request was approved by the Regimental Colonel but it also has to be approved by the Brigadier General and Division General and then it goes on to General McClellan's headquarters where he must also approve it. If he is a mind reader and knew of my concerns, although kept to myself, of our inaction he most likely would tear it up and let me sit here on my ass even longer wondering why we are not put to use for what we volunteered. Hopefully he is not a mind reader.

We have received a care package as the fellows like to refer to them from home and it contained cakes, pies, butter, shirts and other presents. Josiah was upset that there were no candies in the package until John happened to turn it upside down and some peppermint drops fell out. I don't think I have ever seen Josiah move so fast as he did. I believe he caught every one of them before they hit the bare ground in the tent. We all had a wonderful tension-breaking laugh over it. I fear that a few more pounds will be added to all of us with these fine thoughts from home.

I cannot believe that all up the line of command the officers had approved my furlough but when it went to the general's office it was turned down. I am beginning to believe he can read my mind and figures I can rot here a little longer. I am going to re-apply and this time I plan on hand delivering it to General McClellan myself and if it is war that he wants it damn well may be war that he gets. To continue to keep me from my family when all the other officers have had several furloughs is unconscionable. He either does not care for me, frankly I don't even think he knows who I am, or he thinks I am indispensable, and I rather think it is the latter as far as my ego is concerned. Even Mrs. Hucksley and Mrs. Brown have come down from our fair village to visit with their husbands. It was not a good time for them to be here unfortunately as it is very wet and muddy but I don't think they really thought too much about that as they were all so grateful to be together. Each couple was given their own private tent for the night so they could renew old relationships if you get the drift. Along that line without being too crude Julia has written me that she is having trouble with her breast as little Joseph is getting a little old to breast feed anymore. I have written her that she needs to wean him off of it as soon as possible so she will be more comfortable.

John and Josiah and myself are all on picket duty together tomorrow so we have saved some of the pie to enjoy when we are out. It is the little things like this that make this situation bearable. Along with the pie we are going to sneak out some nice sausages and the coffee pot so we can make coffee in the pinewoods and enjoy a picket picnic so to say. At this point if I saw Johnny Reb I would invite them to join us and partake and feel none the worse for so doing, they are in fact our brothers if you think of it. Much better in my mind to dine together rather than try and kill each other. Julia has even sent us a red and white warm shirt and John and I have been fighting over who is to wear it but I won out not due to rank but due to girth. Unfortunately it did not fit John too well with his added weight. An even greater gift than the shirt was the fact that Julia said that little Joseph helped pack the box for Papa and that warmed my heart more than the wool shirt.

We still have not been paid for this month and since it is almost the end of January I have not been able to send any money home. If we are not paid in the next couple of days I plan on going into the city and confronting the paymaster about all the men's pay and mine. It is hell enough to be living like this but even worse when we are not paid. One would think we are prisoners rather than volunteer fighting men. It is exceptionally muddy here of late and even though we are not fighting Johnny Reb we certainly are fighting the mud. It is most difficult for man and beast and everything has pretty much come to a standstill for now. I guess as far as the commanding officers are concerned, possibly on both sides, it is another reason to delay any action. Maybe when the weather improves, the mud dries up and the spirit moves them we will be ordered to take on the enemy. If one would have asked me months ago if I thought the regiment was ready for combat I would have said decisively that they were, however after all these months I am beginning to be concerned if they will stand up to the challenge when called upon. They are all good men but they are sadly wasting away in these conditions. Old Doc had to treat a number of the fellows for diarrhea and vomiting and he is not sure what is causing it and is afraid several of those that are the sickest may succumb to their ailments. He is working day and night as I knew he would to bring them through this hour of their need but even Old Doc may not have enough ammunition in his medical bag to help these poor fellows. I am afraid we may be facing another regimental funeral for some of these poor soldiers. I am sure when they eagerly signed up to help their country in what they perceived was its hour of need they did not expect to die of acute diarrhea in some muddy field after many months of inactivity. My frustration is getting the best of me, a soldier if he must engage the enemy would rather be killed in action I believe, than die in a rain soaked tent in the mud of an affliction no matter what it is. I pray nightly that we either move on or that this conflict if it can be called such be ended.

I am sending home by the ladies that have been here for a visit some pine burrs and acorns that possibly Julia and Martha could make little Joseph a chair with. The ladies have gathered up quite a quantity and said they had plenty of room to take mine home also. I am also sending home with the ladies one of my linen coats that I had bought when we were in Elmira as it needs quite a bit of attention and I am hoping Julia will fix it up right proper and then send it back to me. It is more than difficult to keep clothes in any kind of decent condition here in the field. John and I traveled into Washington today for something different to do and I have never traveled over such muddy roads. Conditions here are almost intolerable and I wonder why more of the men are not succumbing to illnesses. I may have mentioned that some of the fellows have been sick, Old Doc was not able to save them all and Lawrence succumbed to his illness yesterday. It is so muddy it is almost impossible to conduct a decent burial service here so at his family's request his body is being sent home for burial. What a terrible waste of a good man and now his family will have to fend for themselves. I am so surprised at my advanced age and living in these conditions that I have stayed as healthy as I have. I had but one cold a few weeks ago and believe it or not being out in the hard rain for 24 hours on sentinel oversight duty cured me of it. Joseph's cure for the common cold is to stay out in the heavy rain for 24 hours. Maybe I could bottle that cure and sell it but I doubt I would have many takers.

We did manage to get our pay after my visit to the paymaster and threatening him with hand-to-hand combat. I really don't think it was the poor fellow's fault however and later on I felt terrible for having made a few threats. I think the fault lies in the higher ups not issuing the orders soon enough for the regular pay. I have managed to send several hundred dollars home to Julia and the family and some of the other men have enclose their monies to go to their families in the same express. I wrote Julia and told her whatever she has extra should go into the bank but if she so chooses to keep it at home to hide it in a very safe place. I also told her with the help of the colonel that I managed to make a little more money this payday so I will be able to send her a larger amount. I will explain this all to her when I see her but for now let us just say it was all legal and above board but just not available to everyone. Most likely this kind of thinking comes from my experience as a New York State legislator for a time. I found that most politicians seem to have a different standard of judgment than the common folk. We live in a wonderful community but in these hard times with so many of the bread winners in this conflict one never knows who might turn to thievery just to keep their family warm and safe and I sometimes think to myself I guess I can't really blame them too much.

I didn't ever think I would see muddier roads, if one can call them that, than we had a few days ago but here on February 1st it is even worse. We had about two inches of snow last night and it is melting and the ground is being traversed by so many men and horses it is almost impossible to get around. Pulling a heavy piece of artillery in these conditions is impossible and the only good thing about that is that Johnny Reb is living in the same conditions that we are so I suspect we will see no action as long as things are like this. Maybe we could wish for 52 weeks of this mud and it would all be over with since no sane man would ever attempt to fight in these conditions. There I go saying "rational man" when this entire crusade is idiotic and about the furthest from rational as any human being could get. At least I can stay relatively clean and dry as I am now boarding with the other officers in Washington at a rented house, which is very reasonable and allows for more privacy and more civilized living conditions. We even have a housekeeper and cook preparing our meals for us and last evening we sat down to a wonderful meal of raw oysters and most excellent cornmeal cakes. My stomach was slightly off for a while after I ate but I have to admit I took several helpings, as it was so good. If these are the conditions that I am forced to live in for the remainder of this conflict then I have a feeling the government may ask that we pay them instead of the other way around for easy living. Nothing can even come close however to home with Julia, the family and Julia's home cooking. I so wish that I were there.

Colonel Draime is also living here in the boarding house and he and I have spent a great deal of time together. We are particularly discussing the current state of affairs in this country and the lack of action on the part of the general staff. The Army of the Potomac, so called, is made up of thousands of soldiers almost all camped out here in the outskirts of Washington seemingly waiting for the Confederates to attack. Colonel Draime and myself both agree that this is a terrible waste of manpower and hope that shortly the higher-ups will order us to proceed to end this rebellion sooner rather than later. He feels as strongly as I do that the longer we are held here in reserve the more we will be unprepared when the time comes. Some of the men have seen it that way also and have drifted away. If they are apprehended they will be dealt with severely but in most cases they have vanished. Very few have taken that route as most all are extremely patriotic and loyal, but a few as I have said have had enough. The colonel and I have even gone so far as to draw up battle plans to present to the general staff if we are called upon to do so. However, I don't foresee that day coming. It seems the general staff is so caught up in disagreeing on strategy that we are never going to get anywhere. I feel a higher power, namely the president will need to intervene to issue direct orders to get things moving. There is some talk that General McClellan who is Commander-in-Chief will soon be replaced and General Halleck will be taking over that highest position. Maybe then we will see some action. It is rumored that the higher-ups are very busy trying to keep Britain out of the war, as there has been some rumors that they may enter the war on the side of the Confederacy. I sincerely hope diplomacy rules here and that possibility can be put to rest peacefully as it is one thing to think about going up against our brothers in the South and a far more sinister thought of fighting both the South and the British.

Would you believe it, Old Doc came to me and said he is not feeling at all well and needs some time to rest and recuperate. He said all this mud and cold weather is getting to all the men and he is working 24 hours a day to try and keep his flock healthy and he said it is a losing battle. The men can't even drill and march daily due to the weather and the mud and so there is very little to occupy their minds so they dwell on their aches and pains. They have taken to music quite a bit and several of the fellows are wonderful banjo players and there is a lot of playing and singing but that can just do so much. Old Doc said he has just had it for a while and needs to go into Washington and spend some time away from all this squalor. He said even the latrines are overflowing and need to be re-dug and insisted that I assign some men to do that task immediately. I thought the officers in the field were tending to that but I guess I was wrong and anyway it is my responsibility so I will issue the orders. I suggested to Doc that he spend a little time as a patient in the hospital in Washington but he said as a doctor they would most likely just put him to work so he thought he might instead spend a little time at the Little White House which he says is back in business. I'm not sure how he found out they are back in business but we all realized that shortly after our famous raid on that house of ill repute they had reformed their ranks and were doing a thriving business again. I asked him how he thought he could get any rest there and also asked him if he had enough money for his board and room. He said that he knew some of the ladies and they would see that he was not disturbed and it wouldn't cost him much of anything since he was so old the ladies knew he would not be partaking of any of the delicacies while he lived there. He said he was a personal friend of the madam of the house so he knew he would be in good hands. I told him he could take a week for recuperation and that was all since the other doctors in the other regiments are also swamped and will not be well equipped to handle an even larger load of sick, tired and homesick soldiers than they already have to deal with. He said a week would be fine and I wished him the best, I sincerely hope he returns rejuvenated, as we need his services so desperately. I also told him I had heard nothing about any upcoming battles to raid the Little White House so he should not live in fear that the army is planning any sudden moves against it. He was reassured by that and bid me a fond farewell. As I watched him trot off in the mud I envied him for a minute or so, not so much as where he was going but the very fact that he was getting away from these appalling conditions for even a brief time.

John has moved into our boarding house also and we are sharing a room. I think all this easy living is agreeing with John as I wrote Julia and told her he has gotten so heavy that you can't see much more of his eyes than you could of some of those fat corn pigs we formally had in our other life. John is so good-natured that he just lets the kidding roll off his back and I sincerely hope it doesn't really bother him. He is often commenting on how a good wind would blow me back home and that doesn't bother me. In fact I have been hoping for a good wind, under the circumstances.

I am sending home pictures of General Porter for little Joseph to keep in his room next to Papa's. I also sent a picture of Commodore Foote, the naval officer who commanded the Gun Boat Fleet. That unit took Fort Henry on the Tennessee River on the sixth instant. The Cameron Dragoons that took ten prisoners yesterday belong to the same division, Smiths, that we are in. It was about ten miles from our camp when they took them so at least some of the men are seeing some action. I saw some of the prisoners being marched to the makeshift holding pens and I could only think that they could very well be our brothers that we are fighting and planning on killing. I also told Julia in the letter that I sent the pictures in; that she should pay cash for the necessary items she needs like cotton goods, coffee, woolen goods and other items. If she were to charge them and pay later then she might well be paying a much higher price since there is wild speculation in some of these commodities. Hopefully this speculation will settle down since the army is well clothed, well furnished with coffee and will most likely not require so much of these items in the near future but I still don't want Julia caught in any trap like that. Cotton is also in short supply since the South has virtually cut off supplies to the North except of course from those unscrupulous individuals that take advantage of the situation and are smuggling it into the North for tremendous profits. Men answer the call and fight and some will die to show their allegiance to either one side or the other and these low life's take advantage. It would serve this criminal element right if both the North and South would team up and take all of them out for a speedy execution. I believe the country would be so much the better off without them. That is the way of mankind sadly however and has always been and I am afraid will always be. Washington is full of goods and equipment for soldiers and many have got too much loose money on them to buy swords, pistols, gloves, woolen shirts and all kinds of such goods. These dealers like the smugglers have fleeced the soldiers, have reaped their harvest and some of them will loose it again and most likely end up being killed by their fellow criminals. Some of these low life's were selling swords for $25 not long ago and they can now be bought for $15 since we have an oversupply. John bought a pair of boots this week for six dollars, which would have cost him eight dollars last week. I even heard of one fellow that spent all his money on spices as he thought he would corner the market on them and then the bottom fell out of the market when an overabundance turned up and he can hardly give them away now. So it goes with massive speculation in times like this by the honest tradesmen and the unscrupulous fellows. I believe they are all opportunists and really have limited knowledge of the way that government and business works, some get lucky but most get burned one way or the other. I have no sympathy for any of them that try to take advantage of this appalling situation.

It is now the 22nd of February and things are beginning to dry up some here outside of Washington. I don't foresee the way things are going that will make any difference in our possibly seeing action as I am beginning to think that the decision makers are intent on letting us all sit on our collective behinds here and in so doing provide protection to this fair city. I do fail to see however how that is going to end this conflict but only delay it's ending. Even if they send some of us into battle to engage the enemy I feel a very large contingent of soldiers will be kept here in a defensive state possibly to the very conclusion of this conflict. Hopefully John will be one of them as I constantly worry what might happen to him if we are called into battle. I don't really worry about myself but I do worry about John and I don't know what I would do if he were to become a casualty. Julia would never forgive me even though she did encourage his enlistment but those were heady days and now most everyone has come down to earth.

I wrote Julia also and told her that I am sending a box of items home with George who is on his way there. He has been so sick as of late that the army has discharged him and he is going to return to his loving family. I don't wish anyone sick but I am sure jealous of his being able to get home. I sent some old books that were taking up too much room in my trunk and I also sent some shirts and a box of collars. I hope Julia has the time to mend the shirts and the collars and send them back before we are moved out. I also sent the knife I had been carrying for over ten years in my pocket and replaced it with the one that Irwin gave me. The one he gave me is a fine knife and has a fine edge on the blade for whittling all these lonely hours away. I told her she should set the old one aside for little Joseph to have when he grows up. I also sent home my commission papers and asked her to put them in the old family Bible along with my certificate of admissions to the bar and a few other keepsakes. Thinking back to some of my schooling I told her that I ran into an old teacher of ours the other day. We were both on our way out of Washington and I thought it was old man Tittues and we had a wonderful reunion of sorts. He had moved to New Hampshire shortly after he finished teaching in our fair town and he said he joined the Second New Hampshire Regiment as a private and has worked his way up the ranks until presently he is a Lieutenant Colonel in the Ninth New Hampshire. He was at the battle of Bull Run and he was severely wounded but has recovered enough to rejoin his regiment. He related to me some of the horrors of battle and said he saw his best friend get shot in the head as he was astride his horse right next to him. He said he didn't think he would ever get over those thoughts or images in his mind and he related that he has a terrible time sleeping as he wakes often with the vision of his best friend falling from his horse. He told me, and I certainly agree, not to be anxious to head into battle for no matter how much the men and I may feel invincible he said that there is no hell like being directly in combat and facing the enemy especially in an open field. He said it was unbelievable that both sides were in the open and marching in lock step towards the other side with rifles unloading on each other. It was total madness and during all this his horse was shot out from under him and the ball that killed his horse went almost through his leg but as I have said he has recovered and is ready to return to the field if called upon. It is because of the loyalty and devotion to duty of men like he that this Union will survive which I am confident of. It was good to see him and talk of home but not particularly in these circumstances.

I heard from Julia again and I wrote her also as I try to do most every day. I told her I was so pleased to hear of all of their good health and suggested that they take plenty of outdoor exercise especially in the morning or whenever it is dry out. I told her they should not be afraid of catching cold, but on cold damp days it is best to stay in. As I think of it I would imagine Julia saying a few choice words under her breath about my suggesting how and when they should exercise. She always said that I thought I knew everything and could even be a doctor. Speaking of doctors we have seen nothing of Old Doc since he went for rest and relaxation about five days ago. I gave him a seven-day pass and I hope he will be back in a couple of days since the men need his steady hand. I hope he doesn't become too laid back in his present situation and decide he has had enough of this appalling living and choose to finish out the conflict in the arms of the madam of the house.

My much-anticipated furlough has never come through. The general staff has told me directly that my services are needed here and that we may be moving out at any time so they are not willing to grant it at this time. I even contacted, through his assistant, the general himself but I was not persuasive enough so here I remain. I will not however give up on the idea and I will keep pursuing it vigorously. Maybe one of these days I will get lucky and be able to again lie in my sweet Julia's arms and rock little Joseph to sleep. I love all my children so deeply that it becomes more and more difficult the longer I am away from them. Maybe I would have been better off being a lieutenant and not so indispensable and then I would most likely have been granted it. I don't know why I am complaining, however with the big bucks I am making and the fact that shortly I may be facing Johnny Reb and staring down the barrel of his rifle while I try to end his life before he ends mine. What folly we have brought upon ourselves.

Along with all the other things on my mind Julia has written me and told me that Sara, who is in her teen years, has become somewhat of a task to handle. She said she has been using some fowl language and is disobedient constantly to her. Julia is beside herself in how to proceed with her. This is one more of the casualties of war that the children left behind in their mother's care do not have a father around to discipline them when they need it. I have written Julia the following advice on the matter and I hope and pray it will be the last of this issue for we all have much more to concern ourselves about than an unruly teenager at this time. We all worry about the men that have volunteered in times like this but we are quick to dismiss the other damage that is done to those left at home with families broken up, fending for themselves and folks having to resort to all sorts of devious things to continue to exist. I in no way think that wickedness is playing any role in Sara's misbehavior but so many families have been displaced with so many suffering both at home and in the field. I wrote Julia the following suggestions.

"Dear Julia

It grieves me much to hear that Sara is a disobedient and mischievous girl. But I have seen it, for years past that unless you pursued a very steady course with her that she would give you trouble. Now you must make a beginning and dear wife if you will but follow my advice in the matter I think there will be an improvement. That is in the first place give her good advice, appeal to her better feelings, and avoid getting angry with her. At all times be firm and see that she obeys every direction and that she does it when you bid her to. Use but few words of command, keep cool and steady yourself and I think you will succeed. I hope you will cultivate kindness towards one another and be cheerful and pleasant and especially should all the children be kind, obedient and pleasant to you. How often have I written to Sara urging her with all a father's love and regard for his child, to avoid rebellious talk and actions, of which I knew she was much inclined? I insisted upon strict obedience in her to you and yet it seems it has had little effect. God forbid that it should ever be said that you and I had a child that would not do right at home, and that we had to call on others for assistance to govern a child. Yet as true as I am writing this letter, sooner than my family at home shall live in turmoil and a child of her age keep my house in an uproar as I have heard it myself and worse than all to strike or resist in anyway her mother. I will write and bind her out to some other person that I know can and will manage her or put her a year or so in confinement in an institution for the purpose of managing such children. I would not ask it if I were home for I would take some such course in our own village to do it and no matter whatever the whole disruptive girl must be checked and at once. I regret to have to write this but as a loving parent and husband I feel it is my duty to set out the standards for Sara and if she chooses not to follow them I will see that she is sent some place where she has no other choice. I love her deeply but feel this is for her own good. Please show her this letter and let her dwell on it for a while and let me know how thing are.

Your loving husband and father, Joseph."

It is easy for me to give such advise from miles away but I fear Julia is the one that has to deal with it. I hope that Sara upon reading my letter may decide that she had better get her act together especially if she thinks I may be home soon or she will end up some place away from home. Time will tell and I pray that I have been some help to Julia in this regard. I cannot wash my hands of it or get it out of my mind however as my family is the only thing in this world that means anything to me. I love them all so dearly. I was talking to Colonel Draime and mentioned this as we share our problems with each other a great deal. In this situation where everyone is so tense we all need someone to share our thoughts with and I didn't want to turn to John on this problem since it is his sister and he had a great deal of other things to worry about at the moment with rumors of our moving out soon. Colonel Draime said he also had heard from his wife and one of his sons, who is also a teenager, was giving her a difficult time. I think it has to do with the fact as I mentioned that so many of the fathers are on active duty in the army and there are few father figures still at home. Most of the men that choose not to serve their country are not very good father figures anyway, most able-bodied ones I personally see as losers and certainly wouldn't want any of them advising my wife or children. The colonel said he thought my mention of possibly having Sara institutionalized might have been a little harsh. I still think it was the proper decision and hopefully it will be a motivation for Sara to behave. Maybe the next war, heaven help us if there is one, mankind should send all the women into combat and let the men stay home and take care of the family. In dwelling on it however I don't quite think that would be fair since in about 100% of all conflicts it is the men that started it and this conflict is no different. Old Doc put it bluntly when I mentioned it to him that we are the asinine ones so therefore we should suffer the horrors of war. The women are left at home to pick up the pieces of the chaos that we men make. If mankind ever truly becomes wise, and every day I think that is never going to happen, at least in my life time, we should turn over all the leadership roles to the ladies and then maybe they would find a better way to resolve conflicts. Old Doc said only in my dreams and I agree with him unfortunately. By the way I failed to mention Old Doc, or as he is now referred as Old Grinning Doc, has returned from his rest and is as fit as a fiddle. He even suggested to me as commander that I rotate all the men through the R and R program at the Little White House in order to lift their spirits. I told him I was sure he was jesting but with him I am never sure. He told me he worked on developing more of his secret codes he likes to have me solve while he was there but frankly I doubt he spent too much time on those. I think after the numbers of sick, both physically and mentally, soldiers that are lined up to see him he will soon request another leave.

Would you believe we had a minor rebellion amongst the troops with their sending three representatives to the officers to spell out their grievances? The rebellion mostly is about these horrible living conditions and the inactivity of so many men living in such close confinement for so long. Colonel Draime and myself agreed to take their concerns to the general staff and hopefully it might just be the catalyst to get things moving. Being March of 1862 and having been here since last July is becoming totally unbearable as Colonel Draime and I have told each other in confidence. We dared not tell the men sent to air the regiment's grievances that we shared their feelings, however we well know how they all suffer. After making an appointment to see the general's staff and going over the concerns we were summarily dismissed with a statement that the general would be updated on these complaints. We were frankly given little or no encouragement that the problems would even be brought to the general's attention. Neither Colonel Draime or I were very impressed by our reception and both agreed that the staff should be able to find the time to address these issues since they don't seem to be doing much of anything else. We returned to the men and asked the representatives to meet with us and expressed to them the response we had received. We did embellish it somewhat for their benefit and we also reminded them that this man's army was not a democracy, and they will, no matter what their complaints, follow orders. They politely said they would return to the men and pass the word, however we were not encouraged by their attitude.

They do have every right to express themselves to us as we have every right to pass the word up the chain of command, but when push comes to shove they will follow orders or be dealt with harshly. If they could have seen the letter that I sent to Julia about Sara they might think different about any complaining, however it is the soldier's prerogative to grumble. I would hope they would all have Old Doc's attitude but then again they have not have the pleasure of living with the ladies for a week.

CHAPTER SEVEN

False Starts

I'm not sure if it was our visit with the general's staff or just a coincident or weather conditions here in early March but we have been issued orders to be geared up. Our brigade had been placed under instructions to hold ourselves in readiness to march at an hour's notice with three days cooked rations. We have heard nothing certain yet but we are preparing the men and the meals and this has certainly taken the men's minds off their recent grievances and replaced it with apprehension and well concealed fear. I think the general and his staff after hearing complaints from Colonel Draime and myself on behalf of the men figured they need to, you know what, or get off the pot and move this massive army forward to engage the enemy. That is what we thought we were brought here for nine months ago so all I can say is that it is about time. I wrote a quick note to Julia and told her that when she hears that we are moving out not to worry herself unnecessarily about our safety. I told her that the same protective hand of Providence that has protected us from sickness for the past many months is still over us and may equally protect us on the field of battle, if we are so called upon, from the pain of injury or death. I told her if we should be called into action and either of us should be wounded that she will be informed without delay by telegraph so she should not borrow trouble in the meantime. That is all easy for me to enlighten her and again my deep love goes out to Julia and all our children in this hour of uncertainty. She has so much on her plate to deal with and she is such a strong woman that I am sure she will cope but it will not be easy. She has John and my continued safety to be concerned about, Sara's unruliness and all we have to worry about is killing our fellow man or being killed. As I equate the two it seems to me the pressures on both Julia and I are about equal since as I have previously stated it is the men that have started this insanity and always have in the past so they are the ones that are destined to end it. I pray it will end soon and we will all be united under God's calming hand.

In Julia's latest letter she mentioned that Brother Charles had paid her a visit and spent some time with her trying to ease her fears and cheer her up. I sincerely hope Brother Charles will be able to dispel Julia's blues as she also mentioned that Martha had wanted to go to Falls and she was against it but she went anyway. Julia needs to remember that Martha is now 23 years old and is strictly out from under our legal control. I think what is occurring is that everyone at home is so concerned about the movement of the troops and our safety. There is so much tension that it is hard to remain calm in any circumstances. I continue to pray for all of them that the good Lord will come to them and ease their anxiety and let them live in relative peace with one another. These times are difficult enough without the constant internal strife going on. I would be so much more stress-free if I knew they were all getting along fine. Colonel Draime and I seem to share the same problems both here and at home so it is so reassuring to have someone about my age and circumstance to share my thought and concerns with and he tells me he feels the same. I wrote Julia and said I approve of Martha's going to the Falls for a short trip and that I will send home an added ten dollars for her too use if that will help. I am concerned that maybe the money is so tight that it is at the root of some of the disagreements. It is difficult enough for young women and young men at home to be struggling with the current condition without asking them to give up their youth and the pleasures therein. I told Julia and the children that they should not do anything to tarnish their enjoyment of life except thoughts of their absent father, husband and brother and they ought to rejoice and be thankful that we and they continue to be in good health. They should look forward, as we do, with a cheerful heart and buoyant spirit to the time in my opinion that is not many months away to our happy reunion. I also told her that if she and the children love me and love one another that she will love them and be reasonable in granting their requests and that they will love and obey her. I begged Julia in my letter to push despondency far from her side, have nothing to do with it, but keep cheerfulness as her every day companion. It is so hard to effectively play the role of a loving father and husband from such a distance from home and I have to constantly remind myself of the strain they are under and as sure as I know that Julia and the children love me as I love them I am sure they, especially Julia, often says under her breath, "easy for him to say." All I can do from here is offer my love and support and pray for the best and also pray to be home with all of them soon. I sincerely hope that the next time I hear from Julia and the family that times have brightened up and they have taken some of my advice to heart and it has helped. That is about all I can think of to say to them at this time and I cannot write more as I am out of candles for seeing to inscribe more letters. I think Julia has enough on her mind now anyway so maybe being out of candles is the Lord's way of telling me enough advice for the time being.

It is now March 11th, 1862 and the Grand Army of the Potomac or as I sometimes referred to it as God's Avenging Army is on the move. We are marching south and it is raining and the mud is getting deeper all the time. I think everyone, including the horses and oxen, are praying for some drying weather and sunshine instead of the struggle we are all having traveling in these conditions. Even old Blackjack is stressed trying to make any time but then again when you are moving thousands of men and all the artillery and food and all the other supplies necessary to keep this massive army on the move it will never go as smoothly as we would like. We are ordered to march to Sewinville where we should arrive just after daylight. I have been ordered to take my men and take charge of the munitions train and I am pleased that the General Staff has the faith in my leadership and my men's abilities and loyalty to choose us to look after the ammunition. Without our ammunition I fear we would not even have the bite of a mosquito. It is not easy to move the wagons full of ammunition, several times they have gotten stuck in the mud and I have had to order 15 or 20 of the stronger men to take hold and they would soon lift it out only to see the wagon get stuck on down the road several more times. After a while it almost became impossible but as it turned out we were only about a half hour late in arriving at our station where we managed to bring the entire weapons supply through safely. When I think that all the effort, money and sweat of making this weaponry and bringing it here safely is for the sole purpose of killing one's fellow man that is almost incomprehensible. If this money and effort only would go into helping one's fellow human beings rather than figuring out bigger and better arms to annihilate the so-called enemy wouldn't mankind be so much better off? This is a dream I often have but when I wake to the raw reality of life and why we are here I am soon brought down to earth and the futility of mankind's efforts to stop their militaristic ways. Men always seem to preach that peace is their goal or that everyone seeks peace but when it comes right down to it I am beginning to feel that those are empty words. So much on reminiscing on what I think should be for the general has told us to be ready to march in a half hour which is definitely not enough time for the men and animals to rest after the grueling march we have just been on, especially for the men and livestock that have lifted so many heavy wagons out of one mud hole after another. I wonder why the hurry after we have been sitting on our collective behinds for months twiddling our thumbs and raiding the Whore House and barns full of hay, they are in such a hurry now. I guess once they finally made a decision they have crossed that threshold of inaction and are no longer restrained by their uncertainties. I wonder how long it will take for the reservations to return once we enter into battle and the causalities begin to mount up. I worry that since we were unused for so long that any major engagement may raise the specter in the eyes of the general's that they must again hold back rather than following up on any advantage we have achieved or hopefully will achieve. These things I shouldn't dwell on since I am not making the immense decisions but only ordering men to lift many times their weight of ammunition trains out of the mud and most likely soon to be ordering them to march lock step into the barrel of the enemies guns. I also had to order some of the men to return to camp and get several thousand loaves of bread for the troops. At some point we may have to move the bakery closer to the front lines but for now we can send a few wagons of men for it. In some of the supplies we have ample amounts, but bread is not one of them so we have to re-supply that every other day.

We were told to march on a moment's notice three days ago and still we are sitting here, so goes the life of a foot soldier. I think many of the men appreciated the few days of rest especially those that lifted wagon after wagon of ammunition out of the mire. The weather has now dried up some and also maybe the general and his staff have finished contemplating their next move and finally decided it is time to move again. Whatever, we are all dressed and in full battle gear, the animals are all hitched up to the wagons and the men are getting ready. Where we are headed, only the general and his staff know but wherever it is I have a strong feeling that this time we are going to take on the enemy.

We were all prepared to march and then we were told that General McClellan wanted to review the troops again so these thousand of fine soldiers all formed ranks and watched the general all dressed out in his fancy uniform ride up and down the ranks on his excellent stallion. I'm not sure what he was looking for but maybe it was an excuse to not move forward at this time or maybe giving him the benefit of the doubt he wanted to try and instill confidence in the men and make sure in his mind that they were ready for what lay ahead. He assembled all the officers after his review and said we would be moving tomorrow and we are to head for Norfolk on foot to Vienna, then by rail to Alexandra and then by water. Seems we will be taking advantage of all the means of transportation including foot power, rail power and waterpower. I wrote a quick letter to Julia and told her we were headed south, not mentioning the specifies for security reasons and told her not to worry for if we were to find any Rebels we shall whip them good and that God will protect her husband and her son. I also sent Julia a small piece of wood from the Fairfax Court House as a souvenir that she should keep as a reminder of this time in the service to our country. At least I think it is service for our country, so far as you know, it has consisted of a raid on a Whore House and a barn full of hay. We shall see what the future holds.

Courtesy of the Library of Congress

As it turned out, we didn't march as originally told because the general's staff didn't think we had sufficient teams for each division to move all the goods that such a large army requires when on the move. We can somewhat live off the land but like a swarm of locust we would soon devour everything in our path and have little left to sustain us or those non combatants left fending for themselves in the south. Would you believe it when finally we were ordered to move out it started to rain slightly and within the first hour it started to pour and with an army that would stretch from Rochester to our fair village you can imagine what the roads look like. The men and animals near the front are faring certainly better than those back further and much better than those that are bringing up the rear. They constantly have to deal with deep mire, heavy rain, stuck wagons and deepening despair on the part of the men. We sat on our collective asses for days when the sun was out and the roads had dried up and then we are ordered to move just as it is about ready to pour. I sure hope the general plans our first major engagement better than he planed this movement. He does have advisors that are paid to give him some idea of the weather but alas I am afraid he may not be listening to them any more than he listens to me. Our division had to halt at the Fairfax Court House as another division was passing us on orders and another had already passed by here. We finally arrived at our campsite for the night and although the ground is so sandy it is afloat, the men are all soaked as they could be but camp for the night we must. This will be an unbelievable night for both man and beast, the only ones that will be able to sleep in relative comfort are the general staff as their tents accompany them or they occupy a confiscated house for their comfort. I think in all future conflicts, unfortunately that may well be true, the foot soldier should have their tents brought up for them and set up or they should be housed under a dry roof for the night and let the higher ups lay out in the open, soaked and having the rain pour down on them, seems only fair to me. The men did finally get their Deambra tents and they set them up and I ordered them to find all the dry wood they could so we could build some fires. Finding dry wood under these conditions is like finding a female at the Whorehouse after they have been warned of our raid. I did manage to get my tent set up and gathered some wet brush and spread it on the ground so that I could lie down. You cannot imagine what it is like to lay in a massive open field in a little tent, soaking wet with thousands of men around you all trying to sleep as they lay shivering in the cool night air in their wet clothes. What supreme idiocy this is when we could all be home in our warm beds with a roof over our heads but I have been down that road before and unfortunately mankind does not seem to listen to me. I did manage to share with John, Henry and Josiah a good meal of pork and some excellent coffee so that helped lift our spirits somewhat. I also managed to burn my fingers when some of the hot grease from frying the pork in our makeshift stove happened to spill out and burn two of my fingers. We shall call this my first battle casualty, however I don't think it will qualify regrettably for a battle casualty furlough. Don't think for one minute that I did it intentionally just looking for some sympathy or a possible furlough but after it happened I had to admit the thought crossed my mind. I did call on Old Doc Peterson to tend to my wound and we had quite a laugh about it as being as I said my first battle wound. He put some ointment on it and recommended three shots of his famous cure, which I hear he prescribes for every ailment that he is faced with. They say he has an entire wagonload of his special, secret cure that follows him wherever we go. When I look at Old Doc and see just how old he is and the fact that he is living in these same conditions I feel ashamed that I am complaining about it. If he can manage under these atrocious surroundings at his age and condition then I certainly can manage and I don't want to hear any complaining from any of the other men. He said he would officially file a report that I was "burned with pork fat" and maybe on my record, if I survive this war, I can get a slightly larger pension from such an egregious injury.

You might call this the saga of floating down the river on a river cruise. We boarded the Steamer Nanskon on the Potomac River this day. Wouldn't you know it now that it is a beautiful sunny day we are out cruising on the river rather than marching on dry land for a change? Whoever is calling the shots on this army's movement sure seems to have their head on ass backwards. We march in the rain and mud and then we sail in bright sunny days. We boarded the boat at Alexandra about 2 PM and have run down the river just below Mount Vernon. I have tried to write a letter to Julia explaining roughly where we are and where we are headed but the boat shakes so much it is hard to keep pen to paper. It most likely doesn't make much difference anyway as no mail will be sent until our destination is reached to protect the troop movement from ever-watching enemy eyes. Of course when you are moving such a vast army with all its equipment, ammunition, food, livestock and other supplies it is a little hard to keep it a secret and I firmly believe Johnny Reb or General Lee and most likely both are well aware of our movements. There are 15 steamers carrying the troops and all the other items and we congregated at a rendezvous point and are now all steaming down towards Chesapeake Bay. It is a good thing that mankind has not developed any more sophisticated weapons of war like underwater boats or anything that might fly in the sky or we would all be history. Isn't it interesting how the progress of mankind is often measured by the modernization of their weapons of war? That certainly tells one, if you think about it deeply, something about mankind regrettably. We have been told we will be landing at Hampton near Fort Monroe.

Would you believe amongst all these men and materials that have been moved down the river the only thing that didn't make it is our pay. The higher ups, which most likely have gotten their pay, have told us we will have to wait a little longer than normal for ours. If we were strictly mercenaries rather than loyal, dedicated and focused soldiers we would most likely have said "screw you to the higher ups, pay us and we march, otherwise we sit here on our collective butts until we get paid." What allegiance these men have to the cause, which I recall was to end slavery, and is now to preserve the union that they will continue to march into the jaws of hell without getting paid, I am sure their families at home are having a very difficult time trying to make ends meet under these conditions. So much for complaining about our pay but remember it is the prerogative of the soldier to grumble about things most of the time as long as they do their duty when called upon. John and I had managed to get a trunk full of unneeded items freighted home just before we marched however. It included a few dollars I had saved up and that I knew Julia and the children needed. It also included a looking glass which some of the men got at Mr. Stewart's House. He was a secessionist officer in the Rebel Army and his wife is the sister of the Jackson fellow who killed poor Ellsworth. The men gave it to John and we sent it home for safekeeping as another souvenir of this great journey we are on. I also included my captain's epaulets for safekeeping and asked Julia to watch over them. The sun is now setting beautifully here on the bay as we steam down. We have about forty miles yet to go and I am sure we will spend this night on board. This is just another beautiful day to be sailing on the waterway, so to speak.

At eight A.M. we all disembarked and it was quite a sight to see as thousands of men left their floating castles and headed ashore. We are going to march about three miles to Hampton just after breakfast, which John and Josiah are cooking up. We are having fried oysters and they are most likely native to the bay we have been spending a few enjoyable days on. Most of our other supplies have yet to catch up with us and our bakery is still far behind but hopefully will be in the area in a few days. The oysters and some very black and very hot coffee will sustain us well on our march this morning. Here it is almost the first of April of 1862, almost a year from the time we were all so caught up in the patriotism of the time and so anxious to enlist to teach the Rebels a quick lesson. I don't believe there is a man amongst us that even in their wildest dreams thought we would still be in the army and certainly never imagined that an entire year has gone by without our engaging the enemy even once. Colonel Draime mentioned that maybe we should just call the whole thing off and go on back to our homes, if only the powers that be thought the same thing. I told the colonel he best keep those kinds of thoughts to himself as the high command would not want to hear such nonsense since they think we are finally going to whip the enemy once and for all.

Our march was uneventful except for Old Doc who became very upset when his wagon full of his special medicine happened to almost tip over when it hit a gully. Fortunately there were many strong backs eager to help right it again as so many of the troops had been prescribed some of Old Doc's special remedy on a number of occasions and certainly felt they may well need it in the future and wanted it to be available. After we righted the wagon and calmed Old Doc down we all had a good laugh over it. Believe me a good laugh is the best medicine when one is marching with thousands of soldiers towards what may well be the last day of some of our lives. If the last months are any indication however we may well sit here, drink of Old Doc's medication, and wait and wait and wait.

It is a pleasant day and we have set up all our tents on the banks of the beautiful James River about two miles above Newport-News and nine miles or so from Fortress Monroe where we are eventually headed. The mail has also caught up with us, even before the bakery, and John and I received some wonderful letters from home. There is nothing, absolutely nothing, and I say this as a soldier who has been living in appalling conditions for months with my fellow men that can lift the spirit more than letters from home. Letters that blessedly report the continued good health of all those left behind. The support of our loved ones, as it is with all the men, is at this point what keeps us going. When we were first caught up in the tumult of patriotism, that is what drove us, but after so many months of living like this it is the letters from our loved ones that keep us going. John and I have taken pen in hand and written all the family at home, even little Joseph, however, we could not divulge to them exactly where we are. We could only tell them when we left the camp and our means of transportation. I am sure this causes them great anxiety but those are the orders and of course they are given for a very good reason. I support one hundred percent those orders but doubt very much that Johnny Reb and his leaders are not well informed of our movements either through direct covert contacts or through spies in our ranks that I firmly believe we have. Some men will do almost anything for money and I am sure some have been bought off to pass on information on our movements and our strength, etc. I hope such individuals meet an unhappy ending either by our troops or by the enemy's troops. This great number of soldiers are firmly knit together and have become brothers in this conflict so to a man they would not take lightly to anyone who is furnishing information to our enemy. I would not envy any man who was caught doing that and as an officer I would look the other way when they were harshly dealt with by the troops. There are about 40,000 men moving toward the enemy in our regiments at the present time and it is amazing that we can even move that many at any one time.

We have now marched to Big Bethel and are camped out on lowlands awaiting even more troops to join us. The Rebels have retreated from our advance, as I am sure our vast numbers have frightened the living daylights out of them. Don't get me wrong because I certainly don't mean to imply they are cowards, or anything but soldiers of the highest order and discipline and much to be feared, but such shear numbers as our ranks have swollen to be would scare off even the bravest of men. I am sure their leaders are waiting for the most opportune time to either attack or defend and from all I have heard over these many months in the service they are strong fighting men, afraid of nothing. When you think of it they are really no different than we are so why are both sides so anxious to engage each other. What madness this is as I have often said.

You would think we would have learned not to camp out on low lands. It has started to rain hard and we are again trying to sleep in almost impossible conditions. As I have said, whoever is planning this movement needs some help since when it pours we are on land and when it is sunny and nice we are sailing. They need some guidance from the likes of myself. There I go again, as Julia would say, blowing my own horn. I think the commanders must have heard my complaining or maybe it was mental telepathy. Whatever it was we have now moved thousands of men, equipment, food and tents to higher ground to see if we can dry out this army for what lies ahead. Wouldn't you have thought we would have originally camped out on higher ground just for common sense sake? There I go again talking about common sense when we are ready to slaughter each other. Will I never learn? All this laying on wet ground in wet clothing has gotten the best of the Colonel and he has been taken to the hospital at Fort Monroe for some much needed rest. I told him before he left that all he needed was some of Old Doc's special medicine and he would be good as new. Unfortunately he was not at all well and I am worried about him. In the meantime I am assuming some of his duties as well as mine, neither of which is too time consuming as we are now sitting on our behinds again here in Virginia rather than sitting on them back at Camp Griffin. Fortunately most of the men are in fairly good health considering these conditions. However we have had a few seriously ill, they have been sent back to Washington to the hospital there and I worry several may not make it. Living in such conditions with so many men in close proximity is always a major worry as far as illnesses and their rapid probable spread is concerned. Old Doc may have been right in worrying that this madness may take more lives from illness than from fighting, at least at the rate we are moving to engage the enemy at this point.

I wrote to Julia and the children and told them what a beautiful part of the country this is along the James River. I could content myself to living in this area at any time in the future. The saddest thing is to see the utter destruction the Rebels have brought upon this land. As we approached, they have burned every building to the ground and destroyed livestock and crops so that our advance would be made even more difficult. What a shame when those that actually live in this area are forced to burn their homes and the homes of their neighbors and friends. I am sure in time this area will rebuild and become again as beautiful as it was. It is so sad that we can rebuild that which has been destroyed but not those brave souls that will be permanently maimed or killed. Many a fine residence in Hampton Village has been destroyed. Homes that stood for years against the ravages of nature are now brought to ruin by the devastation of man. I told her that John and I are sharing a tent and we have fixed up very good beds with some dry grass that has been cut and put in our ticks and on the bed stead's made with crotches and pine poles. I sent the letter along but in it I told Julia that we have no postage stamps here so she would have to pay the postage on the letter, which I am sure she would be happy to do. The postage service is not all that efficient, however I guess under the circumstances they are doing the best they can. The army realizes that the men not only need something on their stomachs to be an efficient fighting force but also letters from home to lift their spirits in these melancholy times. Not only do we have no postage but also we are short on bread, some other supplies and as I said the Rebels devastated the area so we cannot forage off the land as we might. We have not been paid for quite a while but down here there isn't anything to spend our money on anyway so it doesn't make a lot of difference except as many of the men have said they would like to send money home for their families as I am sure they all need it.

It is now April 3rd and almost a year since the call went out and we still sit. I am in charge of the picket duty this night and I am actually looking forward to it to relieve some of the boredom. Seems strange that I would look forward to moving up to a forward area when the chances are much greater for engaging the enemy but almost anything would be better than just sitting around any longer. This great army of the Potomac should be renamed "Hurry up and Wait" as it seems that would be more appropriate. I usually have to assign the men for picket duty but as it is now they are all volunteering for the same reason that I am looking forward to it. I really don't expect we will be engaging the enemy even out on picket duty so I will pack a little lunch and Blackjack and I will enjoy the ride and the picnic, so to speak. The colonel has returned from the hospital also and is feeling well again. He told me of so many sick and some dying soldiers that had contracted illnesses and that the doctors were generally unable to help them. They must not have heard of Old Doc's magic medicine up at the hospital yet.

I decided activity, as I have said, it is the best for keeping the men occupied and myself as well so we don't dwell on our aches, pains and our thoughts of home. I have been particularly busy, as I have no field officer to assist me, as our newly appointed major is not yet here. On Sunday we moved the camp to another site on even higher ground and Monday I had a brigade drill. On Tuesday we went out about five miles to near Bethel where we were led to believe we would engage the enemy but as we arrived we only caught sight of a few of their pickets and they vamoosed at the first shots we fired. We then withdrew and on Thursday we had a parade and a review of the entire division, thirteen regiments of infantry and three batteries of six guns each of artillery. That all seemed to do the trick at least temporarily of keeping the men occupied and not dwelling on their illnesses and memories of home. I did hear that young Francis who had been sent back to the Washington Hospital had succumb to his illnesses. I feel sorry for him and his family, as I am sure he or they never dreamed he would die a slow death in a hospital rather than a quick death on the field of battle. It was such a waste of a young life. Losing even one soldier saddens me as we have all become like one massive family in this task we have undertaken.

We are currently about eight or ten miles up the James River above Fortress Monroe on the north side of the river. We are told that we are going to advance up the north side of the river between the James and the York Rivers. We currently have about sixty thousand troops in this expedition and it is an awesome force to see and a major challenge to move such a large force. The necessary supply lines, food, tents, ammunition, etc. for this many men are unbelievable but it sometimes seems it all comes together and even with many glitches we eventually move on. Looking around the countryside I have seen the peach and apricot trees in full bloom and many of the garden flowers that have not been destroyed either by our vast army or the Rebel retreats are truly beautiful. A reawakening of the earth in the spring is something truly amazing and I thank the Lord for his allowing me to again be able to experience it here in 1862 even under these circumstances. Such beauty amongst such evils of mankind. I wrote to Julia and described some of these beautiful trees and flowers and also reminded her to send her letters for John and I to 33 Regiment, New York Volunteers, Smiths Division, Fortress Monroe, Virginia. Hopefully they will all catch up with us in a timely fashion. I even picked a few of the prettier flowers and sent them on to Julia and the family to try and cheer them up some that their father, son and brother were not in any immediate danger since they had the time to stop, smell the roses and pick a few.

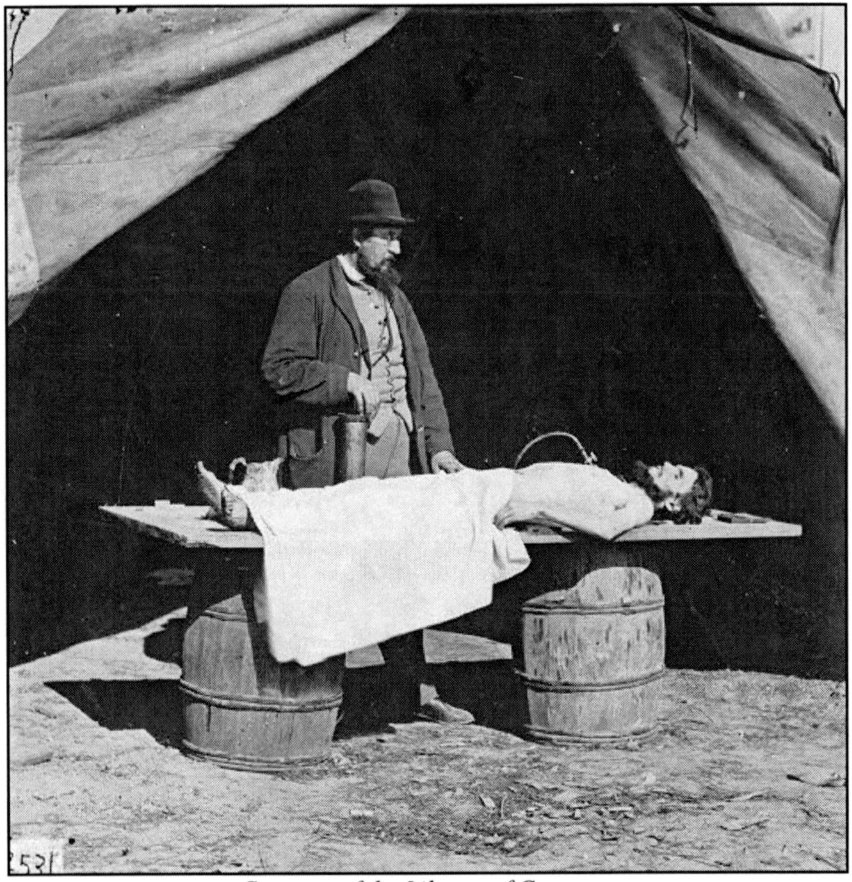

Courtesy of the Library of Congress

CHAPTER EIGHT

Engaging The Enemy

It is Sunday April 6th and our Sunday morning music is the sound of rifle, musketry and the whistling by of balls and shells in our ears. Every now and then we are even rewarded with a crescendo of artillery fire to add to the music of the morning. While those at home are listening to the sounds of the church bells we are listening to the sounds of mankind slaughtering each other. It is such a far cry between these two extremes. Leading up to this a couple of days ago we advanced with 240 men as pickets and engaged their pickets at daylight. My men wounded one of theirs and one of our men left ranks, chased them and in their haste to retreat they were putting their spurs to their horses. A Rebel lost his hat in the rout and my man retrieved it. He plans on keeping it as a souvenir of his first engagement. Hopefully he will live long enough to see it in his old age and bring back memories of his time with his brothers in the service. After this brief engagement we moved on up and came upon the enemy's works at or near Warwick. We found them abandoned. The defenses they had built were very formidable with a very large barracks overlooking the road where it crossed the creek. I was surprised they gave up so easily without a fight as these fortifications looked like they were easily defendable and I would have thought they might have made a stand there. I worry that General Lee, being the wily old fox he is, may well be drawing this vast army of ours into a trap as we keep advancing and they keep retreating. He is a cunning leader and I wouldn't put it past him to be setting us up. I trust that our leadership is up to the task of thinking one step ahead of Lee and his other commanding officers. We spent the night in the area of these defenses and in the morning before daylight we headed out again. This land is covered with trees and more trees. In our state back home there is much cleared land and often an horizon to see but here all we see is timber and more timber, it is almost as plentiful as the mud. It is very difficult to move such an army through these conditions and we are finding it very slow going. We do have a road to move on but with the recent rains and the fact that it is very narrow it makes it even more difficult. I thought I had seen the most weighty and deep mud ever put forth by Mother Nature but the mud holes on this road are indescribable. The men have had to work constantly to cut timber and make causeways to move the artillery over. Such slow going and such constant cover have given Johnny Reb. the chance he needs to try and pick some of us off as we struggle forward. Their rear pickets and our forward pickets have been exchanging gunfire for most of the day with a few casualties on both sides. Old Doc has been kept busy along with the other surgeons patching up a few of the men. Fortunately none of they're wounds so far seem to be life threatening. Old Doc's steady hands and a little sewing thread was all that was needed so far. He gave the men some of his special medicine before he sewed them up and that seemed to relax them for that ordeal. I shudder to think what it will be if we suffer hundreds of casualties and he and the other surgeons are called upon to amputate limbs and dig balls and bullets out of some of the soldiers' flesh. I don't believe a hundred wagons of Old Doc's special medicine will be enough to ease the horrendous pain of those moments. I pray it will not come to that and we will all be spared, on both sides, the agony of such ordeals.

Most of the exchange of gunfire has been between Company B, Company A of our regiment and the 49th. Since the colonel has been sent back again in a very ill state I have been in command. As the days wear on we have been engaging the enemy even more and they are becoming expert marksmen from behind the trees and it is becoming very difficult for our soldiers to get a clean shot at them. We have had two killed today in our ranks, both from the 49th and three more wounded. Jackson and Williamson have both been shot in the legs but Doc has patched them up and they are both back on full duty. With that kind of allegiance and commitment of men like that I don't think Johnny Reb has much of a chance in the long run. Lewis had his tobacco box shield in his pantaloon pocket or else he would have had a wound in the groin. It is remarkable and God works in mysterious ways to protect some folks. The ball hit his tobacco box and it stopped it from entering his body. Even though God protects some and is the giver of all miracles I am sure He does not look down upon this situation with anything but tears in His eyes for mankind. Since I believe He is a compassionate God I pray that this will soon be over and He can smile down on the good side of mankind if there truly is such? While I was out directing the forward pickets a spent ball hit Blackjack in the rump and made him jump. Fortunately it was spent and did not enter him and I managed to stay in the saddle even when he bolted. I was rather surprised that I am still on his back but again the Lord was with us. I have even written to Julia and the family this evening. Even war is not going to stop me from writing to my loved ones, and a ball struck not more than ten feet from where I was sitting while I was writing. Henry, Josiah and John were all in the tent with me at the time but they were all mercifully asleep so they didn't even hear it and none of them were in any danger thank God.

On the other side of the creek the enemy has two forts and a large number of rifle pits and breast works. This afternoon or tomorrow, whichever the high command decides, we shall pitch into them and there will be a merry time of it for a while. After a brief opening encounter again the enemy decided to retreat and pull us even further into the south. We did have some killed and wounded on both sides and I designated some of the men to see to the proper burial of those poor souls that were killed, both Northern Soldiers and Southern Soldiers. Nothing is a more heart-wrenching task as to bury your fellow soldier in some far away field from his home and loved ones. We wrap them in a canvas, lower them slowly into mother earth and the Chaplin and I say a few words, which is never enough, over their gravesite. It is almost impossible to describe what I and the men are feeling as we perform this task. The same respect is shown to those Southern Soldiers that have taken their last breath on this earth. What a waste this is for both sides of this conflict. We did have one desertion during this encounter and Old Moses has not been seen or heard from since. We think he was unharmed and decided he had enough of this and is most likely headed home. I wrote to Julia and told her in my letter that he may soon show up in our fair village and advised her not to give him any comfort and certainly not any money as he has left his fellow soldiers and does not deserve any assistance. In fact he deserves the hangman's noose. Unfortunately I doubt if the authorities will catch up with him so he will most likely have to only answer to his own conscience for the rest of his life. Who knows maybe he is the smart one. Time and history will tell us all.

Can you believe it is again raining and of course with the rain came more mud, I am having difficulty deciding which is more to be feared, the Rebel soldiers or this cursed mud. I have come to the conclusion that I think I would rather face the Rebels than this constant mud. This army has suffered mightily from the constant exposure and Old Doc is having a hell of a time keeping up with the various ailments running from sore, blistered feet to constant diarrhea. There is no way with all the rain that Doc can heal the sore feet especially since each man has only one change of socks but he has had some success with the diarrhea with his famous medicine which we seem to miraculously have an almost unlimited supply of. I don't know what we would do without him, I do know there would be a lot more sick, dying and dead soldiers if it wasn't for his skill and courage. I will be forever grateful to him, as many of us owe him our health as well as our sanity.

The high command has decided to move this vast number of men a mile or so back so that we can set up some makeshift tents and maybe get some much-needed rest. It seems if the Rebels can't stop us the weather sure can. John and I have managed to stay relatively dry and under a tent whenever possible and with the Lord's help we have both remained healthy. In moving back the mile or so we also had to move the great cannons and artillery and one can just imagine the backbreaking work that was. I really again question the high command as it seems to me we were relatively safe where we were in this weather since the Rebels couldn't move any better than we could. It seems to me that our command is constantly over cautious most of the time. The patriotic folks of our fair hometown could hardly have rested peacefully if they would have known of the weary, wet and hungry soldiers of this division. It is a great wonder that many more have not fallen ill from the constant exposure and not being able to dry out for days on end. I have been ordered to take 250 men and try and get some of the provisions moved up to our current position. As I said it is backbreaking work and John and I are as worn out and tired as the next man as we also have pitched in many a time to try and free a bread wagon or a coffee wagon, etc. from these cursed mud holes. I wonder sometimes if it is the Lord's way of telling us to stop these thoughtless ways and go back to our homes and let time work these issues out. A wagon of beef that the mules just could not pull through all the mud needed a solution so I thought up an innovative way to get all that beef into camp and asked each man to put his bayonet on his rifle. As they came by the beef wagon some of us stuck a large piece of beef on each bayonet and then we marched it all to camp that way. When a man's stomach is empty he will do almost anything to reach food or move it for his fellow soldiers. I thought as I watched the caravan of men with bayoneted beef that it was a much more humane use of bayonets than thrusting it through some poor fellow from the Rebel side. Our Chaplin has held a prayer meeting to ask the Lord for some drier weather. I'm not sure under the circumstances if that will be a curse or a blessing as it may lead to more engagement.

It is now mid April 1862 and we are about four miles from Yorktown. We are spread out mightily in a section of woods waiting for the next turn of events. Yesterday I was in command of the pickets and we encountered the enemy over on the right side of our line. Several of the men were killed on both sides and Doc told me about one of the wounded, whom I vaguely remembered from back in our days camped out around Washington, was asking for me. This poor young man had been shot severely in the stomach and Old Doc was by his side but shook his head as I approached so I was sadly aware that nothing could be done to ease his pain or save his life. Old Doc said he had mumbled that he wished to see the lieutenant colonel and of course in his last few moments on this earth I was moved to his call. It turned out it was the young soldier who I was called upon to be one of the court-marshal judges who had been arrested for frequenting the Little White Whore House in Washington. I bent down beside him and held his head in my arms as I tried to comfort him and he whispered with a breaking voice in my ear that he wanted to thank me for my compassion during that ordeal and then he asked me if he was going to die. All I could think about at that moment was what if I was holding my son's dying head in my arms. I uttered a prayer for him and it seemed to calm him somewhat. What is there to say in this situation? Even the greatest minds that ever walked this earth could not have uttered any words to ease this poor young man's pain and suffering. Old Doc took me by the shoulder and moved me away as he new I was not handling this well even for someone of my rank. I walked away and could not bring myself to look back as I knew shortly I would be ordering a burial party to wrap this poor young fellow in a canvas, dig a hole in mother earth and lay him down. It is one thing to have the officer's report to me the numbers of dead and wounded as it is somewhat impersonal but when you hold them in your arms as they take their last young breath it becomes very up close and very personal. It even crossed my mind that I hoped he had consummated his manhood at the Little White House before this terrible ending of his young life. What insanity have we brought upon ourselves? This poor fellow who was only 17 years old will never again see a sunrise or the stars in the heavens. He will never lie in his dear wife's arms and feel her warmth beside him. He will never enjoy the laughter of his children. He of course is not alone since heartbreaking deaths are occurring more and more frequently on both sides as mankind acts out his inhumanity towards each other. Fortunately John and I, Henry and Josiah are all well. Josiah, having been under the weather is quite smart again and ready to go, at least as much as any of us are ready.

We still have not received our pay yet even for January and February let alone March. It is now April 17th and I desperately need to send home money for Julia and the family to live on. Even though as an attorney and state assemblyman in my past life my family is still urgently in need of money to buy the essentials. Many of the men's families of course do not have even the meager means of ours, they are truly upset and I think in some cases ready to revolt if they don't get paid soon. It is amazing that most of the men are still willing to fight, in some cases die for this cause and country even without being paid on a regular basis. I have had a number of them approach me and I have sent dispatchers to the high command asking them to rectify this situation but have heard nothing in return. It irritates me to no end that my requests come to naught but it is an even greater abuse to not even have the courtesy of a response, even one in the negative. We poor soldiers it seems are at the sole mercy of those higher ups who are using us as they see fit without much consideration for our well-being and that of our families at home. There I have gotten that off my chest and even shared the frustration with Colonel Draime who agrees with me one hundred percent. I guess we are lucky to be fed the essentials on a regular basis let alone be paid. I have written Julia and told her to try and make do without dipping in to our bank account, which is drawing interest unless she is totally forced to. I am confident she will do her best to get by until I can send something. It is becoming harder and harder to have letters sent and of course received from home as we are often sent on ahead overseeing the forward pickets, and the mail of course does not come up that far. I don't really blame the mailmen for not putting themselves in harms way and I sometimes think John and I should have volunteered for the postal department of this war instead of the front lines.

We have held the burial service today for those that were killed in the recent engagement including the poor young fellow I tried ever so awkwardly to comfort in his greatest hour of need. What a sad time for all of those assembled when the Chaplin read their names and said a few appropriate words over their graves before the parties assigned the task to cover them up for the last time. I saw many a man with tears in his eyes as the various names were read and knew they were saying goodbye to fellow soldiers that had become their friends and brothers in arms. How many times will this scene be repeated before this lunacy ends?

It is becoming more and more difficult to find the time, the paper and pencil to put together letters to Julia and the family as we are now on the front lines and engaging the enemy almost constantly. I have spent many a night with all the men sleeping on the ground, if you can call it sleeping. I did manage to find a pencil and a sheet of paper and before the light faded I put together some words to home. I always feel as long as I can keep in touch with our loved ones that somehow it will keep John and I safe. It is like having a connection to something that is structured and sane rather than this folly we are now living with. I sometimes lie on my back at night and look up at the stars, when it isn't raining, and wonder if Julia is also sitting on the porch looking up at the same stars and I feel connected. I have even made up a makeshift bed by taking fence posts and propping them up against the fence and laying branches over them and sleeping, or at least resting on them. John and Josiah are sleeping under them as I told them since I outranked them I was to get the upper bunk. Henry would most likely be squeezed in there also if he weren't out on picket duty almost every night. I pray for his and all our fellow soldiers safety. Talk about ingenuity, Old Doc rigged up a small tree house and even had an improvised roof over his head. He claimed he had done it himself but I really think he had some of the men help him. He is so admired by all the men that I think they would build him a castle out here in the so-called wilderness if they had the time and the means. I kid him often of the easy life he is leading. In these conditions my rheumatism is beginning to bother me quite a bit. It wakes me up with its aches and pains and usually I get up around one in the morning and take a walk around the camp amongst the sleeping soldiers. Some of these beautiful moonlight nights I let my mind wander to better days and more beautiful places that I have been fortunate to visit with Julia. I so ache for her and the family. I also look at the men sleeping and my mind slips into deep thought of wondering who amongst these fine fellows may not be with us tomorrow night or the night after and so on. Which ones will be killed and which ones will be wounded. As sure as I am wandering amongst the living I will soon also be wandering in the midst of the dead and dying. I have to be careful not to get too melancholy about it here in the middle of the night or I might decide to hell with it all, as it truly is a nightmare, and wander off never to be heard from again. These kinds of thoughts I must try and keep from my mind if I am going to be leading these men as they go into battle. The morning ended well however as we had some good black coffee, some hard bread and some bologna sausage most of which had been sent down from the fort. There is nothing like a full stomach to change ones outlook on life even for a short time.

It is a beautiful April morning here on the 18th and the sun made its usual appearance in the heavens even though I feel the

Lord may look down upon this carnage and think maybe he should just shut off the sun and give up on this great experiment of this earth and those who dwell upon it. I guess I wouldn't be all that surprised if it happened with what I am seeing mankind do to each other first hand. I did manage to find a stub of a pencil and a piece of wrinkled up paper and I took a few minutes to drop a note to Julia. If I get it back to the fort some time today it should go out to home tomorrow. I also am in the hopes that I will hear from her today or tomorrow. I told her that our tents and trunks have finally caught up with us and we have set them up and its just like home again. Who am I kidding, certainly not myself or anyone else in this man's army? I even made up a spring bedstead for sleeping and hopefully things will be quiet for some time and we can settle in here. I sometimes think I complain too much, earlier I was upset that the high command had us sitting on our collective butts far too long, now I am hoping they decide to do that in this location so we can settle in some before the fighting resumes.

Maybe we will patent the special bedsteads, as they are quite unique. We cut four strong sticks, even stronger for Josiah's bed and each has a crotch on one end. We then drive them into the ground as far as we can; we then cut some poles and lay them across the top and the end. With this well-timbered land we have little difficulty finding these parts and the seven-foot poles we lay close together end-to-end. Since the poles are not too heavy when you lie down on them they sort of conform to your body so it is not as uncomfortable as it might seem. We also lay some pine bows on them for even a little more insulation. What wonders it does for my rheumatism not to have to lie on the cold hard ground each night. This rheumatism is slowly consuming me and I fear that someday it may become my downfall. Unfortunately John is also having problems as well as Henry and Josiah. The only one who doesn't seem to be bothered by all this hard living is Old Doc but then again the men, as I have said, treat him like royalty.

You would have thought with all this comfort that we invented, the Rebels would have left us alone to get a good nights sleep but they had other plans. I had ordered two of the regiments out this night to build breast works and rifle pits in order to set up an easily defended line when the Rebels decided to try and drive us back. I was called to duty just as I finally dosed off and jumped on

Blackjack and rode up to the front. This was about 1 PM and fortunately I had ordered an increase in the forward pickets to protect those troops that were working on the defensive positions and when the Rebels tried to cross the creek, our forward pickets opened fire on them and they were soon driven back without any casualties on either side. Things seemed to be quiet so I urged Blackjack at a fast pace to take me back to my fence post bed and castle and when I got there I lay down again and was almost asleep when a runner came up and woke me and said the Rebels were again advancing on our troops. I jumped on Blackjack and headed out at an even faster pace than before and was soon in the thick of a fight. I decided we have had enough for one night and dispatched a runner to tell the battery to send a few artillery shells the Rebels way and maybe then things would be quiet. It worked wonders as one shell landed just beside the creek and that was the end of about eight of the enemy and the rest decided to give ground. I ordered the forward pickets to fall back some so the officers on the other side could collect their dead and dying, give those that have passed from this earth a proper burial and treat as best they could those that were wounded. We were fortunate that we had no injuries on our side in these battles. Old Doc was even awakened from what many consider an absolutely sound sleep that even an artillery shell going off right beside him would usually not rouse him. This time when the artillery started up, he came up to the front to see if he could help treat the wounded and when I told him we were fortunate enough not to have any he asked if he could approach the other side and see if he could help them. He said it didn't make any difference to him if the soldier was from the Army of the Potomac or the Confederacy that a man was a man and the color of their blood was all the same whatever they believed in. By then the Rebels had fortunately picked up all their dead and wounded and I told Doc to stay put as we will surely need him and his skills too much in the future when I shudder to think our side will also suffer the further pains of warfare.

CHAPTER NINE

Stalemate

Our current location is called Camp Winfield Scott after one of our most famous generals. Our tents are all still up and there is only the occasional firing of artillery about a mile to our right and a mile or so to our left. The Rebels respond in kind after our shells are fired. I don't believe either side is inflicting any damage or casualties to the other side but just practicing and honing their respective skills. After the recent skirmishes it is refreshing to be able to just rest for a while in our tent and catch up on things that have been going on here in camp and the planning for what lies ahead. Our mail is now reduced to every other day so we are not receiving, nor can we send letters everyday, as we have been used to. Seems the government cannot keep up with the mail demand and of course as I have mentioned they are not doing a very good job keeping up with our pay as we are still waiting. What a way to run a country, I sure hope we learn from this entire experience for the future, as the saying goes, if we fail to learn from our past mistakes we are bound to repeat them, or something to that effect. It didn't make much of a difference however on the mail as I tried to write Julia and the family but I was so close to being out of ink that I had to keep dipping my pen in the ink jar constantly to write even one word. I tried to borrow some ink from others in the regiment and found that just about everyone was out. That certainly proves how much each of us cherishes writing to home and how much we all enjoy getting those wonderful letters. The only ink available was from the knapsacks of those poor fellows that had fallen and those were buried with them, as it would have been an insult to those brave lads that were lost to take any of their belongings from them. Wherever they are going I am sure they will be well provided for as I am sure the Lord runs a much more organized operation than our government. We will add missing ink to our shortages along with the loss of mail delivery and of course the fact that we still are months behind on our pay. What a way to run a war. What must we expect next, at least to this point we are being fed on a regular basic, however, I sure wish they would issue some clean socks to the troops as the collective stench from so many unwashed feet and socks that in many cases are months old is unpleasant to say the least.

I have been directing the picket lines for the past several days and up to this point things have remained quiet. After finishing my duties overseeing the pickets I was told by the colonel to take charge of the fortifications that we have been building 24 hours a day. They are coming along well and are truly a sight to behold. I hope the Rebels are watching these fortifications going up and realizing it would be suicide to attack us here. I think they were hoping to unseat us from this location with their earlier skirmishes but as they were driven back and we have increased the strength of these defenses I am sure they are thinking better of any attack at least from the front. We have spotted a few of them on horseback scurrying through the woods but they are moving so fast and so far away that we cannot get a clean shot. Just as well as I for one have seen enough death and dying to last this poor soul the rest of his life. The Rebels also have a fort on the other side of the creek so I don't believe we are planning on anything so foolish as to attack that well fortified position either. I guess one might call this a stalemate and all the better for it, maybe if we are lucky it will last until this brainless conflict is brought to an end. This is not to say the leaders on both sides of this issue are brainless only to say that their passions are misdirected in my opinion into waging war rather than pursuing a peaceful solution no matter how much time it might take. Would one believe it but when I was out on Blackjack overseeing the protection of the men building the ramparts that it started to rain and rain it did. This is beautiful country but it seems it rains about every other day, maybe that is the Lord's way of saying stop this thoughtlessness, go home and love one another and spend your life with your families helping your fellow man rather than trying to take his life. The men are so wet that their feet have been wet through their boots and socks so at least we might say they have partially washed their feet. In everything there is a good side, except this cursed war.

I kept the regiment out of sight for some time and then at nightfall we moved some sentinels up to within about 200 yards of the Rebel fort. The ground was mud and water and the night cold and windy and not fit for man or beast. The forward sentinels numbered 33 men and they were all volunteers and it continues to amaze me how men will volunteer for such dangerous duty. Maybe each man thinks he is invincible or something to that nature, unfortunately time will have a way of showing many of them that they are not. Some of the men lay down on boards or rails that they collected that were left over from building the fortifications but most of them just walked to and fro just to keep their circulation moving and keep from becoming totally chilled. I for one have not lain down at all this night as I have a sinking feeling that we are going to see some action and the Rebels will take advantage of this cold and miserable night to try and make our lives even more wretched. John is also out here and he is laying on a couple of old rails that we collected and I loaned him my blanket from the back of Blackjack to try and keep him somewhat comfortable. The blanket however is wet so I am sure it is not much comfort. I am sitting here on my faithful horse in the middle of this wet, cold and depressing night looking down upon my son who is lying on cold rails and shivering and I am worrying about whether he will see the dawn and I wonder why we are here. In the morning I am going to march the regiment back to some shelter of the woods and a ridge and maybe if the sun comes out we can all get some much needed rest and dry out. As it turned out I was on duty for 56 straight hours and I only dozed off a few minutes every eight hours or so while sitting in the saddle. Blackjack is such a fine animal that I believe he senses when I doze off and he adjusts his stance so that I will not fall. We are like one when we are together, I could not ask for a more faithful mount to help me try and live to tell the tale of this horrendous conflict.

Now that we have camped again under the ridge and in the woods I plan on getting a good eight hours sleep while the colonel takes over for me. I have so much faith in Colonel Draime that I will sleep soundly as I hope he rests when he puts me in charge. We avoided any direct contact with the Rebels for at least the time being. Rumor has it that the siege of Yorktown, about five miles to our right would commence this morning but we have heard up to this point but a few guns in that direction. I have said a silent prayer for the soldiers on both sides, as I am sure many will be killed or wounded in that conflict. I think we will be held here since we are protecting our defenses and also keeping track of the Rebels in their ramparts across the creek unless things fall apart in that siege and they need reinforcements.

Wouldn't I know it, I lay down on my makeshift bed which I was so proud of and found that some of the poles were quite crooked and with only a comforter on them it was not restful. Tomorrow I plan on assigning several of the men to cut some dry grass and stuff my comforter with it and also to find some poles that are not crooked. How can I possibly function in these conditions? When the regiment calls upon me to perform I want to be well rested and of course I want the men well rested also.

John, I, Henry and Josiah are going to travel over to the 98th Regiment this day and pay a visit to a few of the fellows we know from a couple of the towns near our fair village. I understand that Lieutenant Carlson and Lydies Hayden are there and we have not seen them in some time. Word has it that they have also seen quite a bit of action and I want them to bring us up-to-date on what they have experienced. When we got there we also ran into Colonel Dugan and had a pleasant reunion with him. Unfortunately he told us that Lydies had been killed several days earlier in a skirmish they had with the Rebels. He said he was out on picket duty and got separated from his fellow pickets and the enemy surrounded him and an officer thrust his sword through him. By the time the rest of the pickets got to him it was too late and the Rebels ran like jackrabbits from our superior force. The Colonel said they gave him a proper military burial yesterday and sent what little belongings he had home to his wife and family. How heartbreaking that must be for the family to receive notice that their husband and father had been taken from them forever and all they have to show for it is a pouch of tobacco and a tin cup he used for coffee. Of course they also were sent the pen and paper that he had on him as all the men have for writing home. The higher ups have replenished our supply of ink and writing paper and I sincerely hope poor Lydies was able to write a letter to his loving family shortly before his death and at least they will have that to cling to in their wretchedness and as they try in vain to make a life for themselves and scrap a living off the land without Lydies there. What have we fashioned upon ourselves?

When we returned I decided I had enough of this war and went in the tent and retired to my makeshift bed. I wasn't quite asleep when I started to feel something crawling on my leg and it turned out that a whole colony of cockroaches had decided they liked my straw stuffed comforter as much as I did. I jumped up and decided after pulling out some of the straw that there were so many of them it was useless to try and clean them out. I threw the comforter out and decided to try sleeping on the ground instead and finally fell to sleep with dreams of cockroaches crawling all over me. We have encountered many rodents and bugs on our many nights in the open and on the move but these bugs unnerved me some. Not only are we fighting the Rebels but also the insect world. We may be fortunate enough to beat the Rebels in the long run but we will surely lose to the insect world, as we are so vastly outnumbered in that conflict. The only good thing about this day is that we were sent a five pound piece of cheese and it was absolutely mouth watering. I would have liked to send part of it home for Julia and the family but of course we do not have anything close to a speedy express mail system and I fear it would turn quite rancid before it got there. Under these circumstances we decided to eat it all ourselves so John, Henry, Josiah and I made short work of it. We cut it into four equal parts to share and I noticed Josiah was eyeing the pieces quite carefully to make sure he didn't get short changed, as if he needed any of it. I sincerely pray that the Rebels don't decide to attack for many reasons but one of them is if we had to retreat rapidly I fear Josiah would not be able to keep up in his present condition and would unfortunately become a casualty of this campaign. I sometimes sit in our tent and wonder if Johnny Reb and his fellow soldiers are enjoying sharing some special food and I also wonder if when they lie down at night if the cockroaches also bother them. Seems we are so alike, North and South, it makes one stop and wonder why we are trying to slaughter one another. I could just as easy be sharing the bedbugs and the cheese with a few fine fellows from the Rebel side as I am sharing it with our soldiers. As it turned out the next day Josiah ended up in the fort hospital with a very severe case of the runs. He was so weak when I visited him that he could hardly talk. He did joke a little however that he didn't think it was the fine cheese that we had yesterday. It must not have been the cheese as the others of us are quite healthy. There are so many bugs running around the ranks, and I mean the types that make one very sick, that Old Doc can hardly keep up with the demand of his time and skills. I said a little prayer that Josiah would be feeling much better in a couple of days, be able to take hold, and eat quite well. John is very upset over Josiah as they have become the best of friends during this conflict and he would be crushed if anything happened to him. John said if Josiah succumbs to his illness he would have rather seen him die on the battlefield beside him than to pass away from some unseen illness in the hospital. John said he would rather be with him and both of them be killed than have it end this way. I reassured John that Old Doc can work magic and I think Josiah will be up and fit as a fiddle shortly. One knows when Josiah is not feeling well when he refuses to eat anything laid in front of him.

It has been raining again and all of the men are wet and muddy, what a way to exist. Most of them are trying their best to get some much-needed rest and have hunkered down in their makeshift shelters the best they could. There are of course a couple of hundred fellows out as pickets to make sure those sneaky Rebels don't try and use such a night to gain an advantage. Even though the men are so wet and muddy I know if they are called upon they will answer the call and be a force to be reckoned with. As it turned out about 3 A.M. the moon came out and the clouds cleared up. I strolled out of the tent quietly so as to not awaken any of the others, spent some time looking at the heavens and I finally located the North Star. I then dropped my gaze to the horizon in the direction of our fair village, closed my eyes, dreamt that my loving wife was also standing outside looking at the same North Star and it was drawing us together. Oh what I would give to be lying in her arms this night but alas linking to her via the North Star is as close as we can be on this night in April of 1862. I miss her and the family so much that it makes my heart ache.

As many things are extraordinary in times like these I have to relate a story that was told me by one of the men the other night. He said he had gone down to the watering hole, which is halfway between ours and the enemy's lines, to fill a number of canteens for he and some of his fellow soldiers. It is strange that both sides are using this same watering hole and it has been an unwritten agreement that when either soldiers from the North or South are at the watering hole no hostilities will be carried out at that location. It has even become so structured that the Rebels get to use it from midnight to noon and we are free to use it from noon until midnight. Strange that two enemy forces in some cases, craving to kill the other fellow, are so tolerant of the need for all the men that water is essential to our lives and we are free to collect it without being afraid of being attacked or killed when doing so. I have even made the trip to the watering hole many a night to fill a number of canteens for John, I, Henry and Josiah. I even offered to fill Old Doc's canteen but he never seems to need any water and most say that he needs little of it as he has such a great supply of his favorite medication, which he partakes of, that it satisfies his thirst. He has never divulged his secret formula but whatever it is it has kept many a man from ill health and also kept many a man from deserting when they feel so downhearted and lonely for their families. Old Doc gives them some of his famous cure and they are back in a fine frame of mind for the near future. I could never figure out where he gets so much of it but I would suspect that he sends orders to the supply officers and indicates it is an absolutely essential medicine for his flock. So much about Old Doc and his magic medicine.

CHAPTER TEN

Notes From The Watering Hole

The other night I went down to the watering hole to fill our canteens and low and behold there was a folded piece of paper there that had been left, I thought, by one of the our men. Out of curiosity I opened it and was taken back when I noted who had signed it and I read the following passage, "Depart from evil, and do good, seek peace, and pursue it. Palms 34:14. Yours in peace, Captain Tyler, Eighth Regiment, Army of the Confederacy." I could do nothing but just sit there for several minutes reading this over and over again. Here was a note from a soldier of the Confederacy who could have been a friend, a fellow church member, or even a brother and he was leaving a note one minute at this spot and the next minute he may well be trying to kill my fellow soldiers or myself. I dug down deep in my thoughts and felt that this fellow had many of the same misgivings as I did about why we were here and that he also would have given almost anything to be home in the arms of his wife and surrounded by his children. I decided to leave him a response and left it addressed to him in the hopes that no one else from either side would intercept it. "But the meek shall inherit the earth; and shall delight themselves in the abundance of peace, Psalm 37:11." Yours in peace, Lieutenant Colonel Joseph. I left my note partially concealed under a rock so that expectantly only he will find it. As Captain Tyler certainly was, I also am a student of the Bible and know many of the passages by heart having read them over and over again as we burrow ourselves deeper into this conflict. I did of course think briefly about the question of communicating with someone from the other side but after dwelling on that question for only a few minutes I said to myself, "the hell with it". If we are ordered to kill our fellow man then I will take the liberty to communicate with him, even an officer from the other side but I did have some misgivings about giving my last name so I stuck with my first name only. Always the cautious one I am. Neither Captain Tyler nor myself divulged anything of any nature that could be construed as giving any kind of aid or comfort to the enemy. If I am to be judged someday by a higher authority than that which is leading us on this earth then I say fine. I will freely try and ease the anxiety of a fellow human being and at the same time to grasp some reason amongst this living hell we are in even if he is on the opposite side. Maybe I would call it a little insanity in an insane world. As I wandered back to camp on the back of Blackjack I wondered if he would receive the message, if he would live to read it and of course would he reply. We are both it seems seeking the same thing which of course is that elusive peace. I decided not to mention it to anyone else and we shall see from here where it leads. I would not be concerned telling John, Henry or Josiah, as I trust they would all support me but I would not want to involve them in case any overly ambitious officer might construe this entire event in some way other than what I have mentioned.

Back to reality even though I cannot get Captain Tyler's message out of my mind. I know that I will be back out of curiosity in the hopes of receiving another message. I was pleased when the general held a meeting this morning of his officers and told us to avoid firing or provoking the enemy in any way as he feels that the men need some much needed rest and time to dry out for a couple of days. I certainly would not be the one to try and talk him out of his request as none of the other officers did, in fact I would have been most contented if he had asked us to avoid conflict for the rest of this year when hopefully this nightmare will be behind us.

It is now almost the end of April of 1862. It is a year since this entire issue came to a head and so many of us at that time were overwhelmed with loyalty that we couldn't wait to sign on the dotted line so to speak and go off to what most of us contemplated would be a grand adventure, safe and secure and over very quickly. Here a year has gone by and it seems like an eternity to so many of us. What we thought would be short-lived has turned out to be an extensive conflict with many dying on both sides already with no end in sight. What have we wrought upon ourselves?

It has been raining now for about three days and we finally have some sun to help us dry out and also lift our spirits. I was ordered to take the regiment out for reconnaissance this morning at 5:30 AM and remain out until mid afternoon. I was ordered to support two regiments of General Hancock's Brigade and fortunately we did not connect with the enemy and we all returned safely back to camp. Most of us were dried out a little after being out in that elusive sun for most of the day. General Hancock's Brigade did suffer some casualties, counting three men who were wounded and suffering and one poor fellow who was killed. This means another funeral for the chaplain to preside over and I wonder how he can keep his sanity with all the burials he officiates at. He must have a great faith in the good Lord that these poor young men are in a better place when they fall to the Confederate's fire. I have great faith but it is shaken daily when I see the death and dying of so many fine young men on either side of this conflict.

When we arrived back at camp, I asked John, Josiah and Henry if they need their canteens filled and they all looked at me strangely wondering what the attraction was for me at the watering hole but none dare ask. I just told them in response to their looks that I needed some more fresh air and I also needed to be alone for a little while. I think that I convinced them as all of us are living in such tight quarters with thousands of other men. We all cherish a little private time as often as we can find it. I went to the watering hole with I must admit great anticipation and was not disappointed for there under the rock I found another note. I opened it not knowing what to expect and read the following. "To every thing there is a season, and a time to every purpose under the heaven. A time to love, and a time to hate; a time of war, and a time of peace. Ecclesiastes 3:1,8, Yours, Captain Tyler, Confederate States of America." I sat there on Blackjack and pondered this passage from the Bible and wondered if Captain Tyler had so studied the Bible that he knew all these passages by heart. More than likely I surmised that he was a student of the scriptures and also carried with him, as most all the men do, the Holy word. I also let my mind wander to the meaning of this scripture and the implication of hate, war and peace and found it disturbing that peace was mentioned in the same scripture as hate and war. Far be it from me to be gifted enough to understand the scriptures but in my simple interpretation I think the meaning is clear. Mankind finds himself at some time or another in any one of these conditions. We continue to think of ourselves in the role of peacemaker's and living in a peaceful world but we also are capable of hate and certainly as these times dictate we are proficient in the art of war. I believe it is the good Lord's way of reminding us of our infallibilities as well as our strengths and in so doing is hopefully leading us down the road to a peaceful coexistence. I reached in my saddlebag for my scriptures as I needed to find an appropriate response to the good captain and even though I consider myself also a student of the Bible I needed to refresh my memory. I found a passage and pondered for a moment whether to write it to him. Several of the other troops during this time came down to fill their canteens and looked at me strangely as to why I was spending so much time there but in answer to their unasked question I just said that I was supervising the water hole during our time of use. I guess they bought that explanation but one will never know as several of them were shaking their heads and grinning a little as they left. They were most likely thinking that Lieut. Colonel Joseph had gone over the hill. I would certainly not be the first soldier or the last to escape this madness by letting my mind find another more peaceful place to live. Several of the men even in our regiment have had this happen to them and they have been sent back to the hospital in Washington in a very bizarre mental state. I wonder if they will ever be sound again and if this war will leave them in a permanent state of emptiness not much different than spending eternity in a quickly marked grave in some farmer's meadow on some unknown battlefield. I chose the following passage.

"Captain Tyler, Confederate States of America. Peace I leave with you, My peace I give unto you: not as the world giveth, give I unto you. Let not your heart be troubled, neither let it be afraid. Joseph, Army of the Potomac." I rode off wondering if he would find the note, if he would answer it and of course wondering if either he or I would live to see another sunrise.

I decided to write Julia and tell her about my encounters at the watering hole. Since the mail has become more regular and since I am confident only Julia's eyes will see it I feel comfortable in telling her about it. Since she is such a Christian lady I am sure she will find the humanity in our exchanges. I also told her generally where we were camped and what our current situation was and that John, I, Henry and Josiah are all safe and well. Josiah is especially well as he is consuming as much of our rations as the rest of us put together. He continues to round out, as John likes to tell him when they are jostling. Anything to take our minds off where we are and why we are here. I suggested she find a map of this area and draw a line on the map from Yorktown in a Southeasterly direction towards the James River where it elbows towards the North. In so doing she will have a map of where we are encamped in the middle of that line. I told her I feel confident that there will be no general battle in this location for some time to come. I also told her that it is generally thought that General McClellan will not make an attack for some weeks but hold the Rebels here until General McDowell and General Banks have made further advances towards Richmond or close to the Rebel Army now in front of us. General McClellan seems to be again somewhat cautions about committing his troops into any engagement and I for one am not arguing that point after what I have seen previously. I also told her that miracles of all miracles, our paymaster has finally arrived, we will be paid tomorrow and that I will be sending money home in my next letter. I closed by telling her that John was asleep safely next to me and that I will soon retire for the night with buoyant spirits trusting that you are all well at home and will have sweet sleep and pleasant dreams.

We are hearing that the Union Forces have captured the city of New Orleans so that lifted all our spirits that maybe finally some progress is being made in ending this conflict. I for one do not think the Confederacy can long stand up to the overwhelming strength of numbers and resources of the Union. Some of the men are becoming anxious again to engage the foe and with the information of the taking of New Orleans and other victories of the Union some of the men are anxious for a good chance at the

Rebels here in Virginia. I for one can wait but if called upon I will perform my duties as I always would. I put in a package to send to Julia $390, $350 was for her and the $40 was to be given to the Einfiels as he asked if he could send some of his pay in my package. John also sent $175 and he asked that Martha put $150 out at interest and with the other $25 pay his note at Henderson's and Hibbards, which is about $21.75. He also said that Martha could keep the rest, which was kind of him. I am trusting that this money will tide the family over these difficult times until again our government finds the time and money to pay us. We are also owed two additional months but only God knows when we will ever get that if at all. I also sent in the same package $450 to be distributed by Julia to all the families as stated in the letter, the men having sent money home to help their loved ones through these times. It is refreshing to realize that they all feel comfortable trusting their money to myself and of course to Julia but they have nothing to fear, as their money with us is secure as it would be in the bank. I sent her the following breakdown of the distribution after having John, Josiah and Henry help me figure it all out and make sure that each person was mentioned with the correct amount of money. I was fearful that someone would have been shortchanged or forgotten and the last thing I wanted was for any of these fine men to think that their commanding officer was not looking after their best interests.

Clinton Palmer's wife	$45
Mrs. Edith Bennett	$40
Jacob Wisner	$60 (Sent from three of his friends with a note to tip one for them.)
Mrs. Lucy Stickles	$30
Hiram Tiffany	$25
Margaret Johnston	$25
James Harris	$40
Mary Adams	$30
Sarah Health	$35 (Sent from the pay of her deceased Husband, small consolation that will be regrettably.)
Rebecca Jackson	$30
Enos Davis	$45
Willits Herendeen	$45
	$450

I trust Julia will distribute it immediately especially to Sarah Health where as I noted it will be little compensation for the fact that her beloved husband has been killed in this conflict. Her brave husband fought gallantly and died with tears in his eyes, as told to me, telling his fellow comrades as they were trying to comfort him speaking of how much he loved his dear wife and three wonderful children. What folly is this as I have said so often before?

CHAPTER ELEVEN

The End of Fellowship

I felt a tremendous urge to again visit the watering hole to see if Captain Tyler had left any kind of a response. I was not disappointed as the next day at about the same time that I normally stopped by to either fill our canteens or just to make sure we were observing the unwritten rule to respect it as a small beacon of peace in an otherwise mad world I found another note. As my trembling hands open the note I was not disappointed. Captain Tyler had written the following; "Joseph, I fear this is my last opportunity to communicate with you as I will shortly be moving on, to where I do not yet know, but hopefully a more tranquil place. I believe we both share the same desire to see an end to this lunacy and soon return to the comfort of our wives and families. I know not what has brought this insanity upon us; my family, I must admit, have been slave owners in Virginia but two years ago our patriarch saw the light and freed those that we had kept in bondage seeing the practice as hideous as it was. You and I shall never know if slavery would have eventually ended on its own or if the many thousands who have been already killed in this war and regrettably most likely the additional thousands yet to die will have accomplished anything. To weigh these thousands of deaths against giving the issue time and God's will to heel we will never know. Persons much more powerful than you and I have chosen this route and those answers will never be known. But enough of my rambling, thank you for helping to comfort my soul and may God bless you and yours and keep you safe. Those of us that walk in darkness will hopefully live to see a great light. Might I suggest in closing that I will be standing outside the entrance to the White House in Washington two years from today and if events allow I would look forward to meeting you there. Let us pray we may keep this date. Yours in peace, Captain Tyler, Confederate States of America."

I felt a certain sadness knowing that this would be our last communication as it was such a journey from reality to exchange our notes and know that someone on the opposing side shared my views of this conflict. But as always in life everything has its time and the time for our exchanges to end is now. As I turned Blackjack to ride back to camp my eye caught some movement in the trees across the pond and as I looked I was startled to see a Confederate officer sitting astride his beautiful horse and looking my way. As I stared wondering if this was a surprise attack on this place of peace or if I was seeing an illusion. The officer's next gesture was to draw his sword from its saber and for only an instant I feared I would be in combat and then an amazing thing happened when he lifted his sword to his forehead and in so doing saluted me. I immediately realized it was Captain Tyler and his way of paying his respects to a fellow soldier and to say goodbye. I drew my sword and in turn saluted him as we both reluctantly turned and rode off to our destiny, never to see each other again. I did note in my diary the date however and in my mind I may well, if God is willing, be outside the White House gate on this date two years hence. What are our destinies? For a fleeting moment it crossed my mind that maybe Captain Tyler was intending to meet at the Little White House where the ladies reside but I quickly dismissed this thought. I am sure he means the White House where President Lincoln resides. It also crossed my mind that I wondered if Captain Tyler thought he would be standing there as a victor in this war but that thought quickly passed also. Even if he had meant the Little White House I would have had to ask Old Doc to go with me as I am sure he could find their location if in fact they are still in business. What a stupid question that is, if in fact they are still in business. Old Doc always seemed to have a great sense of direction when it came to these ladies, of course he always maintained he was only taking care of their medical needs and not collecting compensation in any other way than hard cash. I pity anyone who would believe that.

We have had a few days of rain again so as far as any battles it has been relatively quiet. I was awakened this morning from a restless sleep hearing cannonading and bombardment to our right towards Yorktown. I was told that it had been going on all night but one gets so use to it even in a restless sleep it sounds like music to put one asleep. That is a terrible way to think of it when you realize what these shells might be doing to one side or the other. Once up John told me that breakfast was ready so the four of us sat down at our makeshift table. We have but two knives and two forks which we must share but there is never any arguing over them as we have done this for so long. Our table consists of an old cracker box about 14 inches above the ground and each of us has a tin cup and a tin plate. John had fixed good coffee, fried pork, cold boiled rice fried and Hardees. Hardees are what the men call those square pilot bread loves. Unfortunately some of our dishes and utensils were left at New Port News and have never caught up with us. We are better off than most of the men as many are eating with their fingers since their utensils were long ago set aside and never found. We have also had some very good Northern potatoes this week, which we bought at the Brigade Commissary as we do most of our provisions. I would have thought that the government would be providing the food for this army but as with so many other government involvements this one also is, I feel, all fouled up. As you can tell I am just a little upset with the fact that we have to buy much of our food from our meager pay, which often is months late. As an officer I can purchase anything on hand at what it costs the government. I paid 85 cents per bushel for the potatoes, ham for 9 cents and coffee for 10 cents. Sugar cost me 11 cents, and all these provisions last us quite a while. It is a good thing that we have full stomachs for the command has ordered us to march immediately. We have been told to march on Williamsburg and that we will be engaging the enemy.

It turned out to be an horrific fight and as I ordered the men to engage I said a prayer for all of them and even asked the Lord's help for the poor Confederate soldiers whom we were marching towards. As the Southerners would say this was a "right smart fight." We whipped the Rebels handsomely on the right flank where we were, and the ground in front of us was thickly strewn with killed and wounded. I am pleased to say that the 33rd came out ahead of any regiment that was engaged at this point. Three of the companies, including Company B were not in action having been left in one of the Rebel forts as a guard about a quarter of a mile to the rear of where our line was. The Colonel was with four companies a little to the right and front in the woods as skirmishers. I was in command of the other three companies on the field and an additional 50 back on the road guarding and helping our division wagon train through. The 33rd was not in a very good condition to make a very big fight of it but for all that they did nobly, one company on the left in the woods had to retire and the three under my command withstood the fire of the Rebel's well.

Courtesy of the Library of Congress

As it happened the Rebels came upon us rather unexpectedly even though we had been ordered to move up and engage the enemy. They came upon us so quickly that our artillery had to retire to get a better position and also two of our regiments retired to obtain a position of advantage. Once I established that our positions were defendable, I ordered a halt, ordered the engagement and the men fought bravely. The Rebels at one point came within 25 rods of us with horrific fire but the men held their ground and gave not an inch. The Colonel came upon us and I suggested that the only way to halt this assault by the Rebels was through a charge. The Colonel agreed with me and I ordered the men to take the fight to the Rebels with a total engagement. It was a sight to behold as the men ran forward with muskets firing, bayonets flashing in the sun and to a man shouting at the top of their lungs their defiance of any assault on they or their fellow soldiers. I must admit that it was an exhilarating moment and it crossed my mind at that moment that mankind has a strongly controlling attitude which when properly directed works for the betterment of mankind. When misdirected it may help explain why there have been so many thousands of wars in all of recorded history. I guess that is too simple an explanation of mankind's history of warfare and I certainly am not the one to think I have found the hidden flaw in man that leads us to this forbidden place so often down through the ages. Enough of this philosophizing, as Julia would remind me if she was here, you are just a simple fellow from a simple town living a simple life and you are certainly not Plato even though on occasion you seem to maybe think you are. Julia always has a way to bring me back down to earth.

As concerns the charge at the Rebels, although I am sure they are brave to the last man, they certainly did not expect this charge especially by a smaller force and they were putting off on double quick right after it happened. Once they had left the field of battle and the smoke began to clear we saw the many dead and dying on the field of battle. This image will never leave my mind as long as I live, an image of total wretchedness and certainly hell on earth. We counted a Rebel colonel, a lieut. colonel and a major of their general staff that had been killed. We also took three captains, two lieutenants and 151 prisoners during this engagement. We counted 70 dead on the field of battle and watched as the Rebels dragged off from a more distant part of the field of battle some of their dead and wounded. Our part of the fight was, as I mentioned, of short duration, but most magnificently done, if I can use that word to describe such destruction. Again the excitement of the moment soon gave way to the realty of what we had wrought upon our fellow man and ourselves.

General McClellan sent his compliments to our regiment in the morning for a job well done. During the night the enemy left the remainder of their fortifications, to I assume, lick their wounds and regroup for the next fight that I fear will surely come. Old Doc is now the savior to many as we have had one captain killed, 28 soldiers killed or missing and thirteen wounded, several of which Old Doc tells me will surly die. In thinking about this horrific scene afterwards I was amazed of the relatively few numbers of our killed or wounded compared with the enemy and it appeared to me remarkable. Maybe tomorrow or the next day will see a different outcome but for now I will thank God for helping us through this. John came through unscathed, as did Josiah and Henry even though all three of them were in the thick of the battle. I cannot imagine writing Julia of the injury or death of our beloved son in this insanity.

Courtesy of the Library of Congress

The sun has come out and the Chaplin is busy with the burial parties saying his words over the dead and dying, and Old Doc has been at in for over 24 hours without a break tending to those he feels he can save. The screams from his makeshift hospital as he was amputating the arm or leg of some poor fellow with only his special medicine to ease the pain were dreadful. Several of the ladies that still lived in this area are helping Old Doc tend to the dead and dying and are truly a blessing from God. One of the younger officers was upset as they thought they might be spies for the Confederacy and came to me with their concerns and I immediately told them to set aside their concerns and think only of those suffering as I had seen first hand some fair lady holding the hand of one of our dying comrades and the look in his eyes as he gazed upon her. There is no replacement for the love and caring of a motherly figure when anyone is suffering, be it a child an adult or more than any a dying soldier. I told the young officer I did not want to hear again of his concerns and to put himself to use in helping Old Doc in the hospital. In addition to this problem I was extremely upset when the higher ups allowed a photographer onto the battlefield after the battle was over and they took pictures of the dead and dying. I confronted one who called himself Mathew Brady and questioned what he was doing but was abruptly told that the general had approved it. I see it as an affront to the memory and dignity of those that gave their lives on the field of battle but Mr. Brady told me that he and the general feel this living misery needs to be recorded for history so hopefully it will not repeat itself. There are a number of things that I don't agree with the general on and this is certainly one of them. I sincerely doubt that seeing the pictures of the dead piled up will in any way influence man to stop his madness. I wish it were so but alas I think not.

Courtesy of the library of Congress

In a rare moment of reflection when I was alone in my tent after the unspeakable events of the past few days I took out my pipe which had been given to me by Julia a number of years ago as having been an old family heirloom and sat there looking at its beauty as I enjoyed the smell and taste of the tobacco. I looked at this beautiful instrument with its hand-carved horns, dogs and antelopes plus other adornments and wondered how the hands of man can create such beauty. Those same hands are also capable of creating such ugliness as the living picture of a battlefield after a battle. As I evolve through this life, if the Lord sees fit to allow it I will always think of this battlefield whenever I take a moment to remember and take out this beautiful work of art and light up in a moment of reflection. I was quickly aroused from my thoughts as

John, Henry and Josiah came into the tent and Josiah announced that it was time to eat as only Josiah could. It seems no matter what the circumstances Josiah's stomach always is calling him. We shall partake and pray for all the dead and the dying on both sides and prepare for the many services that the Chaplin will be holding tomorrow as the bodies are respectively being prepared to enter their final resting place. The Colonel consulted with me and we decided that the 28 killed, as the final tally came to, will be interned in a common grave, as time does not allow our individually burying all of them. As they were in this life and especially in this army they were friends and brothers in arms and as such will be buried as friends and brothers in arms. I pray they will all find peace in a better place under the forgiving hand of God. This is a beautiful place where we are now camped as it is on a 300-acre wheat field on a slight rise and is surrounded by a pleasant view. It is about three fourths of a mile near the banks of the York River and about six miles above Yorktown. If I were to choose a final resting place the beauty of this land would be near the top of the list and I chose an area near the top of a rise for the burial site hoping the souls of our poor departed comrades would approve. As we all gathered to listen to the Chaplin's final words and have the names of each of the brothers read there was not a dry eye amongst us. It is at times like these that we so need each other and at times like this that I wish I was in Julia's arms as I am sure I would give in to the great urge to cry uncontrollably for my fellow man and all of our shortcomings. As I said I hope these poor fellows are in a better place, that the sacrifice they have made and that all of their families that are left behind will now make was worth it. Only time, much beyond my time, upon this earth will answer that question. Our fight of the other day and the victory was more decisive and a more wonderful repulse of the enemy on our part of the field than even I could imagine. It was a terrible blow to the Confederacy and a most brilliant achievement of the Army of the Potomac, and it turned the entire action of the day. Only in my dreams do I dare imagine that it is the battle to end this brutality but yet again I so hope it is the beginning of the end. Here in May of 1862 we have been at war for over a year and it is in my opinion a year too long. Blessed are the peacemakers, as they shall be called the children of God, or something like that. I don't have my Bible handy to check the accuracy of that statement but I hope you will forgive my taking liberties. If only mankind would work as hard at peace as they do at war what a glorious world we would all inhabit.

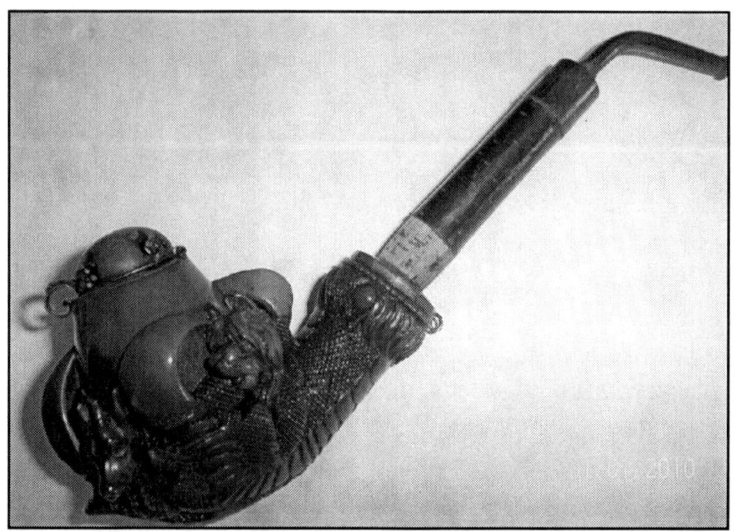

Courtesy of the Library of Congress

CHAPTER TWELVE

The Second Major Battle

It seems we are only going to get a short time to rest as the enemy can be seen on the other side of the field and it looks like they are preparing to attack again. They have regrouped and it looks like there are about twice as many of them as the recent struggle we were in. I would have thought that they had enough but I guess it is the nature of man to seek revenge and feel that today will be his day on the field of battle. As it turns out our artillery is about 400 yards in front of our regiment, the Seventh Maine is on our right, the Fifth Wisconsin is on the right side of the artillery and the Sixth Maine and the 49th Pennsylvania are on the left. The artillery has kept up a brisk fire as we currently have six pieces engaged and they have been firing from 11 AM until about 2 PM when General Summers who is already engaged with the enemy towards the James River sent word for our artillery to cease firing as the enemy, as I was informed, were sniping him hard. I ordered the artillery to stand down and from 2:00 PM until about 5:00 PM they only fired infrequent shots if they saw the Rebel troops passing from fort to fort on some distant part of the field about a mile or more in front of us. We were facing a large clearing of some three miles in area, and that is about what we can see in front of us. The Rebel works and the Rebel Army extend far to the southwest beyond what we can see from our vantage point. They look like a fearsome force and I am surprised that to a man our forces seem overly anxious to take them on. I'm certain it is because of our recent victory that the men feel indestructible but I fear they may have a rude awakening since it looks to me as if we are heavily outnumbered this time, even more so than the battle of the other day. Out of the corner of my eye I caught sight of Mr. Brady with the general in the rear and wondered what he was contemplating to record for histories sake. I am saying a silent prayer that he will not have pictures of the piles of dead and dying soldiers to send to the newspapers that crave more pictures to go with their stories of this conflict. This battlefield, if it turns out to be so in the next few hours, is slightly rolling but relatively open and I cannot see any ravines or any obvious place for cover for either our troops or the Rebel forces. Again it looks like it will be a right smart fight, if I can use that word to describe a frontal assault by either side across open land. Seems to me very strange that we and the Rebels, namely General McClellan and General Lee seem to look for open land to launch an attack wherein it gives no cover to the men that are actually doing the fighting and the dying. If I was the general I think I would find more protection for our troops as we faced the enemy rather than just marching towards almost total loss and annihilation on both sides. I was even of the thought that as warfare evolves maybe someday mankind will not be so dim-witted in picking this type of battlefield situation. I of course am only alluding myself to think that I would ever be a general and as I have said before Julia would certainly bring me back down to earth in rapid fashion if she knew of my illusions. As I thought more about this I reminded myself that I pray that mankind does not evolve further in the art of war and that this war will end all wars. Why am I eluding myself, mankind has fought thousands of wars in recorded history. I can only pray and hope for what most likely will be a bleak future.

The Rebels even dammed up the creek so as to form several large ponds between ourselves and their forces so it would make it harder for our men to cross and especially hard for our artillery to move through if in fact they were to come up to this vantage point. I believe at this time we will keep them in reserve until we see what develops. A short time ago the general held a meeting of his officers and raised the question of our position and how vulnerable it was at present. He even went so far as to question the propriety of maintaining this location or pulling back to a more defensible arrangement. There are only five regiments available at the present time and three companies of ours are in the fort a short distance to our rear. About 50 men I have assigned to assist the wagons along with our supplies and I also have sent out some skirmishers and I firmly believe they will all give their greatest effort when called upon. If the general had asked me personally I would have told him from what I see unfolding that it is a little late to think about repositioning ourselves in a more secure setting. Again he seems to be somewhat indecisive and that of course can spell many a death warrant in war. As our meeting broke up and Blackjack and I returned to our point I was starting to decide if we should consider bedding some of the troops down for the night and all of a sudden I heard artillery from the Rebel side and we looked towards them and they were advancing on the double quick out of the woods in the back of the clearing and they extended their line of battle across the entire open field and proceeded to come down on us. One line of theirs consisted of Calvary and the other the foot soldiers. There was no hesitating in their intention and it certainly was far to late too think about re-establishing our line of defense to a more invulnerable position as the general had suggested. The last I saw the general he was headed back to his command post on the double quick and leaving the rest of us to deal with what certainly looks like a blood bath and not Rebel blood. Colonel Draime and I each took positions on either end of the field and we directed our troops to commence firing but it had little effect on the circumstances. Our men all stood their ground and their fire was extremely deadly as many of the Rebels are falling upon the field. I fear Mr. Brady may well have more than enough pictures of the dead and dying for his newspapers. Even though we are taking a terrible toll of the Rebels they continue to advance across the open field directly in the line of our fire. They are about 20 rods in front of our most advance troops and it looks we may well lose this day. I caught a glimpse of John to my right with Henry and Josiah with him and they are firing and reloading as fast as they can. I had a moment of admiration for all three of them, especially John, as I saw what a fine young man he had become. That feeling was quickly replaced by the realization that he and his fellow soldiers are in the direct line of fire and could well be killed or wounded in the next few minutes. I immediately appraised the situation and I feel the only way to save this day is an immediate charge. I signaled the colonel who was within eyesight at the other end of our forces and ordered a charge. I was stunned as to a man my troops and those directly under the colonel stood to a man and with a scream loud enough to make the air tremble they rushed the Rebels. Old Blackjack carried me into the heat of battle and with my sword raised I charged ahead of the men and into this nightmare. At his critical moment thanks to the brave hearts of our band not a man faltered but on they rushed and the entire line, seeing our 33rd charging the enemy, took up the cry as orders were passed along. It only took a few minutes it seemed and as the smoke cleared I was not disappointed by the decision to charge this superior force as the Rebels were running in every direction.

Colonel Draime rode up to me and we exchanged a salute to one another on a job well done, if leaving hundreds dead and dying on a battlefield is a job well done. I quickly checked on John, Henry and Josiah and only Josiah was slightly wounded as a Rebel bullet had nicked him as we were charging forward. The wound did not seem too serious and he told me that if needed he would be ready without delay to take the enemy on again. This type of loyalty and courageousness can never be bought or taught, it is inbred in good men.

We have pulled back to regroup as the battle has ended and when I spoke to Colonel Draime I mentioned that it seemed that the battle only lasted about ten or fifteen minutes, the colonel remarked that it had lasted nearly an hour and that the general was on the far left flank and was amazed as he saw our regiment charging and he had sent word that this action saved the day for the Union.

I wrote Julia the following letter a few days later when the smoke had lifted and the dead and dying were being tended to.

"Dear Julia, my beloved,

I could not believe that it lasted more than a few minutes, but how we dropped them. I was astonished myself when the smoke lifted and I could look beyond and around us and see the number killed and wounded Rebels and it appeared to me at the time to be the work of a few minutes. There at the same time so few killed or wounded on our side, the seventh and sixth Maine had some hurt, they were upon the right and left flanks. But this was an even chance, what fighting men call a fair fight, neither party having the advantage of position, being in open fields which sometimes has been rare in any major conflict in this war. The Rebels having always fought us from behind walls of earth and wood and trees in smaller skirmishes up until now. I was informed today that there were eight regiments that made the attack on us. I saw prisoners myself from five different regiments, but this I do know from my vantage point during the battle. They had two lines of men coming down upon us either of which was nearly the length of our one line. They certainly had many more men than we had and they had been brought into the field for the express purpose under the command of two of their generals to drive us from the field and capture our artillery. The same good results along the line as we had in our area would have most effectively used up their army on this peninsula. As I have been told and observed they desperately needed to capture our artillery as they do not have the industrial base in the South to build the quantity or the quality that the North has being that they are mostly an agricultural society. I sometimes wonder then how they thought they could defeat the North but then again one could argue in some respects that they didn't start this conflict although they planted the seeds for it.

Our wounded men and most of theirs were brought in before dark, and as far as the surgeons working with Old Doc they all agreed that the men from both sides are being cared for as the need arises and time allows. Julia, it is unbelievable that one minute we are killing and wounding our fellow man and the next minute we are trying to make them whole again. What insanity is this? I was pleased to see our men without being ordered about, going over the battlefield helping up and leading in those of the Rebel wounded that could walk. The stretchers were at first used to bring in our wounded and when that was finished we carried some of the Rebel wounded in for treatment. Some of course were shot up so badly that even Old Doc's skills will be inadequate in trying to help them. Their only hope at this point is the prayers of the Chaplin and the prayers that they are headed for a better place along with their comrades that were fatally wounded. I saw many of our men pouring water from their canteens in cups and giving it to those that had fallen on the field of battle no matter which side they were from. The enemy I can happily say was in no way maltreated, they were cared for and made as comfortable as the circumstances, time, place and their condition would allow. Early the next morning Colonel Draime and I sent one of our companies into the woods where our skirmishers had been to pick up any that were found there. Unfortunately they found a number of dead and some wounded and they brought them in. The dead were buried as quickly as possible in mass graves as there is no time to dig individual graves with the enemy regrouping. The wounded are being cared for and the screams from the hospital tents bear out the agony some of these poor fellows are going through. Even if they survive, their lives will never be the same again. I have even heard that some Southern heartless witches have boasted of having drumsticks and finger rings made from the bones of Yankees as hard as I find that to believe. Irregardless we have the gratification of saying in reply, we cared for and administered to the comfort of your dying and wounded, as decently as civilized people ought to do. We buried your dead with prayer and reference and we would not allow any loafers to insult your comrades when they are our prisoners. Julia, can you imagine my saying, as civilized people, that certainly is a contradiction of what we just experienced and will most likely experience over and over again. One last thing, Josiah was slightly injured but will be fine in a day or so and Henry, John and yours truly are just fine.

Thinking of you and the children constantly,your affectionate husband,

Joseph"

I'm not sure who is busier now, the Chaplin or the doctors. I don't believe I would want to be in either's shoes at this point. I am not even sure I am comfortable in my shoes having to order men into battle to the fate that has befallen them and certainly will befall them in future battles. The excitement of the moment these last few days has been replaced by a disheartened frame of mind for me. As I lay in my tent trying to catch a few moments of rest I cannot erase from my mind the images of the battle. I fear that the good Lord is looking down, as I have said before, upon his great experiment of humans on this earth and wondering where it all went wrong. He is most likely wondering if He made them too violent, short changed them in the acumen department or if it was just a grand plan that has again failed. I pray he is a forgiving God as I myself have run through more than one of the enemy with my sword and will never eradicate from my memory the terrified look upon their faces and the screams emanating from their souls. In several cases they were but young men not as old even as John. I wonder as I lay here if having been responsible for taking the lives of our fellow men will condemn me to everlasting hell. Is there a difference in God's mind between our being ordered to kill our fellow man by leadership in a time they choose of war as compared to taking a human life without the excuse of war? I doubt if God sees it that way and I fear I am damned for eternity, if that be the case I pray that those responsible for this slaughter on both sides will share that same fate with me. I fear I will find ample company in hell, even though it is not the company I seek, if all those that over the centuries have been responsible for wars are already there.

CHAPTER THIRTEEN

Camp In The Field, Near New Kent, Virginia

I have finally received a couple of letters from home from Martha and Julia and they were most welcomed. It is now the 11th of May and it has been about two weeks since mail has been delivered. I am beginning to think that it represents negligence on the part of the quartermaster department in not delivering our mail more promptly. As I have previously stated, soldiers survive to fight another day on a full stomach and on letters from loved ones. When either is disrupted there is hell to pay. I have reprimanded those who are responsible for this and told them maybe they need to get their collective asses in gear and not be so fearful of getting too close to the action. Hopefully my harsh words will make a difference however I fear that those in charge are not terribly concerned about the feelings of one Lieutenant Colonel in such a vast army.

One of the other officers told me this morning that he had seen the New York Herald newspaper and it had many pictures of the dead and wounded which I continue to think is disrespect to their memories but unfortunately it is not my decision to make. The paper reported that the battle was concluded and victory won by a splendid charge of the 43rd New York Regiment. That of course is an error as the charge was made by the 33rd New York and not the 43rd as reported. They should check their facts as the 43rd was not even on the same side of the creek where the battle was fought and had no part in it; they came over in the evening, as did another

10,000 men. Maybe the Herald was a little bias as the 43rd is made up of mostly men from the Albany area but also some from the New York City area where the paper originates. I guess my pride is getting in the way of logic again when I take issue with exactly who was responsible for ending this particular battle. The important thing is that it is ended and no more blood is being spilled by either side at least for the time being.

At the battle General Hancock had the Fifth Wisconsin, Sixth Maine, 49th Pennsylvania and my 33rd New York Volunteers. He also was in command of the Seventh of Davidson's Brigade. No other troops or artillery were across the creek or engaged with the enemy at that time or place. As I wrote to Julia it was a brilliant execution carried out by the brave fellows of the 33rd that saved this day and none others. There I go again tooting my own horn but it wasn't myself that deserves the credit but the men, especially those that fell and are no longer with us or will be wearing the scars of battle the rest of their lives. They are the true heroes.

We are getting some much needed rest these last few days while I send teams to York River for provisions. Our supply train is catching up with us, the bread makers and the wagon loaded with Old Doc's medicines which he is dreadfully in need of as he has used so much to deaden the pain of many a wounded soldier both in mind and body. The toll that injury to the body takes is incalculable but the toll that is inflicted on the human spirit and mind can never be healed even with gallons of Old Doc's special cure. In all of those that are fortunate enough to survive this war it will stay with them forever and if I survive it I will never again sleep in peace. We have been told to prepare to march again any day with three days rations and we will be marching towards Richmond. We are currently about 35 miles from there and we all expect that any past battles will pale in comparison to what we are facing if and when we attempt to cause its downfall. Men who have little or no chance of winning this overall war will fight to the last man to preserve Richmond. I fear any such battle will be devastating and I pray that some treaty or resolution of this conflict, even if it is temporary, will be found before this has to happen. As I look around this countryside and see the leaves blossoming out and the corn coming up here in mid May of 1862 I think of the rebirth of the earth and look forward to that day, hopefully not in the too distant future when we will see a resurrection of peace on this earth. Our Chaplin has said a prayer for all the troops as well as all mankind that it will be so. What started out a year ago to be a grand adventure of maybe a month or so has developed into a never-ending nightmare.

Julia's last letter was extremely anxious as to when I was coming home on furlough. It has been over a year and still I have not seen my beloved wife and family. I doubt that any able-bodied officer will now be granted leave with the upcoming assault on Richmond to take place shortly. I am hoping that once we take Richmond and things quiet down it will give General Robert E. Lee and the other leaders of the South pause to contemplate whether this lunacy is worth any more blood being spilled.

It is strange the things that happen at a time like this, the small things we think of, home, family, friends and the day-to-day events that we wonder about. I have a prized knife that Irwin gave me before I left our fair village, Irving being one of our oldest residents. He always said he was so old he had fought in the Revolutionary War but everyone in town sort of doubted that claim. His claim was even expounded upon on many a Saturday evening when he would buy a round of drinks for his many friends at the local pub. When he found out I was leaving to head up the local group of soldiers he presented me one evening with his favorite hunting knife, said it was for good luck and would keep John and I safe. Several times in the recent few months on the other side of Lees Mills I had lost the knife but each time I was fortunate enough to stumble upon it. It has become a symbol for me as I guess I am somewhat superstitious and think it actually is keeping John and I safe. The other day I reached for it as I often do to see if it was safe in my pocket and low and behold it was not there. I sort of panicked and I searched every pocket and even my boots to see if I had left it in the side of my boot. Later on in the evening I had given up entirely when, I guess that is my lucky knife, I put my hand in my back coat pocket to get my tobacco again and my hand struck the knife. I was so pleased that I jumped clear from the ground and shouted, which startled some officers that were standing nearby. It was a strange occurrence as I had taken the tobacco out a number of times during the day and had not felt it there. How it got there I will never know but my lucky knife is back and that is what is important. It is strange the small things that we cling to in times like these. Small things, like a lucky knife, mean so much to each of us, especially when we do not have our families to comfort us. I will sleep well this night knowing that luck is still with us and will hopefully spare John in particular and myself in the upcoming battles. I told Old Doc about it and he smiled slightly and took a rabbit's foot out of his pocket, held it up and just looked at it and I knew the meaning in his expression. I think if I went to thousands of the troops in this army each man would have some simple possession that they cling to. Maybe it reminds them of home and better days or reminds them of their loved ones, whatever it is important to each individual.

We marched about five or six miles this day and we are camped in a large 300-acre wheat field with about 60,000 other troops. This is a formidable assembly of manpower and as I stated I hope it gives the Rebels pause to consider their position and possibly call for a cooling off or a conference of the field leadership to talk to each other rather than kill or be killed. If I were a Rebel officer and saw this gathering of so many armed men and artillery I would try and encourage the generals to reconsider their position of defending Richmond at all costs. I fear all costs, but their own hides, to put it very bluntly. As Napoleon was quoted as saying, " Soldiers win the battles and generals get the credit," I fear that may well be the case in the very near future. Sixty thousand troops on the march is a sight to behold but not a sight I want to see for long. Hopefully this will be the end or nearly the end of this lunacy.

I have been informed that this beautiful spot that we are encamped on is none other than the Custis Estate where George Washington courted Martha who later became his wife. It is a beautiful spot with acre upon acre of clover as far as the eye can see and the clover is just beginning to blossom. As I sit here enjoying my wonderful pipe I am contemplating what George Washington would think now of his country and its warring ways. I am sure like all other leaders that he thought the war he was involved in was "the war to end all wars." I think over time that statement has been worn out and maybe it is time to come up with a new one at the end of each conflict. Maybe it should be "the end of this war is the beginning of the next" or something to that effect.

I have also been told that this estate now belongs to the Rebel leader General Lee who in my opinion chose the wrong side in this clash. This has been a quiet time as we are camped out here and the leaders on both sides are contemplating their next moves, or I should say, the next moves for we unfortunate foot soldiers. I still consider myself as one of the foot soldiers even though I ride Blackjack, as my attachment to the men has never been closer as we have faced the enemy and our true colors have been tested and found not wanting. In fact it is a time to rest and for the first time since the beginning of April of this year I have slept soundly in my drawers rapped up in a blanket in our tent. Since April first I have always slept with my coat on and fully clothed even with my boots on, as I never knew when I would be called upon to lead the men in battle. It feels so good finally to rest soundly and for a time anyway not to worry about being immediately attacked. Unfortunately amongst this many troops camped out in the open we have rampant disease and Old Doc along with all the other medical men have their hands full trying to contain the unbridled illnesses which are ravaging our ranks. Old Doc in all his wisdom was certainly correct when he told me that this conflict could see more men die from disease than from bullets. It is horrifying to see the ill and their suffering and know that they signed up to face an enemy with a rifle and not an unseen enemy which would take them down without their being able to defend themselves from such sickness. The doctors are doing their best but regrettably they do not have the medicines to halt these ever-expanding afflictions.

Courtesy of the Library of Congress

I have not been informed if we will be leaving here shortly or not, frankly I could spend the rest of the war, short as I hope it will be, in this beautiful spot. It is almost impossible to move a large army, as this is with the 60,000 troops, horses, wagons, supplies and of course the artillery. When we do march we plan on moving the artillery and equipment of about half the force for half a day and then the other 30,000 troops, etc. will start out and rejoin with the original 30,000. It is important not to have the entire regiments separated for too long a time in case of an all out attack by the Rebels, therefore the high command has restricted the distance between us for everyone's sake. I do feel having been in the thick of battle that the forward 30,000 troops and artillery would be more than enough to handle anything the Rebels would throw at us but the higher ups are again in my opinion overly cautious. Since it looks like we may lay siege to Richmond I think it wise that we wait as long as possible so that the women and children are allowed to evacuate. As in so many wars in the past many of the victims have been women and children either by accident or far worse by design. One might call this a "Civilized War" when it comes to both sides trying to protect women and children if any war can be called "civilized." I wrote Julia again a long letter of our situation and told her that I expect we will shortly be taking Richmond and after that I believe the Rebels will lay down their arms, as this will most likely be their last stand if in fact they decide to make a stand at all. I further told her that after this engagement I fully expect furloughs will be granted more liberally and I will be able to come home for a short visit. It has been many months since I have seen Julia and the family and my heart aches for them. It would be even better if the Rebels, as I stated, lay down their arms before any major battle instead of our being called upon to invade Richmond and hopefully end this war. When I think about it I looked around at this immense army of ours and wondered, if we invade, how many of us and the other side will lie dead after such a battle. All of these potential lives hinge on the decisions of a few higher ups on both sides and I hope cool heads prevail and peace be at hand.

As it turned out here on May 15th, 1862 while we are awaiting orders it has started to rain and rain heavily. The only good thing about it is that the ever-cautious high command has decided that the rain makes an undesirable condition to attack in so we have been ordered to stand down at least for the time being. Our camp as I have said is quite comfortable considering everything and while we camp here other troops are being marched up to join us and this fearsome force is ever growing larger. I even managed to purchase some fine cheese from the supply wagons that came up along with two excellent hams and I also have been told that they will see that I can buy some more coffee and sugar tomorrow. All the comforts of home, who am I kidding? I was sort of hoping that the generals would send myself to negotiate a peace with the Rebels and the thought crossed my mind that Captain Tyler and I could spend some time hammering out the details over a cold tall one. Frankly I think he and I could soon come up with an acceptable peace that both sides could agree upon, especially the foot soldiers that will be bearing the blunt of any combat.

John, Josiah, Henry and I took this opportunity while standing down to inventory our goods and just where things stand. We have brought into our tent many a cedar branch and are using them for not only carpeting but also as feathers for our beds. They are surprisingly quite comfortable under the circumstances. We have arranged all our furniture and fixings consisting of our trunks, a satchel each, a haversack in which we carry our rations, a canteen, two swords, a pistol for John and myself and our carbines. We also have a shoe washbasin, mightily needed with all this mud, horse brush, shoe brush, horse blanket and other odds and ends. When I look at it all I wonder how we can all fit in this one small tent with all these goods but we have it well organized and blessedly we all get along fine so it makes it much easier. When I see Old Doc and his arrangement I really wonder who outranks whom as he has his tent as I have said all to himself with his trunks, doctor tools, special brew, etc. Absolutely no one in this man's army would deny Old Doc as many comforts as could be afforded as he is so loved and admired by all the men and of course I think each man thinks when they see him if tomorrow or the next day will he be digging a bullet out of my flesh or cutting off one of my limbs. If it sadly has to happen to a man they would rather have Old Doc than any other doctor operate on them.

We have been ordered to march here on May 19th and unfortunately we will have to leave this beautiful southern plantation where we have been camped out. I think to a man we could all have spent the rest of this war in this spot but alas it is not to be. It is hard to describe the movement of such a vast army, regiment after regiment are on the move, battery after battery and of course the squadrons of cavalry. They have all been breaking camp starting at 5 AM with a never-ending movement it seems. Some of the troops, cavalry and artillery have been ordered to head due South towards Richmond and our group, including the 33rd New York Volunteers are marching West and I have been told we are to proceed about six miles and make camp in a pine forest at that spot. As we marched we passed some absolutely breath taking plantations and some beautiful fields. These people had such beauty, regrettably some of it was built on the back of slavery, but I would have thought rather than give this all up and go to war they could have decided amongst reasonable men to end the atrocious practice of slavery and work together to better all their lives, both free and slave in an equal society. Here I go again thinking that mankind is rational and could actually do something like that without going to war. As I have often said, only in my dreams.

This is one of the saddest days of my time in this man's army. As we left our fair village and have spent so much time together all the men have become brothers as we have faced dangers together and stood up to them as the brave men of the 33rd. I particularly have grown strongly attached to Henry, Josiah and of course John could never be replaced as my beloved son. I also consider Old Doc as one of the originally five of us that signed up for this great exploit as my closest friends and confidants. When you are faced with never knowing what tomorrow will bring and living with constant danger close friends are truly a gift from God. Sorrowfully today I have said my goodbyes to Henry as we are going our separate ways. His resignation has been accepted by the high command upon my recommendation. After having been together in the service of our country for a year, and been on duty so much together we are parting ways. He and I as well as Josiah and John have marched on grueling long treks in all kinds of weather and faced the enemy together. It is with tremendous regret that I parted with him today. I could but say a few words to him as we parted, not because I had little to say but because I found my heart was getting too full. I could not say all I desired to him as I took his hand to bid him goodbye without opening a fountain of tears. My feelings ran so deep that all I found to say was "God's speed." He also was choked up and found little he could say or we would have found ourselves, both officers of the Army of the Potomac, crying our heads off in the middle of thousands of soldiers. As he rode off towards what I truly pray will be a time of healing in our fair town I thought of how well he has served his country and that there was no truer or braver officer in the regiment. John and Josiah are also having a very difficult time with his leaving. Unfortunately the Captain's health has been poor since last fall, by spells he would appear quite smart, but of late, I have seen that he was daily growing more and more feeble. Many a day I have seen him nerve up and go on duty and on a march when I knew he was poorly able to do so. His great desire and determination has been from first to last whenever the regiment was to march with a prospect of meeting the enemy, to always go with them. His nervous system regrettably has become so weakened and unbalanced that I think there was little or no prospect of his getting much better with the great burden of the companies well being on his mind and of course on mine. The fatigue and excitement of the campaign has become more than he could handle. Under the circumstances I had no choice but to recommended that he be released from service. I don't think anyone in this army would have been more devastated to be told he could no longer handle his post than Henry. He pleaded to be allowed to stay but it had become very obvious that he could no longer function and was a danger to himself and to those who he commanded and led. He will be sorely missed and hopefully with much rest and his loving family to nurse him back to health he will soon recover. It is a heart-rending day when a man like Henry realizes he cannot stand up to the constant pressure of the circumstances we are all in. I told him it took a brave man to admit when he needed to step aside and finally convinced him of the wisdom of leaving. I believe in his heart as he left he felt after a few weeks of recuperation that he would return to his fellow soldiers and brothers in arms to take his rightful place. I know in my mind this will not happen and pray he will be able to live with the reality of his fate. There is none braver than Henry but each man has his limits and regretfully he has reached his. I constantly wonder what will become of the four of us that are left to face each new day and its perils, hopefully we will all be able to march in the Civil War remembrance parades in our old age in our fair village. Henry, John, Josiah, Old Doc and I but there are many obstacles that we will have to face before that wonderful day happens. I think it would be fantastic for the five of us and Captain Tyler to all reminisce about these days sometime in the future over a tall one at the tavern. Only the Lord knows our destiny, whether it be to survive and die in our beds of old age, die on the battle field or die in the hospital tent of some grave disease. I pray that we all will die in our beds of old age including Captain Tyler. I am so despondent over the loss of Henry that I needed to be alone and so I saddled up Blackjack and just rode away from the camp for a while. I am sure it is not the brightest thing to do with the possibility of the enemy lurking nearby but I just didn't care as I needed what I would call uncluttered time to collect my thoughts and gather myself together for what may lay ahead. I reached in my pocket for the pictures of Julia and the family to comfort me and I was shocked that they were not there. I then remembered that I had given a trunk to Henry to take home for me and I had forgotten these valued pictures were in the trunk. I must write Julia immediately and ask her to return them for without them to calm me I am not sure I can go on much longer. With Henry leaving and now the loss of the pictures it is indeed a distressing day for this officer. My only consolation is that I hope to be able soon to see them all in person rather than through pictures as I mentioned I am hoping my time for a furlough is at hand.

I think I had ridden several miles North when I came upon a freshly dug grave and a crude marker. I dismounted to rest and sat down beside the grave to ponder life's mysteries. I noticed that someone had put up a makeshift cross, with a Confederate hat hanging on it and burned into the cross was, "Damien Cavanaugh, 16 years of age, too young to die." I am sure a fellow soldier of the Confederate States of America and a fellow friend had left this poignant message for the entire world to see. As was the case with the young soldier who I sat in judgment for back in the day of his court marshal I found myself shedding a tear for this ill-fated young man. So many young folks, even children in my opinion, have been recruited into this conflict, God help us all. Too young to die certainly tells the entire story as I am sure this young man saw little of life and its many pleasures and pitfalls before his untimely death at the hands of a Union soldier or an incurable disease brought on by living in such close confinement and in such dreadful conditions. I grieved for him as I would grieve for any soldier of the Army of the Potomac and finally remounted Blackjack and with my mind free at least for the time being of Henry's leaving I rode back to camp in a melancholy state of mind.

I also had sent home with Henry in my trunk my heavy overcoat cape, as I definitely do not need it in this weather. I asked Julia if she could sew the collar and hang on to it as I am sure this conflict will be over long before next winter sets in but then again I have been sure before that we were near the end. I always carry a blanket on Blackjack and of course enough food for he and I for at least three days so I am sure the blanket will suffice if I need it but I doubt that I will. I also sent along a piece of copper and some handmade nails from the ruins of the old church at Hampton. This beautiful old church, which had stood for many a year, has now been reduced to ruins. I also enclosed a corkscrew, a little old knife, the code of Virginia, some books and a little article I picked up at the Rebel Fort at Lees Mills on the morning of the 4th of May. Included with all this were a sword I had recovered and two small pieces of black marble. The black marble was from the tombstone of one Captain John Mills, his tombstone said he died in 1701 at the advanced age of 128 years and was buried near the church at Hampton. The tombstone was badly broken and the marble was lying on the ground so I picked it up. After this cursed war is over I plan on researching Captain Mills' history as I find it hard to believe he lived 128 years. I doubt I will be so lucky especially as I am in the middle of this horror although I would assume from the title of Captain that Mr. Mills was also involved in a conflict and survived it. I thought for a minute that was an asinine assumption with mankind's history of making war on one another so many times over the centuries. Heaven help us all. All these keepsakes will hopefully comfort me in my old age, if I reach old age, as I look back on this great journey.

I was ordered early this morning to be the officer of the pickets and I went out with the troops at 4 AM. It has been a quiet time and we experienced no hostilities and returned to camp unscathed around 6 AM. We are now marching West by North for a few hours. Since it is so hot in this area which is currently about 11 miles North of Richmond our commanders are ordering the troops to march in the early morning only for a few hours so as not to bring on too much heat exhaustion on us all. I certainly agree with them on this score. Men that are totally fatigued would be of little value in a frenzied battle. We are now near Chickahominy, Virginia and it seems all we are now doing is marching and counter marching. I have been on duty for about three straight days with little or no rest except that which I can snatch in the saddle on the back of Blackjack. I thought we were gathering to lay siege to Richmond but that does not seem to be the case at present. Our commander seems reluctant to commit so many troops into such a conflict, which surly will result in hundreds if not thousands of deaths on both sides. All the commanders have been ordered to record all of the troops under their command and Josiah and John have undertaken this task. The 33rd New York

Volunteers left originally with 1,000 men and we currently are down to 911, having lost a number in combat, a few have wandered away and many have succumbed to disease, some of which are still amongst the living but not fit to serve.

We did experience a smart brush with the Rebels at Mechanicsville, which I estimate is about five miles North by West from Richmond. I was in advance with three companies, G, K and B when we discovered the Rebels just before sunrise. I at once issued orders to open fire on them and the battle was upon us. We brought down a few of the enemy and then the rest of them scampered for buildings, fences and trees from which they kept up a constant fire upon my men. At about the same time two pieces of their artillery opened up on us and inflicted some damage. I ordered a brief retreat to better cover behind a ridge and sent back word to the general on the situation and the location of our engagement. I suggested he move some or our artillery into a position to respond to the enemy artillery and he immediately took my advice and they opened up a fierce volley at the Rebels. This did the trick and they soon scampered out of the buildings and took off into the trees for a safer spot. The general also sent up the 77th regiment and that regiment and those of us that were engaged went ahead into this small village on the double quick to search for any of them that were left but they were all gone. They left a large number of knapsacks, blankets and some other items in their haste to withdraw. Unfortunately I had one poor fellow of Company K killed, three wounded and one of Company G wounded. Several others were hit but not seriously and had holes in their clothes and shoes but no other wounded of the three companies. The 77th had one killed, nine wounded and two of their artillery horses were killed, one having had a ball pass entirely through its body from front to back and in exiting injured one of their soldiers. We saw a number of the Rebels either killed or wounded but we did not attempt to stop their troops from removing them to the rear under cover of the woods. Two of the dead Rebels were left and our Chaplin and Old Doc and his staff are tending to the dead and wounded. Hopefully those that are wounded can be made whole again as I cannot imagine going through life especially a young man missing a limb. Sometimes when I think of the killed and wounded if the wounds are to leave one permanently a cripple or worse it would maybe have been better to die in battle. After the clash finished and the field had been cleared of the dead, wounded and dying I sat there on Blackjack and looked out over this potentially beautiful spot and wondered what had been wrought here.

Is man's stupidity infinite or does it just seem that way to me at this point in time and in this place. I dismounted Blackjack and wandered over the field, knelt down and picked a double yellow rose and some honeysuckle to send to Julia and the family. I wanted to find some beauty even in this wretchedness so the sights and sounds would hopefully not again return in my nightmares and I, if so blessed, would be able to think of Julia holding the rose and the honeysuckle and looking pretty as a picture as I remember her. It is the small things in this war that keeps one sane.

I visited the hospital tent when I got back to our base of operations and Old Doc was again performing his miracles on those that had been wounded. He told me that they all should eventually recover and none of these injuries were threatening their lives. He had given a number of them ample doses of his special medicine before he dug bullets out of them and most seemed to be somewhat serene so whatever it is in his therapy it certainly has a calming effect. Some say it is nothing but moonshine but I think it is a special formula that he has developed over the years and he keeps his secrets to himself. I was concerned about Old Doc's condition however as he looked exhausted and he even looked as if he might be as old as Captain Mills must have looked when he passed away at 128 years of age. I worry about the strain on him and hope he will be able to stand up to it. He is a saint amongst men and to a man in the regiment he would be deeply missed if he were not able to continue or if anything happened to him, God forbid.

We are now camped out a few miles from Richmond at New Bridge, Virginia and I have been out on picket duty for a straight 24 hours with Blackjack and 300 men. At first the weather was pleasant but shortly after we got out there it started to rain and rain it did. I have seen all kinds of rain in the time I have been in this army but I don't think I have ever seen such a downpour as it is at present. It has been raining for almost 15 hours and the flats where we are camped are flooded, not a man or beast is able to stay dry.

The only good thing I can say about all this rain is that it will impede our march any further towards Richmond for the time being. We were supposed to cross the river on our way to opening up an assault on the city but that is now impossible and I believe the Rebels would have easy pickings if we were to try that, as we would be open, unprotected and very vulnerable in that situation. I am beginning to wonder if this vast army, which unfortunately is losing more of its men in battles and disease daily, will ever assault Richmond. It seems that either the weather or the reluctance of our leaders is keeping us from moving ahead. I for one could not be more pleased as I have said it will be a slaughter on both sides as the Rebels I am sure, being the brave fighting men that they are, will fight to the last man to defend their capital.

Now that I am back in my tent I decided to write a letter to Julia and the children in the hopes that the mail delivery will soon be back on track and it will get to her shortly. I did receive a letter from her a few days ago, which I am carrying in my vest pocket close to my heart.

"Dear Julia and all the family: June 4. 1862,

I have just gotten dry and rested after having been out on picket duty for the past 24 hours. More than two thirds of the time it poured rain. A great quantity of rain has fallen within the last 24 hours and the flats are totally flooded where this vast army is encamped. We expected to all have crossed the river today but this rain will necessarily retard our march further towards Richmond and hopefully what will come to be the end of this gruesome conflict. I received your most welcome letter a few days ago and carry it with me at all times even though of late it has been difficult to keep it dry. When I could I have taken it out and read and re-read it many times over. It was a great source of pleasure to me to hear from you and the children and to learn of the good health of all of you. There are but few hours of the day or night when I am awake but what I am thinking of you all at home. Many times last night when I was walking up and down in front of my picket reserve when all was still, save the lonely sentinel patiently and watchfully pacing to and fro upon his beat, the falling rain, the croaking of the many frogs and the chirp of the crickets my thoughts turned to home. I was thinking of all of you and how much love I have bottled up for you and the children and it was really a source of pleasure to me to imagine that I could visualize all of you comfortable and sweetly sleeping. Do not for one minute think that I was thinking I had a hard lot or that I was repining at my situation. Nothing of the kind I can assure you for as we have often shared in our letters the trials and tribulations of those left behind at home in many a measure are just as troubling and a tremendous strain on all of you. It is only through our love for one another that you, the children, John and I can someday be reunited again in our fair village. During this time I finally laid down under an apple tree and slept from nine until 11 for a few hours rest but by then my blanket was so wet I could not rest the remainder of the tour. I seldom sleep at all when I am out on duty even for an extended period of time as there is a great responsibility resting upon my shoulders and all the other officers and men to see that all those under them attend faithfully to their duty and most especially to command the men in case of an attack. The line of picket guards is the outpost guard. They have under their care and vigilance the line between the sleeping soldiers who number in the tens of thousands and the Rebel's, so not only their lives and that of their companions on duty rest with them but all of the resting soldiers they are sworn to protect. They have to watch against the advancing enemy, against spies that might try and infiltrate our lines and also anyone on our side that might try and pass through to convey information to the enemy. As such is our duty and of course as I have said, your burden and duties at home are equally demanding. In the hope that you and the children will find rest and peace in this night and every night I remain your loving husband and father.

Joseph."

CHAPTER FOURTEEN

Diversions

I keep hoping I will be able to write Julia and tell her about the fall of Richmond and the end of this senselessness but alas it has not happened. We march a few miles every few days and then we camp out with only minor skirmishes with the enemy on occasion. Here it is the seventh of June and I just finished writing another letter to home and as it is late I decided to go to bed and try and get some rest. At about 2 AM the orders were shouted out, "Turn Out, Turn Out." And we were told to get ready to move in 20 minutes. Hardly time to take care of ones bodily needs but to a man we were ready when the 20 minutes were up. We were ordered to march to the East, South East and we marched about ten miles in that direction. We crossed the Chickahominy River on the railroad bridge and then we marched five miles west, southwest and we finally camped out on the south side of the Chickahominy. We are about a mile away from where we originally started from but it is not my place to question the high command although it seems we took a long way around, marching about 15 miles in several directions to reach this spot where we can almost see where we formerly were. Maybe the high command had some intelligence about an enemy force they did not want to risk this army at this time in a location that required this circumvented maneuver. Whatever was the case they didn't consult me but we are now here and have been ordered to settle in, set up our tents, send out pickets and dig latrines, the latter being most likely the most important.

Courtesy of the Library of Congress

I have been told that this march became necessary as far as the command determined because of the great amount of rain and the fact that they did not want this colossal army to have even a more difficult time crossing over the river in case the rain continued for some time, since that seems to be the case usually here in the South. Our engineering troops are building more bridges and some corduroy roads leading into and away from each bridge. It is amazing the skill and hard work of the engineers in constructing the bridges and roads in such a short time, which are so vital to the smooth movement of such a mammoth army. They have also built a footbridge over the flats by driving posts into the mud, which are plentiful, and laying cross pieces diagonally and then laying planks or timber to form the surface. They are built very substantial and we could not even move this huge army without them. With all the construction of roads and bridges and the higher ground we are now encamped on the Rebels would not, in my opinion, be wise to attack us here. I fear if they did, it would be their "last ditch."

After we settled in I rode over to Colonel Draime's tent and we reminisced for sometime. I had not had much time to spend with him and I wanted to renew old friendships as we had shared so much in the past and leaned on each other through the thick and thin of this conflict and of our personal lives. He did mention that he had gotten a letter from home and in it his wife had mentioned that Julia and I had the smartest boy of his age in our fair village and that certainly lifted my spirits. It is so considerate of her to take the time to say such a wonderful thing and I am sure she realizes how small gestures mean so much to those of us on the front lines. I cannot wait to write Julia and tell her and I am sure it will please her to no end to know what a wonderful job she is doing raising young Joseph. The only problem with writing or receiving letters is that we are shifting camps so often that the mail is difficult to send or receive. I guess I can't blame the mail department since when this is happening and we are constantly on guard it is difficult for them to do their jobs. We all miss the regular mail as I have said so many times it is the bond to sanity that keeps us all going in this nightmarish situation.

Our present camp is now called officially, Camp Fair Oaks. I am not sure who is in charge of thinking up names for our various camps but they certainly have come up with some unique ones. There are many fine old oak trees in this area along with beautiful cypress trees and many other species. I might have picked another name if I had that responsibility such as Camp of the Muddy Flats, but as usual they didn't ask my advice even though they should have. Fortunately we have had a few days of nice weather and things were beginning to dry up so that we were in hopes of being able to start moving the artillery and all the other equipment that such an immense army needs. All of a sudden the heavens opened up again and a cold rain, which was almost as cold as we experience in the North, came hammering down. It is making everyone's lives miserable and things are again becoming unfit for man or beast. Maybe it is the Lord's way of saying, "I am giving you humans a few more days of respite so hopefully you will all come to your senses and stop your warring ways before it is to late. I fear it will only delay the inevitable, however as I have grown more and more cynical about mankind's ability to think rationally and come to a peaceful conclusion of this conflict. I shudder when I lay in my bed and have time to think about the numbers on both sides that are here today enjoying the friendship of their fellow soldiers and tomorrow if we attack Richmond many of these same fine fellows, both North and South, will be laying on the battlefield dead or gravely wounded in agony and most likely maimed for the rest of their lives either in body or mind. I sometimes wonder if those good folks at home are wondering why this gigantic army has not brought on the fall of Richmond and the end of the war but we have been moving and have had minor engagements about as fast as the weather permits. I do think our leadership has been hesitant to commit troops and I believe that can lead in the long run to disaster but only time will tell. At some point the waiting game must be over and we must proceed to end this. I was talking to Colonel Draime again and he agreed with me that we should either attack or fall back to Washington and let the leaders fight it out. As the good colonel and I both agree we would surely be running this war differently if we were in charge but President Lincoln has yet to realize our wisdom and appoint either one of us to be commander-in-chief. I think he would secretly be concerned that we might choose to finish it by gathering together officers on both sides and having many a tall one while we end it for good and let time heal the rifts that have come between us. Mankind never seems to let time work things out, as they are much too impatient.

I wrote Julia and suggested she purchase her May and June butter that will last her through July and August. I also suggested that she purchase her sugar, tea, coffee, lard and ham as I think the prices will be going up somewhat in the near future. I suggested also that she and the children wear their woolen clothing as long as they possibly can since very little wool is available except that which is being smuggled by some unscrupulous individuals and the prices are very high. I asked her to send me some more postage stamps also and I hope she has money for all these items, as again it has been several months since we have been paid. At the end of my letter I had second thoughts about advising her on such things from as far away as Dixie and I apologized so she wouldn't be too mad at me. I am sure she can manage her affairs equally as well as I can and I should learn to keep my thoughts to myself. Hopefully she will still love me and forgive me.

We are finally getting a drying out here in mid-June and I hope it continues for quite a while. I don't think I ever have regretted seeing it cloud up and rain as I now do. After living in the out of doors for more than a year, many days with rain and mud, the last thing we need is more rain but then again I don't control the weather even though I sometimes think I should along with a lot of other things. When it starts to rain I become very melancholy along with about 60 thousand other men at this location. When you think of 60 thousand men all having the blues it is not a pleasant thought and if I were Johnny Reb I think I would stay clear of us. Maybe the Rebels are used to so much rain so it doesn't trouble them but it sure bothers us.

We are still camped out in the same position near the Chickahominy River. The Rebel pickets are less than half a mile from our camp. Our pickets at a portion of the line are within 300 yards of theirs, each in front of woods with a narrow wheat field in between them. Occasionally one of the Rebel pickets will try and pick off one of ours but the distance is too far for any accuracy and I have ordered our pickets to save their ammunition for when we need it. There has not been any artillery exchange by either our side or theirs so things for the time being are relatively calm.

We have been here near a week now and things are heating up with more that a hundred shots being fired at our men every day. As yet, as I have said, no one has even been wounded. I'm not sure what the Rebels think they are accomplishing by wasting so much ammunition but that is their business and not mine. At each break of day the general has ordered that our entire force turn out and stand in a line of battle at the edge of the clearing until sunrise. This is to dampen the enthusiasm of the Rebels in case they are thinking of a frontal assault on this vast army. The other night I was sound asleep about one when a heavy volley of musket fire on the picket line to our left suddenly aroused me. I sprang from my bed, I was fully clothed as usual including that my boots were still on, and I ran from the tent and shouted as loud as I could, "**TURN OUT, STAND TO YOUR ARMS**." This order shouted out by Colonel Draime and I at the same time and then you could hear these words echoing along the line in both directions and also to our rear. Within a minute or two there were long dark lines of our men dressed out in full battle dress ready to take on any enemy. It was quite dark and I suddenly recollected of seeing the bright full moon in the evening when I retired. All of a sudden I realized that the moon could not have yet passed our meridian at this hour and when I looked up I expected to see the moon's fair face veiled by a cloud when instead it was an earthy shadow. There was almost a total eclipse of the moon with only a small semicircle on her eastern limb being visible. I called the attention of the officers and men to it and miraculously there was no more firing from either side as we all stared in awe at this magnificent event. We all pleasantly, both our soldiers and that of the enemy, enjoying this stunning event for a full half hour while it passed. I laughingly told the officers of having read of the superstitious of some people in parts of the world that at the time of the eclipses they beat pans and fire guns to drive away what they imagine as evil spirits. Maybe some of the pickets thought the same thing and fired their guns to try and ward off any evil spirits that were accompanying this event and that is what aroused everyone. And then again maybe they just discharged their muskets hoping to wake us all up to see this striking sight. I doubt if anyone from either side would admit it but whatever it was it saved many a soldier from both the North and the South from either being killed or maimed that night. Again as I lay down on my makeshift bed I thought maybe God in His infinite wisdom had decided we should all take a few minutes to reflect on the beauties of this earth and beyond while we engage in this living disaster that we are all experiencing. Whatever the case I for one and I am sure thousands of others on both sides felt a relief and a blessing that we avoided conflict that night.

Colonel Draime is ill so I am in charge of the regiment at present. I hope he gets well soon and I hope the illness, be it mental or physical is soon behind him. Would you believe it whoever is in charge of naming our campsites has decided to change the name of this present one from Camp Fair Oaks to Lincoln Camp. It is now the middle of June and we are still stalled at this location awaiting orders to move on or maybe retreat since we never seem to be willing to get into that mammoth battle that will hopefully decide this conflict once and for all. General

McClellan has issued the order for the name change and I am wondering why, perhaps President Lincoln is planning on visiting us here, and General McClellan wants to make him feel at home and maybe he also wants to make some points with him because rumor has it that the president is becoming frustrated that we are not on the move and engaging the enemy to bring this to a swift conclusion. Time will only tell as it does with so many things. I for one am ready to take on the task of attacking Richmond. I didn't think I would ever be saying that but we have waited, planned and sat on our collective assess far too long. We have marched, toiled, fought and watched and many have fallen under the hardships and I myself am becoming weary of it all. We have been 14 days in this present position and nothing seems to be any closer to a resolution than it did months ago. Frankly I think it is time for our commanders to either make some decisions or step aside and let someone else lead these brave souls. As I mentioned we are all up at three in the morning and standing to our arms in line until sunrise. This with guard duty, picket duty, building roads and bridges and other duties it is taking a heavy toll on the men's attitudes, tiredness and mental well-being. If I were a swearing man I think I would tell the leaders it is time to either go or get off the latrine if you get my drift.

Here on the 19th of June we are again under orders to hold the regiment in readiness to march at a minutes notice. The same orders have been passed down almost every morning and we end up staying here and doing the same mundane, tiring tasks as we have been doing now for weeks. Colonel Draime has returned from sick leave and is now in command again of the regiment. I had been told that if he were unable to return I would be appointed to command in his place. I would not shirk that duty but I am grateful he is feeling well again and has returned as we have become very close and I believe he needs me as I need him. We are all brothers in arms. I decided since we did not move that I would take this opportunity to write to Julia and the family.

"Dear Julia and Children,

John and I have been disappointed in the last few days of not receiving any letters from home but then again the mail delivery system is far from efficient. I guess they do their best that they can under the circumstances but it would lift everyone's spirits if they were a little better organized. I sometimes think the only area of government services that is efficient is the military since most of the other government operations keep stumbling all over themselves. I am not even sure anymore if this military is all that efficient since as I have said we do nothing but sit on our collective behinds and wait and wait and wait. It even has been sometime since we have been paid again and you would think that for men that are willing to lay down their lives for their government they could at least pay us on a regular basis so we could send some money home. I am in hopes that we will be paid soon and I can send along some money for you and the children to use for the items I am sure you are in desperate need of. We have been under orders almost daily to be prepared to march and most likely, possible before you receive this letter, we will have done so. You may well read in the newspapers or telegrams of our advance and of battles fought. I beseech you, if that be the case, that you not allow yourself to be unnecessarily troubled about our safety, but trust in God and pray that He in His great goodness, will, as He has thus far shielded us from the swift flying missiles of death. Pray that He will preserve our health and safety as well as all of you at home. We have great cause for thanking our Heavenly Father for protecting and sustaining us thus far, and ought to be encouraged to hope and trust for a continuation of that protection.

It is now sunset and how I wish I could be sharing that with you and all our family. I am careful not to allow myself to repine at my separation from you, or dwell too much upon the subject. I cheer myself up with the hope and pray that we may soon be together and it may again be sunshine where now in our minds it appears to be nothing but dark clouds.

With more love that any human can process for his wife and family

I remain your loving husband and father,

Joseph."

Here it is almost the end of June and nothing much has changed. It is raining off and on which is certainly not new, the leadership is still unsure of what they want to do, the men are tired, bored and have sore feet and aching backs and I and the colonel continue to wonder what we are doing wasting so much man power and time. At least this day we are finally getting a little relief from the heat and rain and we are experiencing a cool breeze from the North, which must be coming all the way from our fair village in Upstate New York. There is still some occasional fire of muskets to our right and to our left but as far as our present location all is quiet. We can see some of the forward pickets of the Rebel forces across the field but they remain as quiet as our forces. In fact several of our troops asked if they could pack a picnic lunch and venture out into the field with a white flag and ask some of the Rebels to join them for cookies and cake. I thought about it for a moment and almost said, "Go for it," but decided I had better not. I am not sure it would make any difference to our just gathering dust here day after day. There is some artillery fire from General Porter's Artillery a mile and a half up the Chickahominy and the Rebels are returning shell for shell but as I hear it no one is injured and most of it is just to let the other side know we are ready if they wish to engage us. Most of the time I have the men standing to arms just in case but beyond giving them something to do to ease the boredom it is not accomplishing much. The colonel is under the weather again and in the hospital so I am in charge of the regiment and trying my best to keep their minds occupied so if called upon they will be ready. The health of our regiment is generally good, as we have not lost any men to enemy fire or disease recently compared to some of the other regiments. It seems the longer these thousands of troops are camped out in one spot the more disease shows its deadly march through the ranks. Old Doc and many of the other doctors are having their hands full trying to keep up with it and he tells me it is a losing battle in many cases. John is well but Josiah has been feeling under the weather and we hope he will be fit as a fiddle soon and in Josiah's case particularly, be able to sit up and take nourishment.

Courtesy of the Library of Congress

Courtesy of the Library of Congress

Courtesy of the Library of Congress

Courtesy of the Library of Congress

Courtesy of the Library of Congress

CHAPTER FIFTEEN

Blood, Sweat, Death

Here on the third of July we are at Starks' Landing and we have been in several major battles with the Rebels over the past few days. I am pleased to say that we have whipped them badly each time they attacked us. We had far fewer casualties than the Rebels. I understand from the reports handed down to me that they did take a few prisoners but mostly those that they took were either ill or frankly drunk. Being drunk is not acceptable in this army but regrettably does happen on occasion and frankly I am not surprised it doesn't happen more often with the mental pressure on all of us. It is difficult to comprehend unless one is here on the battlefield the horrendous trauma that falls upon both sides in these battles. The South has men of great pride that are throwing themselves at our troops in the hopes of driving us back from this location. The shouts of the soldiers on both sides, the screams of the wounded and the horrifying look upon the faces on both sides as they rush into battle is frankly hell on earth. I doubt if those looks, screams and the utter terrifying expressions on the faces of the dead and the dying will ever leave my thoughts. There is no way to describe it unless you have been here and seen it first hand and I pray that will not be the case for our children and grandchildren. Mankind is unfortunately sick to the core to engage in such as we are going through. I have little faith in the future of the human race after existing through this living torture. All of our men fought bravely and as I have said they were victorious in each of the several battles that were fought. Josiah fought bravely and was not wounded but has fallen terribly ill both in mind and body and I have ordered that he be taken back and by boat delivered to Fortress Monroe where I pray the doctors will be able to help him. I consulted with Old Doc about him and he insisted I send him back as he said his chances of surviving were not likely if he were required to remain in this place of wretchedness. I plan on following up on his transport and condition as soon as time allows me after I receive all the officers' reports of the ill, wounded and killed in recent fighting. Again Old Doc will try and work his miracles and the Chaplin will be busy saying the final goodbyes to those less fortunate. The smell of death will never leave this soldier or I am sure any of the other soldiers in either the Gray or the Blue ranks.

Our ranks continue to thin through disease, wounded, and killed but those that are left are up to the task and fighting courageously. I have sent out some messengers to try and locate John as he and I became separated in the last battle and as yet he has not turned up. I pray that the Lord will watch over him and return him to me soon. There has been so much confusion it was hard to keep track of anyone and we are just now compiling the lists of the dead, wounded and missing. I pray that he is not in any of those categories as I don't think I could go on if he were and I don't think I could ever bring myself to write Julia about the loss of our son. I tried when we all volunteered to talk John into staying home and taking care of his mother, brother and sisters but he would have nothing to do with that as we were all so caught up in the loyalty to our cause at the time. If I could only turn the clock back I would have insisted he remain at home as it will be traumatic enough for Julia and the family to possibly lose me but certainly not both of us. I am sure that thousands on both sides, except those too stubborn, pig-headed or just downright stupid are thinking the same thing at this time. Tens of thousands already have been killed or maimed and there seems to be no end in sight as I am sure many more tens of thousands will find the same destiny sadly. The strains of war run deep on both sides after the fighting of over a year.

I received the reports of the officers on the dead, wounded and missing and John blessedly is not on any of the lists. We are missing about ten men from the roster and John is amongst that ten so hopefully they will show up soon. Several of the officers have taken out search parties to try and locate them. I am sure that they did not wander off for I know that John and the others that are on that list to a man would never retreat or run off from the battles we have been in. They are all made of solid oak and have never displayed anything but total bravery in our previous battles. While I await word on John and the others I saddled up Blackjack and rode back to the disembarking location to see if Josiah had been transported yet to Fort Monroe. After riding through thousands of soldiers, tents, wagons, artillery, cavalry and a lake of mud, which makes things even worse, I finally reached the hospital tent where Josiah was. I found him there in the grip of death and was told that all of the wounded were being transported back to the fort for treatment before any of the sick in mind or body could be taken. I tried to pull some strings and frankly pull rank but they insisted on taking the wounded first and honestly I could not argue with that reasoning even though Josiah was as wounded as the next man having stood shoulder to shoulder with his comrades in repelling the enemy advances.

While I was in the hospital trying to comfort him I witnessed one of the most terrifying, intense and heart-wrenching scene that I have ever seen and hope I never have to see it again. There were tables set up about breast high upon which a number of the wounded had been placed. They were screaming and they were all facing the amputation of a limb or more. The surgeons and their assistants bless their souls for being able and willing to perform such surgery, were stripped to the waist and drenched with blood. The assistants were holding the unfortunate fellows down while the surgeons were armed with bloody knives and saws and cut and sawed away with frightful rapidity, throwing the severed limbs on a pile as they completed their gruesome work. They then immediately went on to the next wounded soldier who was screaming and repeated the entire procedure not even having the time to wash themselves or their paraphernalia off. They did try and give the long-suffering fellows some chloroform but in most cases it was totally ineffective in deadening the pain. I do not believe even if they had access to Old Doc's famous remedy it would have been any easier for them. Many of the limbs that had to be removed already had gangrene set in and the flesh in most cases was rotting away and without the limb's removal the poor fellows would have most certainly died. The mini-balls that have injured so many of them do a gruesome job of tearing the flesh open in large sections. Many of these brave lads are just boys and are so young to be facing such horrifying prospects of living without one or more limbs for the rest of their lives even if they are fortunate enough to survive the surgery and the healing process afterwards. I firmly believe standing here watching this hell on earth that all the leaders that are responsible for starting this war and any other war should be forced to see what they have wrought upon their fellow human beings. If they could have only seen into the future maybe they would still be sitting at the bargaining table and trying to find a peaceful solution to this conflict.

Josiah stood and fought until he could stand no more from his illness and then was carried off the field shouting that he did not want to leave his friends and brothers in arms. Old Doc thinks he has Typhoid Fever and is not optimistic for his survival. I have already lost to mental strain and general fatigue Henry and I fear now that we may lose Josiah. I said a silent prayer that the doctors at Fort Monroe will be able to bring him around and that his internal strength will prevail and he would be able to return to all of us. What an absolute waste this war is on both sides. Old Doc says more men are dying under his and the other doctor's care, from diseases that they have no knowledge of how to combat, than from the Rebel bullets and shells. For the thousands of men living here in such unsanitary conditions it is impossible to keep them healthy. I and the other officers have tried our best to enforce the rules of sanitation with new latrines being dug almost daily and other means to protect all our health but our efforts are sorely wanting when it comes to the battle between man and the mysterious hand of disease. That battle in my opinion, reinforced by Old Doc many times over, is definitely a losing battle. We may beat the Old South but we will never beat the unseen enemy in the way of malady.

When I returned to camp I was delighted as John was there. He and the other nine missing soldiers had been surrounded by the Rebels and cut off from the rest of our regiment for several hours. They had all fought valiantly and four of them were killed before the captain and reinforcements arrived to drive the remaining Rebels away. I am more proud of John than ever for his bravery and his leadership in that harrowing experience. I could not, as I have said, accept that John be badly wounded or killed and could not also accept that he be taken prisoner as I have heard many horrific stories about conditions in the Southern prison camps. The South has barely enough to feed and take care of their soldiers and citizens let alone tend to the needs of the thousands of prisoners they have taken. The chances of surviving this conflict are very remote if one becomes a captive compared to our chances on the battlefield which daily become more precarious.

The general came by, extended his hand to me, gave me a very hearty shake of the hand, and very earnestly thanked me for the manner in which I had commanded the 77th regiment and in bringing it so well through such troublesome times. I heard a number in the brigade say today that the 77th never had done so well before. It requires a good deal of firmness and energy to keep the regiment square to its work, especially when shells are flying thick. It is my honor to lead these men as there are no finer in the entire Army of the Potomac and I will always be proud of them and forever in their debt no matter how long the good Lord allows me to live. I mourn the loss of any one of them as if they were my own.

Are we any closer to the end of this conflict than we were a year ago or a month ago, I pray that we are but I have my doubts. I need to bring Julia up-to-date since I am sure she will have been reading in the papers about our recent engagements and she needs to hear it from myself that John and I have been spared. I am not going to mention to her about John's missing and almost taken prisoner as it would likely unnerve her and with all her other fears on her mind she does not need anything else to agonize about.

"Dear Julia and Children:

I hope you are having a pleasant and enjoyable Independence Day. The soldiers here are all too tired and worn down to feel much like celebrating. There was a salute fired at twelve o'clock by some of the artillery and some of the bands played some patriotic songs including the "Battle Hymn of the Republic" which certainly stirs men's souls. Although we have had our breakfast and later expect to eat our supper of hardees, as the men here call them, pilot bread with coffee and pork, I for one do not repine or think or wish that I had some of the good things upon which those at the North are feasting on today. I hope you are having a fine feast even though we have not been paid for some time as you are aware and therefore I have not been able to send any money home. I do hear that we are supposed to be paid shortly so I am in hopes of being able to send you the funds in my next letter.

I eat my hard bread, meat and drink my coffee and I am satisfied. This constant duty, marching, watching and fighting of the past 30 days and certainly that of the last seven days has caused me to feel quite tired and used up both mentally and physically. Speaking of being worn out I was wondering how Henry was faring since he returned home. I fear he may never recover enough to lead a normal life, like all the rest of this fighting it is a dreadful waste of a fine and brave man. As I previously mentioned I am totally washed-out along with the thousands of other troops that are camped here and those that are fortunate enough not to be sick. I plan on getting some real valuable down time and trying to regain my strength and hopefully all of the others including John will do the same. I am sure the Rebels are just as depleted and tired as we are so I think we are all in for a quiet time for a while. We received your's and Martha's letters of the 30th today and we were blessed to take delivery of them. We were so pleased to hear from all of you and we read and re-read the letters several times. I was even more anxious to get a letter off to you as I am sure you have heard and seen newspaper reports of the horrifying fighting that has been going on here over the past days. I wanted to make sure you knew that both John and I have been spared from being wounded or worse. Josiah has been taken back up to Fort Monroe however and Old Doc Peterson thinks he may have Typhoid Fever as many of the men on both sides are succumbing to it. Please say a prayer and ask our minister to have the congregation pray for him this week. We have figuratively lost Henry and I now fear we may well lose Josiah.

Just as we were relieving the pickets on Saturday morning and as most of our division were already back or had fallen back a short distance, the 33rd had been ordered out on picket duty and had but just arrived upon the line of the 49th Pennsylvania, on their right, when suddenly we were all attacked and a most tremendous bombardment came down upon our whole brigade front by the

Rebels. Some 20 or 30 pieces were playing upon us repeatedly, and two of their regiments of infantry rushed upon our picket line. For a moment it looked like a giant death grip was upon us all. The fighting began and the 33rd and the 49th Pennsylvania fought bravely and retired while fighting to a breast works we had built in front of our regimental camp. As we regrouped about 300 men of the 33rd and some of the 49th poured fire into their ranks and we brought two pieces of artillery into the battle and got the range on them. As the fighting progressed over what seemed like a long time, men were piling up on the battlefield and many were screaming with an ear splitting, frightening shriek as more and more lay wounded and dead. In the face of our assault the Rebels broke ranks and ran and the battle was soon over. A. J. Bennett, Lewis Knowles, George Gardner, all of Company B were killed. Sergeant Lours was taken prisoner and John Clemmons was missing and most likely taken prisoner, as we could not find him amongst the killed or wounded. Our regiment had 12 killed, eight wounded and ten missing and presumed all of those had been taken prisoner. Among those killed were Lieutenant Church and Captain Hamilton was captured. John was on the line to the right with Company B at the time of the attack fighting next to Knowles and Gardner and only God knows why they fell and John survived. We did lose some men as I mentioned but the Rebels lost at least five to one and some say ten to one to our losses. We captured a number of their men including a colonel, a captain, two lieutenants and many more, more prisoners than our total loss both in dead, wounded and missing in action.

Knowing that you, as I said would hear something of this daily fighting, I knew that you and the children would be greatly troubled in mind until you could hear of our safety, hence my great desire to get a letter to you. Any letters from you any day of this tiresome march would have been grasped and read with delight and would have tended to perhaps have kept us a little more wakeful when on the night marches but as it could not be so I did not repine. My thoughts were divided between my family, my country and asking God's protection and blessing on both. You know that I am not one that complains very readily of hardship or exaggerates, and I do not complain now but am thankful that the retreat was managed and fought so well by our brave men.

I will say that I do not think that any army ever had a much more severe and trying time occupying a position and some portion of the line fighting the Rebels in order of battle all day while our trains of wagons, ambulances and artillery could retire, and then march all night, and occupy a similar position the next day. I don't believe anyone except those that witnessed and experienced it can comprehend the very great achievement and fatigue necessarily attending it. We were at the battle of Savage Station, aptly named for the carnage that happened there, but not immediately engaged. We had been in line of battle with other divisions for some hours waiting for the Rebels when about 5:00 PM thinking they were not coming our division and some others moved on. We had gotten about a mile and a half when the battle began. We immediately marched back and were just getting into the action when those already engaged drove the Rebels from the field and this second time they did not return as they were badly whipped.

Julia, my love, I have unloaded my soul to you and feel a heavy weight lifted from my shoulders knowing that you will read and understand my fears and rage over such a waste of fine young men on both sides. I pray to God we will see each other in the very near future. Forgive me for rambling on so long but you are my salvation in good times and bad.

With all my love to you and the family,

Joseph."

I wrote on the edge of the envelope to tell Martha she need not be so stingy about sending me postage stamps, as I will pay her when it amounts to one dollar that is if the government decides ever to pay us.

Sometimes on those long nightly marches in between the daily battles I pray for a telegraph or carrier dove or any other means of conveying to my family "ALL'S WELL" but alas it is not possible. Mankind has progressed in their weapons of war and means to fight them but has yet to find a quick and expedient way for us to keep in touch with one another. What a waste we bring upon ourselves. It disturbs me that I realize that the morning papers at home will carry stories of the battles going on here even though they are sometimes days old and that the family can only be anxious over our fate until they get a letter from either John or I.

Thousands have fallen in battle and many thousands more have fallen from disease and yet in most cases the families are notified days if not weeks after it has happened. As I related to Julia and the children, this has been a great movement and great battles, which I cannot get out of my mind. I pray that I will be able once again to sleep in peace without the nightmares of such horrifying visions. The Rebels as I have said attacked us at different points on our line almost daily with great boldness and recklessness. I have heard from fairly reliable sources that part of the boldness was from whiskey, which had been generously taken before some of the battles. I am not putting down Johnny Reb. as he is a fearsome fighting man and from what I have seen to this point his bravery is beyond question, but as I said, the smell of whiskey has been noticed upon a number of them that were captured, killed or wounded. In every instance our forces meet them with ferocious fighting and repulsed them with losses to them of three to five greater than ours. I cannot speak higher praise for those of us in Davidson's Brigade, Smith's Division and Franklin's Corps. Many a night when I marched our pickets back into camp after our tour of watch was over and I would order them to keep their belts and boots on as any minute we might be attacked and it shall never be said that we were not prepared.

I wrote the following recollections of the fighting in my diary for upcoming generations to ponder particularly those leaders who will in the future have the power to send men into battle against one another. Hopefully they will think long and hard about such decisions and have what I refer to as a well-measured response, avoiding all out warfare at all costs. Only the wisest of leaders will be able to clear that hurdle.

"Our artillery performed superbly and on one particular day up to 30 pieces of artillery from the Rebel side opened up on us. At the time we had 18 of our guns, which had been stationed on a ridge, about 15 rods directly in front of the regiment and amongst them were six 12-pound guns. These guns and about six to our right and six to our left immediately opened upon the Rebel positions and for nearly an hour these weapons never ceased firing. If some ladies or gentlemen of the nearby villages or some of the ladies and gents from our fair village had been looking on I fear many of the ladies would have fainted, the men would have stood aghast and the horses would have run away. Bang, Bang, Whiss, Bang, Spiraling and Whirring through the air came shell after shell and round shot and they cut many a limb from the few standing trees in front of our camp. Crash went another cutting through the body of a tree ripping and tearing as it goes, others had ripped though the tents and one struck just in front of Company B throwing dirt over all the company. Bang bursts one, over the heads of Company H, another in front of Company D and C and along the entire line of our regiment. There went one through the Major's horse, entering the front and exiting out the back. A grape shot just killed the quartermaster. I told Winfield to take Blackjack as far back as he could on the double and he rode him back in the nick of time as a shell landed where he had been tied minutes later. I told the men to keep their heads down but to keep steady. I also ordered them to take the wounded back to the next ridge and I said to walk as you are just as likely to be shelled running as walking and the poor fellow that you are carrying does not need to be roughly handled. This entire scene was one of unbelievable confusion and revulsion. Even in the middle of all this grief I saw men laughing over the plights of others as revolting as that sounds. The Artillerymen, many of which have seen a great deal of service performed admirably and even with all this shelling, not one of our gunmen was killed. There were several artillery horses killed but our guns dismounted three of their guns for good and our guns kept up their constant bombardment well after the Rebel guns had been silenced."

I also noted in my diary that President Lincoln visited our camp after the major fighting was over with. He reviewed the troops and I am sure discussed the future engagements of this vast army with the general and particularly whether we will be flung into the caldron of hell in attacking Richmond. As I said earlier in my recollections, send the sons of politicians first into conflict and then send the politicians and if more fighting is then necessary send the fighting men to finish the job. If such were the case I doubt if there would be anywhere near the conflicts mankind has seen and will see unfortunately in the future.

I believe the visit and review by the president lifted the spirits of the men after the grisly events of this past few days and they seem to be more cheerful now as they have been able to get some rest. I also am hoping to get some rest even though the nightmares of these past few days will never leave me, as I am sure they will never leave any of the men.

I have applied to the command for a furlough so I can finally see my family and my dear wife after more than a year. Several of the men of the 33rd have applied for leaves for various reasons and I approved them up to 25 days and the senior command also approved them. I have asked for 20 days and we shall see if I am granted it. I am somewhat concerned as the major has also asked for a leave since he was just informed that his wife is seriously ill and not expected to live but only a few more weeks. The strain of families being separated and those at home having to fend for themselves is taking a dreadful toll on everyone. In addition, not being paid and able to send money home for your loved ones to live on is also very much contributing to both mental and physical breakdowns. I would not for one minute even though my heart aches for my wife and family interfere with the major's request under the circumstances. General Brannon is also expected to leave the brigade shortly and that will also put the officers staff in short supply for a time.

As it turns out they granted the major's request for a 25-day leave of absence and I pray that his presence will help his wife recover. The major and I discussed his wife's symptoms with Old Doc and he told us he thought she might well recover if the two of them were brought together even for a short period of time and this brightened the major's day immensely. When the major had retired to his tent to pack the necessary items for the travel, Old Doc just looked at me with that look of the wisdom of the ages and I knew his poor wife was on her death bed. Miracles do sometimes happen however and I truly believe maybe it will happen in this case. The major and his wife are genuine folks and loved by all in our fair community so I am sure he will have a lot of support when he is lucky enough to arrive home. I also received an answer back on my request and the command granted me a seven-day pass. A fat lot of good that will do me. It would take about four days of the seven to travel to and from home and cost me about $30 so I am not even going to mention it to Julia in my next letter as I am sure she would have seen three days together as an answer to her prayers and not understand why I am reluctant to take advantage of it. I signed up in April of 1861 to serve my country and the duration of the service was agreed on as two years. Since it is now July of 1862 I have about nine months left in the service. I will continue to attempt to receive a leave for at least a minimum of 15 days every month from now until the end of my term of duty. Hopefully it will happen sooner rather than later.

Even though I didn't get a chance to go home we at least have been paid and therefore if I can't send myself I can at least send some money for Julia and the children. That may be small consolation but at least it will help with all their needs except to be held by their loving father. Our pay today is for the period up to April 30th so the government is still a couple of months behind but after being in this man's army for over a year and seeing how the government operates I am not at all surprised. It is my humble opinion that very few endeavors that the government undertakes can be called efficient and successful. Hopefully in the future this will change but I am not optimistic as politicians, remember I was one, seem to only think of themselves and being reelected than thinking of what is right for the average folks. So much for getting on my soap box and preaching how I think things should be run in Washington. I often feel that those in charge of fighting this war do not know anymore about it than the average fighter and in fact sometimes after the living torment that those of us on the front lines have been through I think even the lowest private could manage things better than those currently responsible for the decisions. I need to write Julia a letter and send it along with my money. John and many of the others in the 33rd are instructing me to properly handle their funds and send them home along with mine. There are fewer of us left to send anything home as we started out numbering 1,000 and we now number 819, having had over 80 killed, over 40 wounded and lost the remainder to disease and to being captured by Johnny Reb. What a terrible waste it has been as we move further on into this clash.

"My Dearest Julia,

We have finally been paid up through the end of April and I am sending along with this letter a packet of money for you to use and or deposit as you see the need. I understand from a couple of the men that have recently returned from their furloughs that the bank is only paying about 5% so if there is anything left over from the $350 I am sending you I would suggest you talk to Mr. Lovett and see if he will extend us 7% on our funds. The banks seem a little cheap only offering 5% so it is best to shop around. You mentioned your desire to buy our own home and I would rather you wait until I return so we can search for one together. I realize it is difficult to wait all this time but I am thinking if we cannot find a real bargain of a house at say around $1200 then we should consider buying a few acres outside the village. We could then build a house plus a barn, and enough land so that we may have a good fruit and vegetable garden. We could also buy a cow, pigs, a horse, and maybe I will be fortunate enough to bring Blackjack home with me although I would expect the army will claim they own him.

I am happy to be able to inform you that both John and I are in relatively good health. John has a slight case of diarrhea, which is not unusual living under these conditions as I think at least half of the army has the same affliction. Old Doc has sent for another supply of his legendary medicine and he guarantees it will cure the runs. He has had to use so much of late to ease the pain of those poor fellows that have been wounded that we are running short. I told the supply officer that this was a priority and it should take precedent over all other requests. All of us that at one time or another have partaken of Old Doc's famous remedy agree, even the high command, that this takes priority over all other needs. I think we are all concerned that if we are unfortunate enough to be drawn into another battle those that may be wounded are going to need all the help they can get and Old Doc's medicine is as good as it gets in easing one's pain both in mind and body. I am sending along with this $1,111.00 to be distributed as I have outlined. I appreciate your doing it and ask that you make sure those whose fathers and husband have been killed receive their amounts first. I cannot imagine the grief of the families that have lost so many fine men and even if it is of little comfort at least the money being sent along will help provide for them for a short time. Heaven help them all as they have in most all cases lost their breadwinners and time will become extremely hard for those left behind. I am sure all the good folks in our fine community, the ministers, congregations and all the merchants are doing all they can to ease the suffering of these families. Even though I have written the families of every one of our fallen hero's a personal message telling them what courageous and valiant men they were, I would ask that you convey my sympathies as you see each of them. I realize Julia that I am asking a lot but I know that you are more than willing to do this and that your comforting manner will in many cases help these unfortunate folks to be able to move on if ever so forlornly.

After counting and organizing all the funds and doing most of it under candle light I am growing weary and my eyes are aching so I will wrap up this letter to you. I dream about stepping in to our home and catching you all still in bed. What a merry little time it would be for I do think you would all be asleep and thankfully dreaming fine thoughts of our family and your husband and son.

I have enclosed a gold dollar for Little Joseph and I trust he will have a pleasurable time finding something to spend it on.

With much love and affection to you all, I remain your devoted husband and father, Joseph"

As it turned out the paymaster had money left over and so he paid the officers the extra month he owed us. I would suspect that the final tally of those brothers that have fallen on the battlefield had not yet reached the paymaster so he brought more with him than he needed. This is not money that the widows or families are entitled to and since we are still a month or more behind in our pay I gladly accepted it. I would never have accepted it if I thought it was denying some poor family of a brave fallen soldier what was coming to them. As it is I would suspect if we did not take it as money due us it would have gotten lost in the transit back to headquarters as so many other government functions end up. The waste rampant in government is beyond comprehension and I trust that will end with this war when hopefully wiser men take over the leadership of congress and our country. I wrote Julia and told her it was on its way and she should invest any extra she had at the highest and safest return. I am sure she will as she has a good business head on her shoulders and when I was a practicing attorney and state assemblyman she kept our books and did an admirable job of it. She has a fine business head upon that beautiful body. She is an all around wonderful wife and mother and I am so fortunate to have had her give me her hand in marriage. With some of the money John and I received that we did not send home we brought some fine tea, cheese and lamb for a number of meals. Our ranks have thinned and now when we sit down to our meals only John, Old Doc and I are around our makeshift table. Josiah has not returned and Old Doc as I mentioned does not expect that he will make it and I do not ever expect to see Henry back in the field and I pray that one day I will see him back in our fair village and be able to reminisce with him about these harrowing days on the field of battle and our great friendships we have made with such exceptional brothers in arms. I will never forget to a man those of the 33rd New York Volunteers as they have shown their mettle many times over when called upon. Old Doc was telling me the other evening at supper that we are now losing as many men to disease as to the actual fighting with the Rebels and he suspects that figure could go as high as three dying of disease to every one of us that dies in battle. It is difficult each day to face the possibility of facing off against the Rebels let alone worry about what malady lingers around the corner that may lay any of us in our grave. I and all the other officers are strictly enforcing all the sanitary codes of this army and have even gone beyond the basics the army requires but with so many thousands of men living out-of-doors constantly and with little or no opportunity to move to healthier areas the ailments are everywhere. Our general staff, I understand, is becoming alarmed by the manpower losses but they have reconciled themselves with the fact that we have been told by informants that the proud and brave men of the Confederacy are faring far worse than we are if that is imaginable. God help us all and I pray nightly that this lunacy will soon end and all of us, both Northern and Southern soldier can pick up their lives and return to their loved ones. I did ask Old Doc if he wanted to move in with us for companionship but he just winked and said he would prefer his own private living quarters especially now that his famous therapy supply has been replenished. I can't say I blame him in the least since I have used it to cure whatever ails me a number of times over.

Courtesy of the Library of Congress

CHAPTER SIXTEEN

Camp Near Harrison's Landing

As it is at present we have settled in here by Harrison's landing and expect to be here for some time. I am hoping since we have settled in that the mail delivery will become a little faster. As of late it has been taking about eight or sometimes ten days for letters to be received from home and for ours to reach the family. That is far too long and I have again spoken harshly to the postmaster about the dismal service his department is giving these fine men. I think I got through to him this time and he assured me that things would improve. I told him frankly if they did not he would be carrying a musket and be on the front lines in the next battle along with all of his staff. It is amazing how an intimidation like that can motivate men.

It is extremely warm and humid here at Harrison's landing and that is making it even more difficult for the doctors to try and deal with all the diseases that are so rampant in this vast assembly of men. I frankly think we would be losing less if we were in battle rather than sitting here on the banks of the James River and biding our time but the general has not again asked my opinion. Hopefully this heat will ease up soon and with it the sickness that is plaguing the men. It is so heartbreaking to watch such strong brave men, who signed up to fight an enemy, or so they were told, and instead they are dying from all the diseases that are impossible to conquer. Old Doc said it is going to get much worse before this is all over with. The colonel, major and the adjutant are all sick as well as John feeling under the weather. Old Doc is beside himself in trying to ease all the suffering. At his age I am amazed that he is still on his feet and able to deal with all the grief. Not only is he dealing with all the grief, trying his best to heal those amongst us that are ill, he is also staying amazingly healthy himself. It is either a miracle or he is going through his famous medication at an alarming rate and I would think that alone might bring him down but I pray his wisdom and steady hand will remain available to help us all. Fortunately John is not as ill as many of the others so I am praying he will be back on his feet soon. Hiram Kelly of our fair village is very ill and I have obtained a 30-day pass for him to hopefully go back home and recuperate. He has given me a hard time about going as he is one of the bravest men I have ever known and he does not want to leave his fellow soldiers but I am insisting for his own good and I do believe we will see him back here shortly.

Courtesy of the Library of Congress

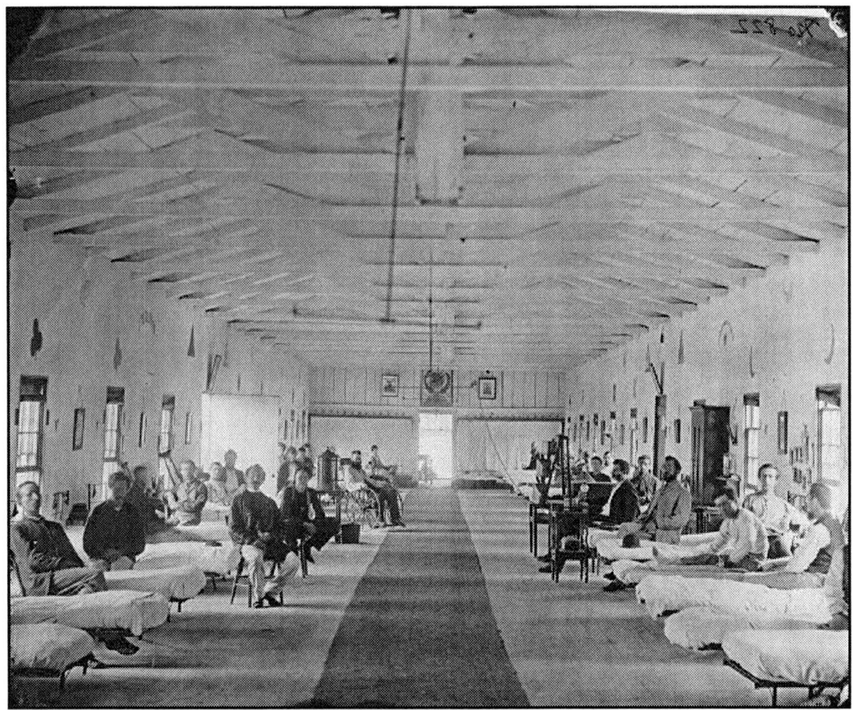

Courtesy of the Library of Congress

I was just thinking how lucky we have been with the weather lately even though it is very hot and humid and all of a sudden we were in the midst of a terrific cloudburst accompanied by very high winds. A great deal of lightning also has accompanied the storm. The heavy rain, high winds and lightning have cooled the air and I believe purified the camp and I believe it will ease the spreading of infirmity and help everyone out. The winds did do some damage to the colossal number of tents on this vast plane but it seems everyone is pulling together and getting things shipshape again. I held on very tight to the inside pole of the tent while Old Doc and John held on to the outside during the short lived high winds and through all our efforts we avoided losing anything. John as I mentioned was under the weather but still threw his weight into the task, as I would always expect of him. Several good things came from this God given storm, cooler weather, purification of the camp and the fact that the Rebels experienced the same calamity and should slow down any efforts on their part to attack us. Our command doesn't seem to need a reason to avoid conflict since we have not been ordered into battle for some time and there are no rumors that we will be any time soon. John has also felt well enough to be out on picket duty the past few days and he reports everything has been quiet with little or no sight of the enemy. Maybe we will get lucky and sit out the rest of the war here although I hear that some major fighting is taking place in other areas of this clash and I feel sorry for the men on both sides that are suffering through that.

With some of the money we were paid a short time ago I have been trying to buy a coffee pot and other necessary utensils along with some good meat, coffee and butter for our needs. So far there has been very little for sale and I am going to write Julia and ask her to buy some of our needs and package them up and send them on down to us. I also plan on asking her if she could send along the time baker that is up in the pantry on the top shelf as I remember it well. It is strange the small things one remembers when they are in this hellhole and they are what keep all of us slightly on the right side of sanity. I also want her to send some good dried apples and some towels, which we also desperately need. She will also send me a coffee pot, which will hold about three quarts and have a nose on one side with the handle on the opposite side so I avoid burning myself like I did with the pork roast. We also need three tablespoons, forks and knives for John, Old Doc and I. Would you believe I also am going to ask her to send some pepper, a quarter of ginger, a pound of cream of tarter and a pound of soda? In her last letter she said she was making some of her mouth-watering home made ketchup so I think I will ask for some of that. To finish out my requests I need her to send some writing paper, yeast cakes, a yeast stick and a dozen pair of colored cotton socks if she can still buy cotton socks in the middle of this war. I will ask Julia to send it express to myself, Colonel of the 33rd New York Volunteers, N.Y.S.V. Smiths Division, Harrison's Landing, Virginia. As an afterthought I may also ask her if she can buy ten or fifteen pounds of some good cheese to send that along also. John, Old Doc and I have a craving for that and it would be great to get some but I will ask her to make sure it is not hard or sour, as I do not want to pay the freight on spoiled cheese.

As you can see, our government certainly sees to our needs? Julia should be running the government, as I am sure it would be a lot more efficient and we would not be begging our families to send us the bare essentials on a regular basis? Hopefully we will not starve to death in the meantime since we do have some very fundamental essentials that are necessary for all our survival furnished by our very efficient government. You might note I am saying that with a great deal of sarcasm. This shortage of the proper food and clothing is also a mighty contributor of all this ill health that is so unbridled I know I can depend on Julia and the family when I need them and that is more than I can say for our government.

If the other officers were not so sick and I was not totally in charge I would have taken some time to go to Fort Monroe and visit Josiah but as it is I can only rely on information that is second hand from others that were recently their either visiting the sick or being there sick themselves. Several of the men have told me that Josiah is still hanging on even though Old Doc is amazed and thought he would have succumbed long before now. He said he knew he was a strong man with a great deal of inner faith in the Lord's blessings and that hopefully that is carrying him through this crisis and he may well be able to return to his friends and comrades in arms shortly. Even better maybe this entire nightmare will soon be over and he and all of us can return and rebuild our broken lives after enduring the hardships of the past many months.

After writing the letter and finishing it so it would go out in the 6 A.M. mail I was informed that the mail department has moved up the time for mail to leave our camp to 5 A.M. so it will have to wait another day. I believe my little talk with the postmaster about putting him on the line in the future must have made a very lasting impression. I am sure he did not think I was kidding and frankly I was not as he and all his staff would have soon been up with the rest of these brave fellows on the front lines if he had not gotten off his ass and also insisted his staff do the same. The least they can do for those of us that are actually doing all the fighting is provide our cherished letters from home in a timely fashion.

Some of our forward pickets had a brief encounter with the Rebel pickets this morning. They reported to me that one of the

Rebels had been killed, several wounded and our losses amounted to one man shot in the left leg, which Old Doc is seeing to. This is the first encounter for some time and hopefully will be the last for a while. It has been relatively quiet here and I hate to see hostilities begin again as so many will be forever devastated. I continue to say my nightly prayers for an end to all this lunacy.

John and I were surprised to see Lieutenant Chapman from our fair village show up in camp today. We had not seen him since the Williamsburg battle and we had plenty to talk about concerning that engagement. He is well and I was very pleased to see him. We talked at some length about what we considered some of the mistakes of our commanders in the field during that engagement and someday when this is all over with I hope to gather together my thoughts on that clash and what could have been done differently to avoid the shocking loss of life and limb from the orders that were given. It is always easier to look back with hindsight on an event as it becomes mush clearer in one's mind after time has passed and you reflect on the events leading up to, during the engagement and directly afterwards. I do feel strongly that things could have been handled differently and avoided such a loss of life and maybe when I am growing old and gray I will take the time to reminisce about it. That is if I am granted old age and gray hair or if I end up lying in some quickly marked grave somewhere in Virginia or beyond, another lost soul of the Civil ??? War along with hundreds of thousands of others who have sacrificed everything. John and the lieutenant have gone over to one of the other regiments to buy some mackerel as we hear they can be bought for about two cents a piece. They are fresh mackerel so we shall have a fine dinner tonight and we have asked Lieutenant Chapman to dine with us. I am looking forward to it, as it is always pleasant to have a guest at our dinner table that has shared the dreadfulness of this time with us all.

I was reminiscing this morning that in all the months that this war has been going on neither John nor I have once been entered on the report as sick that day. There are days when one or both of us feel under the weather but we still have managed to report to duty and still function as we have been used to. Some of the other officers are still unwell including the colonel, the adjutant, and the major. General Davidson even went north several days ago for the benefit of his health. He assigned me as commander of the brigade during his absence since I am one of the few officers that are still on their feet and able to lead if called upon. I do not take the assignment lightly and appreciate his confidence in my ability. I must write Julia and the family and tell them as I have heard it said that some of the men have mentioned, and it was reported in at least one paper, that I was appointed Brigadier General of the entire brigade. Sort of sounds nice, Brigadier General Joseph but I don't quite think that is what he had in mind when he left for hopefully only a short time.

Martha wrote me concerning the money that I sent home recently to be deposited in the bank and distributed as per my instructions. I must not have made myself completely clear as Martha thought the extra $250.00 was ours and to be deposited for us. I regret not being clear as it belonged to a number of the other men from the division and they had entrusted it to me to have it deposited so it could be earning some interest while they were away fighting. I must write her and clear up the confusion, as these men will be looking for their funds when they are mustered out if of course they are still amongst the living. If they should perish I have a complete list of them and the amounts they entrusted to Martha. We will see that each family is given the money plus any interest it has earned. God knows that they will need it then even more than now if their loved one and bread winners do not return home. I will send the letter to Julia and the family and ask her to go over it with Martha. I also must, as I stated, set her straight on my temporary promotion so she doesn't think her husband is now the commander and might want to make army life my career. That is the last thing on my mind and certainly not my desire at all. I have seen enough of death, suffering and dying to last me ten lifetimes.

Courtesy of the Library of Congress

"Dear Julia and my beloved family:

I regret to inform you that I have been feeling somewhat indisposed for nearly a week past, but having so many things to attend to with my regular duties and my new duties as acting commander, which by the way is only temporary until the commander returns from sick leave. I am not sure if I am the lucky one or the unlucky one as I, even though I am feeling somewhat ill, still am on my feet so all the duties fall on my shoulders as the others are all on sick call. Old Doc assures me I am one of the lucky ones as he said so many of the ailing in fact may not make it with such rampant ill health amongst all of the men. He told me even with all my added duties I am certainly better off than being in the hospital tent with the afflictions that are raging there. John is also feeling slightly down but I believe we are of good stock, particularly John as he has the greatest, strongest mother in the world. I am cooking for the three of us tonight some excellent tea, baker's bread, and blackberry and I have even been able to get some pancakes to rise fairly well so all of that has built up John's and my resistance. Old Doc miraculously can eat almost anything and it does not seem to make much difference, as he always seems to stay healthy even at his advanced age. I frankly am surprised he moved in to our tent as it somewhat restricts his access to his famous treatment but then again he spends most of his days and many a night in the hospital tent tending to the wounded and the ill and I would guess he may partake slightly himself as well as sharing it with those poor souls lying there.

Please go over the recent accounting of funds with Martha that she deposited in the bank to draw interest. I had inserted in the express a sheet of paper with the names of those fellows who gave me their funds to send home to be invested and it must have gotten caught up in the wrapping of the express and she did not see it. I have added a sheet attached to this letter of the same accounting and that should clear up the matter. You and the family must have really thought I was named commander and received a large increase in pay to send that extra money along. This money of course belongs to many of these brave lads and eventually either they or their loved ones, depending on who survives, will need it at the end of our period of service.

I recently received the package you had sent with the yeast cakes, butter, soda and excellent cheese along with all the other requests I had made from you and I sincerely thank you. I even had a friend recently give me a bottle of Claret Wine, which the three of us immensely enjoyed. Our bread, baker's bread, is sent from Fort Monroe to the regimental hospital for the use of the ill. They also allow any that is not needed to be purchased by the officers so I was fortunate enough to buy two for us. It is good bread but I would have thought the government could at least furnish it without our having to buy it but then again they didn't ask me even though they should have. I am sure at this point in the letter you are smiling at this temperament of your husband as you are so well used to and so patient with. I hear also that they are going to try and bake some soft bread at Fort Monroe for those ill fellows as the baker's bread is very hard and in many cases these poor fellows do not even have the strength to chew it at all. You mentioned also in your last letter that you would try and send us some more tea but my thoughts are to hold off on this as the officers can purchase tea at the commissary cheaper than the express costs to send it. I appreciate your thoughts but other items, which you have sent, are much more appreciated, as those cannot be purchased here or at the fort. I am paying 69 cents a pound for reasonably good tea so we are taken care of in that department.

One other article that I am in desperate need of is a pair of spectacles. Would you believe I lost mine on the march from Yorktown to Williamsburg and have managed without them ever since. I get along all right during the day such as writing orders and letters but at night I can hardly see by the candlelight and so I need another pair sent down. You will have to get Mr. Nottingham to make them and if my memory serves me correctly he fitted the size and magnification to Mr. Tiffany who it seems has the same eye boundaries as I do. I was hoping the government would furnish me with a new pair but alas all they seem to basically provide is guns and ammunition but not many other necessities of life. I cannot read the fine print of the newspapers and maybe that is a blessing for most of it is filled with battles, names of those poor souls that have fallen and more war, war and more conflict. I look forward to the day when the newspapers will be filled with stories of peace, tranquility and more serenity although it doesn't look like it will be anytime soon.

Colonel Draime has sent me a letter and expects to be back here within the next ten days, as he is feeling much better. I was relieved to hear from him, as we need all the able-bodied manpower that we can muster with so many men down. We especially need many of the officers back as so many have reported to the hospital or gone north to recuperate.

All for now as I am headed to the hospital to visit the wounded and ill and find out from Old Doc and the other doctors what the current state of affairs is. Pray for our continued safety, an early end of this horror and the poor souls that are in such agony in the hospitals.

With more love than the entire universe can hold,
Joseph"

As I had mentioned John was feeling somewhat indisposed but has finally shaken off the tribulations that plagued him. I think it was most likely a combination of a slight case of the runs and also a larger case of homesickness. Being homesick is a major problem for many of the men especially as we have so much time on our hands lately without any action or movement. The high command has us sitting here at Harrison's Landing and it looks like we may well be here for some time to come. It is a blessing and a curse as inaction is great for relieving the possibility of anyone being killed or wounded. However it leads to men being bored stiff and beginning to feel sorry for themselves. It also leads to the men having a great deal of time to just sit and worry about their aches and pains and wonder if every ache or every pain is the beginning of Typhoid Fever or one of the many other illnesses that are so rampant. I truly believe if we are kept in this one position too long that we will succumb to something that will fell us all. So many men in such a relatively small place with sanitary conditions in many cases less than cattle would enjoy. Even though I have the men digging fresh latrines everyday the stench and I am sure the disease emanating from them is overpowering us all. These are all good men and they do not deserve to be living in these conditions for any length of time however it is the way of the foot soldier especially in this conflict. I have been told that there are tons of boxes at Fort Monroe that have been sent from families back home to their loved ones that are camped out here. Word has it that the express company has not the means to transport so many boxes up the river to this location and therefore many of the men are going without bare essentials that their families provide them. I wonder some days if we will not have a mutiny on our hands over this and the general living conditions but I know these men well and they are loyal and brave to the core and would never even have such a thought cross their minds. Maybe I shouldn't go quite that far as I am sure it has crossed many a mind but being the stout lads they are that is where the thought dies.

Colonel Draime has spoken to me about his going back home and trying to recruit men to fill the many empty spaces that so many that have died, gotten ill and wounded have left us with. This may not be an easy task as the government has tightened up the regulations for serving. When this chaos all started the government was willing to accept anyone no matter how young or how old and that very fact is contributing mightily to so many that have been plagued with all the various illnesses that are afflicting us. Some were so frail that there wasn't any coherent reason to allow them to join up. Even the old, young, sick and frail were caught up in the patriotism of the time and the government needing manpower looked the other way unfortunately. Some of the other regiments have sent officers home and have had some success in filling the missing ranks even though support for this war, as in all wars, has waned considerably from what it was when we were all caught up in the nationalism of the times over a year ago. Those at home are of course reading about the tremendous casualties and having I am sure second thoughts as to whether they wish to join this insanity. However I suspect that the colonel if he goes will be able to recruit some fine fellows that will be of great help when we go into the next battle which I am sure is imminent and as always will see many of us perish or have our lives ruined forever. I must write Julia and tell her that he may be coming home to recruit and that he has insisted I remain here and lead the troops. I am sure Julia would wonder why I am not coming home for that duty and I want to inform her before she hears it from someone else. I was going to write her this morning but the flies are so thick after about 5 AM in all the tents and of course the hospital that I cannot sit for too long and have to get out in the open along with all the thousands of others. Since our tents have no netting for keeping the insects out they are so bothersome that I must keep one hand free to keep brushing them away from my arms and face constantly. Old Doc said that he is sure they are carrying many of the diseases that are afflicting the men. In fact the other day we were discussing the terrible state of affairs in these camps that is almost impossible to control living like we are forced to. He said the men are ailing with dysentery, measles, small pox, pneumonia and malaria plus others that he is not even sure what they are. The doctors are all working it seems 24 hours a day trying to help so many that are laid up but it is a losing battle with men being assigned each and every day to digging more and more graves. Old Doc as I have often said is a very wise man and he has all along said that the chances of not surviving this conflict are much greater from disease than from the Rebel's mini balls. Very few of the doctors that are serving have had as much formal medical training as Old Doc who was fortunate to train for four years in Europe. Many of the other doctors have only gone to school for a couple of years and many of them say they have learned more in a little over a year in the field with the troops than they could have leaned in 20 years of schooling. To a man however they feel totally inadequate to do much more than comfort the sick and patch up the wounded as best they can. Many women are now serving in the hospitals and are a Godsend to those unfortunate fellows. Without the help of so many fine ladies our casualty rate would be even higher. We all will forever be in their debt. Some of the newspapers have referred to the doctors as "butchers" but believe me when I say they are anything but. They are strong, compassionate and brave souls that are giving their all to help relieve the appalling torment of so many. Many a night Old Doc does not come into our tent until well after midnight having been on duty for about 18 to 20 hours straight. We arise at 5:00 AM for the morning drilling of all the regiments until about half past six and John and I try to be as quiet as possible to allow him to get a few more hours of much needed rest. I have to mention that even though the rumors when we first joined up and were at Camp Granger was that Old Doc's snoring would wake the dead it is the furthest from the truth. He is so dead to the world each night that I don't believe he makes even the slightest sounds and even if a cannon went off in our tent I think he would sleep right through it.

We had a long discussion the other day when in a rare moment he wanted to talk and share with someone. He again reiterated his shocking concerns which have been born out that more of these fine lads will die from disease than will die or be wounded by the enemies' bullets and shells. From what I have seen in the hospitals I cannot dispute what he is saying and of course I never would, as he is by far one of the most gifted of all of those of us in this man's army. Old Doc also had some devastating news for John and I. He had received a letter from friends at home informing him that Henry had thrown himself in front of a train. They said he had been so distraught of late in both body and especially mind that he could not function. Many in the community had tried to help him and they mentioned that none tried harder than my wife, Julia. The friends also told Old Doc that Henry was so despondent that he had let John, Josiah and I down and all these other amazing men that daily lay their lives down if necessary for their country. I told Old Doc that I was not surprised to hear of his demise since I above most of the others knew just how distraught he was when sent home. If I had thought he would have fared better here I would have let him stay but as it was he was not only a danger to himself but also would have put his fellow soldiers in precarious positions if allowed to enter into battle. Maybe I should have been wiser and let him stay and perform some behind the line duties but knowing Henry as I did he would have found a way to be in the front in any future conflict. Old Doc could see how overwhelmed I was and told me the decision I had made was the correct one. With command comes many difficult decisions and this was one of my most difficult.

And then there were four, John, Old Doc, Josiah and myself, and each day I fear of hearing of Josiah's passing. Old Doc had brought some of his fixer upper with him, for want of a better phrase to describe it, and we tipped our glasses, John, he and I to Henry's memory, bravery and friendship. I then led the three of us in a brief moment of prayer to our loving Lord that he will take Henry's soul into heaven for he was one of the finest men I have ever known. My dream of someday tipping a few at the local tavern with the original five of us plus Captain Tyler is forever shaken.

To take my mind off the terrible tragedy of Henry's untimely death I awoke at 5:00 AM as usual. As I mentioned it is impossible to sleep beyond 5:00 AM as the flies become so thick that they wake everyone up. These low lands, swamps and waterways are so stagnant that it is the perfect breeding grounds for the flies and of course that is one of the reasons that Malaria, Typhoid and all the other diseases are so rampant. John was already up and Old Doc was sleeping peacefully with an old blanket pulled up around his head so that the flies could not get to him. Putting in the hours he is at the hospital I doubt even a thousand flies could keep him awake the few hours he is able to lay his head down. I mounted Blackjack and rode around all five regiments to make sure all able bodied men were out drilling this fine morning. They drill from 5:00 AM until half past six each and every morning. It helps break the monotony of the days as well as keeping an edge on their fighting ability in case the Rebels decide to hassle us again.

I managed to arrange a brief furlough for John, I wished him well and told him to give all the family lots of hugs and kisses from me. I so wish I was going with him but it cannot be at present as the regiments are so short handed of officers, some home recruiting and others laid up sick. Is it a curse or a blessing that I seem to be able to maintain my health when so many others are falling by the wayside? Old Doc said not to complain as it was a God-given blessing even if much responsibility is resting on my shoulders. During most of my waking moments I picture the romping and fun times John and little Joseph will have together if only for a brief time.

The command issued orders this morning to be ready to move today at 2 P.M. but almost as soon as the order was given it was countermanded. I am not privy to why the order was cancelled but from the rumors flying around I do believe we will be moving out within the next 24 hours, at least those that are still on their feet and able to move. I have ordered all knapsacks sent to the landing and they are to be put on the transports so everyone will be ready to move at a moments notice. I have also ordered that we take with us six days rations, two days in the haversacks and four days in the wagons. The colonel has not yet returned from his recruitment drive so a great deal more of the responsibility of seeing that the regiments are ready to march and ready to fight if called upon is resting on my shoulders. I guess I should not complain, as I seem to thrive on it.

I did have a most pleasant surprise this afternoon however when lo and behold Josiah showed up in camp looking fit as a fiddle. Old Doc and I were sharing a pipe full of tobacco in a brief quiet moment for each of us when Josiah walked up to us. Neither one of us could believe our eyes particularly Old Doc as he looked like he has seen a ghost. He has seen so many poor fellows die a horrible death from the fever that he couldn't believe it. He certainly is of solid oak stock to be strong enough to beat Typhoid Fever. He greeted us with a cheerful "Happy to be back," sat down, pulled out his pipe and I shared my tobacco with him. The three of us reminisced for a leisurely couple of hours, talked some about Henry, before everything returned to normal and the routine of army life. The Lord has answered my prayers in having Josiah back and well. And now there are four of us again. Unfortunately Josiah has experienced severe hearing loss and his eyesight has also suffered to a great degree. I talked to Old Doc after Josiah had left to visit with some of his fellow soldiers in arms about whether I should recommend he be discharged as not being fit for duty. Old Doc in his infinite wisdom just looked at me and mentioned Henry, what happened to him and the fact that even if I did recommend he be discharged he would never leave and wait in the background even if no longer was an official soldier of the Army of the Potomac and the next fight he would be right up there with all his brave comrades. All I could say to his astuteness in his recommendation was "thank-you and what an appalling waste of good men."

Josiah it seems has returned just in time as we have been ordered to get the regiments ready to move. This vast army started to move all its wagons, artillery and a few lead troops out at about ten this evening, the 14th of August 1862. The movement of so many men and all the wagons and artillery makes for slow going and a very dusty time of it. Our division is bringing up the rear and we cannot believe how dusty it is and what a slow march it is. I hear little complaining however as we all know what our responsibilities are and are more than willing and able to carry them out even though we are dangerously shorthanded. Josiah was not quite as recovered as he put on and after a few miles I ordered that he mount one of the mules to proceed as I could see how weak he had become. I admire men like Josiah as they always give all to the cause, whatever that cause may be, and even if it is a terrible nightmare as this has turned out to be. We marched about five miles the first night and we have bivouacked for the night without blankets, it is a very cold night and many a man is curled up trying their best to keep from freezing and rest as best they can under these terrible conditions. Everyone was bugled awake at 5:00 A.M. and most of the men were only too happy to be aroused as they were cold and shivering and were more than ready to recover their circulation as soon as possible. The only thing that could make this any more trying and miserable would be more rain and I pray that won't happen. Today we have marched about 17 miles and we are bivouacked about one and a half miles east of the battlefield of Williamsburg. That is certainly bringing back some ghastly memories of our recent engagement with Johnny Reb at that site. I am hopeful we do not repeat that battle again.

It is now the 19th of August and two days since we were ordered to march and we again are awakened at 5:00 A.M. and we marched the troops to about a mile and a half east of Yorktown near the York River. It has been an extremely dusty march otherwise the weather has been comparatively cool which has aided the men under the circumstances. Josiah has held up rather well considering all he has been through lately and was thankful to be able to ride the mule. Unfortunately he has lost almost 100% of his hearing either as a result of having had an encounter with Typhoid or being in such close proximity to so many of the artillery pieces going off. So many of the fellows are experiencing the same problem and I fear some times when we need to yell out important orders that so many may not hear them especially above the sounds of battle. With so many of the troops feeling less than 100 percent, we have quite a number riding mules, and horses when available and on the wagons. We have had to abandon quite a few along the way and they have all been transported back to the temporary hospitals that have been set up as we moved such a colossal number of men. Orders have come down that the brigade will not be moving from this spot today and this will give everyone a chance to catch a little well needed rest and wipe some of the grime off of themselves. In discussions with other officers of other divisions I have heard of none being molested by the Rebels on this march, which frankly I think was very wise of the Rebels as most of these able-bodied men were just itching for a fight. It is hard to imagine after months of such living in squalor conditions, fighting and dying and such rampant infirmity that these men are still ready and more than able to engage the enemy.

I understand tomorrow we will most likely move out and go almost to Fort Monroe where the fighting ability and readiness of the divisions will be ascertained. I recently dreamt that I had heard from Colonel Draime and John and that they had recruited about 140 fine fellows to fill our ranks from those that have been killed and those that had succumb to diseases. It turned out to be only a dream, as I have not heard that they have had any success up to this point, hopefully soon, as we need healthy able-bodied men to fill these ever decreasing ranks. As it turned out on the 24th I received orders to prepare the brigade for readiness to move and we proceeded to Fort Monroe to prepare for embarkation. As it turned out everything went efficiently and we entered the ships that awaited us and went on down near to the Aquia Creek area. The entire brigades movement went relatively smoothly for such a large task and the steamers were most efficient. We experienced no hostilities and are awaiting further orders when the high command makes up its mind what we are to do next. If they were to ask me I would say let us get together with our Southern brothers and have a couple of drinks and decide this insanity is all behind us but alas they will not.

I never believed that moving so many men, horses, wagons, mules and artillery would have gone so smoothly but with everyone's cooperation and the cooperation of the weather the ride up the river was invigorating to the spirit and well being of the men. It seems to a man our emotional state has improved.

The colonel and John have both now returned from home and brought a few fresh recruits with them. I could not wait to be alone with John and hear first hand of the family and especially little Joseph. I pray that little Joseph will be spared the horrors of warfare in his lifetime but I am not overly optimistic as mankind as I have often said has an inherent flaw whereby he continues to enact inhumane hostilities on his fellow human beings. John told me enthusiastically about the family, their continued good health and their continued prayers for all of us. My conversation with John made me extremely homesick and I am going to double my efforts to have a furlough granted soon.

I had to immediately take pen to paper and write to Julia and the family as writing always makes me feel closer to them.

"Dear Julia and Children:

John has brought me up-to-date on all of you and especially your continued good health. John said that little Joseph even gave him a big hug and kiss upon his leaving and told him to pass it on to Papa. I had to draw the line on that however as I feared if anyone saw us they might wonder what their Lieut. Colonel Joseph and his son were up to. I settled for rubbing my hand over the spot on John's face where the kiss had been planted and then touching my hand to my lips. I immediately broke down and fortunately only John was in the tent with me or others might again be wondering if I had gone over the hill. If Old Doc was here he would certainly have understood but I fear others might not. I am going to double my efforts to acquire a leave of absence however rumor has it that we may be going into a major conflict shortly and since many of the officers are ill all of the rest of us are irreplaceable at this time. I always thought in life it would be wonderful to be irreplaceable but never in my wildest dreams meant it to be under these circumstances.

Love to all,
Joseph"

Today is the first of September and we are on the march about 4:00 A.M. and marched about six miles through Fairfax and as we went along that way we heard cannon fire going on in front of our position. I fear as I have said that something major is about to happen and I know our loyal brave souls are up for whatever Johnny Reb throws at them.

I marvel at the enthusiasm of these new fellows and well realize until they experience combat and see the stench of death after a battle their enthusiasm will be as short lived as they may well be. We need them desperately but I also feel a deep compassion for them, as I well know what awaits some of them. The scars of battle, even if they survive, will live with them always as it did poor old Henry and many may never get over this living nightmare.

As we moved on further towards Fairfax we were hearing more and more battle sounds ahead of us. We understood there was a great deal of fierce fighting going on and as we proceeded we began to see many of the dead being carried by and many of the wounded struggling back. Two officers rode up to me and put out their hands to shake mine and also called me by name. They were so covered with dust that I could not recognize either of them. As it turned out one was Dr. Lanner, a member of the New York State Assembly when I was there. He had sat on my left hand during our many meetings of the assembly. The other was one of his assistant clerks and they had Colonel Pratt under their charge as he had been severely wounded in the recent and ongoing battle. The poor colonel was in terrible shape and Old Doc who was riding in his magic medicine wagon looked at the colonel and then at me and just shook his head. Another fine man who will never again see the light of day, the stars in the sky, his children's laughing faces or all the other wonderful things that make life worth living. As we parted, we proceeded and were crossing the rim when we received orders to counter march. We were told that the Rebels had turned our left flank and after that there was considerable confusion.

There was mass disorder and I was ordered to round up as many stragglers and prisoners as I could and after a short time I had more men under guard than I had guards to watch over. In retrospect I think it would have been wiser for the commander to order a full frontal assault on the enemy in order to throw them off guard and regain the advantage, however as usual, I was not consulted and I followed those orders that were handed down to me. In my opinion our leadership continues to be too hesitant to commit our resources, which if he would I think might end this lunacy sooner rather than later. We were then ordered to camp for the night and I took the opportunity to drop another note to Julia.

"Julia and my dear children,

My dear wife and children, hope on, trust in God for a continuation of his protection over us, and that we may yet have a happy, joyous reunion of the family circle. In the meantime I beg and beseech my family to live in peace and enjoy life, as you might if we were all together. I beg and pray that our children, as is their duty to both you and I Julia for the months and years of care and toil we have both bestowed upon them, or for their maintenance and education, and the duty they owe us as parents that they will not disregard our admonitions and counsel. That they will show proper respect to you in my absence as well as if I were present. And my dear children, one and all, honor your parents and if you love your parents and for the regard you have for your absent father please let him toil out the remaining time of enlistment, the hard duty of an officer in this war, without adding pain to toil and if you would have peace of mind when the remains of your parents may be moldering in the grave. Respect your mother, and under no circumstances insult or ill-treat her. Do not, I beseech you, be deceived by the soft words of flatterers or the deception of hypocrites; do not as you value your peace of mind, or mine, listen to any who would speak evil of your parents. None but those you should shun who would ever attempt to set a child against its parents. Beware of all such for the time will come when you may know their real character and unless you shun them in time the virus they may have engendered may poison all the future of your early existence, if it should not sting your conscience unto death. When I left home I believed and I think truly that my children were respected, that their reputation was good. If they, God help us, during my absence shall so conduct themselves as to tarnish that fair reputation, disrespect and slight their mother or go and associate with disreputable persons thereby disgracing themselves and I. How a two edge sword that would be to pierce my heart and how could I think of returning to that pleasant village to meet face to face with old acquaintances but to see the pity in their faces for me on account of the acts of my children. I realize I have said more than enough and I pray that the good Lord's calming hand will be upon all my family and that my children will use their good judgment and respect their mother and father.

I am not sure what possessed me Julia to go on like this but believe me sincerely when I say that any words I write to all of you bring me closer to you and that my family means more to me than life itself. Do not fret if you hear of a major battle happening in the area in the next few days, as divine intervention will surely watch over your husband and son as the good Lord has in these many past months.

With all my love, as deep as my heart.

Joseph"

This war is taking a terrible toll both on the soldiers being killed, wounded in the heat of battle, or dying a horrifying death in some makeshift hospital from some terrible disease. It is also taking a terrible toll on those left at home without husbands and fathers to offer guidance and support. Please God, let this madness end.

CHAPTER SEVENTEEN

Every Man Has His Day

We are camped near Rockville, Maryland and have been on the march off and on for the past several days. There is no question that we may soon be facing a major battle as we can hear constant shelling ahead of us and it is said that General Robert E. Lee of the Confederacy is planning a major offensive in the near future with the desire of driving this vast army further north. There are so many rumors abounding that even a couple of the men who I thought we could count upon have gone absent without leave. I have sent word home to the authorities that if they show up there they should be immediately arrested and incarcerated until such time as they can be brought to trial for desertion. Some of the newer recruits having heard so many horror stories from those hardened soldiers have decided this is not for them. The meager pay that the government is paying, at least on occasion when the spirits move them, is not enough for some of these fine lads to face such a colossal experience such as we have been through and will shortly be experienced again. For those casehardened veterans they well realize what we are facing as they have faced it before, and if luck would have it and they have not gone completely mad, they are ready to face it again. I am sure the same uncertainties are swimming in Johnny Rebs' mind as they face what may be their last days on this earth also. The battle lines are being drawn and we shall see who lives, who dies and who is victorious. How I wish we could end this over a tall one at the local pub but alas it is not to be so.

It seems that our general seems to remain cautious about committing troops but the day is rapidly arriving when he may have no choice. General Lee continues to push into Maryland and even this poor soldier knows that there is only one way to stop him. I would rather see this vast army mount a major offensive than wait to be attacked and then be ill prepared or totally on the defensive.

Here on Sept. 16th, 1862 we remain camped at Pleasant Valley, Md. and it is ironic that we are bivouac in a place with such a name as Pleasant Valley. I am sure under more peaceful times this truly is a place of lovely living but certainly not currently. This is a valley of death and dying as a major battle is taking place just west of the ridge ahead of us. General McClellan is still holding us in reserve and many of the officers feel we should be committed or this encounter may well be lost. Since again the general does not call on me for advice all I can do is try and reassure the men and remain ready if called upon. This morning Hooker's Corps has been ordered to move so it is now 6 AM and we are joining the rest of these brave men to be thrown into this caldron of hell on earth. It has been passed down to us as we march forward that this is becoming the bloodiest battle so far of this war here at Antietam. As we move forward we are passing hundreds if not thousands of men being carried back behind the lines for treatment. There is no time to bury the hundreds that have already been killed and as we approach the battle field all of us to a man is trembling inside as we gaze upon this hell on earth. I have ordered the men to engage the enemy and we have made a direct frontal assault on Johnny Reb. He is a fierce fighting man and men around us are dropping like flies. I tremble to think of the nightmares if I am lucky enough to survive this firestorm that I will be living with the rest of my life after ordering so many fine fellows to their certain death. Blackjack is as dependable as ever as we sweep down upon Lee's left flank and men are dropping rapidly on both sides. I managed to drop a couple of the rebel soldiers as I pierced them with my sword and I was fortunate to escape the many shells being fired from every direction. There is an old church here in this field where we have temporarily taken cover while we regroup for battle. We are licking our wounds and taken stock of how many men we have left and in what condition they are. The general has ordered us to mount a major assault against the Sunken Road to hopefully turn the tide. I fear this day may be lost if we do not follow up on our advantage since we have managed to pierce the Confederate center. It is now that these fine young fellows who have been so brave in enduring the hardships of combat, disease and all sorts of other evils should be allowed to follow through on this gain. I begged the commanders to allow us to again take the fight to the enemy with a full frontal assault as we did in past successful battles but General McClellan has again decided to be overly cautious in my opinion and we have not taken advantage of our temporary gain. I have lost track of John and Josiah in the fierceness and confusion surrounding this living nightmare and pray that they are still amongst the living. So many have already dropped that it seems there are more dead on the field of battle than there are standing and still fighting. I can remember when our fine minister at home in our fair village would preach on the total desperation of those sinners who have and will end up in hell. His description compared to what I am seeing today does not even come close to what eternal torment may be if it is anything like what is unfolding around me. These scenes of killing and being killed, men being bayoneted and driven through with swords is unspeakable. What have we wrought upon ourselves?

Courtesy of the Library of Congress

Our courier has told me that General Burnside's Corps has now entered the battle and has crossed the stone bridge over the creek and is rolling up the Confederate right. We are outnumbering the Rebels it seems as much as two to one but they will not back down. I keep hoping and praying for this carnage to stop but it seems it continues to escalate. I have ordered what remains of the 33rd into battle again and as I look out over the field of battle it seems as if there are only about half of the number of men left in the 33rd that started this day. It crossed my mind that I wish the leaders who were responsible for starting this carnage should be here watching this butchery or better yet be part of it. It is one thing to receive a written report on the battle of this day or any other day with the number of killed and wounded neatly written out on a report and it is a far more devastating image to see it in person. This day is slowly coming to a close with gunfire continuing to sound from every direction. I do not believe the Lord will look down upon this moment in time with any compassion for what mankind has wrought upon themselves. I firmly believe that the devil may well look upon this day as another victory in the eternal battle between good and evil.

Courtesy of the Library of Congress

Courtesy of the Library of Congress

As it is now dusk and those men still standing are literally falling asleep on their feet as if in a trance. Skirmishes continue along the entire battle line and General McClellan has decided not to take advantage of the gains our vast army has made and we seem to presently be fighting a stalemate with those that are still able to fight. I still have not been able to locate either John or Josiah and I fear the worse as so many bodies are lying in the fields and along the Sunken Road. I have ordered some of the men to bring in the wounded and Old Doc and the other doctors are performing their miracles of trying to save those they can and trying to ease the pain of those that will not survive this night. As I sit here on Blackjack looking over this bloodbath I find I cannot fathom mankind's inhumanity to his fellow man. I am sure this place and this battle will long live in the history of this country as one of the most brutal, bloodiest and deadly battles ever. There is not a man amongst us that is not in total shock as this battle winds down and the slaughter can be gazed upon.

It is now the 18th of September and the major battle seems to be over. There are still some skirmishers fighting on both sides but most of the battle now is to help the wounded off the field of battle, tend to their suffering and try as best to ease their pain. I have asked the captain to organize burial parties and with so many to bury on both sides the Chaplin's will be busy for days to come. Everything I am seeing and my feelings are that this battle is over with and the Rebels are moving back, caring for their dead and dying and moving their wounded to makeshift hospitals south of the river. I believe this could be called a standoff, as neither side seems to have gained an advantage from this massacre so I ask myself WHY? I doubt if I live to be as old as Methuselah I will ever be able to answer that question.

Courtesy of the Library of Congress

The officers and men assigned to the gruesome task of counting the dead have reported that it is estimated that well over 20,000 men have become casualties of this conflict over the past several days. The horror of this spot on this earth is indescribable. Old Doc has reported to me that there are thousands wounded amongst the Union troops and I am sure there are just as many or more amongst the Confederate troops. He doubts that many will survive as the medical personnel are so overloaded with men to take care of that many of these stout lads are sadly being neglected.

He said they are trying their best to serve all these brave souls but with so few doctors and orderlies it is humanly impossible to treat all of them. I have ordered the men to begin to prepare the mass graves for the several thousand men and boys that have fallen in this battle and as they lived closely with one another these past many months they will now spend eternity with their fellow comrades in arms. I pray to God that I will never again experience anything as depraved as this scene of carnage that all these brave souls, either Union or Confederate have experienced these last few days. God deliver us all from this carnage.

I am frantic over the whereabouts of John and Josiah and I am searching each and every report that comes to me to see if their names are entered therein as either wounded or missing. I cannot bring myself to consider that either of them or both have succumbed to this insanity. I have spoken to many of the men as to there whereabouts and Collins told me that he thought he saw them on the right flank near the sunken road and it looked to him at the time that they might have fallen into enemy hands. He is not sure but he recollects that he and several of the other men had shouted to them to watch their backs as the enemy skirmishers were surrounding them but John seemed to acknowledge the shouting above the commotion of battle but they said Josiah didn't seem to hear their warnings and I am sure if this is true it was because he had completely lost his hearing. Colonel Draime told me that he had heard also that John was surrounded and it looked like he was about to be captured in all the disorder and that it was reported to him that Josiah charged the Rebel soldiers screaming his head off at John to retreat and in so doing Josiah was run through and shot several times. I am beside myself, as I cannot find out the facts only what folks seem to think happened and until I locate them I will not be able to rest.

I checked again today, the 19th with Old Doc and he had a complete roster of all those that had fallen forever and today are being buried in several mass graves. I scanned the names in great anxiety and found sadly that Josiah's name was therein recorded as having paid the ultimate sacrifice for this cause, which daily I am questioning more and more. I found a record of where he had been laid to rest with his comrades in arms and knelt and said a prayer for a brave man and a true friend. I am not surprised that he died trying to save John, as they were as close as any two soldiers could ever have been. What a tragedy that Josiah survived all these months, overcame Typhoid Fever and then is killed on this field of battle. He had, as most of us do, a number of months to go in our enlistment and yet he will spend eternity here at Sharpsburg, Virginia. I must write as soon as my hand has steadied to Josiah's wife and family. I am somewhat relieved that I do not see John's name on the casualty list and am beginning to wonder if he was indeed taken prisoner in the confusion of the battle. I know as sure as I am standing here on this field of tears and wretchedness that John would have never deserted and I pray that under the circumstances he has been spared and is a prisoner of the Confederates. And now there are three, myself, Old Doc and I include John as I want to believe John is alive and still with us.

It is now the 21st of Sept. and as far as we all can tell the Rebels have left completely. The commanders are taking some credit claiming this was a victory for the Army of The Potomac but being in the thick of the fighting and having seen the utter butchery on both sides I would say at the least it was a draw as battles go. It certainly was not conclusive as far as seeing any end sooner than later to this conflict. I am still beside myself not knowing John's fate and I spent some time with the Chaplin this day and also spent some time with Old Doc again going over all the records of those killed and wounded and still I am not any closer to finding out his fate. I dare not write Julia until I have more definite proof of what has befallen him. I told Old Doc and in his unbounded understanding he said he would figure out a way to find out if John had been taken prisoner. I am not sure what he has in mind but in my desperation I am not going to question him. When I write Josiah's wife and family I will ask for now that they not mention any of this to Julia and the family. Knowing Josiah's strong wonderful wife and his amazing family I know that they will honor this small request for now. I have received a letter from Julia and she mentioned that they had heard of a great battle and they were so anxious to hear from myself and John that God had again watched over us. I fear I will have to either not write her for awhile which will even give her more anxiety or I will have to choose my words very carefully until more is known of his fate. I sent the following letter to Josiah's family.

"Dear Agnes and family,

I realize by now you have been notified of the untimely passing of Josiah. It was my heart felt privilege to be associated with him these many past wearisome months and I have always considered him as a true friend and fellow soldier. There was none braver or more loyal than he and I would have laid down my life for him in an instant if called upon. Very few men that I have known in my lifetime I consider to be saints but Josiah in everything he did was truly a blessing. If this country, both North and South had more fine men like him then I firmly believe this conflict that we are enmeshed in would have been resolved over a table of bargaining rather than the massacre that it has become. Josiah was the kind of man that was comfortable in his own body, never asked others to do anything that he was not willing to do himself and when he spoke he spoke with understanding

I wanted you to know that Josiah died trying to save John as his fellow fighting men have told me. The fate of John is still unknown so if you would be so kind please do not mention this to Julia or the family, as I will be writing them shortly. John and Josiah were inseparable and both helped the other get through these gruesome days we have seen these past many months.

This is a hellish war and Josiah gave his all, be proud of him as he loved you and his family deeply. I will truly miss him intensely and I stand ready to assist you and your family in any way I can in the future. Josiah is now with our Lord and I am sure he is looking down on us all with that sly sense of humor and watching over us.

May God bless you and yours.

Joseph"

I am so distraught I mounted Blackjack and headed back to the makeshift hospital to see if Old Doc had found out anything and I was told by one of the other doctors that he had mounted up and with a white flag had ridden off in the direction of the regrouping Confederate lines. I could not believe my ears and now I fear for his safety as well as John's. The doctor I spoke with said that Old Doc along with the other doctors and orderlies had done everything possible to relieve the pain and suffering of those poor wounded fellows and so there was nothing immediate that required his attention over here on this side of the battle field. I felt better about his trying to go over to the Rebel side then, as he would not neglect his duties for my concerns about John. As it is he never neglects his duties as lately he has been working about 22 hours every 24 hours as all the doctors and orderlies have. I pray for his safety and that he will be able to find something conclusive about John's fate. In the meantime since it is now the 23rd of the month and we are camping out at what is called "Camp in the Oakwood's" I decided I could no longer put off writing Julia and the family. I have received two letters, one from Julia and one from Martha begging for information on our well-being. Martha said she had heard that Josiah had perished and that made them even more anxious. It is certainly not fair of me to try and keep any information I have at this point from them so I will put pen to paper. I will strive to make the letter as casual as I can so hopefully that they will not sense my current immense anxiety about John and what has happened to him.

"Dear Julia and Children,

I am sorry I have not written sooner but the events of the last few days have been so horrific and have occupied one hundred percent of my time in helping to bring all the proper records up-to-date and care for those poor fellows that have perished or been wounded. At the present time there is no marching or fighting going on so time is beginning to drag and I am beginning to feel melancholy so it is wonderful hearing from my loved ones at home and their continued good health and happiness. This part of Maryland appears more like portions of our state than any parts I have been in yet, the farm houses and buildings are good and resemble ours very much. The land is good, the farming done well and everything looks thrifty and indicates industrious people. The timber is principally oak and hickory. The woods in which we are camped, the camp name being "Camp in the Oakwood's" which is certainly an appropriate name. The woods are very fine, really magnificent large stately oaks with a few hickory and small trees. Even with all this it is still open enough to drive a four-horse team anywhere through it.

I understand from Martha's letter that you have heard of Josiah's passing along with a number of the others from our fair village. The fighting was fierce for a couple of days and took a heavy toil on both our army and that of the Rebels. Not much was frankly gained by either side, as I believe our leadership was too hesitant to follow up on any advantage. Therefore I would call this battle a stalemate which under the circumstances of those that have fallen on either side it has been such a waste, gaining no advantage, and certainly will not in my opinion do anything to end this conflict sooner than later. I do believe as does Colonel Draime that if our command had taken full advantage of our total manpower and attacked Lee's army as it was regrouping and retreating we might well have put an end to this lunacy.

Old Doc sends his regards and has been a miracle worker in helping ease the suffering of so many of the fine lads that are under his care. He even had to order more of his fine therapy as he was running short. I am sure you remember his wonder cure from his days of doctoring in our fair village. He has currently gone over to the Rebels' lines under a flag of truce to request records of those fellows who fell prisoners during the recent clash. The last I talked to him he was planning on taking John with him as he felt John's fine nature would lend itself to negotiations with the other side. Since they have as yet not returned I cannot report further on their condition but I am sure they are just fine. As soon as I get more information I will send it along immediately.

Do not I beseech you unnecessarily worry about your husband and son's fate as the good Lord has watched over us so far and I believe as firmly as ever he will continue to watch over us in the weeks and months to come. Give little Joseph a hug for me and sleep well and dream well of your loving husband, father and brother.

Deep love to all,
Joseph"

I was concerned about my evasive comments in the letter about the whereabouts of John but until I am informed for sure I will not unduly worry Julia and the family. I hope she would understand and if Old Doc has any luck and returns unscathed then I should know soon enough. I dare not think anything but, "and now there are three" as I am afraid I might somehow influence the situation as far as John is concerned. With Henry's passing and

Josiah's untimely death our numbers are rapidly sinking as they are with the entire regiment. What started out to be a great adventure to many of these brave lads has now become nightmarish and to many the untimely end of their days.

I dared not tell them that the brave men of the 33rd now number less than 600 when all the dead and wounded that will not see any further service are tallied up. We started a little over a year ago with a complement of 1000 men and are down to less than 600 at present.

Here on the 30th of the month I had expected at least one letter from home after the recent letter I had sent. I am again deeply disappointed however as we still have not received any letters from home even though we have been camped in the same spot without any activity now for over a week. I have checked and been told by division headquarters that they had sent a man to fetch the mail up to us and yet we have not received any yet. Frankly I can scarcely realize I am in the Untied States, as our government does not even seem to be able to deliver the mail in a timely fashion. How can they run a war, if what is happening could actually be classified as managing a war, when they can't even have the mail trains run on time. Many of the survivors are beside themselves, as they know their loved ones at home are trying desperately to communicate with them as they are with those at home to little avail.

Each regiment has dispatched an officer to Washington to bring up any new recruits and stragglers and any that have healed enough to rejoin the front lines. Heaven knows we can use all the help we can muster under the circumstances. I fear what might happen if we are engaged in another major battle with Johnny Reb under the thin ranks we now have and with more rampant diseases we may well have even fewer shortly.

Courtesy of the Library of Congress

It has been over a week since Old Doc took on his mission to try and find out the fate of John along with others from our division that are still on the unknown list. Many names of these stout lads have not shown up on the deceased list or wounded list and we are all anxious about them. I fear he may have met with fowl play possibly at the hands of some Rebels who have not and will not follow the rules of war. Rules of war, seems when I think of such an irrational statement as, rules of war, I wonder where again mankind is headed. It has been true that the Confederate soldiers have overwhelmingly been humane and have followed this convention for the most part so I am clinging to the hope that he remains all right and will return with some information. Both sides have generally respected the symbol of those moving under a white flag and I pray that happened in this case.

I mounted Blackjack and rode up to the hospital to see if anyone there had any news of his whereabouts and low and behold as I entered there was Old Doc and one of the orderlies said he had just returned a short time ago. He looked up and saw me enter with a sign of both apprehension and relief on his face. I had difficult reading anything into his expression and could not wait to engage him in conversation as to what he found out if anything. He took me by the arm and walked me into a private part of the hospital where we could be alone and I was terrified of what he was going to tell me. He could sense my trepidation and immediately told me that the information that he had obtained showed that John had been taken prisoner and was, as far as the officer who was assigned to assist him from the Rebel Army said, unharmed. This officer even went so far as to tell him that he would personally send a directive to the administrator of the prison of war camp where he will be incarcerated in to watch over his well being. I almost fainted and Old Doc had to steady me when he told me all this and I thought for a minute it was the best news I could hope for, as I feared he had been killed and buried by the Confederate Army after The Battle of Antietam. My greatest fears having been calmed I hugged Doc and I am sure he well realized why I was so grateful. He went on to tell me he had not seen John but took the word of one Captain Tyler who he was assigned to that he was all right. He said Captain Tyler had been a perfect southern gentleman, most helpful and understanding and seemed to somehow sense the apprehension in the officer who was the father of this prisoner of war. I thought for a minute this might have been the same Captain Tyler that I exchanged notes with at the watering hole but then I realized there may well be many Confederate Soldiers named Tyler as that is a common southern name. I cannot believe it was the same Captain Tyler but the Lord works in mysterious ways and maybe it was. Old Doc went on to say he was prolonged in relaying the information since he had volunteered to help out in the Confederate Hospital where he was taken by the good captain and told that they were hugely understaffed to help those dead and dying Rebel soldiers. Doc said he was not surprised that the blood was the same color flowing from the Southern Soldiers as it is flowing from the Northern Soldiers. His efforts to ease the pain and suffering of fellow human beings is praiseworthy in my eyes and that shall remain our secret as some over zealous officer might see it differently.

I dare not say, "and now there are two" as I now know that John is alive and even though he will be facing many dangers of disease in the Confederate Prison he will at least not be facing flying bullets and shells. I pray to the Lord for his survival and release in what I continue to hope will be a short time until this madness ends. I must now write Julia and tell her what I have found out and hopefully I can ease her concerns, as I am sure she may be extremely apprehensive ever since my last letter. Again I plan on being as nonchalant as I can under the circumstances so as not to convey to her and the children my fears and anxieties. I decided I would write directly to Sara and mention it in that letter so it may ease the fretfulness of the moment.

"Dear Sara and family:

It is now the fifth of October and we are still camped near Bakersville in Maryland. Everything is quiet and has been for some time since the great battle of Antietam. It has been some time since I have heard from you and you have been unusually quiet of late. Well, I trust you have been a good girl and have been studious at school and have had most of your time usefully occupied. Since I had not received any letter from you lately I concluded that perhaps you were making a diligent effort to improve your writing skills and perhaps you intended an agreeable surprise for me soon in a well-written letter. I hope and trust that you will strictly obey every order and direction and follow every word of advice and council imparted to you by your excellent teacher, Miss Hanse, to whom I would appreciate your giving my highest regards and say to her that I am happy to know she yet remains a teacher at her old post and that you are now under her guidance.

In a letter I received from you some time ago when I believe we were in Alexandra you asked me about taking lessons on the piano. I am sorry I had not addressed the issue sooner but will take this opportunity to do so now. I trust in free pardon from a loving daughter for neglecting to address the issue before now. My dear Sara I can assure you, as I often have before, that I am not only willing but very desirous of doing anything and all that I can consistently with what means I have had or will have for the benefit, improvement, and happiness of our dear children. My only concern would be that you not neglect your other studies and duties to solely concentrate on the music. I have always felt you have natural abilities to do multiple tasks and so I see no reason why you should not pursue this dream of yours. Upon the condition of your being a good girl, obedient in all things to mother and your teacher, studious and attentive in school then I give my consent and authorize mother to make such arrangements. I will most willingly and cheerfully pay if I can but hear favorable reports.

We have remained in this campsite for over two weeks now and the inactivity is making time drag, it is so tedious doing nothing. We have not had rain in some time and I think we will need some as unpleasant as it is to those of us living in tents before the river rises and we can be moved.

That is about all I can think of to transmit for now. With a strong continuous desire for your improvement in your studies, and general cultivation, and your comfort, health and happiness I remain your loving father.

I am affectionately yours,
Father

PS: Please let mother and the entire family know of the good news I have just received from Old Doc. As I recently mentioned to your mother in my letter Old Doc took John with him under a flag of truce to the Confederate side to receive records of those soldiers that had been either killed, wounded or captured by the Rebels. Both sides in this war have respected the flag of truce and he has returned. Old Doc told me he was assigned to a Captain Tyler; mother may well remember my mentioning him before in correspondence. Old Doc told me he could not bear to think of mother and the family both possibly losing a father and a brother particularly after the horrendous fighting at Antietam so he arranged that John, much to his anguish, be held prisoner by the Rebels in the understanding that he will be well treated. This way he will no longer be in harms way for the remainder of this conflict however long it lasts. He said John was very crestfallen about leaving his fellow soldiers and comrades in arms but as it turned out he was not given a choice and I thank God that Old Doc in his infinite wisdom was able to arrange this. Gather the family circle and say a prayer for John's continued good health and safety and also for my health and safety. I will let you, mother and the family know as I may hear more about John's whereabouts in the near future but believe as I do that he will soon be released as this madness ends and again be home to join the family circle and the love and devotion of all the family.

Father"

I am deeply concerned as to the approach I took in telling the family of John's being taken prisoner and at some point in the near future I will try to clear up the entire incident. I wanted to break the news to them as gently as possible and I thought the explanation I offered was best for the time being. I sincerely hope that Julia and the family do not in our fair village say evil of Old Doc as he above all others deserves only the highest honors. I know that he would accept and well understand the rational in my explanation and not think ill of me for presenting it in this fashion. It would be difficult for anyone who has not experienced this living torture to understand my contentment at knowing that John will no longer be in the sights of some Rebel soldier's musket or some artillery shell. Even in my most disconcerting nightmares in my lifetime nothing comes close to describe the events of the past weeks. God help us all or mankind I believe is doomed to be a great experiment of the Lord's that failed miserably.

I heard from one of the men who had received a newspaper from home that the paper was quoted as saying that General Smith's Vermont and Maine troops retook and held possession of a portion of the field from which our troops had just been driven at Antietam. The fact is and it is especially important to me for our strong departed brothers in arms to set the record straight and I intend to write to the newspaper a true accounting of what happened. The true story is that our brigade, the 3rd was the only troop of Smith's Division actually engaged and we were the troops that recovered and held this position for 26 hours. A brigade from Conch's Division and this brigade one knows is composed of the 20, 33, 49 & 77 New York Regiment and the Seventh Maine relieved us the next day at noon. With all their casualties they only numbered about 200 but they all fought bravely and should be given the credit for their stand. I had 332 stout lads with me in the 33rd and I had a number killed and 41 wounded which is about one out of every seven men; a frightening death and wounded toll.

After we took the position there the troops laid for 26 hours and not a man was allowed to leave except to bring water and not even that until nightfall. No one was allowed to make coffee or anything of the kind. We experienced light artillery fire for most of this time. The enemy shells burst over and about us and a continual shower of grape and canister rained upon us. Fully half of the loss in the 33rd was from the artillery and the remainder from our first encounter with the Rebels. In the evening I took with me my officers detailed for that purpose to establish a line of sentinels in front of the regiment. The distance between the Rebel Infantry and us was about 250 to 300 yards. I advanced my sentinels to within about 100 yards of them. It was a ghastly place to position anyone on duty since they were directly amongst the dead and the dying and the groans of the men was something that will never leave anyone as long as they may live, if in fact any of us live beyond this lunacy. My own wounded I had made sure were all attended to but there were those of this fight still there in the morning and from where we were to the enemy lines there was continuous wailing and moaning. We could at that point do little for them except to give them what water we had to try and ease their pain and suffering. Both our men and those of the Confederate Army were lying there and as we listened to this living hell on earth I thought to myself that those that had been outright killed were in many cases the lucky ones that day. Later that day I returned to the headquarters of the regiment and the most difficult part of that trip was being careful not to tread on the dead. As I have thought before and repeatedly think, if the Lord's judgment is that I am to be condemned to hell for eternity for my taking others' lives in this conflict then I fully expect it will be no worse than that which I am observing currently both in sound and sight. If I were an artist and wanted to paint my impression of everlasting torment then I would set up my easel on the far hillside and paint the picture I now see in front of me. What would be a fitting title for my painting, "MAN'S INHUMANITY TO MAN?"

Early the next day the prisoners were set to work burying the dead and it was a gruesome task, so many disfigured bodies of so many fine men and boys. As I mentioned before in my humble opinion we should have been permitted to advance on the Rebels and it would have been a most complete and final crushing of them. Everyone I talked to, soldier or officer thought the same thing and to a man we felt we would have whipped them so they would have been satisfied I think for a good while to come. I went on a little too long as I usually do in expressing myself but I wanted to convey to the newspaper the total and horrible truth of this encounter with Johnny Reb.

We have now been ordered to move to Hagerstown here on the 11th of Oct. The men have been ordered to strike tents and it is particularly tough on the new recruits that are still with us as it has started to rain and those of us that have seen months of this conflict, miserable weather and all the other obstacles thrown in our paths take it in stride but the new recruits are finding it is a lot more difficult than lying under a solid roof at night and only listening to the rain playing a tune than to actually have to march and sleep in it. Hopefully and if history is any guide they will soon be hardened to it.

Julia had told me some time ago that she had sent me a box containing some much needed supplies, especially since our government is still failing to pay us for the past several months. I heard from the quartermaster that a number of boxes have been stolen and they are going to try and recover them. It is hard for me to imagine the low life's that would steal supplies from soldiers that are fighting and dying for their country but as I have often thought mankind is flawed and capable of any wickedness. The weather is not only wet but it is also rapidly growing colder with a brisk wind from the North. Many of the men have not even been issued tents and only have their coats to try and keep themselves warm and with those wet from the rain it is becoming a nightmarish night. Fortunately I do have a tent to pitch, which again is being shared by Old Doc and myself. I sometimes feel guilty that I am sleeping in a tent on a makeshift bed of straw while some of the men are sleeping, if you can call it that, out in the open with rain and cold moving into their bones with every passing hour. I even have written Julia to buy some of Allen's make of red flannel and make me another pair of drawers to help keep me warm and healthy. It has been some time since I have received a letter from home and I worry about Julia and the family's reaction when they read my explanation of John's fate. I will write her again as soon as there is light to see to write by and again try to smooth over the state of affairs to hopefully ease her apprehension.

"Dear Julia and Family

It is now the 15th of October and we are camped near Hagerstown, Maryland. I recently was ordered to take my regiment and the 77th and go to the Cave Town Turnpike Bridge which crosses the Antietam Creek which is about two miles North East of our camp. I ordered the men to guard and watch that point to intercept any portion of the Rebel Cavalry that visited Chambersburg that might be driven in that direction. We were assisted by two pieces of artillery and spent several days in that location without seeing neither hide nor hair of the enemy fortunately. I have now returned to camp and low and behold the box, which you shipped out by express three months ago, had finally arrived, another wonderful example of the efficiency of our government. As usual they cannot even keep the trains running on time as I have often said. I opened it immediately and looked at the wonderful cake you had made and shipped and could only imagine how it looked and smelled when it was sent. I will not even try and describe to you how it looks and smells after three months. There was also something of a round hard mass of blue mold with a paper around it and there was another item with yellow spots on it which I believe was once lemons but now is only God knows what. I conclude that you had as you told me sometime ago also sent some donuts but they were rotten to the core. The bottled goods seemed to be preserved and the butter was melted and separated and rather strong but it has worked OK for cooking. The tobacco and plugs, which were sent on by Mr. Walton, I also appreciate and they of course were not spoiled and I will enjoy them immensely. I shall think of him many, many times as from day to day I press out and eject the essence of the "weed."

Julia I cannot express how grateful I am for these items and knowing that you and the children packed them with your loving hands. It is unconscionable to understand why, when we in the field so cherish letters or gifts from home, our government cannot deliver them in a timely fashion. I have not opened the honey or preserves as Lieutenant Carter has lately been sharing the mess with Old Doc and he had a can of nice peaches and a small can of excellent honey that he opened last night and shared with us. We all look forward to sharing those items you and the neighbors sent which are not spoiled. I have not yet drawn the corks from the catsup bottles so I cannot report yet how that survived over the past months.

I have nothing new to report concerning John's well-being but I am completely confident he is being well-taken care of and especially since Captain Tyler told Doc he would personally take an interest in him. I pray daily to thank the Lord that John is no longer in harms way as so many of these fine lads have fallen forever or have wounds, either or mind or body, that will never let them lead a normal life.

We had a good laugh the other day when Matthew Qunne stopped by. You probably remember Matthew from our fair village, as he was quite a character both in looks and speech. The parts of the young America coffee pot were on the trunk and he eyed them for a moment and said to us, "Colonel what in the devil is them things for there?" I told him it was a coffee pot and he replied. "A coffee pot, upon my soul a pretty looking lot of traps for a coffee pot, I'd not give my old black one for a dozen of them even if it has no civin." None of us knew what he meant by civin, but we were afraid to ask. He went on to say, "What good is that thing in camp or on a march, the first time a mule lays down or runs again or trots it's all gone to the devil for sure." He then examines the baker and says, "Who the devil ever invented that kind of a stove, where in the devil do you put the fire?" I replied that we did not put any fire in it. "Well how in the devil is ye going to cook wid it then?" I explained the process of baking and roasting in it and that they were years ago used successfully when he says; "I's traveled a good bit in this world and never the likes of that did I see before, never such a stove as that. What does ye expect to do with all these things, I'd wash them up and sell them tomorrow." That ended and then he finished up by saying, "Good luck to ye all."

I thought you might enjoy his comments since we know him so well and his conversation is usually quite colorful. It was a light moment in an otherwise dreary existence. I have had a couple of the men fix me up with a makeshift bed with some more straw on it and I think I will rest soundly tonight. We managed to buy some items for our mess, vegetables, good bread, and chickens; we bought the chickens for 20 cents each. We also bought some eggs and poor butter. We are able to buy more here than at our last camp as it is good farming country and more is available.

My candle is about used up so I must stop writing for now. A very pleasant night to you all and to John wherever he may be. Sleep well and have pleasurable dreams.

Your loving husband and father,

Joseph"

I was finally getting much needed rest along with all the men when I was awakened from a comfortable sleep with notice to get the regiment in readiness to move at once here on the 22nd of October. Within a half hour we were assembled and on our way to Hagerstown and thence on to Clear Springs, Maryland, which is a 14-mile march. We arrived at this location around eight and took up positions. Davis's group had been stationed here and has been ordered up the river to Hancock and our brigade is temporarily assigned to duty here to replace his group. We are nearly three miles North of the river and one of the regiments goes each day to perform picket duty at the fords of the river and culverts under the canal along the river for nearly three miles, one company at each point. I also assigned two companies at the points I thought most vulnerable. I have been out with the regiment for about 20 hours and trying my best to keep the men's moral up and keep them on their toes. We continue to be shorthanded as far as officers are concerned so it means those of us that are still well and able to perform our duties are stretched very thin. It was the upper ford that we are now guarding that Steward's Calvary crossed.

After I was able to assign one of the officers to take charge I headed back to camp upon old faithful Blackjack and I managed to get a few hours of much desired sleep. All of the men are exhausted and I am sure more than one of those stout fellows out on the picket lines may be keeping guard with one eye closed and I for one cannot hold it against them knowing what we have all been through. When I awoke this morning I was delighted as a young soldier, no more than a boy, delivered three letters and one box from home for me. These immensely lifted my spirits and my hands nearly trembled as I opened each of them. In the first one was a painting of Julia that had been done by our dear neighbor Barbara and it reassured me that time and worry over the fate of her husband and son had not taken a toll on her incredible appearance. I have heard some of the men say that have been furloughed that they have been shocked at the changes in their wives even over the months that we have been engaged with the enemy. It seems that the long absence and the precarious business we are occupied in has brought about premature old age. What a toll this conflict is taking on us all, those at home and in the field. I will carry the likeness in my coat wherever I go over the next weeks and months and when melancholy finds me I shall take it out and hold it close.

The second letter was from Martha and she had added a geranium and its leaves to the letter, which gave off a stunning odor when I opened it. The little flower was as fresh as when she packed it in the envelope with her loving hands. I sat here a minute or two and looked at that beautiful little flower and wondered how God in his infinite wisdom could have created such beauty and with the other hand tolerate such evil as we are now experiencing.

The third letter was from little Joseph, who had gathered Julia said, some items from the neighbors to send and it included some excellent honey and some ketchup. As we have bought a few fat hens from the locals we plan on feasting on them tonight. It will feel great to be able to sit down with Old Doc and any of the other officers that choose to join us and have a fine meal of chicken with ketchup and some fine honey on the side especially as a cold wind is blowing in from the North, I will rotate the men on picket duty several hours early as they have no shelter to protect them from the wind and the conditions make it horrendous out there. At least here even those that do not have tents as yet will be able to craft some makeshift shelters.

The adjutant has been unwell and forced to resign along with Captain Bigilow who has also been extremely ill both in mind and body. What we have been through and lived through over the past weeks has been more than enough to permanently damage not only the fiber of oneself but the minds of many of the men. These resignations will leave us even more shorthanded but I am still doing my best to get a furlough and be able to visit my dear family at home.

I have written the authorities at home and told them to be on the lookout for one William Danville as I hear from some of the men that he is boating on the canal. He was one of a few that deserted shortly before the last great battle and I trust he will be most severely dealt with when apprehended. It is even more inconceivable in my mind to think of these few unscrupulous characters who have chosen to cut and run while so many brave lads are daily laying down their lives for the cause either on the field of battle or in the hospitals. If I were to serve as judge and jury for the likes of him and a few others the gallows would be very busy indeed.

CHAPTER EIGHTEEN

A Change of Command

Here at the end of October I am hearing rumors that General McClellan may be on his way out. I remember thinking when he reviewed the troops months ago that he was cut from solid steel, would make a fine commander and bring this conflict to a rapid conclusion. As I have often thought since however and many of the other officers have shared with me he often seems to be somewhat indecisive. Whether it is he or his staff that is advising him I will never know but frankly I think we need a hard drinking, cigar smoking, fowl mouthed son of a bitch in command to finally take this fight to General Robert E. Lee and get it over with.

It has now turned very cold again, almost cold enough to freeze our water buckets. We are experiencing a cold rainstorm, which is making it even more insufferable. Many of the men are and will suffer a great deal for want of sufficient clothing, as we have not yet been able to get a full supply of winter coats or drawers. Many of their shoes are poor and most have no overcoats and only a little shade tent to shelter them from the storms. I have done everything up to threatening to shoot the quartermaster myself but the government in their own inefficient way doesn't seem to be able to provide the necessary clothing to those that are sacrificing all any more than being able to pay them so they can send a little money home to their desperate families. If I was not brought up by parents of solid oak I would have thought more than once of saying, "the hell with this" and go boating on the canal myself. I wonder how Johnny Reb is making out with his government supplying their needs; surely it can't be any worse than what we are seeing. Most of the officers also have no tents as we did not expect to be in this location this long and therefore they have not yet been brought up. I have asked several of the officers to share Old Doc's and my tent. We will be crowded but I know they would do the same for me if our positions were reversed. I continue to be wrapped up in as many blankets as I can find as this cold gets right into my bones and once there it is almost impossible to get it out. If I live to be an old, old man I do not believe I will ever be warm again. Again I am hoping to be granted a furlough but I am waiting for our overdue pay before I again apply so I will have some funds to take with me to give to Julia. Possible if we do have a change in command it might make it somewhat easier for me since I sometimes think the good general may well be a mind reader and not take kindly to my inner most thoughts of his failure to follow up on recent advantages we had gained against the enemy. Only time will tell, I sincerely am praying for a leader that will make a difference in bringing this clash to a rapid termination. This is far from being a game and it needs to be concluded immediately or sooner as anyone who has seen the horror of the battlefield will agree with.

Here on Nov. fifth we have been on the march for two days and halted near Harpers Ferry. We crossed the river and are now about 36 miles South of the Potomac. It has been a hard march as the weather is still cold and rainy. The Rebels are continuing to return to the South and we are being held as part of the Reserve Corp. I have had my tent set up and Doc and I have enjoyed a fine meal of sweet potatoes that Julia told me were packed by little Joseph and also some pies, cakes, ham, chicken and some fine grapes. I think I may be fleshing up somewhat with all this easy living? We also had a dish of fried peaches which one of our fine neighbors had sent along and enjoyed them enormously. If it weren't for all these thoughtful items from home we would all be living on grass and roots and our existence would be even more precarious than it already is.

We have arrived finally at this spot on the Manassas Gap Railroad, which is about half way from Manassas Junction and Strassbury Front Royal. Our Sutler that follows the army and sells us food, liquor and many other needs has left for Alexandra to refill his supplies. It has been snowing for about two days and it is about as cold as it was at any time last winter at Camp Griffin. I would have thought our being in the South we would be seeing some more moderate weather but alas unfortunately it is not to be. It is so cold that I opened the bottle of whiskey that Mrs. Cuyler had sent in the last box and Old Doc and I had a merry time of it trying to keep warm. We have a few bottles of whiskey stashed away but in this man's army it is not wise to open any more than one at a time, as it seems to disappear rather rapidly.

We have been notified that General Burnside has been appointed by President Lincoln to replace General McClellan. I know little of his abilities but from what I hear he may not be the answer we are all praying for to end this madness. I will of course reserve judgment and hope for the best. General Burnside was present with his corps at the battle of Antietam and was criticized for not moving his men more aggressively against a much smaller Confederate force. Whether such criticism was warranted I was never fully informed on or possibly General McClellan was trying to cover his own hesitation and using Burnside as a scapegoat. Whichever the true answer is will never be completely known but one thing I have heard and firmly believe is that General McClellan's staff officers were and are very loyal to him and I fear for the lack of support General Burnside will receive from them now that General McClellan has been replaced by the President. I don't know much about the new general but from what little I have heard I don't think he is the hard drinking, cigar smoking, and fowl mouthed son-of-a-bitch that this army needs at this point. I will of course follow his orders as issued immediately and do all I can to support him, only time will tell. I also heard General Burnside did not want the responsibility of overall command but that the president insisted on it. My advice to the president is to stop experimenting and hoping to find the proper leader and hire the hard drinking, cigar smoking, fowl mouthed, son-of-a-bitch that I recommend, only time will tell. I decided to write Julia and the family and mention my feelings to them about the change in command. They will most likely be especially disappointed that I was not named the commander-in-chief since I always seem to have all the answers but it was not to be. I might fit the drinking criteria, although not hard drinking; I certainly fit the cigar smoking, along with my pipe. Some might say I am a son-of-a-bitch at times but none would say I am fouled mouth so I guess I don't qualify.

"Dear Julia and children:

It is now the 13th of November and it is cold and wet. I have heard nothing more about John, which I consider the best of news under the circumstances, as I am sure we will hear of any prisoners that are ill or sick during their incarceration. I have the pictures of all of you in front of me as I write this and it brightens my day considerably. I am sending along a small box containing some relics of the Battle of Antietam and a few shell casings that I picked up at McCoy's Ferry that the 33rd guarded for about a week. That was the place where the Rebel Cavalry, before we arrived there, had crossed at the time of their raid to Chambersburg.

We have not been involved in any recent fighting, thank the Lord, and that suits me just fine. You may have read in the papers that General Burnside has replaced General McClellan. I understand that some of those in New York made considerable blowing about it and misrepresented the feelings of the army. There is one thing that is true, that General McClellan has had no occasion to complain nor has any other general in the Maryland campaign any cause to complain of their subordinate officers or men. The troops marched early or late and bravely over and through mountain passes and over fields, met, fought and whipped the Rebels every time when ordered on. The officers and men generally have confidence in their commanders, but many have been tired of what appears to them to be unnecessary delays.

I know that you continue to be upset that I have not been able to receive a furlough but rest assured I am continuing to try. Possibly with this change of command my chances will improve. Since we have been on the march and crossed the Potomac and on into Virginia this has been an active campaign and with a shortage of officers I could not be relieved at this time. Until I can receive such leave continue to hope and trust the good Lord Almighty will continue to watch over John and myself. He has to date heretofore in this war shielded and protected us and with your continue prayers I am confident he will continue to do so.

We have just used up the last of the dried apples you sent on a while ago and we have had some of the other fruit and relishes sent by you and the neighbors, bless all your souls. We had some roast beef yesterday for breakfast, lunch and supper that we had bought locally and used some of your delicious ketchup on it. The cup of jelly that your loving hands made and little Joseph put in the box I have not yet opened but Old Doc and I are greatly anticipating opening it. I have them all safe in my trunk and some in my haversack for use when we march.

I am sending this along via the Chaplin who is headed home for a short visit due to family illness and he has told all the troops that he will deliver any letters to our fair village when he arrives. We can all save a little on postage by his generosity. I cannot think of any more news at this time. I hope and pray this letter reaches all of you in fine health and happiness and pray that it will remain so.

More love than the shining of all the stars in the sky,
Joseph."

We are still camped here for the last four days and at present I am not hearing of any plans to deploy us for the time being. With the change of command at the top I am sure there will be a re-evaluation of our troop levels, strengths and also that of the Rebels. I sincerely hope that this hesitation does not go on too long as I have said many of us felt with the old command many advantages were not followed up on and we are eager for things to change towards a final ending so we all may get on with our lives, both Northern and Southern Soldier.

We have managed to kill a wild turkey and also we bought some chickens from our Sutler so we are managing to eat well. Old Doc and I have set up the old baker before the fire this night and we are baking biscuits, roasting beef, cooking the chickens and the turkey and we also have stewed tomatoes and peaches sent from home. We even added some sweet corn and with such a feast we invited Colonel Draime and several of the other officers to dine with us this evening. It helps to pass the time and we can all share our frustration with the lack of progress. It seems that this war to the high command is like a chess game with check and counter check ongoing without any final follow up or resolution to the match. I would if I had the opportunity be happy to tell them that this is no chess game but a matter of life and death and they are occurring mostly on the line not at the headquarters so please as one of the officers said at supper, "move or get out of the way and let someone who can get the job done be put in charge." War is not an experiment where you appoint different commanders in the hope that eventually you may find one that can get the job done. Leadership is appointing the RIGHT man to get the job done.

There I have gotten that off my chest as well as all the other officers having a chance to vent. Old Doc only sat there and in his wisdom I am sure he was thinking something like this. "Fools, don't you realize this is mankind's destiny to fight never ended conflicts until someday we all destroy ourselves?" Even though the rest of us argue the merits of certain leaders and commanders Old Doc has the answers although any sane man does not want to hear them and dwell on them as to the dismal and grave future of the Lord's great investment in mankind. I fear Old Doc will be correct, as I have said before there is a flaw in all humanity that may well lead us all down the road to annihilation at some point in the future. I want to believe in the good of all men and for a bright future for our children and their children but in my worst nightmares I find myself agreeing with Old Doc. Maybe if all the leaders, present and in the future, were as wise as he is we could avoid obliteration but unfortunately wisdom does not seem to follow politics and those that are chosen to lead. I have to get off this subject or I won't sleep for a week as I will wake up in a cold sweat but it is also good to be able to vent with your fellow officers and let it all hang out, so to speak, for even for a short time.

It is now the end of November and we have been here for 12 days. The teams are bringing up provisions from the mouth of the creek and we cannot move forward until we get up to this point at least eight days of rations. That is a lot of ammunition, bread and all the other necessities for such a large gathering of men and it takes considerable time and effort to fulfill it. The provisions necessary for this immense army is as much as our fair village would require for at least 15 months to take care of all its people, excluding the ammunition, I pray. It would also take all the grain and hay for the horses than all the horses in our village would require for at least three years. There is a railroad that runs from

Aquia Landing to Fredericksburg and the withdrawing Rebels destroyed it but our men have it almost repaired so we will be able to move supplies via that means. It is also difficult for the men that are trying to move the materials, as it has turned very cold and ice forms in our buckets each night that measures a quarter to a half-inch thick.

Today I went over to the regional headquarters and spoke to General Vinton about the possibility of my getting a leave shortly so I can finally visit my loved ones. This separation, which has now gone on for over 17 months, is taking a terrible toll on me during the nighttime hours when I should be sleeping. The conditions that we are forced to live under and the visions of the dead and dying during and after our recent battles is more than enough to send any sane man into insanity. Home and the love of one's family are like a strong medicine that is prescribed to try and heal a ravaged brain. When I arrived, the general was in a passionate discussion with several of the other officers. He was polite and asked me to join them. He told me that the Army of the Potomac had recently executed two Confederate prisoners who were found guilty of recruiting men within the lines of the Union forces. He said that the South had taken prisoners two combatants, Captain Flinn and Captain Sawyer and they were threatening to execute them in retaliation of the executions of their officers, Corbin and McGraw. This was another example of mankind's callousness to his fellow man in the game of catch up, where one side says or does one thing and then the other side must retaliate or they think they will be perceived as weak. Several of the officers were arguing very openly that such brutality adds nothing to the cause of either side especially when it is in retaliation of a deplorable act by one side or the other. The general was taking the other view that it was necessary in order to keep a proper balance in this conflict but I failed to see his reasoning. It is one thing to engage in these endless and mortifying battles and see men permanently marred for life or worse yet outright killed and it is another thing to hang combatants when captured. I immediately thought of John but also was relieved to hear one of the officers say that only those of the rank of Captain or higher were involved in this cat and mouse game if I can take the liberty of calling it such. It was mentioned that they would not be surprised if headquarters, or directly from Washington, orders come down to take into custody two officers who are either presently held as prisoners of war or capture two officers who may well be hung in retaliation if the South does indeed put to death Flinn and Sawyer. I pray I do not become involved in such a tangled web, it is enough to be sent into battle and have those that you are trying to slaughter also trying to slay you and quite another thing to take the life of unarmed soldiers. I want no part of it.

After the discussion was over and I admired the general not so much for his position but for the fact that he allowed subordinates to openly express their points of analysis and seemed not to hold any animosity towards any of them. It takes an intelligent and courageous man to be able to feel comfortable disagreeing with others and not holding their views against them if they differ from yours. The general agreed with the fact that I was long overdue for a furlough but said at present we were so short of officers he could not afford to let me leave. He also said he had heard first-rate reports about my leadership whether it be in battle or during those periods between battles. This was reassuring of him to say however it did not get me any closer to being with my beloved Julia and family. He did however promise me that he would not forget my request and as soon as possible he would find some manner of releasing me from duties for even a short visit home. I also spoke briefly to him about the fact that those of us in the field had not been paid for some time and many of the men were asking and saying that they desperately needed to have some money to send home to their struggling families. I felt I had asked enough of him and he agreed to look into that also. I left him with the feeling that here was an honest man who was also a gentleman whose word you could rely on. I thanked him for his courtesy and his time and rode off on Blackjack back to camp.

We are now camped near Belle Plain, Virginia and it is cold and wretched. In the army, no matter what army, it is usually hurry up and wait and we have been doing a lot of that lately. We have had no general engagement since the battle of Antietam and time is dragging, men are falling sick, conditions are deplorable and yet we wait, wait, wait. I have to ask myself as do many of the men and officers what the hell are we waiting for. We are not growing stronger in these conditions with many more succumbing to illness and it is such a waste to not do what we came here to do. It is now Dec. of 1862; we have been in this army, which was to save the Union and end slavery for 19 months and this conflict is no closer to a resolution than it was when all these brave men and I volunteered to serve. I still have five more months to go on my enlistment with the government and at the present time I have, at least for now, decided two years of this living torment will have been more than enough. As I have said over and over again, "IT IS TIME TO END IT." I think I will feel better if I put pen to paper and write Julia and the family as it always makes me feel closer to them like looking at the stars in the heavens at night and imagining that they are looking at the same beautiful stars that God created.

"Dear Julia, Martha, Sara and Little Joseph,

Winter is certainly upon us here in the South and I am sure it is upon you all in upstate New York. I trust you have put up plenty of firewood to keep you all comfortable and as you mentioned in your last letter old man Higgins cut and split about 10 cord for you so that should hold you for some time. If you need more don't hesitate to ask him even though we have not been paid in a while I will send funds as soon as I can. If you have to ask him to give us some time to pay I am sure he will agree to it, as he knows we are good for it.

I was so pleased to hear of the progress of Martha and Sara and their fine letters recently. It is restful for me to know that you are all getting along famously and it relieves my anxiety greatly to realize that you are thinking and praying as one that this will soon end and we can all get back to our normal lives, whatever that is after such an experience.

I did take an opportunity to speak to General Vinton about the possibility of a leave of absence and he regrettably said it was not possible at present with so few officers still on duty and so many being ill in the hospital. He did however say that he will not forget my request, that if anyone deserved time off it was I and he would try to find some way to allow me a furlough if even for a short time. I so look forward to seeing all of you that even if he only gave me a few days and I could spend at least an hour in yours and our children's arms I would take it. I miss you all so much, I miss our fair community and I also look forward to again someday enjoying the routine of a normal life.

All of us here are ready to move on as fast as possible, and anxious to have the matter of the campaign in Virginia brought to a speedy close or at least strike a decisive blow to the rebellion here. If Blackjack and I continue to survive the upcoming battles as we have in the past I may soon be able to get home and see that smart boy you say you have got up there in our fair village. Give little Joseph a hug and kiss for me.

You mentioned a couple of the officers from one of the other regiments have been home for some time and you wondered how come they could get leave and I couldn't. Frankly my dear they are what we refer to as absent without leave as their furloughs were up some time ago and they have failed to return. I believe some warrants have been issued for their arrest, however I also feel that if they returned voluntarily all would be forgiven since we are so short handed. Under those circumstances I certainly could not enjoy a visit home even as much as I want to be there. None of the officers of the 33rd have taken it upon themselves to do such a fool hearty thing. I am proud of the company I brought into our regiment, with but few individual exceptions they have performed their duty admirably and shown themselves to be brave soldiers and they all are a credit to our fair community and the wonderful folks who reside there. They are also an immense credit to this country for standing up for what is right, even though I often think the ends may not justify the means in this case, and may well have been solved over time without such carnage. We are all proud of our regiment; no man belonging to the 33rd is ashamed to have it known anywhere. We have introduced ourselves so many times to the Rebels that I think they are about as well acquainted with us as any regiment in the service. The 5th North Carolina, 8th and 9th Georgia are particularly familiar with our gallantry. The 5th North Carolina we certainly gave such a lively reception to at Williamsburg that they have not since attempted to renew their acquaintance with us. The 8th Georgia, which we first became acquainted with at Williamsburg along with the 9th Georgia, attempted to restore the relationship at Mechanicsville but they soon took to their heels. If you can believe it those two regiments again introduced themselves to us on the 28th of June, which involved a portion of our regiment on the picket line. Our boys saluted them with occasional volleys on the route to our camp and then our boys headed to their camp and they became so uncivil as not to allow a man of the 33rd to enter so our boys knocked over about 162 of them and sadly about 80 of those perished. We saw some of them again at Campton Gap but at Antietam we introduced ourselves to the South Carolina and Alabama regiments. These are true fighting men to be proud of and have shown it in battle time and again. They enlisted for the meager pay of $11 per month and many months they have never been paid and the two dollar enlisting fee which the government promised them has never been paid and yet they still will fight to the last man. We are ready to show books compared to any regiment in the service.

I have closed my eyes and seen you Julia warm in our old bed with that smart boy sleeping soundly beside you having dreams of riding his hobbyhorse. I trust yours, Martha's and Sara's dreams are also pleasant as mine will be tonight thinking about you all.

With much love to you all I am yours affectionately,

Joseph"

CHAPTER NINETEEN

Battle of Fredericksburg

Here it is the 15th of December already and we are marching back from a raging battle taking place at Fredericksburg along the Rappahannock River. We are all tired and care worn. I didn't think I would ever again face another bloodbath like Antietam but what we experienced over the last several days was just as grisly. The Confederate Army had taken up positions under General Longstreet in early November along the far side of the river. General Lee ordered that the troops were to occupy a range of hills behind the town reaching from the Rappahannock River to the marshy Massaponax Creek further to its right. General Jackson's men also arrived on the scene about a week after Longstreet's Corps and they were dispatched about 20 miles down river from Fredericksburg. The Confederate Army was therefore well entrenched along the river in the hopes of delaying or outright denying our forces from crossing over the river and continuing the fight further into Virginia. Since Lee's Army was not sure of where General Burnside would attempt to cross the river he felt he must protect as much of it as his forces would allow. We have been engaged in skirmishes for the last few days on the front lines to try and ascertain the enemy's weak points. It seems that General Burnside, as rumor has it, is having difficulty with his staff in formulating a plan of action. I have to ask myself have we gone from the hesitation and uncertainty of General McClellan to the hesitation and indecisiveness of our new general. I was in hopes that we would be ordered to proceed, cross the river in pontoon boats or by whatever means possible and take the fight to the enemy. General Burnside had ordered the engineers to begin to build the bridges in the vicinity of Fredericksburg on the 11th of the month only to have them driven back time after time for the next few days. The musket fire from the river front houses and the yards on the Rebel side effectively drove our men from the river many times with many casualties. We tried our best to protect the bridge builders but the enemy was well entrenched behind solid walls and other coverings and it was virtually unattainable. Regrettably there were a total of nine such attempts to complete the bridges over the river all-resulting in failure and heavy casualties. No commanders could have asked more from these brave men that attempted the unattainable under the circumstances than that of these courageous soldiers. I was at the time unsure of why the general had not first softened up the Rebel side with artillery but again he failed to ask me.

Courtesy of the Library of Congress

Courtesy of the Library of Congress

I have had a little rest if you can call it that, tossing and turning with the images of the dead and dying in my dreams. Finally this day the general and his staff have called upon the artillery chief, General Hunt, to move his big guns into position and ordered him to blast Fredericksburg into submission. General Hunt has opened up with over 150 big guns and the city is slowly disappearing. The devastation is mind boggling, we have reaped the whirlwind, and again if one ever wonders what it would be like to spend eternity in hell they need only to gaze upon the total destruction of this once fair city. I am sure General Burnside wanted to avoid such obliteration but sadly in war that is the way of things, kill or be killed. What insanity this is.

As I watched this constant bombardment of the guns vomiting forth their terrible projectiles into every street, house and corner of Fredericksburg I said a silent prayer for the brave Rebel soldiers as I had said a prayer for our boys as they repeatedly tried to finish the pontoon bridges. I was told when the onslaught was halted that over 8000 shot and shell were unloaded on this once fine city. I was again ordered to take my men to the river and assist the engineers in finishing the bridges. They ventured guardedly onto their unfinished bridges and were commencing to add to them for the 400 foot crossing when I was stunned to hear and see the muzzles flash again from those cobble-strewn streets and even more of our engineers, some mere boys, hardly old enough to be out of school fell into the river and their blood was forever mixed with this once serene river. The general's staff ordered the immediate withdrawal and everyone scrambled to the safety of the slight hills in the back. I wondered what our next orders would be and if the loss of so many fine men was worth the effort but the president is urging a full assault into Virginia in the hopes of laying siege to Richmond and ended this lunacy. I am fearful that until that time we shall see no end to this war.

Courtesy of the Library of Congress

General Burnside and his staff again went into their council of war and when they issued orders it was for volunteers to ferry themselves across in those clumsy pontoon boats that were supposed to form the foundation for the bridges. I offered to lead them but I was ordered to remain back as we had already lost a number of officers. Men of our regiment, some from Michigan and others from Massachusetts volunteered and those of us left on our side of the river did our best to cover the brave advance of these valiant men into the jaws of hell. I have never witnessed such bravery as I have amongst the men here and at Antietam. I have only to wonder what all this sacrifice and heroics would accomplish if it were directed to curing what ails mankind and finding answers to many of mankind's problems such as diseases and crippling illnesses. If it were only channeled in that direction rather than here on the field of battle with the express purpose of killing one's fellow man.

It was amazing to watch the street fighting that erupted as soon as some of our daring fellows made it safely across. It was, I would call it urban warfare, not seen before in this war where the two sides often advanced against each other over open fields. Once a number of our men landed and established a so-called beachhead on the far side of the Rappahannock the enemy snipers beat a hasty retreat to their main line of defense. Once the far side was secure the engineers set upon the task of completing the bridges and we all eventually crossed into what was left of Fredericksburg. What a terrible toll this battle has taken, I certainly cannot imagine the toll on both sides if the Army of the Potomac lays siege to Richmond and those brave Confederate soldiers decide to fight to the last man. It is beyond my comprehension that General Lee and his staff have not decided to ask for a meeting to try and resolve this without further loss of life on both sides rather than face such unspeakable fatalities. As I have said before however there is a flaw in mankind that sometimes lets destructive traits come forth rather than those of reason.

Old Doc is busy again and working his miracles as only he can do. Of all those wounded that are being cared for by the number of fine surgeons the lucky ones, if you can call them that, are being cared for by Old Doc. He will certainly not get any sleep to speak of for the next week or so and I hope he can survive the pressure he is now under. General Burnside has asked General Lee for a truce so that both sides can tend to their dead and wounded and Lee has agreed to it. One of the staff of General Burnside mentioned that it was the civilized thing to do to agree to the truce so that all those that need assistance can be helped and those that have taken their last breath can be laid to rest. As I sat in my tent awaiting orders to attend to the dead or the prisoners that have been taken I lit up my pipe for a brief time and thought to myself, a civilized gesture. We kill each other for several days and then we consent to a truce to take care of those mangled bodies of the brave men on both sides. I would think this is anything but civilized and if a truce can be agreed upon under these circumstances how come it can't be permanently decided upon? I just sat there and shook my head and thought to myself, "has this world gone mad?"

So much for my melancholy mood and my totally inadequate understanding of man's colossal shortcomings, it is far beyond this mortal soul to figure it all out. The final toll in this conflict which has been reported to me and this is only at this point an estimate is that our side has suffered over 12,500 men either killed, wounded or missing and presumably taken prisoner. Of the 12,500 almost 1300 have been killed, 9600 wounded and almost 1800 missing. Old Doc and his staff will have to as I said work their miracles and I am sure he will run out of his famous healing medicine before these days are over. Our 33rd, which started out 15 months ago with 1,000 men, now has less than 400 left in its ranks. What a terrible toll! I heard also from reliable sources that the Rebels suffered over 5,000 casualties, 600 plus killed and over 4,000 wounded with 600 plus being taken prisoner. I would not consider this a victory for the Army of the Potomac; in fact I would consider it as a massive defeat. Since it is the first major battle that General Burnside has overseen I wonder how long President Lincoln will leave him in that position, more experimentation in trying to find the leader who can finally put an end to this.

General Vinton has ordered that those of us remaining in the 33rd take charge of the 600 or so confederate prisoners. The prisoners outnumber my men since the battles and diseases have taken such a horrifying toll. I ordered that the officers were to be separated from the regular soldiers and was surprised to find we had captured almost 60 officers up to the rank of general. The general in question turned out to be none other that General William H. F. Lee, the son of the commander of the Rebel forces General Robert E. Lee. Our commander ordered that I send a detachment of men to accompany General W. H. F. Lee to Fort Monroe where he will be held in close confinement and I have been told he will be one of those hung if the South carries out their threat to hang Captain Sawyer and Captain Flinn. I do not envy his position at all since he is not only of the rank of general but also a son of the infamous leader of the Confederates, General Robert E. Lee. I will be interested in following this state of affairs as it progresses. Colonel Draime has decided that this prisoner requires special attention and he will take him personally with an armed escort to Fort Monroe.

The men I have chosen and the colonel has agreed upon are brave and loyal soldiers and can be entirely trusted. I was concerned that the general might not arrive at the fort alive, since emotions are running so high, so the men were specially selected for their loyalty. We had a number of volunteers from our regiment and others but by the look in the eyes of some of the men I don't think General Lee would have gotten very far. This way I am convinced he will arrive safely, what happens to him after that is up to the Fort Royal commander and of course the route that the South chooses to take with our two captains. Oh what a tangled web we have woven in this cat and mouse game. In addition to this aftermath of the Battle of Fredericksburg I was reviewing the prisoners and seeing to their well being as I have insisted that none of them be maltreated, as I would expect the Confederates would do the same for those of the Army of the Potomac that were taken prisoner. That is one of the reasons why I continue to have faith that John is well and will again rejoin us in our home in the not too distant future. As I rode Blackjack to evaluate the state of affairs under which we were temporarily housing the prisoners I thought I recognized a Rebel officer that I had seen before and sure enough it turned out to be Captain Tyler. I was relieved that he was still alive and he nodded slightly as I passed by, not wanting to acknowledge our previous association openly.

I finally here near Christmas have a little time to myself so I have decided to write Julia and the family and again reassured her of our continued safety. What a way to celebrate the birth of Christ but to kill and be killed by our fellow man. This is totally insane, as I have so often had occasion to mention.

"Dear Julia and children;

As the good Chaplin who was recently discharged and sent home told you I have again miraculously come through this recent battle at Fredericksburg unscathed thanks to the Lord's blessing. It grieves me not to be able to immediately send you a letter proving of my continued safety for many a day when we are in battle and was pleased that the Chaplin delivered the information. The mental suffering of my family and those families of other brave lads after they read in the papers that there loved ones have been in a major battle is beyond belief. An understanding anxiety hangs about my mind until I know that my family has received word of my continued safety. When I know that you have heard a great load that depressed my mind is lifted and passes away. As you have mentioned in your letters these battles are appalling to contemplate with the numbers killed and wounded. They are truly ghastly enough when the absolute facts are told but when over anxious individuals or newspaper reporters, who generally keep at a safe distance to the rear, as do all these sensational letter writers, it makes it even more ghastly to read and is reprehensible. Too often the reports are gathered for the first time from chicken hearted, cowardly officers and men who either sculled away to the rear before the battle began or after the first volley the regiment received sneaked off to the rear to protect their sorry assess. When interviewed by reporters and writers in order to cover their shame they often give a most exaggerated account of the great slaughter of our men as if they were in the middle of it. They always add as a matter of course that their regiment is "ALL CUT TO PIECES." Such reports are then published in the papers of such editors that are over anxious to send forth-sensational articles often for the sole purpose of selling more papers. This only adds greatly to the anxiety of the loved ones at home. This practice of false reporting causes such fear amongst those left at home that it is wicked and heartless and those responsible should be dealt with in no uncertain terms however they seldom are brought to justice.

Courtesy of the Library of Congress

I was so relieved that the Confederates prior to this massive battle were holding John, as I fear he may well have ended up as one of the casualties if he had been involved in it. John has given his all in many a battle and should hold his head high when he returns to the family circle and our community; he has absolutely nothing to be ashamed of. So many have fallen over the last week or so. I had not taken off my boots or coat and relaxed in my makeshift bed for over a week. I, like all the rest of the men that remain, have been sleeping on the cold frozen ground fully dressed and ready to be called to action any time. We now have a few tents set up to help shelter those brave souls that survived and last night for the first time I managed to take a few hours rest. I had a very bizarre dream or maybe I should say nightmare last night, which I need to share with someone. Old Doc of course is working almost 24 hours a day to tend to the wounded so he is not here to share it with so forgive me if I mention it herein.

I dreamt that on the field of battle there were two soldiers, one a Union soldier and one a Southern soldier and they were firing their muskets at each other over a period of hours without inflicting any damage on the other. After some time they happened to glance around and noticed the entire vast battlefield was deathly quiet except for their occasional firing. What had at one time been a gigantic clash with thousands of combatants on both sides was now as quiet as a church mouse. Both men noticed this at the same time and thought to themselves, "Why has everyone gone and left me here?" They then realized that all the other thousands of brave lads had perished and were lying motionless upon the fields, which once was the home of many beautiful trees and flowers that God had created. Simultaneously they both threw done their muskets and stood with great difficulty and cautiously approached their adversary. When they met in the middle of such destruction they each sat silently on a stump of what once was a beautiful old oak tree and now, having being shelled many times, was nothing but a remnant off its former self. They looked at each other realizing they were the last two soldiers left out of the many hundreds of thousands that started months ago in this conflict, placed their hands on each other's shoulder and wept. I then awoke with a start and realized where I was and vividly remembered the dream and wondered if that is what is in all our future. Thank you for letting me share this with you.

It is still very cold here as I mentioned and we now have managed to forage a small amount of wood and build some fires to keep us warm. So many of the troops are foraging that the wood that is available will not long last but while we have a little it is a welcome relief from the cold.

We are moving on tomorrow to camp near White Oak Church here in Virginia and hopefully it will give the survivors a brief time to rest, gather their thoughts and try and make their peace with God. It will not be easy with what we have all recently gone through but I pray that the Lord is a forgiving God and we will all, both Northern and Southern soldier not be condemned to eternal torment.

My light is rapidly fading and so I must say goodnight my beloved. It always makes me feel closer to you and the children when I write and I hope this night I, John and all of you will dream pleasant thoughts.

Your loving husband and father,
Joseph

PS: I plan on talking to the general again soon about a leave and since we are now camped in the rear of any action I think my chances might improve."

Yesterday I had an opportunity to again discuss the request for some time off to spend with my family and the general was receptive to the idea. He complimented me on the bravery and daring of our regiment and I told him it was not me he should be complimenting but those brave souls that are still standing. He indicated he planned on reviewing the troops soon and would personally thank them all for their gallantry. He said he was formulating a plan in his mind that he could present to headquarters to be able to honor my wish and it had to do with the issue of Captain Flinn and Captain Sawyer being held as I have said by the Confederates with their threat of hanging them. He mentioned of course that General W. H. F. Lee was being held in solitary confinement at Fort Hood with the understanding that he would be hung immediately if Flinn and Sawyer's sentences were carried out by the Confederacy and he said that Washington wanted another Southern Officer to be selected and brought to the Old Capital Prison in Washington to also be held in close confinement and be executed along with Lee if the South carries through on their threat. He said he may be able to arrange my leave if I were to go by way of Washington with said prisoner and he would shortly issue the necessary orders if command approves. His staff has been directed to select the officer and will soon do so.

We remain camped here at White Oak Church awaiting further orders. I have not yet heard from the general about my leave and hope that he has not forgotten his words to me. The more time that goes by the more concerned I become that it is not going to happen. It is becoming most difficult as I had gotten my hopes up so thinking I would soon be in the arms of my beloved Julia and children. I still say a prayer to the good Lord that the general will come through. The sun has finally come out and dried things out a bit and it has lifted the spirits of all the men. We had steady rain for several days and I need not describe how that affects everyone both mentally and physically. It is becoming more difficult to obtain any of the fine foods and relishes, etc. that we would like since we are camped away from any markets to speak of. Our Sutler's still have available some goods so we make do the best we can. I have managed to cook a good beef stew in which I put some potatoes we had and a few onions. Old Doc has now finally gotten caught up at the makeshift hospital and is able to spend a little time with me and we have also invited several of the other officers to share our mess. We will therefore celebrate News Years Eve sitting around our tent with our beef stew and discussing the current state of affairs and whether General Burnside will in fact have had a rather brief career as the General of the Army of the Potomac. It was by and large agreed that President Lincoln would in all likelihood look for someone else shortly after the disaster at Fredericksburg. I mentioned to all that I thought the president should try and find a hard drinking, cigar smoking, fowl mouthed son-of-a-bitch to lead this fine army, or at least what is left of it to a rapid conclusion of these hostilities. We certainly all agreed that we do not need any more hesitant leaders at this time in the war. Too many have already given their lives on both sides to not have the proper leadership for so many brave fellows. I firmly believe we shall soon see some changes again, maybe this time I will get the call except I will have to drink more and become more fowled mouthed so if I am selected I asked everyone not to let my family know and especially Julia as I would face a rolling pin across my forehead if and when I ever get home. Everyone enjoyed a fine laugh over all the speculation. It is amazing that men can still laugh amongst all this revulsion; it most likely helps keep us sane at least to some extent.

I mounted Blackjack and rode around the camp several times today to ward off the boredom but it didn't help much. When the mail was finally delivered I was excited to receive a box from home and several of the other officers also received boxes and so we decided to again gather, open our surprises and share them with each other. Old Doc had not received any since he has no family back home but he did share abundantly with all of us his famous cure and so when we finally opened the boxes we were in very high spirits. I was in such good spirits after sharing our bounty of boxes with Doc and several of the other officers I decided to share my thoughts with Julia and the family.

"Dear Julia, Martha, Sara and Little Joseph,

I did not think that those of us that are camped here at the White Oak Church would be able to surpass the fine meal that we all shared on New Years Eve but tonight we outdid ourselves and it has raised all of our spirits. I received the box that Martha sent and the colonel received one also and a third was sent to the major. In them were an abundance of wonderful things for us to share. When we heard they were at Falmouth we sent an orderly for them while we wiled away the time with a game of Euchre and they arrived in great shape. In the first one there were some delicious pies which the colonel partook of, one in its entirety, and after eating it we all were amazed to see him crawl over to one of the rough and ready beds of pine bows, roll up in his blanket and fall immediately to sleep with a smile on his face and some pie still left on his lips. We had some delicious canned peaches and low and behold we had some frosted cake the ladies had sent on to us. What nick-knacks for men sitting around over smoking log fires outdoors in the woods? We all had a hearty laugh, which we all needed, seeing each other in this situation with a chunk of frosted cake with white frosting in our hands and partially on our faces and then knowing that shortly we would be turning around, rolling up in our gray blankets and retiring for the night on our pine bows. Old Doc said in a good natured way that we all acted like a bunch of kids at the playground but he said it was great therapy from the torment we have all been through and seen in the last months. He said that the white frosted cake was better for us than all the therapy he could offer both in word and in his famous cure.

We so appreciate all of you ladies sending us so many fine things to make the life of a soldier bearable. As you have said, the ladies at home pity us and want to do what they can to make our path of responsibility as cheerful and comfortable as possible and I suppose you all think that if we do without cake and sweet meats too long we may become too soured and cantankerous. But when I think about it we use a considerable amount of sugar in our coffee just to avoid such an outcome and of course a lot of syrup on our pancakes when we can get it. The new boots that you the ladies sent and the two pails of butter will also make our lives a little easier. We have been able to buy some butter locally for 50 cents a pound but it does not measure up to the quality that you send us. We are living well enough for soldiers and I have no regrets at present except not being able to be home with all of you. I feel as well as I have at any time in the past 15 years so all those goodies from home must be agreeing with me.

You mentioned again the possibility of buying our own place and you said that the Gallups House is a better-looking residence than what it really looks like. If I recollect it is low between the joints having been built many years ago, the kitchen is small but it is pleasantly located with a large lot. I would be willing to give them $2500 for the Gallups House but not any more than that. As you also mentioned the Camdee place is for sale for $3000 and it has ten acres and is much newer than the Gallups but I still would hope you would think about a small place in the country, which of course would mean more walking to get to town, but we could have land enough to keep a cow, a horse and a couple of pigs which would add very much to our comfort and lessen expenses of living. Keep me posted on the progress of purchasing a property and keep in mind that I would not be willing to purchase any of them except at a bargain price.

The general has indicated a possibility of a leave for me, which would involve transporting a Confederate prisoner to the Old Capital Prison in Washington on my way home. As I believe I mentioned to you in a previous letter there is a cat and mouse game, for want of a better term, going on between our commanders and the Southern commanders over the previous execution of two prisoners held by our army and the threatening execution of Captain Flinn and Sawyer by the Confederates. Our side in this contest has incarcerated General W. H. F. Lee in solitary confinement to be hung if the South carries out their threat. The general has indicated one of the officers recently captured at the Battle of Fredericksburg will be chosen to be taken to Washington, held in solitary and immediately hung if the South carries through on its threats. He has told me that he may be able to work out my leave through this association. I pray to the Lord that I will be able to soon depart for home on furlough but I am despondent about accompanying any Confederate soldier to his possible execution. I will keep you informed as I hear more.

I am concerned that you mentioned you were afflicted with a bad case of diarrhea and I asked Old Doc what he would recommend. He said he would strongly recommend his special cure-all but since you do not have that available he said he would try the following. Avoid eating much meat, and only that which is cooked to a very tender state for easy digestion, avoid eating rich cake and heavy bread; in fact only eat what is easy to process. He said you should eat all the green apples you want during the day but none in the evening rather go to bed hungry. Chew the apples or whatever you are eating well and for medicine make milk porridge and season it with a little nutmeg and sugar if you like. Have a dish of this prepared each day and take a little of it frequently during the day and if you take some in the evening it will be rigorous. Eat no cheese or pickles nor any such hard substances until you a feeling better. Use light bread only. Doc said follow his advice and you should be feeling 100% shortly. He also mentioned again that if this all does not work he would send you some of his special brew, which will cure whatever ails you in a very brief time. I paid Old Doc for the advice as we opened up a bottle of that fine whiskey that came in the last box from home and after a little while neither of us were feeling any pain, after what we have all been through we may all end up permanently intoxicated. I guess I am still trying to qualify for the commander-in-chief's job and decided to start with some hard drinking. Do not misunderstand as this is related in jest and I am still your very straight husband Joseph who on rare occasions tries to deaden the pain of the memories of battles gone by with a little of the spirit.

I have rambled on long enough as I must try and get some rest, as I am to be in charge the next few days of the pickets. We are not expecting any major engagements but are always trying to keep the remaining troops on their toes. We will also be drilling for several hours each afternoon to keep things sharp. These brave fellows who have been to hell and back many times over certainly do not need any more drilling but it helps occupy their time as we wait for the headquarters to order the next move. I do not expect to be moving from here any time soon as hesitancy is usual the order of the day. Things seem to be at a stalemate possibly while the president again tries to find a new commander for his Army of the Potomac.

I will if time allows contact you immediately if I hear anything positive about a leave or I might just show up on your doorstep one of these days and surprise all of you. Little Joseph would most likely not even know who it was on the doorstep so maybe you might want to warn him that the stranger may in fact be his father.

Wishing all of you very pleasant dreams I remain your loving husband and father,

Joseph.

PS: I heave heard nothing pertaining to John which I consider the best of news."

Here as we enter the middle of January in the year of our Lord, 1863 we are still sitting near White Oak Church waiting for orders. There is more and more talk of General Burnside being replaced and that along with some nasty weather is holding up any further movement towards Richmond and an end to this madness. I am not sure if the weather is more indecisive or the leadership but whatever it is time in my opinion to move on.

CHAPTER TWENTY

Condemned

As I was sitting in my tent enjoying a pipe full of that fine tobacco sent from home a courier asked for me and told me that the general wished to see me post haste at headquarters. I immediately jumped on Blackjack and rode off trying not to get my hopes up that this might mean I will finally head for our fair village and my loving family. When I arrived he and his staff were in another deep discussion about the commander-in-chiefs position and again he asked me to feel free to join into the thoughts being passed around. Several of his staff were urging him, General Vinton, to contact the president's staff and offer his services for the position and from what I know of him I agreed he might very well be the one we need at this point. He himself however was modest and said many times that he was far from qualified to lead such a brave lot of men from such a lofty position. He said he would rather be on the firing line standing shoulder to shoulder with his fellow soldiers and that would never be acceptable to the president for a commander-in-chief. After the hearty discussion he dismissed his staff and he and I were then alone in his tent. He told me he had some good news for me and that they had finally chosen a Confederate prisoner to be taken to the Old Capital Prison in Washington to be held in solitary confinement until the president orders his execution. He directed that I should pick five of my most loyal soldiers to accompany said prisoner, men that can be fully trusted, and keep in mind that those five men could also spend a few days at home after we fulfill our duty and deliver the prisoner. I told him I would have no difficulty finding the five as all my men are loyal and I will and continue to trust them with my life. He said the transfer will take place the day after tomorrow and now that the railroad is completely rebuilt to Washington we will be leaving on that rather than by horsepower. I was especially pleased to hear that since the weather is so unpleasant and I was beside myself with joy as I rode back to my tent with the idea that I would soon be in Julia's and my children's arms and the family circle would be almost complete and hopefully soon fully complete when John rejoins us.

I could hardly restrain myself when Doc came into the tent to share the good news and he was very excited for me, however he cautioned not to get my hopes up too much as one never knows what lurks around the next corner especially in this man's army where it seems uncertainty is the norm rather than the exception. We again took out the precious bottle of whiskey and toasted the success of my upcoming furlough. He said he would have liked to accompany me but he has no family to return to there and he is very much needed here as so many are still hurting both mentally and physically from the wounds of Fredericksburg.

The long awaited day has arrived and the contingency of soldiers I assigned to accompany myself and the prisoner have gone to the improvised prison to bring the officer to my tent so that the general's instructions can be properly posted to him. I wish the officer no harm but I want him to fully understand the regulations, which I am laying down so that we have no untoward incidences on our way to Washington. As usual I take my assignments very seriously and this is no exception. It is my desire to deposit this officer as soon as possible at the old Capital Prison to thereby await his fate without any problems.

My sergeant arrived and said that the prisoner was shackled in the wagon outside awaiting transport to the railroad siding. The sergeant also had the written orders from General Vinton and the sergeant said they had not been formally passed to the prisoner yet as the instructions from the command was that I was to read him the orders when he was in our custody. I emptied my pipe and put it in my knapsack and walked out of the tent with some apprehension since I knew I was most likely transporting this gentleman to his certain death in Washington as the South has again threatened immediate execution of Captain Flinn and

Captain Sawyer. I am not sure what we are supposed to do if that happens while we are on route but whatever, I do not intend to have these brave men of mine act as a firing squad for some arbitrarily chosen unfortunate Rebel who as luck would have it was selected to face his untimely demise. The sergeant told me all that this prisoner knew was that he was being transferred and he was not told why. Old Doc was as curious as the remainder of the men so he was by my side when I left the tent and he was absolutely shocked as was I when in the wagon was none other that Captain Tyler. He nodded slightly as I approached with a slight smile and my legs almost gave out under me. Why of all the Confederate Officers has he been the one selected? I was told and I well believed the general that the choice was strictly arbitrary and that it was just the luck of the draw so to speak that he was chosen. After our experiences at the watering hole and then Old Doc's discussion with him about John's fate this was the absolute last Rebel officer that I wanted to transport to a most certain death. I accepted the sealed orders from the sergeant that the general had passed down and for a moment I thought I was going to be sick and Old Doc seeing this told the men that he and I had something unfinished in the tent that we must attend to so he led me out of the sight of the assembled men and Captain Tyler. I wished for a moment that some other officer was to escort him to the top-security prison but of course I could not ask that of anyone else and if I didn't go it would be the end of my chances to be in my loving family's arms. Doc just stood there for a moment and said in his infinite wisdom that it was an order I could not refuse and in the Lord's mysterious way maybe it was meant to be. I gathered my thoughts as we stood there for a minute and over me came this horrifying image of all the dead and dying from the battlefields screaming, "END IT NOW!" I wasn't sure what the meaning of such a revelation was but to convince me in some strange way that transporting Captain Tyler to Washington might in some way hasten the end to this lunacy.

There was no way I could relate to any of the men the history of this captive and myself so I stood straight and proceeded and I think I said a silent prayer that Captain Tyler and I would still meet outside the White House on May 3rd, 1864. As my legs steadied and Old Doc's prudent words resonated in my mind along with the vision of so many brave lads that have perished I exited the tent and felt that maybe this was God's way of balancing things out somewhat and I proceeded to read the good captain the following.

"To the commandant of the Old Capitol Prison, Washington,

Be it directed that the prisoner, Captain Tyler of the Confederate States of America, has hereby been ordered to be transported to said prison under armed guard and once arrived is to be isolated in solitary confinement until such time as orders are issued by the Union Command that he be taken out and hung in retaliation of the threatened Confederate execution of the Northern officers, Captain Flinn and Captain Sawyer."

I hesitated at this point and wondered aloud why either side is now executing combatants except on the lunacy of the battlefield. Captain Tyler's expression did not change upon hearing of this almost certain sentence of death and I almost wanted to salute him, and I would have if the other soldiers were not there. Several of the other soldiers seemed to falter for a moment upon hearing the orders as these brave lads are willing to face the Rebels on the field of battle and either kill or be killed but I could see in some of their faces the hesitancy of carrying out such a senseless assignment. I believe some of them could picture themselves being used as a similar pawn in a situation like this.

I took my leave of Old Doc and he smiled as only he could in his astuteness and we headed out for the train siding. I told the sergeant to unshackle Captain Tyler as I was sure there was no intention on his part to try and escape and with the armed guard it would be foolhardy. I had no intention of transporting him from here to Washington in chains, as the fate awaiting him was a shackle in itself without his having to bear the indignity of restraints for the trip.

Once on the train I separated the men from Captain Tyler and myself and sat with him alone in the rail car. I believe the sergeant was hesitant to leave us alone but upon seeing the expression on my face he ordered the men to the next car. I was wondering if the good captain had any news of John's whereabouts or condition so I finally decided to ask him. I wasn't sure he would want to talk but he had no hesitation and told me the last he had heard he was fine and being kept in a prison in Richmond which was far more humane than the vast outdoor prisons that the South has been forced to set up. He said that disease was rampant in the outdoor prisons so he had asked and it had been granted that John be incarcerated in a Richmond jail. This set my mind at ease and I thanked him for his kindness. I told him I would find some way of trying to repay him and was already searching for something I could do to ease his suffering. We talked for some time and he mentioned again that he agreed that slavery was a repulsive practice and that no man should ever be a slave to another but he said the South was slow to accept this even though some of the slave owners where beginning to see the light and liberate their slaves. He agreed as we talked that the process was moving slowly but that in fact it had started and we both wondered aloud if all those brave lads that have died and been scared for life in this conflict were worth the sacrifice or that time might well have healed the insults of slavery without such bloodshed. We agreed that was a question that would never be answered since the path taken by the leadership on both sides was one of death and destruction. He mentioned reading one time that Plato, the Greek philosopher from centuries ago had said, "**ONLY THE DEAD HAVE SEEN THE END OF WAR**." Our thoughts were amazingly similar that mankind is and always has been too anxious to settle their difference with the sword rather than the bargaining table.

I told him I had been granted a furlough due to the transport of him to the prison in Washington and also mentioned my absolute loathing of the reason. He asked me how long I had served, in which battles and also asked about my family. I was comfortable to share my family pictures with him and how anxious I was to be finally united with them if even for a short time. He showed me a picture of the love of his life and told me they had recently been married in a church full of Confederate Soldiers in Tappahannock, Virginia and after the ceremony a massive storm hit the area and he and his new wife, Sally Chinn, had to run for their lives and swim the river along with many of the soldiers to escape the ravages of the storm. He said if nothing else it was an interesting way to start what he had prayed would be a long and loving marriage full of wonderful children and beautiful memories. I thought as I looked at the picture of his beautiful young bride that this marriage may well end within days if the government deems it so to take his life.

For a fleeting moment I thought of allowing him to escape but then the realization that I would soon be hung in his place cured me of that thought. I did however in my mind come up with a plan to at least ease his upcoming mental suffering somewhat even though I could be most likely brought up on charges if my plan was exposed. I thought it was the civilized thing to do under the circumstances. I also had great hopes that General Robert E. Lee would pardon Captains Flinn and Sawyer especially since the North now held one of his sons who would be hung if the Confederate threat were carried out. This pardon would then spare Captain Tyler and then maybe we could still meet outside the Whitehouse and reminisce over the carnage of the past years in May of 1864. I cannot believe that General Robert. E. Lee would let his own son die in such a useless match of gotcha.

I asked the sergeant to step in and watch over our prisoner and retired to a private area where I organized my thoughts. I took out the orders that had been given to me, read them several more times, and then put pen to paper and wrote the following order.

"To the commandant of the Old Capital Prison, be it directed that the prisoner, Captain Tyler of the Confederate States of America has hereby been ordered to be transported to the Old Capitol Prison in Washington under armed guard and once arrived is to be placed in said prison in the general population until such time as orders are issued by the Union Command that he be taken out and hung in case the Confederacy carries out the inhumane act of executing the two Northern soldiers, Captain Flinn and Captain Sawyer." I thought to myself "a little sanity in an insane world" and I had no trepidation of carrying through on this slight adaptation of the orders. Of course hopefully I will never know but I believe in my heart the general's mind was never fully in agreement with this cat and mouse game that each side is playing anyway so hopefully this will not come back to haunt me. It was the least I could do for someone who had been so kind to John and myself in such an out of control world.

We arrived and with a heavy heart I handed Captain Tyler over to the commandant of the prison with the orders, which of course I had slightly altered. Captain Tyler as he was led away said to all those assembled, "The Lord is my helper, I will not be afraid, what can man do to me." I saluted him and was amazed as those brave and loyal lads with me also raised their hands in a salute. I believe to a man they understood the utter damnation of this act of man against man. I dismissed the sergeant and his men, as they were to board the train for a short visit home and thanked them for a job again well done. I slowly left the prison as my legs were weighty with a heavy heart and headed for what I prayed will be a wonderful visit with my dearly loved family.

I have only three days left of my furlough so I hurried to catch some transportation back to our fair village. I was dropped off after the train rides about three miles from the community and not wanted to waste any time and having marched so much in the past months I doubled timed it to home. If I do say so myself it wasn't bad for an old fellow well into his middle age and as I entered the village several of those that were out in this cold January weather of 1863 noted my passing and many stopped to thank me for my service and welcome me home. A few of those that had stayed behind, I will never know if they or I were the wise ones, hung their heads or turned away as they did not want to come face to face with me. This was all well and good, as I have no thoughts at present except being in my loving family's arms. As I approached our house I thought for one fleeting moment that they may all be out but when I knocked on the door Martha soon answered it. I thought for a minute that she did not recognize me and then in an instant she gasped and I thought she was going to pass out. I reached around her as she faltered to steady her and as I did I heard Julia from the kitchen asking who was it that was at our door. When Martha collected herself she literally screamed to come immediately and I believe Julia, Sara and little Joseph thought some evil had entered the house by the shriek from Martha's voice. As they rounded the corner from the kitchen and saw me I could not have expected anything more from them that the expressions of love and caring on their faces. Julia and Sara threw themselves at me but little Joseph hung back and I am sure he was wondering who this stranger was. As we all embraced I looked over Julia's shoulder at Joseph and this prayer quickly crossed my mind, "Lord please keep little Joseph far from the insanity of war in his lifetime." I immediately shifted my mind to the pleasures at hand

and could not let either Julia or the girls go and after a few minutes Julia told me that it was time to let go as I was hugging them so tight I was interfering with their breathing. As we reluctantly separated and Julia turned around she said, "Joseph this is your Papa." The expression on his face will stay with me forever and all of us broke out laughing. He slowly allowed me to approach him after I told him how much I enjoyed the items he had helped everyone pack and send on to us. As I mentioned specific items that I had received he seemed to understand who I was and he gave me a hug and a kiss that I will also carry to my grave as so precious. Julia said we were going to have a feast to celebrate my homecoming and sent the girls to the market for a fat turkey to roast. She then asked me how long I had and I hesitated to tell her so I repeated the story of transporting Captain Tyler, whom she remembered from my letters, to Washington. I thought she was going to break into tears at this inhumanity especially after his help to John. We then discussed John and I filled her in as best I could being as cheerful as I might concerning his situation. Pressing me on the length of stay particularly since she recognized my tentativeness I finally had to break the news that it would be three days only. I reminded her immediately that my commitment to the government would only last a few more months and I had definitely decided not to extend my enlistment any longer. She brightened and we embraced for several minutes while little Joseph looked wide-eyed at his mommy and newly found Papa.

Julia asked me if she could invite Henry and Josiah's wives over for tea on my second day here and I of course agreed. She said she was also inviting several of the other ladies that either still had men fighting or had lost loved ones. I was somewhat apprehensive as I didn't quite know what to expect particularly from Henry and Josiah's wives but I accepted her judgment. As it turned out it was a very cordial get-together and both wives gave me a warm embrace and told me that in no way did they hold me responsible for their husbands' deaths. They said that both of their men had voluntarily signed up when patriotism was so rampant and that neither had anyone influence them and it was their decision. I repeated to both and to the other ladies there that these two fine men who I was very close to had made their families proud and were heroes in the eyes of myself and the regimental commanders. The ladies said they were both receiving small life benefits from our government which was hardly enough to live on but that it did help and in each case they and their oldest children had gone to work to help the families get through these trying times. One of the younger ladies who I did not know and had some time ago lost her husband in the conflict said that she was looking around for a new man but most of the worthwhile ones were still serving in the military. This brought a laugh and a lighthearted moment to the tea. After they had all left I hugged Julia, Martha and Sara and we all shared a tear or two over the senselessness of this entire clash and those fine brave lads that forever are molding in their graves along side their comrades. Little Joseph just looked at us and wondered what was the matter and again I said a silent prayer to the Lord to spare him of such evil in his lifetime.

Martha asked us on my third and last day home if we could all ride over to our neighboring village and visit some of our relatives. I thought that was a smashing idea and so we hitched up the sleigh, headed over and had a fine day. A day like any normal family spends in the time of peace, which I pray is just around the corner. When we arrived home Julia cooked a fine supper of leftover turkey, peaches, cranberries and a wonderful apple pie, which I had not tasted in a long time. We retired early and as I lay in Julia's arms I was afraid to go to sleep, as I was afraid I would have nightmares of the torment of the battles I have been in. As it turned out Julia realized my anxiety and talked me to sleep like only she could do.

This morning as I prepared to leave again for the front I pleaded with all my family that there be no tears and reminded them that I would be home for good in a few short months. As the carriage arrived to take me to the train station I asked that we all say our goodbyes on the porch of the house so I could remember them there in my dreams and trust that this vision will keep me safe and sane for the months remaining. After many hugs and kisses, many more than we exchanged when this war started and many of us thought we were going off to a great adventure which would be over in a matter of days or weeks, we joined hands. As we joined hands little Joseph looked on and then walked over slowly and took my hand in one of his and Julia's in his other tiny hand and we all smiled at this. If the wisdom and innocence of our youth could only carry on into manhood we would all live in a better world. We bowed our heads and Martha led us in prayer for my continued protection, John's continued well-being, all the families continued good health and for a rapid final end to this conflict. As I turned and left the comfort of my family I dared not look back as the tears were streaming down my face not knowing if I would ever see them again. Old Josh who was kind enough to drive me to the train just looked straight ahead and knew not to bother me in my time of sorrow.

The return trip was uneventful and I arrived back to our camp here at the end of January only to find out that General Burnside has decided to mount another offensive against Lee's Army and has ordered that the troops and artillery move about ten miles down the river to cross over and engage the enemy. General Burnside has issued the following order, "This grand and auspicious moment has arrived to strike a great and mortal blow to the rebellion, and to gain that decisive victory which is due the country." I wondered to myself if this plan was an attempt to try and regain favor with the president after the recent disaster at Fredericksburg but I also supported his notion of delivering a final and decisive blow to Lee's Army.

So we began this ten-mile march, the ground was frozen and well able to withstand the weight of the artillery pieces but I sensed in the air a breeze that was sending chills up my spine, as I was afraid we may be in for a regular nor'easter. We had gotten close to the point where we were to cross, the heavens opened and a rain came down like none other that I have seen in all my months in this conflict. The ground, which had been frozen, gave way immediately and the mud became so deep that only the strongest of the horses and men could manage to move. Nothing I have ever seen in the past, and we certainly have seen rain and mud from Washington all the way to Virginia and into Virginia, could even come close to this situation. It was difficult for my mind and I am sure all the others too fully grasp what we had entered into. We were completely halted and even the Rebels who had built fortifications on the far side of the river awaiting our crossing were putting up signs saying "**Burnside is stuck in the mud**," "**This way to Richmond**" and "**Yanks, if you can't place your**

pontoons we can send help." I could even hear the laughter from the Rebel side as we became further and further stuck in this cursed mud. I could not help but think to myself here we were ready to kill the Rebels and they were ready to kill us and here we are stuck in the mud and they are laughing at the situation. It's like at Fredericksburg when after the battle the general sent over emissaries to ask for a cease-fire so the dead and wounded could be attended to. Here we are ready to do the devils' work and in a blink of the eye we have found some peace amongst the horror of this war. Why couldn't it be permanent?

The General would not give up however and ordered extra rations and liquor distributed to the men in the hopes those things would lift their spirits but I along with all the other brave fellows took a deep swig of the liquor and almost fell over in the futility of this effort. I am sure the general sees his career as the Commander-in-chief going down deeper and deeper in the mud so to speak so he just will not give up. He refuses to give up and I have even seen him grabbing on to a rope and trying to help pull the pontoons into position, which of course is a futile effort. Finally myself and many of the other field officers convinced the general's staff to advice him to retreat and move our men and equipment back to camp as best we could. This terrible storm will not let up and when I saw the general ride by on his fine steed under these circumstances I don't believe I have ever seen such a forlorn figure, covered with mud with his head hung down realizing the fate that awaits him. Without this dreadful storm he may well have been successful and we could have well driven the Rebels back towards Richmond. One never knows what fate awaits them in life but here I saw a broken man and my heart went out to him. It is impossible to describe the chaos that followed when the orders were finally given to return to camp. Horses and mules were dropping dead like flies as they could not move and many a man had to be helped by those stronger fellow soldiers or we would have left men mired and dying in this cursed mud. I believe in the annuals of history this action may well go down as, "**THE MUD MARCH**." And it will be aptly named. One of my lieutenants came up to me as we prepared to try and return the ten miles to camp and said, "It is continuing to get colder, raining even more and I have seen enough mud to last me 100 lifetimes, I have had more than enough of winter campaigning and on top of all this my diarrhea is growing worse." I think this exposure and the fact that many of us burned our temporary huts back at camp since we thought we were on our way to Richmond will kill thousands of our brave boys from exposure and disease. I fear he is going to be totally correct about the consequences of this abortive campaign. As we trudged back to camp we became a disorganized group of soldiers trying to move artillery and supplies and keep ourselves alive. I heard many a man shout out, "The Hell with Burnside" and "Burnside is Bad Luck." I heard some fellows shouting out, " The men have no confidence in General Burnside as we all remember the horrifying bloody Fredericksburg and on top of that this current horrendous situation, why he should resign." Finally what was left of this magnificent army, covered in mud with many dead animals left behind and men dragging their rifles and looking as crestfallen as I have ever seen them headed back to camp. Many of the artillery pieces I had to assign as many as 12 horses each to in an attempt to move them and since some of the horses were perishing we had to keep rotating them. The noise coming from the ranks of, "get up, get up, hey there, up, up, go along, go along," was a futile effort to move ahead. I ordered some extra mules that were still on their feet to be hitched up to the wagons and they repeatedly fell into the mud trying their utmost as beasts of burden, and what a burden this was. I saw several of them that all you could see of the mules were two eyes and two dark spots that had been their ears, other than that they were completely covered with mud. One of the mules had fallen and sunk into the mud and the driver was sitting beside the mule holding his head out of the mud as it was going to suffocate shortly. It was a wasted effort and I ordered the driver to move on and he did so reluctantly and left the mule to its fate. I saw three of the fellows get so stuck in the mud that they had a hard time extracting themselves and one of them, a slight fellow could not get out. He was a weakly looking youth and seemed to me to be no older than about 15 and I wondered to myself what the hell is he doing here in this nightmare. I asked the two fellows that had extricated themselves if they could reach him and they said they couldn't. I approached on Blackjack and the young man hollered, "don't come any closer colonel with your horse or you will lose him, I think I can get out" but the harder he struggled the more he sank. One of the men tried to get to him but it was no use and I thought for a minute he would be left to depart this life as the mule did in some mud hole in this God forsaken war. The other man then hollered that he had a small tent in his knapsack and he would roll that up and try and throw one end to the poor lad and it seemed to work and we managed with his hanging on for dear life to extricate him from his almost certain grave. I wanted to tell the two fine lads what a brave thing they had done but the poor young lad was clinging to them in tears and thanking them for saving his life so I quietly rode away as best we could in this mire.

As I was riding back to camp Blackjack stumbled over a stump in the mud and dark and I went down rather hard. I hit my head but most of the damage seemed to be to my right shoulder and right arm. With the rheumatism that I have been suffering from that fall certainly does not bode well for my future health. I managed with the help of several of my brothers in arms to regain the saddle and Blackjack seemed none the worse for the experience so we finally made it back in one piece.

So is the way of things, I have no doubt that if this storm had held off we would have successfully crossed the river at several points as the General had planned and we would be currently chasing the Rebels to Richmond. The general would have than been hailed as a hero. Things can change in this lifetime in the bat of an eye. The only blessing of this tempest is the fact that even though some will eventually die from disease and exposure none died from bullets or shells on either side of the line. God works in mysterious ways.

CHAPTER TWENTY-ONE

"Fighting" Joe Hooker

General Burnside has had, as we speculated, one of the shortest careers of any commanding officer in any of the thousands of wars that have been fought by mankind throughout the ages. General Joseph Hooker, Fighting Joe Hooker, has been named by President Lincoln to take up the call. Maybe finally we are getting the right leadership to end this, as I understand he is a frequent if not a heavy drinker and some have said his headquarters is a bar and a brothel. Maybe he is the kind of commander I have been advocating for and will get the job done. Only time will tell, if he is not then his career may well be as short as General Burnsides was and we will continue to go to the grab bag and try again to find the appropriate leader. I can only hope we have found him. It has been some time since I wrote to Julia and the family after the few wonderful days I spent with them so I am going to take pen to paper and send them a letter. It was not possible to write during our ill fated "**MUD MARCH**" or for some time afterwards since we were taking care of so many of the exhausted and sick men but we have moved on now and have the time.

"Dear Julia and Family,

I apologize for not having written before now, the end of February here in 1863, but as you have read in the papers and communications General Burnside's attempted assault on General Lee was a catastrophe and that and the upheaval following the abortive move has taken all of my time. Old Doc, the regiment and I have now returned to the camp near Falmouth to await further orders and I finally have time to renew your acquaintance. Colonel Draime has also accompanied us but is quite ill and Doc is extremely concerned about him. So many of the stout lads have fallen ill from the abortive attempt that General Burnside ordered. As you have read he has been replaced by General Hooker and we all have high hopes that he is the stalwart soldier to lead us to victory.

We are quite comfortable in our place of abode and we have some fine things to nourish our stomachs with sausage and that great butter that we recently received from home. I think of all of you each time I partake of it. Old Doc says you make the best butter he has ever tasted and I am sure he has tasted a lot since he has lived several centuries. Please don't mention that when you write back as he sometimes, not often, is a little sensitive for such a wise man. Thank you also for the looking glass but unfortunately it broke which of course might mean I will have seven years bad luck. I can't believe any bad luck I may face can be in any way as ghastly as what I have lived through for the past 20 months so I am not going to worry about it. As it turns out I really don't want to spend any time looking at myself anyway as when I do I think I look like I belong in a cage after these past battles.

Enough of that, as always I am very grateful for your kindness in sending things along which we desperately need. We have not been paid now for several months so as soon as we hopefully are I will send some funds home. I was sorry to hear about little Joseph's fall from his hobbyhorse and his hurting his mouth. I would suggest that you feed him all the beef he can eat and do not overcook it, as this should hasten the healing. Also several kisses from Papa might help it if you would please handle that for me.

Our command recently exchanged with the Rebels in this "**CIVALIZED**" war a list of prisoners and John's name appeared on it so he is well and fit. I understand there is some talk of exchanging some prisoners and have even heard that Captain Tyler has been transferred to Fort Lafayette in New York so hopefully that is some measure of good news. I have heard nothing more about the threats of the Confederacy to hang Captains' Flinn and Sawyer so continue to pray that injustice is behind us.

I have slowly recovered from the fall from Blackjack during the recent disastrous march and my head has completely healed but my arm still bothers me and the rheumatism is certainly not going away. Old Doc says it will most likely bother me for the rest of my life. He said I may have developed it anyway but living out of doors in all kinds of weather conditions he told me does a great deal to aggravate it. That wasn't very encouraging that I have to look forward to rheumatism the rest of my life but then again so many of these valiant lads lie molding in their graves so I should be thankful and not feel sorry for myself.

I have had the men spruce up the campsite both to make it more presentable and also cleaner so hopefully the illnesses that are our constant companion will abate. It also keeps the men busy when they have so much time on their hands.

Thanks for keeping me up-to-date on the Jones property; I have enclosed a note to Edmund Jones asking him for a full description of it so we can make an informed decision as soon as I get home at the end of my tour. Only in my dreams, both daydreams and those at night, that thankfully replace the nightmares can I see the social sunshine we enjoyed during my recent trip home.

We are all looking forward to spring and it is refreshing to hear the birds more frequently now that the weather has broken somewhat. I even hear the crows in what is left of the forest after the battles making merry as they feed upon the leftovers of this vast army's supplies. Without such leftovers I would judge that their prospects of getting enough to eat, in this part of Virginia, no better than was that of the Israelites in the wilderness. With all the butchered and dead animals they have to feed on I am sure they are getting fat and lazy and when we move on the easy feast will have ended and then they must fend for themselves.

I appreciate the condensed milk that you and Mrs. Draime sent down; it would have cost us about five dollars to buy that much locally so it was wonderful to receive it. Please thank her for me and of course you know how much I appreciate your thoughtfulness.

I have certainly rambled on long enough, you must think there must have been a great lack of sound thoughts in my head for being so long-winded but I always feel so much closer to you and the family when I am either writing or reading the families letters.

Love, as deep as the oceans, to all.
Joseph"

I finally am beginning to count the days until my tour of duty will be up in May. It is just a little over two months and should fall on or about May 14th. I have to await the official word from headquarters but I am confident my discharge, as well as all those remaining in the 33rd, is moving through the system towards that gleaming day. To have this insanity behind me and hopefully with the help of Julia and the children I will be able to erase at least some of the horror I have seen over this past many months. I know I will never be the same man as I was when I became caught up in the patriotic spirit of the day back in April of 1861. The first thing I plan on doing when I am mustered out is hold my loving family in my arms, the second thing is to inquire of the war department of John's well being, third will be to visit Captain Tyler at Fort Lafayette and the fourth and probably the most important thing is to pray to the Lord for an end to this lunacy. I am not sure if the second thru fourth assignments will be done in that order, but whatever, I plan on following through on them all.

Julia is still writing me about our buying our own place which pleases me no end as I take it she is confident that I will be returning home alive and well soon. I also would like our own place but we have to agree on it and that may be difficult as she wishes to remain in the village and I would prefer the country. Maybe we can compromise and find a place just outside the village. I have finally sent home some money as we were recently paid for December and January and told her to deposit what is left over after she pays the bills in the bank at 6% interest. Seems somewhat of a low rate to put one's money to work at but that is about all we can expect right now.

John Quinn is also headed home for a furlough since things are presently quiet on this front. I have written home to Martha and asked her to buy him a pipe, for not more than one dollar, as he enjoys his pipe smoking and he has been so good to us here even under the most trying of circumstances. He always has the coffee ready for us, as soon after we reach camp no matter under what conditions so we are forever grateful to him. It is the small things in such a horrific environment that keeps a person from complete madness and we are in his debt. I am sure the ladies will also invite him to partake of one of their fine meals with them also and I will be grateful for that.

It is still very cold here as the month of March ends, we are about 60 miles further south than we were last March but it is much colder this year, which makes the living out-of-doors especially difficult. I can picture myself with little Joseph on my lap sitting by the pot-bellied stove in our fair abode and rocking him to sleep with the warmth of his body, the fire in the stove and the love in my heart. We have managed to set up our baking ovens for our soft bread in makeshift holes dug in the sides of the hills. The bakers make about 1200 loaves of bread each day to feed the troops and along with that and any extra that we can buy locally we are getting along fine.

At present we have received no orders from "Fighting" Joe Hooker to make a move on General Robert E. Lee and try and end things. Could it be that we have another leader who is too hesitant, only time will tell? I am not prejudging him since he has not yet sent us into battle using a plan of action that he has devised so I will wait to see what happens after that.

Another night has passed and the rotation of the earth has ushered in another day. It is very cloudy with a cold wind from the East, Northeast and even though we have some wood on hand the forest nearby is being picked over very rapidly. Everyone is waiting anxiously for spring to arrive before the wood runs out or there will be one solid block of ice made up of thousands of soldiers in this part of the campaign. The men are getting bored wondering what our next move will be so I have had them gathering wood, drilling and tidying up the camp daily. I think they are as sick of drilling as I am and frankly I see little need for it for these battle hardened veterans but it does occupy some of their day. In fact headquarters ordered all the men to turn out for a general inspection and frankly I think the men would have been happier to be ordered to attack the adversary than have a general inspection but the mud is still too deep to mount any meaningful campaign.

John Quinn arrived back at camp this morning and he said he had a fine time at home especially with the ladies. He was smoking the pipe that I had asked Martha to buy for him and he said he had several fine meals with all of the family while he was there. Old Doc and I invited him to share our mess with us and we had a grand conversation about home. John shared some of his fine tobacco with me and we all, including Doc, lit up and after a while the tent was so full of smoke from our pipes and the fire that we could hardly see each other. It must have done wonders for our lungs with all that smoke but I figured as long as Doc was enjoying it and didn't seem to be worried I wouldn't worry either. There is a lot more to concern ourselves about than a little extra smoke in one's lungs. One good thing is that the sickness in the camp has leveled off which is a blessing.

Julia has written and suggested that she and the ladies would like to come to New York to be with us when we are discharged as a group. I think from what I have gathered from the men they want to return by way of Elmira from whence we started so I am going to write and ask her to be patient. The men feel that returning via the route that we took two years ago somehow pays a final tribute to all those that have fallen so I will honor their wishes. When we left from Elmira almost two years ago there were a thousand of us in the 33rd, as of now if disease does not take any more brave souls, around 400 will be returning if we are not again sent into conflict. I cannot believe with such a short time left we will be but anything can happen especially in this time of war. What an appalling price has been paid for what might have been solved if given enough time. I will always question the need to rush to war before the elbow marks had been wiped off the bargaining table.

The weather has finally broken, the sun is out and I have ordered all the men to hang their bedding and beds to dry out and air. The tents are to be uncovered and they have all been ordered to cleanup and refurbish their habitations. After doing this and watching how the sunshine lifted everyone's spirits the men asked if they could play a round of ball and many games were undertaken. It seemed like we were in another world away from the insanity of this one for a short time. Even Blackjack and I ventured out and watched a number of the games and cheered the 33rd on. After many of the men wore themselves out playing as hard as they fight when called upon we received orders that we all are to be sent out on picket duty and I am to be in charge of this attentive group. We thought it might be a pleasant evening when we left for the duty but lo and behold it started to rain and at times rained very hard. It was a miserable 24 hours for all of us that were out there and if Blackjack could have spoken I think he would have said, "Screw this," and headed for the barn. I guess this is common however for a soldier's life in the field to experience a dreary day of watchfulness on the front. One never knows what tomorrow will bring.

Martha recently sent me a cutout from the newspaper, which was a letter a soldier wrote to the paper about a Lieutenant Colonel in the 33rd. The initials on the letter were F. W. D. and I assumed from reading the article it was one of the men from the Southern area of our recruitment. I had reprimanded him severely on the peninsula and in Maryland and twice punished him, on trial in the Regimental Court, which ruled to dock his pay by $5.00. The last time I reprimanded him for dereliction of duty the punishment was to walk a circle in front of the camp guard for 24 hours, four hours walking and two hours off to rest until the full 24 hours of walking was complete. He expressed in the article what he thought my qualifications to be a disciplinarian were and he had every reason to understand that side of Lieutenant Colonel Joseph. Myself or any of the other officers will not tolerate dereliction of duty especially in the time of battle. His offense was not severe, at least not so severe as to be taken out and shot but it might well have been the next time if I had not taken steps to reprimand him. As it turned out he was one of the bravest and best disciplined soldiers at the battle of Fredericksburg that we had. I will keep the article in my scrapbook of memories, mostly horrifying, of my time in this war. Since we currently are not engaged in any battles but spending what a soldier calls, hurry up and wait time, I decided to write Julia and the family.

"Dear Julia and Family,

I am in receipt of your letter that Mr. Lovett sent to you stating that we could buy the Drake House for $3,300. I want you to know that $3,000 would be my absolute top price as I understand the house needs considerable work including painting on the outside to protect the wood siding, repairs to the fence and many of the rooms need new wallpaper. I believe these expenditures would well cost at least $300 for those that we could not handle ourselves. If Mr. Lovett indicates it can be bought for the $3,000 then you have my blessings on going ahead on it. Take $2,000 from the bank and borrow the remainder at the lowest interest you can receive. I do not feel that we should barter with them about the price as I think we both agree the $3,000 is a fair offer and I do not want to end up paying any more. Keep me informed as to the outcome and my blessings are with you in this endeavor. If you want to wait until I am mustered out so that I am there to assist that is your decision. I think it will take some time for them to get the title perfected and once that is done it will give a clearer title to have the mortgage noted properly.

I was concerned from your last letter to be left with the impression that my visit home has left you more unhappy now at my continued absence. Are you putting on a little affection now, being coy a little, I think so but never mind it is alright. I am feeling very grateful and thank you for the information you gave me of the place your absent husband has in your heart and affection. You asked me the leading question, "If I don't feel likewise." Now I wonder if you really thought of getting up a sort of flirtation by letter, just as though we were two young lovers. Well if you did it is fine with me for I do not think of us as old folks yet and we can still show great affection for each other as was so demonstrated during my recent visit. You must only count the days between now and hopefully May 14th when I can finally leave this nightmare behind me and expectantly return to a normal life, renew my love affair with you and my law practice in our fair village. As we have often remarked the days seem to fly by especially when you are older, I am just jesting about that, but the time will pass soon enough and I will be in your arms for eternity. We currently hear nothing of any immediate plans for engaging the Rebels so hopefully things will be quiet for the next few weeks.

We were recently ordered to have everything in readiness for a general review by President Lincoln of the 6th Corps and three others so I have been diligently getting ready for that. It has been windy and cold with considerable snow so it will not be an easy review for either the troops or the president. I would like to stop the president as he rides by in his review and tell him to return to the bargaining table to end the revolting practice of slavery and the issue of the breakaway states without further bloodshed but he is not seeking my council even though I think he should be. So many brave lads lie molding in their graves, both from the Union and from the Confederacy, that I cannot envision even more falling. Mankind as I have often said seems to have gone mad or maybe just returned to its state of lunacy as it repeats war after war over the millenniums.

I was jovial earlier in the letter especially when I thought of our intimate times together when I was recently home and then I go and ruin it with a lecture on mankind's heartlessness.

Forgive me Julia for the above thoughts and if I had more paper available I would burn this letter and rewrite it but this is my last sheet until you send more so please think pleasant thoughts that we both referred to and leave from your mind my dissertation on my judgment of the evils of man.

Please give little Joseph a hug and kiss for me and tell Martha and Julia I love them dearly and cannot wait to be home with them. Believe me when I say I cannot wait to be home with you Julia and renew our love affair as two young lovers might.

Love,
Joseph

PS: Put out of your mind any thoughts or rumors you might hear of my possible reenlistment, that is out of the question as this soul has seen more than enough of man's cruelty to man to last me many lifetimes."

CHAPTER TWENTY-TWO

Lee's "Perfect Battle"

We are still remaining in camp here near the end of April as I count the days until I am free from this carnage. I was earnestly hoping not only for myself but for those left in the 33rd that there would be no further general engagements of the enemy before our time is up but I hear we are soon going to move on "Fighting" Joe Hookers orders and again engage General Lee's forces. I anticipate that we will be more successful than our last major battle, which was completely bogged down in the mud and was a debacle; hopefully the weather will cooperate this time if we are called upon. They are paying us again and I hope that isn't a harbinger of what is to come, their knowing that many of us will not return so the few dollars can be sent home before scores of us are left thrashing in agony and screaming on the field of battle.

I don't want to be superstitious but I decided to have a photograph of Blackjack taken for old times sake and send a few copies home to the family, I asked one of the officers, who was dressed in a fine uniform, to mount him for me while the picture was taken since I am so disheveled and unkempt that my picture on him would frighten even the most callous amongst us, unfortunately the picture was very grainy most likely since photography is such a new discipline. I was in the hopes of being able to take Blackjack with me when I am discharged and just in case the military denies my request at least I will have a picture of this faithful companion of the past two years.

We have received orders to be prepared to march tomorrow morning at daybreak, April 27th and head for the Rappahannock

River for an assault further into Virginia towards Richmond. It looks as if the high command wants to get one last ounce of blood out of those of us remaining in the 33rd, which now measures less than 400 from its original 1000 that started almost two years ago. I think the command knows what brave fighting men make up the 33rd so they figure since we are so close to being mustered out they want us to have one last crack at Johnny Reb. The men are more apprehensive than I have seen them in the past and I am sure it is because they were almost to the point of getting a final reprieve from any further mayhem.

Blackjack

We arrived at Chancellorsville with over 130,000 troops and prepared to enter the battle against General Lee's forces, which I understand have been estimated at about 60,000. Under these circumstances it seems to me that such an overwhelming force should make short work finally of these Rebels and drive them back to Richmond and maybe end this sooner than later. General Hooker now has the opportunity to prove his grit, lead this great army to victory and this soldier is praying that he does.

Fierce fighting has broken out all along the line and at present it seems like there is somewhat of a stalemate as to which side has the advantage. More brave lads of the 33rd are dropping under a murderous fire from the Rebels and we do not seem to be advancing like I thought we would with the superior force that we have. Intelligence has come down that General Lee has split his army and in doing so has thrown off the advantage we had.

It is now the second day of the battle, which began on April 30th, and there has been no rest for the weary soldiers at least on the front that I am commanding. I have sent word to the general several times that myself and the men are anxious to take the fight to the enemy rather than remain stationary and slowly see men in our ranks and of course some in the Confederate ranks falling. I ask myself of all the evils in war if it not one of the more grievous ones to not take the fight to the opponent but to vacillate in time of bitter conflict thus adding to the death, dying and of course prolonging the hostilities even longer.

The men, all of them and particularly those of the 33rd are fighting like the truly brave soldiers they are but frankly for want of a better term we are getting our asses kicked so far by a much smaller force. I marvel that General Robert E. Lee has been the commander of the Confederate Rebels for the entire duration of the war so far and his brilliance has, with a much smaller force, held off this vast army from finishing its mission. In the meantime we are now with our third commander-in-chief and still we hesitate, vacillate and waver in our determination to advance on our adversary. I had great hopes for General Hooker but so far in this engagement it does not seem that he is the hard drinking, cigar smoking, fowl mouthed, son-of-a-bitch that this Army of the Potomac needs to end this insanity.

We are now into the third day of this struggle having crossed the Rappahannock River and the Rapidan River to reach this place of battle. The objective as spelled out in our orders from Hookers Headquarters was to drive the Rebels back, inflict massive damage, until we arrived at the outskirts of Richmond. As it now stands we have not accomplished any of the above and frankly I believe it is as I have said due to the overly cautious performance of our high command. As I said we had about 400 souls left in the 33rd just weeks away from being discharged and here on this third day we have lost another 100 or so. Old Doc is drawing up a complete accounting as he has time between amputating limbs and sewing up wounds and generally trying to ease the torment of those poor souls that are wounded and have no chance of surviving. He told me that he has had his fill of trying to patch up these brave lads, some no older than boys, and can't wait to be discharged so he can help folks at home with normal ailments, not those caused by the sadism of man.

The fighting does not ever seem to stop and I have run more than one poor soul through with my sword. I think this sword is cursed as it has taken so many lives in this conflict and like I it may end up with me in Hell for all eternity. As we were heading back for a brief respite a group of men approached us carrying the stars and stripes and we thought they were other soldiers of the division but it was getting dusk and we could not tell for sure. We let our guard down and all of a sudden they threw down the flag and started firing point blank at us. This is a new low in this struggle and in the skirmish that followed a ball hit Blackjack just in front of my right leg and he went down. It missed my leg by inches and I was thrown from him. I still had my sword in my hand and as the men remaining in the 33rd saw what had happened and saw me on the ground they let out what I can only describe as an ear shattering shriek and charged the enemy. I rose up not wanting to miss this action and charged into the Rebels also making them regret their treachery. It was all over in a few minutes and many Rebels lay dead or mortally wounded on the field. Unfortunately the men were in no mood to take prisoners and I had to forcible command many that they withdraw after the firing had stopped and head back to camp. These men of the 33rd should never be taken lightly as they are brave, loyal and fierce fighters particularly if deceived. Several of the men stayed with me as I ordered the others off of the field and I knelt down and held Blackjack's head in my arms as he was taking his last breath. He and I have been inseparable for months in this clash and I could not help but shed a tear as his larger than life eyes looked at me and I could only imagine what he was going through at that time knowing, as I believe he did, that his time on this earth was over. He will not be blessed with being able to spend his old age, as I had hoped he would, in a pasture in a picturesque farm in our fair village. Several of the men took me by the shoulder and as Blackjack took his last breath on this earth they led me away and I was a broken man and dragged my sword back into our rest area and asked to be alone for a while. I have cried for every man that perished in this war and Blackjack deserves my tears also, what a terrible waste.

After two more days of relentless fighting General Hooker has ordered that we retreat across the river and so we are in the process of withdrawing this immense army, or what is left of it, from a much smaller force. If I were to sum things up I would say that General Lee's audacity and "Fighting?" Joe Hookers timid performance have led us into defeat in what we all were praying would be the beginning of the end of this clash. One of the men told me the other day that he was going to send President Lincoln a letter and ask him if he would consider asking General Lee to switch sides and then maybe this horrific chaos would be ended. I told him fat chance of that happening as I feel that all these brave armed forces will be drawn into battle after catastrophic battle with no end in sight. The only positive intelligence that has been passed down to us is that General Thomas "Stonewall" Jackson was killed by friendly fire from the Rebels. Robert E Lee was quoted as saying he had lost his right arm in losing Jackson. Unfortunately our side could not even take credit for taking out Stonewall Jackson, which doesn't say much for all the sacrifice of all those poor fellows lying in the hospitals or having died on the field of battle.

Old Doc has reported to me that we have lost over 17 thousand more men killed, wounded or missing in the Union Army in this battle. He said he would have rather hidden this figure forever in one of his favorite codes that he and I have shared over the past two years. In such a disaster however it would not, as he said, be the appropriate time to try to solve a new mystery cipher of his. He just said he is so heartbroken every time he has to write the names of so many fine men on list after list of missing, wounded or dead that he would rather forget the entire record keeping in the hopes it never happened. The missing most likely are now prisoners of war. The rebel fatalities are considerably less, which does not bode well for General Hooker's career as our new commander-in-chief. Doc gave me a breakdown of those of the 33rd that were among the casualties of the first few days of this fighting. I fear that John's name would surely have ended up on this list if in fact he were not a prisoner of the Confederacy. The names of the heroic lads are as follows. Doc told me to keep in mind that these were all brave men that were weeks away from discharge and this list only includes the first couple of days of fighting. Doc didn't have to remind me of that as I said a prayer for each of them as I read their names from his list.

Orderly Sergeant S. McCall	**Wounded in mouth, may be fatal**	**May 4**
Corporal Elisha Lewis	**Wounded in leg, will survive**	**May 3**
Corporal Benjamin Mepham	**Wounded in side, will survive**	**May 4**
Corporal Richard Turner	**Wounded in arm, may lose it**	**May 4**
Private Samuel Adams	**Wounded shoulder, may be fatal**	**May 3**
Private Francis Deyor	**Killed**	**May 4**
Private Michael Elbert	**Wounded in leg, slight**	**May 4**
Private William Brookins	**Wounded and taken prisoner**	**May 4**
Private Royal E. Drake	**Wounded and taken prisoner**	**May 4**
Corporal John Clemons	**Wounded and taken prisoner**	**May 4**
Corporal Washington Everitt	**Wounded in leg, prisoner**	**May 3**
Private William Harse	**Wounded both legs, will die**	**May 4**
Private Thomas Glossender	**Wounded in ankle, slight**	**May 3**
Private Edward Jarvis	**Wounded in arm, will survive**	**May 3**
Private William L. Ingraham	**Wound to abdomen, will die**	**May 4**
Private James Johnson	**Wounded in leg, will survive**	**May 4**
Private John Johnson	**Wound to the hand, will survive**	**May 4**
Private Henry Rimhall	**Wound in hand, will lose hand**	**May 4**
Private Mason Lee	**Killed in action**	**May 4**
Private Thomas Hibbard	**Wounded in ankle, slight**	**May 3**
Private S. B. Risly	**Wounded in leg, may lose it**	**May 3**
Private Chals Truax	**Wounded in leg, questionable**	**May 3**
Private George Wexmuth	**Wounded and taken prisoner**	**May 4**
Corporal Charles Geer	**Missing in action**	
Munson G. Hill	**Missing in action**	
John Hoffman	**Missing in action**	
Joseph Jackson	**Missing in action**	
Joseph Tmax	**Missing in action**	
John Little (Little John)	**Missing in action (only a boy)**	
Jason Vandeworker	**Missing in action**	

John P. Jarvis	**Missing in action**
Charles Eisentrager	**Missing in action**

Most if not all of those that Doc listed as missing in action were most likely taken prisoner and their condition is unknown. These are just those that have fallen or are missing in the first couple of days of carnage. Most of these fine men had loved ones back home and many had families to support that will now have to fend for themselves. I believe some people call the unfortunate families collateral damage, at least those that are most callous about this war and its casualties. I have asked Old Doc for the reports from the last few days of fighting but he has not had time to compile them yet as he is still sewing men up and amputating limbs and trying to comfort those so seriously wounded that there is no hope for them. All of these men of the 33rd were within weeks of being mustered out and now we are down to just over 200 souls from the original 1,000 that started two years ago. About half of the total victims were from diseases and the other half from the enemy bullets, shells and being taken prisoner. Hopefully many will survive the rigors of being in the prisoners of war camps and finally come home to their families, I can only pray for all of them as I daily pray for John's safe return.

I feel I must get a letter off to Julia and the family, as they will be beside themselves as to my fate. I did send a telegram but only God knows if it ever got through to them.

"Dear Julia, Martha, Sara and little Joseph,

We are now camped near Banks Ford here on the 7th of May. We are trying to rest from the past number of days of marching, watching and fighting but it is not easy. We are in the midst of a severe cold rain storm and it is very hard on many of the men as they have no tents or blankets and more than one able-bodied soldier who survived the fierce fighting of the past days has now succumbed to illness and many may not make it without the proper clothing and protection from the elements which our government is supposedly supplying although not too swiftly. I sometimes when I see the misery of all of the men that they and all of us fighting on the front lines, both Union and Confederate are fodder and nothing more, sent to fight and die because the leaders on both sides could not find a peaceful solution to those ills that contaminate this country. What a heartrending state of affairs.

I believe we will be staying in this location or nearby for some time and I do not feel we will have any more fighting to do just now. I think the 33rd has done more than an equal proportion during the late clash and all those battles that have gone before. I salute all of these brave lads, those that have survived and those that have fallen, for each and every man, with few exceptions, have done their duty most nobly. No commander could have asked for anything greater from such a faithful, courageous group of lads. I will remember them always as friends and comrades.

The recent battle was one of the hardest on the men and myself. One of the worst moments was upon the heights when the 33rd drove the enemy from one of their big guns. The Rebels rallied about 100 yards beyond and others came up to join them and they outnumbered us about four to one at this point. We stood our ground, fought them to a standstill even though greatly outnumbered and finally reinforcements came up and the Rebels withdrew. We lost in this one battle 62 lads either killed or wounded, we also lost three officers and after we were relieved and withdrew we were again thrown into an even fiercer clash near evening. In this clash it was so blood-spattered and ferocious that we could not even get to our wounded and many of them were either killed or taken by the Rebels for lack of our having sufficient manpower to rescue them and at the same time hold off the enemy. Even though we call them the adversary, I have to say that no men, on either side of this conflict, have ever fought more bravely or courageously than those in the Army of the Potomac or the Confederate Army. If only all this sacrifice and effort could have been directed towards a more peaceful solution to mankind's problems wouldn't it have be brilliant, but alas mankind unfortunately lacks brilliance it seems.

I am resuming writing this letter here on the 10th of May as the Lieutenant returned and said the telegram did go out on schedule so you know of my safety at this point. I have been extremely busy the last few days so my pen was laid aside and I am now taking it up again. The sun is shining brightly and it is warm and pleasant for a change. I assume you and the girls and little Joseph are at church at the present time since it is 11 o'clock. Today is so different from the scene that was being enacted here last Sunday at about the same hour. What a blessing it is that you and the other faithful members of the church could not see or know what was going on here. All preaching, praying and singing would have been suddenly stopped; voices would have turned to shrieks and wailings. The men were a meager ten rods from the foe and the batteries were belching out a steady stream of flame, hurling lead and iron into the enemy lines and from their side into our line. No human flesh can withstand such an onslaught. After that assault we were ordered again to advance on the next hill. How tired the men all were, numbers of them dropping from exhaustion. And I afterwards heard that one of the sergeants was lying there on the hillside not able to move and he saw me passing by leading the men and heard me shouting, "I know it is hard but for God's sake stick to it for a few minutes more and the victory will be ours." They said he then got up and found the fortitude to move and raced to the top of the hill joining his comrades for this one last battle. This brand of loyalty cannot be bought even with gold. The next day the sergeant lay fatally wounded and only nine days from his discharge.

I further understand that the papers reported myself as having been wounded in this battle but I am sure that the telegram I sent you a few days ago cleared up that confusion in your mind. The papers continue to sensationalize these battles and even though they are all brutal the papers make them out even worse if anything could in fact be more ghastly.

Barring any last minute changes we are scheduled to be discharged on the 14th and I will plan on meeting you in Elmira since those 200 or so of those that are left wish to retrace the steps of the 1,000 men who took up the call to arms two years ago and traveled to Washington from Elmira in what most of us thought would be a great adventure and as it turned out it was a "**JOURNEY INTO HELL AND BACK.**"

I cannot wait to see you and hold you in my arms and renew our love. I believe as you said it is best to leave little Joseph at home with his sisters even as much as I miss them all but soon we will all be together in the family circle.

Love to all,
Joseph"

Those few of us that have survived have finally reached that fateful day, May 14th, 1863 when we are to be mustered out. Brigadier General Thos Neill has called us to one last review and those that are able to stand and be held upright by their comrades are in attendance. He is reading us his farewell as well as given each of us a copy for part of our remembrance of this passage in our lives. There was hardly a dry eye in the assembled group as he read the following as we were all thinking of those friends and comrades that were laid to rest over the past two years. No words can erase that dreadful feeling of loss or those memories that will be with each and every one of us for the rest of our natural lives. I fear as I look over those assembled that more than one of these heroic men may well end up as Henry did when the nightmares become too much to endure. The general read as follows:

Headquarters 3rd Brigade, 2nd Division
6th Army Corps
May 14th, 1863

"The Brigadier General commanding the Third Brigade, cannot part with the 33rd New York Volunteers without expressing to the officers and men of that gallant Regiment who have fought under his eye and command with so much honor and distinction, his regret at our separation and his well wishes for the future.

No words can express what you all must feel, the sense of having fought nobly for your country and suffered bravely for the cause. The memory of those who have fallen is tenderly cherished and your Brigade Commander bids you "God Speed," in anything you may undertake in the future.

Sincerely
Thos Neill
Brig. Gen. Commanding 3rd Brigade"

As I stood there at attention and listened to his words I could not help but think how many times over the centuries of man's existence similar words have been uttered and how many times over the many centuries to follow those or similar words will again be read to the few remaining soldiers from whatever upcoming conflicts they may be drawn into. There was almost complete stillness as the ceremony wound down and the men when dismissed, wandered back to pick up their belongings, and headed for the train siding in silence. I said one last prayer for all those left behind and another for John's safe return. I added a prayer for Captain Tyler's release also and his return to his beautiful wife as I have heard nothing more about the drama which was to unfold concerning the hanging of Captain Flinn, Sawyer and the subsequent hanging of Captain Tyler and General W. H. F. Lee.

We arrived in Elmira at the appointed time and my beautiful wife, Julia, was there with open arms to greet me. I could not wait to embrace her and there were many tears exchanged between the families and those that were fortunate enough to return. I asked the men and their wives and families if I could lead them all in a brief prayer for our poor departed brothers and everyone immediately hung their heads and closed their eyes in reference.

"Dear Lord, bless those of us that have returned, take into your care those souls of our fellow comrades from the 33rd New York Volunteers that have perished. Guide mankind from their warring ways so that our sons and family members that are left behind will no longer have to face the horrors of war that we have experienced. Bless and comfort the families of all the brave men that have gone before. In Jesus name, Amen."

I felt totally inadequate in my prayer but since we had no Chaplin with us and I deeply felt some words needed to be said I trust everyone accepted my thoughts and prayer. Julia told me it was just fine, as did Old Doc. Julia said it was time to put all this behind us and renew our love for one another and the family. I fear that will not be easy for most of us since war leaves its deadly marks not only on the body but imbedded deep in the mind.

We arrived home to a cheering crowd and everyone was in high spirits that the 200 of us had survived and returned to our fair community to take up our lives where we left off. Little Joseph it seemed had grown a foot since I last saw him a couple of months ago and he gave his Papa a big hug and kiss, the first of many to come I hope. Martha and Sara are beautiful young women and I feel the Lord has blessed me in many ways and particularly with a wonderful family that I have returned to.

Thank you Lord

CHAPTER TWENTY-THREE

Memories

The years have taken their toll, it is now 1887 and I am a crippled, rheumatism plagued old man of 71. I am not complaining however since I have been blessed over the years with having survived the recent Great War and having a wonderful family, no man could ask for more. My family has been my salvation over these many years as they presently continue to be.

After my discharge from the Civil War in 1863 I tried in our fair community to restart my law practice without success. It seemed that those attorneys that chose not to volunteer and stayed behind had taken all my clients and so I ended up buying a small farm, a horse, which was not nearly as fine an animal as Blackjack, a cow and a couple of pigs and we scratched a living from the soil and a small pension of $12 per month from the government for the rheumatism I was cursed with from the many months living in adverse conditions outside during the campaign. This was hardly the income I could have been making as an attorney but we got by with perseverance, love and grit, mostly love. Little Joseph, who is no longer little, has been a Godsend as he has taken up most of the tasks around the farm since I am all but bed ridden many days. My beautiful daughters have been married and now have families of their own which is a blessing to Julia and I in our old age.

Many of the other families of veterans and those that perished were much worse off so I think we were in reality amongst the luckier ones. Over the past many years we have attended countless funerals for some of the 200 souls that made it back intact from the war, at least they were intact in body if not in mind. Some of their lives ended abruptly and prematurely due to the ghastly experiences and visions which all of us share. I often ask myself, when I lay awake at night to avoid the nightmares of the moaning and shrieks of the dead and dying which have never left my senses, whether I made the right move by volunteering or if those that stayed behind were the wise ones. That and many other questions I will never know the answer to. It was suggested when I was honorably discharged that I run again for the New York State Assembly but I am a firm believer that a career in politics is corrupting as the saying goes, "power corrupts and absolute power corrupts absolutely." I believe that the people are best served by those willing to spend a few years in the state government or the federal government and then return to their homes and let other fresher, less corrupt minds have their turn.

The war has long been over, President Lincoln appointed more commanders after I was mustered out and sadly was himself assassinated shortly after the war. I left under the leadership of General "Fighting" Joe Hooker who at the time was the third commander of the Army of the Potomac and the president was still it seemed searching for the right man to finally get the job done. General George Meade replaced General Hooker and so on until finally the president found General Ulysses S. Grant who brought this terrible conflict to an end. I'm not sure if he was the hard drinking, cigar smoking, fowl mouthed son-of-bitch that we needed but whatever he finally brought it to a close on April 9th, 1865. This was after many more battle one of which was at Gettysburg where thousands more died on both sides of the conflict. It has been reported that over 620,000 men (and boys) from both the North and the South perished in this Great War. Over half of those that perished died from disease.

The war was originally fought to free the slaves which I have always said was an evil practice and no man should ever be held slave to another. The war then went on to punish the Southern States for seceding from the Union. Here in 1887 we are one United States of America and for all intensive purposes slavery has ended however equality for Negroes is still far from a reality unfortunately. I am certainly not intelligent enough to make an informed thought on whether or not it was necessary to have 620,000 men lie molding in their graves to cure these ills. The questions that have always lingered in my thoughts however are. Would slavery eventually have ended without the sacrifice of so many? Would the Southern States have rejoined the Union at some point in the future without such havoc being brought upon so many? I sincerely pray that in the future responses to evils of this world are measured and greater time is allowed at the bargaining table before such pandemonium is unleashed again. Old Doc is still around treating those folks in our community that so desperately need him. When we last tipped a tall one and reminisced he told me, only as he could, that I am praying for something that mankind is not capable of. What a sad state of affairs.

I did manage to visit Captain Tyler in Fort Lafayette some time after my discharge. I was shocked with his condition as he had lost 40 lbs. and I could well understand why since day after day when he heard the guards coming his way he thought he was to be taken out and hung. We spent considerable time talking over the feelings we both shared of the appalling toll this war had taken on everyone. He told me that General Robert E. Lee had been entreated to revoke the sentence of death of Captain Flinn and Sawyer so as to save himself and Robert E. Lee's son, General W.H.F. Lee, but he was told, and didn't know if it was the truth, that General Lee had said, "If it is my son's fate to give up his life for his country he should submit and comply to it." At that time the authorities turned to President Davis of the Confederate States of America and he revoked the sentences of Captain Flinn and Captain Sawyer. Captain Tyler at the time I visited him was waiting to be exchanged with prisoners held in the South as he had often prayed for his safe return to his beautiful wife. I asked him if we could kneel in prayer and he readily agreed and thanked me for my kindness that I had shown him when I transported him to what we thought would be his certain death. We never did meet at the White House as we had planned but we did keep in touch over the years.

He shared with me a letter he had sent to Captain Sawyer long after the war was over. Captain Sawyer of course was awaiting the hangman's noose in the South while Captain Tyler was awaiting the same fate in the North. I thought it was such a fine tribute to their ordeal I have always cherished it.

"My Dear Captain Sawyer,

Today I received a letter from my friend, General W.H.F. Lee, in which he mentioned having met you and of your kind attentions to his pleasure for his time at Cape May. I have been trying to get your address every since the war closed without success up until now. Two years ago when I and about 100 other veterans were visiting the Bull Run Battlefields with General Rosecrans I made an earnest inquiry about you and the word I received was that you had passed away a few years after the war was over. I was not surprised at hearing this as having gone through the traumatic times of our imprisonment and the constant threat of being executed I knew only too well the toll that had taken on you, General Lee, Captain Flinn, and I. Judge my surprise and pleasure to learn that you are still living. Our time of conversation years ago, after our introduction at City Point, was so limited that I could not ask you several questions that I greatly desired an answer to.

One of the Lieutenants, who escaped from the Libby by tunnel, visited me at the Old Capitol and said he was an intimate friend of yours, and that as I was being incarcerated for you that he wished to manifest his friendship for you by any kindness that he could possibly show me. If I needed anything he would gladly supply it. God bless his noble, generous soul, my heart will ever treasure his kindness even if my treacherous memory has lost his name. He was quite a young man of German extraction. Can you pass on his name to me?

Do you remember showing me a letter written by General Robert E. Lee to a Confederate clergyman, in answer to one by said clergyman, written at the request of the citizens of Culpepper or Orange County? They were anxious to have you saved from the threatened execution on account of your kindness to them while occupying that part of the country? If you have the letter could you please send me a copy of it?

Oh, Captain, that was a dread ordeal through which we passed. It is so impressed upon me that cold chills creep over me when I recall it. I have thought of you thousands of times in connection with it. As soon as I reached Richmond I went to the Libby and inquired for the cells in which Flinn and yourself were locked away in isolation. I could enter fully into your mental sufferings while there.

Your wonderful soldierly letter that you wrote your wife while expecting the death sentence at any time was published in the Washington papers. How fully my heart re-echoed every sentiment you expressed, for I too had a young and beautiful wife, to whom I had only been married a few short months. When you read of the great battle of Manassas you see the Chinn House mentioned. That is where I entered on the pleasures of "Loves Young Dream." I married a daughter of that gentlemen, Mr. Benjamin Tasker Chinn. She can sympathize and enter into the feelings of your wife on receiving that gracious letter. I would love to have a copy of that letter to preserve amongst our family archives.

I have long thought of writing an article on the circumstances surrounding our mutually threatened execution in retaliation. My memory however is so dimmed by the lapse of years that I am almost afraid to go it alone. Would you join me in writing such a narrative of our mutual horrific time, along with that shared with General W.H.F. Lee and Captain Flinn? I think such an article would be interesting to the soldiers of both sides and hopefully lead some of our leaders into greater caution before embarking into a state of war in the future. General Lee mentioned in his letter that Flinn had passed on, how long has he been gone and was his early passing a result of the lengthy confinement and awaiting execution at any time? I was blessed to have a brave officer of the Union Army take charge of my transportation to the Old Capital Prison in Washington when this journey started for me and without his bravery and humanity I fear I would have even had a much more difficult time of it. As it was I lost over 25 percent of my weight and I cannot imagine what it would have been if not for him. I am forever in his debt.

I had some hard campaigning and fighting after I was exchanged, finally following General Robert E. Lee in his last retreat. Fought my last battle at Sailor's Creek in Nottoway County on April 6th, 1865 where Pickett's whole division was surrounded and captured. My regiment, the 8th Virginia infantry numbered only 80 men left in all ten companies from the original 1,000 that had taken up arms in the cause. We had fought the war through together, and I can tell you, "The iron entered my soul when we had to surrender those of us that were left." I surrendered in good faith and I will stand by the "Old Flag", the red, white and blue as devotedly as we followed "The Lost Cause," which will never again be unfurled in anger I pray. We "Shook Hands with the Devil" by entering into such a bloodbath as the Civil War was and I pray my sons will never have to experience anything like that in their lifetimes.

I am now an old farmer with six sons and five daughters which are the blessing of mine and my beautiful wife, Sallie's, wonderful life together."

Do please write me soon,
Yours truly,
Captain Robert Tyler"

Many times I have read and re-read this letter and it brings back many memories some of which I wish I could suppress. One of the better recollections of the exchange of Captain Tyler and many other prisoners that were being held by the North at the time was that amongst those prisoners being held by the South, Julia and my prayers were answered and John was released and returned to the family circle. He was gaunt and had also lost a lot of weight but except for the rheumatism that was also bothering him from so much hazardous open-air living he was fit. He has since married a wonderful lady, has children and is a teacher. He asked me a few times in private how I had broken the news to Mother and the family of his capture at Antietam but I graciously avoided a direct answer and he never pursued it with Julia or his brother or sister's. I know that he was suspicious of what my explanation at the time would have been but being the fine man that he is he let the matter drop. No reason to resurrect the issue with Old Doc still around and so cherished in the community.

I am barely able to get around anymore but believe it or not Old Doc is more spirited than I am. He seems to have nine lives like the proverbial cat and even though he is considerably older than I he still is going strong. I am sure it is a plentiful supply of his famous healing treatment that keeps him so fit and young in his old age. Maybe in his wisdom he actually has discovered the "Fountain Of Youth." He tells me it is only on the outside as inside he has decayed almost as much as many of those we laid to rest.

He came by and told me that the town was going to have the annual Memorial Parade to honor those of us who returned home and of course those that perished and they had asked he and I to be the selected leaders this year in the parade. I told him I wasn't up to it and further more I didn't really like to be the center of attention of anything but he insisted and after all he had done for my family and I over the years I could not turn him down.

The day arrived and I was helped up in to the horse drawn carriage and we paraded down the street with cheering crowds lining both sides of our fair village. I thought to myself as I looked out upon these fine folks that if they could have seen what we saw during that hideous conflict there would be no cheers but only deadly silence. When we came to the end of the parade Old Doc told me he was leaving town and he was going to finish out his days at the "Little White House" in Washington tending to the ladies' needs. He said he planned on ending his days on this earth when the Lord called him in the arms of the madam of the house who he has had a relationship with for many years. Most of the folks in town are not aware of this relationship and he will be sorely missed when he is gone. As he departed the carriage, and I was still in somewhat of a shock from his revelation, he handed me an envelope and told me to open it only after he had quietly left town and he asked me please to not divulge his destination. He said that in the envelope was the sum total of his judgment upon his fellow human beings after living all these years and weighing the good and evil of mankind.

A few weeks later after he had left I sat down with my favorite pipe, lit it up, opened the envelope and it was the following picture with the question below it. It took me a time to figure out the answer that he had given as a puzzle since he always was one to write his innermost thoughts in his favorite codes. He always said it made the recipient use what little brainpower mankind seems to exercise and I for one fit into that category especially at my advanced age. Old Doc was always coming up with deep thoughts about mankind's future. After some time working at it, having had the advantage of exchanging similar codes with him over the past years, I finally cracked the cipher, and as I sat there repeatedly looking at his message and thought of his wisdom, I set my pipe aside and cried.

Why isn't Jesus smiling?

9

2 17

16 18 22

33 4 8 18

21 6 25 11 8

3   13 6 4 9 13 22   1

5 16 11 12 21 7 33

7 21 20 33 12 9 19 9

22 16 14 8 33 26 17 1 13

14 8 16 33 16 18 20 22 13 33

16 23 17 4 19 17 33 26 21 12 22

2

Old Doc

Epilogue

This story is historical fiction but is very thinly guided by a number of letters and stories passed down through the generations of the horrifying Civil War conflict and the appalling toll it took on the soldiers and their families that were left behind. Many liberties have been taken and for all intensive purposes this is a work of historical fiction. Joseph is the lead character with his son John and their three faithful friends including Old Doc. The story follows their lives and their deaths. Two of the friends did not make it through this time of agony on earth and Joseph and John finally succumb later in their lives to the ravages of rheumatism after many months of living under adverse conditions during this struggle. As far as the author is aware Old Doc may still be alive and living with the ladies at the Little White House in Washington. This story is told for the express purpose of thoughts about mankind's future and it is intended to generate numerous questions in the reader's mind.

I wish to thank my loving wife, Lois, for her many hours of proofing this work and her listening to me raising so many questions during the writing of the book.

I also wish to thank my son, Scott, for his help in converting it to the proper media for submission to the copyright office and the publisher.

I also am in the debt of my beautiful daughter and my son-in-law, Ken Romano, for their inspiration for the cover of the book and for a friend, Kathie Spanganberg for her input and assistance in selecting the cover from those ideas submitted by our remarkable family.

I also wish to acknowledge those illustrations in the book, which are noted as being from the Library of Congress and are reproduced here as per their guidelines.

Last but certainly not least I wish to thank Barbara Tyler Ahlfield, my wonderful talented cousin, for the cover creation. Her artistic talent is truly a gift from God.

The book is dedicated to my dear departed sister, Linda, who left this earth in 2007 and is dearly missed.

LaVergne, TN USA
23 July 2010

190568LV00004B/285/P

9 781600 474415